Tom

POWER PLAYS

COLD WAR

Tom Clancy's
POWER PLAYS

COLD WAR

CREATED BY
TOM CLANCY
AND
MARTIN GREENBERG

WRITTEN BY
JEROME PREISLER

PENGUIN BOOKS

PENGUIN BOOKS

Published by the Penguin Group
Penguin Books Ltd, 80 Strand, London WC2R 0RL, England
Penguin Putnam Inc., 375 Hudson Street, New York, New York 10014, USA
Penguin Books Australia Ltd, 250 Camberwell Road, Camberwell,
Victoria 3124, Australia
Penguin Books Canada Ltd, 10 Alcorn Avenue, Toronto, Ontario, Canada M4V 3B2
Penguin Books India (P) Ltd, 11 Community Centre, Panchsheel Park,
New Delhi – 110 017, India
Penguin Books (NZ) Ltd, Cnr Rosedale and Airborne Roads,
Albany, Auckland, New Zealand
Penguin Books (South Africa) (Pty) Ltd, 24 Sturdee Avenue,
Rosebank 2196, South Africa

Penguin Books Ltd, Registered Offices: 80 Strand, London WC2R 0RL, England

www.penguin.com

First published in the United States of America by the Berkley Publishing
Group, a division of Penguin Putnam Inc. 2001
Published in Great Britain by Penguin Books 2001
1

Printed in England by Clays Ltd, St Ives plc

ONE

THEY HEARD THE COPTER LONG BEFORE IT CAME INTO sight, cresting the frozen peaks of Olympus on a southerly course toward Asgard.

Its pilot approached from the rear, nosed down a little, and hailed the team below as he flew past. Some cheerful words over his PA, a flap of a red-sleeved arm behind his windscreen. His large Bell 212 was identical to the aircraft that had dropped them into the valleys, but its National Science Foundation decals showed it wasn't one of theirs.

Scarborough's foot party was no less appreciative of the human contact. They were starting their first full day out of Cold Corners, and if mutual reliance made for good neighbors, this qualified as the most neighborly spot on earth.

All three returned the pilot's wave, their own bright red coat sleeves upraised. Then they watched him level his bird in the crystal-clear sky, skirt the rim of Valhalla glacier, and vanish over the crooked spine of mountains running toward the coast. Away and gone with due haste. The fixed landing and refueling pad at Marble Point was some thirty miles off along his flight path, and he'd want to reach it in time for the early shift change.

Minutes later, Scarborough could still hear the chop of rotors echoing between the scoured brown walls of the pass.

The most neighborly spot on earth, and its quietest, he thought. The polar desert's only native inhabitants were primitive invertebrates. A handful of tiny worms and insects on land, anaerobic microbes under the hardened lake surfaces. There would be no noise pollution from them. Nothing to dent the silence except for the occasional beating of wind against the valley walls and far rarer sounds of human intrusion.

Now Scarborough freed a hand from its clumsy pile mitten, leaving on his thinner polypropylene glove liner, adequate short-term protection on all but the worst summer days. The temperature had been 16° Fahrenheit when his group left camp that morning, torrid by local standards even with a chill factor of $-20°$, and he would need just a few moments to check his bearings.

Scarborough extricated his GPS receiver from his parka and pressed a keypad button. A topographic satellite image of the valley system north of the Asgard range filled his display, its contours reminding him of an old-fashioned ship's anchor. Next, he scrolled down his menu to the "Navigate" option. A color icon representing the object of his search marked its last known coordinates near the deep, craggy notch at the pass's junction with Wright Valley.

Scarborough studied the display a bit longer, his fur-trimmed hood pulled up, his balaclava covering the gray-flecked scruff of beard that would soon grow out into a winter forest. He wore dark polarized snow goggles over the mask's eye slits, heavy-duty wind pants, and neck and leg gaiters for optimal retention of body heat. Here at the bottom of the globe, life was bounded by the cold, shaped by the cold, its limitations defined by how well you adapted to the cold. The threat of hypothermia meant bundling into innumerable layers of gear and apparel before you ventured outside, a tedious routine that packed on thirty pounds of added weight and was the cause of persistent, some might say *epidemic,* crankiness at the station.

As with so many aspects of existence in Antarctica, you either kept a sense of humor about it or went crazy, Scarborough thought. Thankfully most did the former. A wicked hand with a felt-tip pen, his dorm mate had even graced the front of their clothes closet with a masterpiece of graffiti that portraycd them as a couple of sullen, mopish genies who'd been sealed away inside a giant Coca-Cola bottle wearing only their waffle-knit longjohns, a visual pun on the fact that modern polar fleece outer garments wcre made of a synthetic fabric derived from recycled plastic soft-drink containers. Written above it was the title "PRISONERS OF FASHION." Though this king-sized editorial cartoon had been unveiled months before, their Friday night poker regulars still got a sort of rueful kick out of it, using it as a springboard for their own wardrobe laments. Not that Scarborough could recall hearing anyone grouse about being overdressed out in the field.

His location established, he pocketed the GPS unit and glanced across the moraine at Bradley and Payton, who had wandered ahead of him seeking any trace of the rover. Though he'd been careful to stay mum about it, Scarborough shared a measure of their anxiousness. Developed under exclusive contract with NASA, the Scout IV remote interplanetary vehicle was the product of a tremendous investment in dollars, labor, and prestige for UpLink International. Its sudden and complete signal failure during late-stage field tests had everyone involved with the project on edge, and hoping what had gone wrong was something like a defective microprocessor, a programming error, maybe a radio transmission mast that failed to deploy.

Something *simple,* in other words.

In Scarborough's opinion, however, those scenarios

were limp noodles . . . as were the many similar theories being floated at Cold Corners. Scout's critical systems had been designed with multiple redundancies, none more key to its performance as a lab-on-wheels than the telecommunications packet. Information compiled on the Martian surface was worthless if it couldn't be beamed across the void to Earth, making successful data transfer a baseline requirement. The notion that a minor snafu could knock out the rover's entire gamut of backup relays seemed dubious at best, and hinted that accountability for its possible failure was about to become a bouncing ball.

Scarborough's mouth turned down in a private frown under his balaclava. Shevaun Bradley and David Payton were robotics experts who had been on the ice just over six weeks and planned to leave before final sunset, winging off to civilization aboard a Hercules LC-150 ski transport. Not so for Scarborough. Well into his second eighteen-month hitch with the station's winter-over support crew, he had learned from unpleasant experience that tensions could build fast in shared isolation. The stickiest situations often occurred between habituated polies and summer personnel contingents, and part of his role as expeditionary guide was to lubricate the gears, so to speak. He knew Bradley a little and didn't think she'd be a challenge on that score. Payton was another story.

Scarborough made his way toward the techies over wide beds of gravel and patches of bare bedrock that had been scrubbed to a shiny smoothness by time and weather. Stone chips crunched beneath the rubber soles of his boots. Boulders were scattered everywhere around him, many of knee height or smaller, some dwarfing the group's transportable apple hut. The most imposing rocks Scarborough had seen lay back in the direction of camp, a tumbled expanse that had proven sheer murder to negotiate. Carved out of the highland plateau by monumental glacial flows in the Paleozoic, bereft of rainfall for an estimated two million years, the entire landscape might have been transported from another world in some weird cosmic version of a skin graft . . . which, of course, was precisely why it was chosen as the site of the rover's trial run. According to planetary geologists, no place on Earth bore a closer resemblance to Mars.

Scarborough stopped beside Payton, waited to be acknowledged, and was ignored.

He made a loud affair of clearing his throat. "Any luck? We're close to where Scout fell off our screens."

Still examining the ground, Payton merely shook his head.

Bradley was more responsive. "We weren't expecting much," she said. "Scout traversed the area. I'm certain from the feeds it sent before our link broke. But its wheels probably couldn't have left imprints in this stony surface."

Scarborough considered that a moment.

"My sat maps show lots of sand in the lower pass, close to where it hooks into Wright," he said. "Sand cover holds tracks, and the rover's would be damned hard to miss. There're no other mechanical ponies on the range."

His last remark prompted a mild chuckle from Bradley.

"Cute," she said.

Payton finally looked up at Scarborough. "Scout isn't some twenty-five-cent children's ride," he said curtly, sharing none of his colleague's amusement. "We should move on instead of wasting our time here."

Scarborough hesitated. Restraint, he thought As the rover's project director, Payton was used to the golden-boy treatment, and seemed miffed that even an act of God could screw with his agenda. He had urged an immediate start to their recovery mission, but a chain of sudden Force 10 storms with winds blowing at upward of sixty miles per hour—base meteorologists called them *weather bombs*—had imposed a week's delay. A week of hand-wringing and restless conjecture. It was understandable that he'd be wound tight. His superior attitude was more exasperating.

"Okay," Scarborough said in a controlled tone. "Let's go."

And so they did, Scarborough leading in silence for better than a mile. True to his prediction, the pass's terrain changed radically toward its juncture with Wright Valley. Sand the color of tarnished copper first sprinkled its gritty top crust, then fanned out in thicker accumulations, then coated every inch of ground underfoot with dark, heavy drifts. But however useful Scarborough's GPS unit had been in reckoning their progress, it hadn't helped prepare them for the gaining intensity of the wind. It barreled down from the higher elevations, roaring and growling, flinging tattered sheets of sand over them, making every step forward a slow effort.

Scarborough soon found himself concerned that the tumultuous gusts would have blotted out any sign of the rover's path, a feeling that deepened to quiet worry as they toiled onward with nothing for results. It had become almost oppressive when Payton abruptly halted and touched his shoulder.

"Wait!" He pointed. "Over there."

Scarborough and Bradley turned to look. Scant yards to their left a chain of humpbacked dunes extended along the wall of the pass, unmistakable wheel marks threading up and down their flanks.

The group scurried across the sand to inspect them, crouching together at the base of a dune.

"The deeper, the fresher. And these are pretty deep," Scarborough said. "They can't be more than a couple weeks old, puts 'em in the right ballpark time-wise."

"It's our baby, Alan." Bradley indicated a stippled pattern in the tracks and got out her digital camera for some snapshots. "We couldn't ask for better identification."

Scarborough nodded. Scout's cleated titanium wheels would have left just such imprints. And their close spacing suggested the vehicle was too small to be anything but an unmanned drone. Also, his earlier remark to Bradley hadn't been a colorful exaggeration. There truly *weren't* any other mechanical ponies on the range. To reduce the environmental impact of their activities and preserve the dry valleys as a scientific resource, field workers refrained from operating wheeled or tractor-belted vehicles on ice-free ground, making the snowmobiles that towed their supplies and equipment across lake crusts the only motorized conveyances in use. This self-imposed restriction had been observed for three decades before it was formalized in a multinational code of conduct to which the United States was a signatory. In their negotiations to secure approval for the rover's trials, UpLink and NASA had been firm about guaranteeing participant states that they would avoid leaving behind a mess—or in the language of their written application, would "minimize and remedy any disturbances caused to the natural landscape."

Ultimately, though, the good name of Roger Gordian, UpLink's founder and standard bearer, had carried more weight than diplomatic niceties or signed promises. As a practical matter, implementation of any treaty in this freezing, desolate wilderness relied on the honor system. Somebody broke the rules, who was going to catch on?

The story was in the math, and Scarborough had done his calculations long ago. Antarctica's total land area was five and a half million square miles, double the size of Australia, triple that of Europe. With a winter population of about two thousand cocooned in the research stations, and maybe four times that many summer residents, it averaged between fifty and a hundred fifty thousand miles of open space per person, depending on the season. A tough chunk of real estate to police and patrol. Almost impossible, in fact, because the same agreement that regulated experimentation in the dry valleys imposed a continent-wide ban on military bases, effectively forbidding armed enforcement of its protocols.

But none of this presently concerned Scarborough. He rose from his squat, took his binoculars from the case strapped around his neck, and raised them to his eyes. What he saw of the rover's trail encouraged him. Yes, the wind had scrambled the trail. Completely erased entire segments of it. And was dissipating it into spindling little wisps of sand even as he watched. However, it remained plain enough for several hundred yards before cutting around a sharp eastward bend in the pass.

"All right," he said. "Looks like we're in business—"

Scarborough stopped. He'd noticed something out of the corner of his vision. A momentary wink of brightness far above him on the pass's left wall, formed by the great soaring flank of Mount Cerberus. Curious, he turned the binoculars toward the slope for a better look, but saw only a series of naked ledges climbing to its uppermost reaches between vertical thrusts of stone.

"Find something of interest?" Bradley asked, coming over from behind him.

Scarborough waited before he replied. The flash of light did not repeat. Nor could he be sure exactly where it had originated. Then his view through the glasses blurred and he grunted with annoyance. In extreme cold weather conditions, the vapor from your exhalations puffed up into the air, condensed on the optical lenses of your field glasses, and quickly skimmed them with frost. It was the same with the snow goggles. Worse, really, since your eyelashes could freeze together if you removed them. This charming ECW phenomena didn't get mentioned much in survival handbooks, presumably because their authors considered it a nuisance rather than a hazard. Polies knew the distinction could shift in a heartbeat.

He lowered the binoculars, wiped them with his mitten, and slid them back into their case.

"The sun reflecting off a glaze of ice, I think." He shrugged. "Just happened to catch my eye."

Payton had also approached now, his rigid stance the image of impatience. Scarborough hastened along Scout's trail before he could invite another complaint that they were dawdling.

Bull Pass narrowed as it turned east, its walls pressing in close. Shadows spilled down their sides and pooled on the floor of the trench like black syrup. Channeled into rapid currents, the wind seemed to have inflicted its worst punishment upon the crumbled and broken left slope, a slow erosional process that must have begun untold centuries before. In his mind's eye, Scarborough pictured some colossal ruminant grazing away at the ridgeline with stubborn, tireless persistence, leaving a huge projection of stone here, a fallen granitic slab there, spitting irregular mounds of rubble into the breaches. Opposite, Cerberus loomed in stark contrast: dominant, monolithic, its grooved face darkened with mountain shadows from base to icy brow.

It was perhaps thirty minutes later when Scarborough rounded a broad shoulder of rock and first saw the notch about a half mile up ahead. He paused for a long moment, suddenly reminded of the time he'd visited the Grand Canyon as a youngster. His parents had given him an assortment of educational materials in advance of that summer trip. Books, videos, travel brochures, the works. He'd digested them until he thought he had learned everything there was to know about the place. But when he actually stood gazing out over the chasm from the South Rim, Scarborough realized that neither words nor pictures could capture how it felt to see it with his own eyes. He recognized the natural landmarks. Shiva Temple. Hale's Needle. Point Hanover. They looked just as they did in photos, yet were altogether different. This did not seem a contradiction to him. With his eleventh birthday barely past, Alan Scarborough had in a single shot gained a fundamental and lasting appreciation of direct participatory experience . . . as well as an insatiable yearning for it. He'd never since been content observing reality through windows of separation, framed within neatly bordered perspectives, but had always felt the urge to leap outside to where his feet touched the ground. Why else had he eagerly joined the Marines with an ROTC assignment out of college, and on retirement pursued a civilian gig in a land where the Ice Age had missed its final curtain by ten thousand years? Why else?

Scarborough studied the deep V-shaped notch near the

valley intersection with rapt fascination. Like the photos and descriptions in those boyhood references, his satellite readouts had offered detailed information about the area's geographic features. He had come here prepared. But the sheer immensity of the cleft overwhelmed his senses. And stirred his imagination. He again envisioned gargantuan creatures dining on solid rock as they thundered through the ancient pass. What he knew of glacial migrations was momentarily forgotten. Science was Bradley's and Payton's game. His was to see their expedition through the valleys and return them to Cold Corners safe and sound, ideally with the salvaged Martian rover in their possession. He could allow himself a brief flight of fancy. And right now it was easy to believe that the notch in the side of the pass had been left by a prehistoric monster of indescribable scale. Not the same trudging forager that might have munched away at the slope behind him like a fat hippopotamus snacking on reeds and brush. This would have been something more akin to a tyrannosaur. A lunging beast of prey that took vicious bites out of the earth's hide, gulping them down whole, its fangs leaving permanent gouges wherever they sank in.

It looks like a wound, Scarborough thought. *A wound that never healed shut.*

Bradley had strode up alongside him and was peering through her binoculars, but a glance in her direction revealed she hadn't been focused on the notch. Instead she was scanning the ground. As Scarborough guessed he should have been doing.

"I don't get it," she said.

"Get what?"

She looked at him.

"The rover's tracks," she said, and handed over the binocs. "Check them out for yourself."

Scarborough readily obliged, his gaze following the parallel bands of Scout's wheel marks. They coursed across the open sand in a fairly straight line for what he estimated was a hundred yards, and then swung away toward the notch. That didn't surprise him. Rather, it seemed to confirm that the probe had been operational when it reached the area, since one of its selective tasks was to explore, image, and collect geologic samples from the notch's interior. Why had Bradley sounded so puzzled then?

It took a minute before he understood.

Just when the tracks got to the flat apron of the notch, they evaporated. And insofar as Scarborough could judge from his vantage, did not resume at any point beyond.

"Crap," he said. "Seems we're about to lose the trail."

"Yes," she said. "What do you make of it?"

Scarborough was thoughtful. "I don't know. Could be it was scrubbed clean by wind."

Bradley's silence betrayed her skepticism. Scarborough couldn't blame her. His explanation had been pretty feeble. There was a significant distance between the spot where Scout's wheel marks stopped and the entrance to the notch, and the gusts in this section of the pass were blowing a trifle less vigorously than in the last stretch his party had covered. It seemed improbable that the trail wouldn't continue further on. At the very least it should have left some partial remains. But from where he stood, the rover might as well have been swallowed up by the sand.

Scarborough's view through the glasses clouded from his breath, and he rubbed the steam off before it could freeze. Then he wiped his snow goggles. Not that he needed to bother. He knew what he had seen. Or hadn't seen, to put it more aptly. Neither the wheel marks nor the rover would materialize at his command. That magic trick exceeded a Coke-bottle genie's abilities.

"What's happening?" Payton demanded from over his shoulder. "Why are we standing here?"

Scarborough turned to him. The guy was like a perverse talking doll with about four lines of nastiness recorded on its voice chip. Still, he was owed a straight answer. Scarborough would have preferred one that was simultaneously optimistic, but didn't know how to pair his goals. He chose between them, braced for Payton's reaction.

"Scout's trail wipes out short of the notch," he said. "From what we can see, it doesn't pick up again."

Payton looked at him.

"Short of the notch," Payton repeated. Absorbing the implications of Scarborough's words at once. "Which would be approximately where the rover lost contact with base."

Scarborough nodded.

"I don't understand," Payton said. "If that's as far as Scout traveled, that is where it still ought to be."

Scarborough might have agreed that was the logical conclusion. Except the probe *wasn't* there. And though a slew of possibilities had occurred to him, none convincingly accounted for its MIA status.

"We'll keep going. See what's what," he said. "I wish I had a better plan."

Payton thrust a hand at him, palm up. "Pass me the binoculars," he said with derision. "I want to take a look. With my own eyes."

Scarborough was tempted to suggest that Payton might also want to use his own field glasses, which were hanging in their case over the front of his parka. Instead he handed them to him.

"No problem," Scarborough said. "Give 'em back to Shevaun when you're done."

Bradley nodded to Scarborough in a way he interpreted as sympathetic. It made him feel appreciated. And glad he'd curbed his irritation.

They waited as Payton studied the trail. A minute or two later he let the glasses sink to his chest.

"This isn't possible, it—" He suddenly interrupted himself. "Wait. Do either of you hear that noise?"

Scarborough did. It was a kind of high metallic buzz that seemed to drill through the blanketing rush of the wind from an unresolved distance. He glanced at Bradley. The inquisitive tilt of her head revealed she was listening carefully to the sound, trying to pinpoint its source. While the reverberant acoustics of their surroundings made that hard, Scarborough thought it was issuing from the direction of the notch.

Payton evidently thought the same. He brought the glasses back up, aimed them at the yawning, jagged scar in the wall of the pass.

"What the hell is this?" he said. His voice was shaky. An instant later, his hands were too. "Scarborough, do your job. *Will you do your goddamned job and answer me?*"

Scarborough stared at the notch. At first nothing caught his attention. Then an object darted out onto the sand. From a distance it seemed a mere speck. But it was coming on at an incredible speed, growing larger in his vision with a quickness that matched.

Payton continued to stand beside him with his gloved hands trembling around the binoculars. Scarborough did not want to lose a beat getting his own set of glasses out of their case. The buzzing had grown louder and louder, filling his ears as it surged between the stone walls on either side of him. To his unaided eyes, the thing from inside the notch appeared to be a dark cloud of ground smoke churning around a solid and even darker core. At its present rate of acceleration it would be upon them in less than a minute. And he didn't have a clue what it might be.

"I need the glasses," he told Payton. "Hurry."

The techie didn't answer. He seemed oblivious to Scarborough, paralyzed with shock.

Scarborough reached out to take the binocs, but Payton's grasp was unyielding. He pulled harder, snatched them from Payton's petrified fingers, wiped the frost off them.

A glance through the eyepieces immediately told him what had induced Payton's mental disconnect.

The cloud was not smoke but a storm of powdery reddish-brown sand. And the object kicking it up as it raced ever closer was something that should not have been in the pass, the valleys, nor anywhere on the continent. Not for any conceivable reason.

A storm, that's it. Scarborough's thought burst through the door of his memory with haunting irony. The fear arrived an instant later. *A desert storm.*

"Alan, talk to me." Bradley had inched close, her arm brushing against him. "Tell me what you see out there."

Scarborough held up a hand.

"Wait," he said. "I need to be positive."

But that was a lie. Scarborough knew what he saw in spite of his initial disbelief. What he really needed was to pull himself together.

When he'd served with the Corps in the Persian Gulf War, special forces units had used tricked-out dune buggies called Fast Attack Vehicles in advance recon and hit-and-run combat missions. Stripped down to their welded tubular frames and roll bars, their low-slung carriages left virtually no discernible signature for enemies to sniff and chase, which led to their reputation as the earthbound equivalents of Stealth bombers. Accommodating two riders in front and a third in an elevated rear gunner's chair, they held various configurations of roof-mounted antitank tubes, forward and rear machine guns, grenade launchers, and side compartments for gear, small arms, and ammo storage. Back in the day, Scarborough and a buddy had taken an FAV for a workout in the desert and gone belting over dunes and trenches at an uninterrupted eighty-five miles per hour.

Scarborough inhaled sharply, all nerves. He was sweating under his innermost layer of apparel. Sweating *torrents* in the below-zero cold. The wagons had since been redubbed Light Strike Vehicles and given a bunch of munitions upgrades that made them even deadlier, but call them whatever you wanted, one of those swift automotive killing machines was highballing straight at him. He had no time to wonder who had launched it. The vehicle was fully manned and armed. That was enough for him to know his party was in desperate trouble.

He lowered the binocs, looked urgently around for cover.

Cerberus's steep grade was banded by a thirty-foot zone of loose, pebbly scree. No protection on that side. A large block of stone heaving up out of the sand near the fractured left slope was their only bet.

Scarborough grabbed Bradley's elbow. "We have to move, get to that outcrop."

She eyed the oncoming assault vehicle, emitted a breathless gasp of confusion and horror. The LSV had almost reached them. Long kerchiefs of sand streamed back from its spinning tires. The crewmen wore crash helmets, face masks, snow goggles, and wind-resistant camouflage outfits that melted seamlessly into the terrain. Scarborough made the heavy weapon sandwiched between the antitank tubes on its roof as an M-2 .50-caliber machine gun. The man in the gunner's station was gripping its black metal handlebar triggers. In front of the passenger seat's occupant was a pintle-mounted M-60 machine gun—smaller but no less capable of blowing a human being to bits and pieces.

"My God." Bradley was frantic. "That car . . . Alan . . . the *guns* on it . . ."

"*Just come on!*" Scarborough tugged hard on her arm, looked over at Payton. He was still a blank, lock-limbed mannequin. *"Both of you, let's go or we're dead!"*

His shouted warning finally snapped Payton out of his daze. Scarborough motioned him toward the outcrop and then broke for it, clinging to Bradley's arm, half dragging her along at his side. A slight woman, she weighed about 115 pounds under the bulk of her packs and clothing, and would be unable keep pace without help.

Scarborough and Bradley had almost reached the big protuberance of rock, Payton trailing by a step or two, when their attackers opened fire. The rattle of the machine gun was deafening as its ammunition slapped the ground at their backs. Scarborough shoved Bradley behind the outcrop, dove after her, landed on his belly. He heard another crackle of gunfire on the other side, a grunt, and pushed himself to his knees, dirt spilling from his trouser legs. A hurried glance around the rock's edge confirmed what he'd feared. Payton was sprawled on the ground, his garments ruptured with bullet holes, steam rising into the air from his wounds. There was blood on him, around him, everywhere.

Warm red blood flowing from his gaudy red coat into the parched-red cold-desert sand.

Scarborough dropped back into cover, looked at Bradley.

"You okay?" he whispered.

She stared at him wordlessly as if the question hadn't registered. Then a shadow fell over their huddled forms. The LSV had jolted to a halt just beyond the rock, practically on top of them.

He reached out and gripped her arm again. "Are you okay?"

This time she nodded.

"Good," he said. "Listen, Shevaun. We've got to surrender to these people."

Bradley seemed astonished by the idea. She rejected it with a shake of her head.

"No, no, we can't," she said. "We don't even know what they *want*."

"Doesn't matter. We want to live."

She hesitated. "Payton . . . did you see . . . is he . . . ?"

"It's too late for him." Scarborough heard the LSV's engine purring with soft, certain threat. "Giving ourselves up is our only chance. But I won't make the call. We both need to decide this."

She took a couple of sharp, agitated breaths.

Scarborough waited. He could hear the engine purring. It sounded like an eager jungle cat.

"All right," she said. "I'm with you."

He saw her start to tremble, reached out for her hand,

held it. "When we stand up, put your arms above your head. And keep them there. Okay?"

Bradley nodded.

"Don't let go of me," she said. "I can do this. But don't let go."

Scarborough eased his head above the edge of the rock. The vehicle had stopped not five feet away, its crew facing him in impassive silence. Sunlight glinted off the four racked headlamps on its impact bar. He tried to keep his eyes off the machine guns positioned above them, off Payton's limp body on the ground below. Tried to tunnel his gaze onto the man in the driver's seat. He wasn't sure he could continue suspending his panic otherwise.

"We're American researchers!" he shouted. "We have no weapons!"

More silence except for the steady idling hum of the vehicle's engine.

Scarborough swallowed past a lump in his throat. "Do you understand? *We're unarmed!*"

There was another tick of silence. Then the LSV's driver turned to the man in the passenger seat, spoke to him in a language Scarborough didn't understand, turned back toward the outcrop.

"Move away from the rock," he said. His English was thickly accented. "Now."

Scarborough looked at Bradley. He could feel her fingers pressing into his hand through its double layer of gloves, and tightened his own grip.

"Ready?" he asked her.

"Ready."

The two of them rose, slowly, their arms raised high, his right hand still clutching her left. Then they stepped out from behind the outcrop.

"Stop where you are," the driver said, studying them. "Turn toward me."

They complied with his orders, hands linked above their heads, sharing their strength, their courage, facing their unknown attackers together.

That was the way they were standing when the man in the passenger seat trained the long black barrel of his machine gun upon them and also did precisely as he'd been ordered.

TWO

WITH ITS ARCTIC-BLUE BODY, CORAL SIDE COVES, AND
beige vinyl interior, the '57 Corvette roadster was the car
of Pete Nimec's dreams. A bolt of glorious inspiration
captured in streamlined fiberglass and a classy flourish of
chrome, delivering decisive 283 dual-four-barrel go without showoff extravagance. Just over six thousand of them
had hit showroom floors across the USA, and just *under*
two hundred were pumped with Ramjet fuel injection, a
handful out of a scarce, exquisite handful that were still
around and running a half century later.

A '57 Corvette fuelie. Reconditioned to its original
Chevrolet standards, including minor production-line im-
perfections. Probably worth upwards of a hundred, a hundred fifty thou, assuming you could find one for sale or
auction.

And it was Nimec's.

Which is to say, he owned it outright.

Owned it from the crossed-flag badge over its toothy
front grille back to the big twin exhaust pipes at its tail.
Owned it from the removable hardtop down to the wide

whitewall tires. Owned it, his dream car, and by surprise no less, having received it at his condominium with a decorative red bow and handwritten note of appreciation taped to its wraparound windshield, an unexpected present from the man he admired most in all the world.

On any other morning, Nimec would have been in an unsinkable state of bliss. And he had been while driving to UpLink's Rosita Avenue headquarters with his Wonderbar dash radio tuned to an oldies station, while pulling the 'Vette into his reserved underground parking slot, while riding the elevator to his office on the twenty-fifth floor.

But now that mood was heavy and flat, punctured by a single click of the mouse next to his computer.

He checked his watch as his telephone bleeped. Nine o'clock. Gordian would have already arrived at work.

"Nimec," he answered.

It was the boss, as anticipated.

"Pete, you'd better come on up here."

"This about Megan's e-mail?"

"Yes."

"I just read it myself," Nimec said. "Be right with you."

He cradled the receiver and whisked out into the corridor.

Minutes later Nimec entered Gordian's reception room, tipped a brisk salute to Norma, got her nod of admittance, stepped over to the heavy oak inner door that she guarded like a vigilant gryphon, and rapped twice as he shouldered it open.

He stood inside the doorway and waited. Roger Gordian sat at his desk in front of the floor-to-ceiling window with its view of the city skyline and, east of downtown, the solid heave of Mount Hamilton above the Santa Clara foothills. A look at him told two stories. One was about the lingering physical effects of the biological assassination attempt he'd survived last year. The other was about the force of will that had been as vital to his recovery as the gene-blocker codes grabbed during a scalpel raid on the germ factory in Ontario. This was in November, shortly before Thanksgiving. It would always stick in Nimec's memory, the time of year it happened, because Gordian had revived from his coma precisely on Thanksgiving *Day,* his awakening a grace that, like so many, had been attained with terrible bloodshed and sacrifice.

Thanksgiving, not quite four months ago. It seemed longer.

Gordian had gained some weight since his illness, but was much thinner than before. Its ravages had left noticeable marks on his features: the pale cheeks, the slight wiriness of his graying hair, the finely veined skin at his temples, the dark hollows under his eyes. But his eyes themselves radiated an undiminished intensity and brightness. He was better, and with time would be better still.

What troubled Nimec on occasion was knowing that few great losses were ever reclaimed in total.

He tried not to let his thoughts slide in that direction right now.

"You knocked," Gordian said.

"Don't I always?"

Gordian shook his head. "It started after I got back."

Nimec sat across the desk from him.

"Really?" Nimec said.

"Really." Gordian shrugged. "Of course, my observation doesn't imply an absolute preference."

Nimec rubbed his chin. "Might just be a passing fad anyway."

Gordian smiled a little and was quiet. The picture frame in his hands was sized for an 8×10 photograph. Nimec couldn't see the display side from his chair, but realized Gord had been looking at it when he came in.

"With the bad news from Cold Corners, I'm thinking maybe this isn't the right time to thank you," Nimec said. "Except I can't think of one that would be righter. The car, well . . ."

He paused a moment, at a loss for words.

Gordian regarded him from across the desk. "Do you like it?"

"Yeah," Nimec said. "It's . . . choice."

"And it arrived okay?"

"Last night. A guy rolls it up to my building, has the doorman buzz the intercom, tell me somebody's dropped off an oversized package. That I might want to come down to the lobby and get it."

Gordian nodded approvingly.

"He can follow a script," he said.

Nimec looked at him. "You didn't have to—"

"—let you know how much I value everything you've done for me over the past decade? I'm the person who needs to be grateful, Pete."

Nimec kept looking at him.

"Hard to believe it's been ten years," Nimec said.

"To the day," Gordian said.

Another pause.

"Still," Nimec said. "I've got a pretty fair idea what that car must have set you back. . . ."

"I can afford it."

"That isn't the point. . . ."

"Would you have preferred something more conventional? Say, a jeweled tie clip and cuff link set? You've never seemed one for dressing up."

"I'm security chief," Nimec said. "You hired me to manage the protection of our employees and corporate facilities. And I do it the best way I know how." He shrugged. "I wouldn't deserve the job if I gave less."

"Enough," Gordian said. "There aren't many companies engaged in the sort of high-risk ventures UpLink International tackles. I could mention a dozen offhand that would pay whatever salary you demand, without requiring that you be on standby to zip off around the world in a flash. We both know why you're here. Why you *stay*. So ease up and enjoy the car. I was thinking it would complement the old Wurlitzer jukebox and soda bar in that ratty pool hall of yours."

Nimec raised an eyebrow. "Didn't realize you'd heard about it."

"Murmurs and whispers," Gordian said. "I'd be glad to see it sometime. Test my skill at Fourteen-one Continuous."

Nimec gave his surprise a chance to wane.

"You're on," he said.

Gordian nodded, his face becoming serious. He took a slow, deep breath that worked as a kind of unintentional segue.

"Now," he said. "We need to talk about Antarctica."

"Yeah," Nimec said.

Gordian hesitated. He glanced down at the picture frame again, then back at Nimec.

"The missing search team," he said. "Do you know any of its members?"

Nimec shook his head. "I've read their personnel files. That's about it."

"I've met them all at one time or another," Gordian said. "My association with Dave Payton and Shevaun Bradley has been strictly in connection with the rover project. They're top people in their field. And they're our people."

They looked at each other in silence. *Our people.* Nimec fully grasped the connotations of that short phrase. Nothing meant more to Gordian than the safety of his employees in the far-flung regions where UpLink had established many of its outposts. His Dream, capital D, was to bring greater freedom, prosperity, and stability to the citizens of corrupt and oppressive governments by opening them up to information that otherwise might be blocked by their political leadership. Staking his legacy on the old axiom that knowledge was democracy's best tool, he'd brainstormed and funded the world's largest telecommunications network with a fortune earned in military aviation technology. That had involved building and staffing satellite ground station facilities on some very dangerous turf. It had also made him some very serious enemies. Bad guys in places high and low got touchy when their control was threatened. Thus Gordian had spared no cost putting together a global corporate security division superior to the armed forces of many countries. Dubbed Sword, it was conceived as an antidote to their enemies' rabid impulses. A way of staying a step ahead of them. But the unpredictable was always a factor. Sometimes the enemy had the cunning and stealth to lurk beneath your radar until he was ready to strike. Sometimes his claws were sharper, and his reflexes quicker, than you thought. And sometimes it was just a fluke accident that got you where it hurt.

If experience had taught Nimec anything, it was that there was no guaranteed inoculation against human vulnerability.

"What can you tell me about the guide?" he said. "Scarborough . . . that his name?"

"Alan Scarborough," Gordian said. "We were introduced at our send-off for the original outfitting crew at Cold Corners. He's ex-Marine, took officer training at A&M, saw combat as a platoon commander in the Persian Gulf . . . 2nd Division, I think. A strapping, brawny Texan with a personality to match. The type of man that you like right away. And feel you can depend on whatever the circumstances."

"Understandable why Meg would choose him to head the expedition."

Gordian nodded.

"If his party was in distress, I'm convinced Scarborough could manage the situation until help arrived. And he wouldn't need to wait for Cold Corners to launch a rescue effort. There are scattered NSF encampments closer by. Helicopters regularly fly out of McMurdo Station to monitor them and provide emergency aid. Short term, he'd have access to reserve caches of food and medical supplies that have been airdropped throughout the valley system."

"If Scarborough's as competent as you say, I'd expect

him to send out an SOS," Nimec said. "But he doesn't. One morning his team starts out from camp. Next thing you know they're gone."

Gordian took another deep breath, released it.

"Yes," he said. "That's the bottom line."

Nimec was thoughtful.

"There family members we need to contact?" he asked.

"Payton's divorced, with a teenaged son. Bradley's single. The next of kin listed on her employment record is a sister in New Mexico."

"And Scarborough?"

"No wife. No children. No siblings. Parents deceased."

Nimec looked at him.

"Sort of makes us his only family."

"Yes."

They sat without speaking. Gordian stared at the picture in his hands for a long time, holding its frame by the edges with particular gentleness, almost as if it was fragile to the touch. Then he turned it so the photo behind the glass was facing Nimec.

Nimec recognized the sixtyish couple in it immediately. The man had thick, wavy silver hair, an intelligent face, and wore wireless spectacles perched high on his nose. The woman next to him was a slender, fine-boned beauty that age had transformed without diminution. They wore elegant formal clothing, and stood posed before a shimmery portrait backdrop the color of rose petals.

"The Steiners," Nimec said. His voice was low. "Jesus, they made a good-looking pair."

"Yes."

More silence.

Arthur and Elaine Steiner had been maintenance technicians at the UpLink compound in Russia when it was attacked by hired terrorists some years back. Hours before the strike they drove out into the countryside to investigate a power failure and never returned. Their bloody bodies and wrecked jeep were found once the offensive was repelled, in a blast crater torn into the ground by a rocket grenade. They had come to a bad place at the worst possible time, crossing paths with the hit squad, who'd knocked out the electrical lines as they rolled on toward the compound.

"This photo was mailed to guests who'd attended their fortieth wedding anniversary dinner," Gordian said at length. "Their Ruby Anniversary. Did you know that? The traditional symbol, I mean."

Nimec shook his head. "Being single . . . it isn't something I've thought about much."

Gordian looked at him. "For the first fifteen years of marriage, each one is considered a small milestone. The first is Paper. The second Cotton. Then Leather, Flowers . . . and so forth." He sighed. "After that stretch, the special anniversaries are marked every five years. I'm not sure of the reason. But I know the magic number becomes five. I've been married to Ashley for thirty-two years. In another three we'll be celebrating our Coral Anniversary. Then, a half decade later, knock wood, our Ruby. Next comes Sapphire, Gold, and Emerald. Diamond would be our sixtieth. It's an interesting question whether etiquette's caught up with present-day longevity statistics and gone past that. Ash could probably tell us. Women know. Sometimes, I think they know everything the instant they're born."

"A head start like that's kind of hard to beat," Nimec said.

"I'd be happy to finish with a tie," Gordian said. "Those anniversary symbols, Pete. Before the Steiners were killed I couldn't have run them down for you if my fate hung on it. Didn't have the slightest notion what they were, and I'd been married almost three decades. If Norma hadn't reminded me with a scolding that still rings in my ears, I likely wouldn't have known my Silver was coming up. UpLink had consumed so much of my life, I'd forgotten how to share it with the woman I love."

"And when Art and Elaine died?"

Gordian was quiet, sitting with the picture frame still

turned toward Nimec. His gaze seemed at once there and apart, distant and tightly focused, as if telescoped onto some horizon that lay far outside the walls of the room.

"It changed things," he said. "I recall the day their bodies were flown back to the States. They came aboard a NATO plane. An IL-76 transport. There were twenty-three dead. Many were victims of the attack in Kaliningrad. Others lost their lives in our raid on the terrorist hideaway. Twenty-three human beings arriving in coffins. This was at Kennedy Airport, in New York. Waiting for it to arrive, I couldn't feel anything but guilt. I'd put them all in harm's way. Friends, employees. But I couldn't cover them. Couldn't do anything besides wait for that plane to bring them home for burial."

"None of it was your fault," Nimec said. "People can't always be protected."

Gordian nodded.

"I know, Pete. I came to realize it standing there on the tarmac," he said. "It was sunset when the plane touched down, and the light was golden on its wings . . . gold on gray. Then it deepened to orange. And then violet as the coffins were brought out. I'd arranged for a band to be present, and they were playing Bach, an excerpt from one of his Passions. I remember the music. Solemn, meditative. But something about it, coupled with that majestic sunset, helped lift me above the sorrow and despair. Something that was untouchably hopeful. Or that aspired toward hope. And I remember promising myself I'd recommit to my own marriage, make it a testament to the love that Arthur and Elaine had had for each other. Remember vowing I'd press forward, continue using whatever resources and influence I had to do some good in the world. I owed it to them. Owed it every one of the people who'd been killed. They *can't* always be protected from violence. But we have to keep our watch."

Nimec stared at the photo and thought for a while. Then he switched his attention to Gordian.

"Meg was clear about wanting me at Cold Corners," Nimec said.

"Yes."

"And you're with her on it."

"Yes," Gordian said. "Your thoughts?"

"I have to wonder what difference I'd make. Our staff down there knows the territory. They're getting an open assist from MacTown. We've got to believe they're doing everything they can."

Gordian looked steadily at him.

"They're racing against the calendar," he said. "The Antarctic winter is just three weeks off. Months of darkness and bad weather. Once they have to bunker in, that's the end of any sort of investigation. Megan doesn't want to waste time. And she knows what you can accomplish given very little to spare."

Nimec suddenly felt thickheaded. *Investigation,* he thought. He'd misunderstood Megan Breen's request. This wasn't about whether his involvement would effect the conclusion of their search. Wasn't about conclusions at all, but rather undefined suspicions. Megan's, Gordian's, and his own. Antarctica was a brutal place. Nobody went there without a keen awareness of that fact. But the back-to-back disappearances of Scout IV and its S&R team equaled a huge, ominous question mark. And a likely tragedy. Something strange was going on out in the dry valleys, and Nimec was being asked to help get to the bottom of it. That was where his participation could be of important benefit.

The problem was that he considered his principal responsibilities to be with Roger Gordian in San Jose.

"I've got some questions before I hurry to pack my bags," Nimec said. "With Ricci deep in the field, who's left to man home plate? He pressed hard for my go-ahead, and it would be a mistake to pull him back without good cause. In my opinion we don't have it. Not yet."

"Ricci can carry on with his assignment. I don't expect you'll be gone too long. The last flight out of base is in three weeks. And you'll have a reserved seat, I promise," Gordian said. "Meanwhile, Rollie Thibodeau is here to handle things in your absence."

"The way he's been acting, I'm not sure Rollie can—"

"I am," Gordian interrupted. "And I would think you'd have faith in the rest of our local Sword team."

"Not the issue," Nimec said. "We've had some close calls in the past few months. And the snakes responsible are still holed away underground."

Gordian kept his gaze on him.

"I don't need constant babysitting, Pete," he said. "What are your other concerns?"

Nimec paused. It had taken about five sentences to exhaust his arguments. That left him scuffling for a dignified surrender.

"My Corvette," he said "You going to take care of her for me?"

The faintest of smiles touched Gordian's lips.

"She'll be okay." He carefully put down the picture frame. "That's promise number two."

Nimec sat there looking at Gordian for about thirty seconds. Then he gave him an acquiescent nod, rose from his chair, and started out of the office.

"Pete, one final thing . . ."

He turned to face Gordian.

"An old friend of mine with NASA is due to shepherd a small delegation of reporters and Senators around Cold Corners. The timing couldn't be worse, but it's part of a government funding push that can't be called off," he said. "At any rate, give my regards to Annie."

Nimec stood with his hand suddenly tight on the brass doorknob. "Annie?"

"Caulfield," Gordian said. "You remember her, of course."

Nimec swallowed.

"Sure, I'll say hello," he said.

And strode from the room.

THREE

As HE EMERGED FROM HIS EIGHTEENTH-CENTURY ES-
tate outside Rosmarkie for his daily predawn walk, Ewie
B. Cameron, whose fifth great granduncle was the eldest
son of Sir Ewen of Lochiel of the Highland Camerons,
could feel nothing of the legendary courage and fierceness
of his ancestors, but only an awful nervous gnawing in
his stomach that had worsened throughout the long, long
night.

If the documents that plant supervisor had slipped him
proved authentic . . .

No, no, he thought. Their authenticity was beyond
question. He could not seek an out for himself by playing
the willful fool. . . .

If his interpretation of them proved accurate despite
their many cryptic references, verifying the supervisor's
story . . .

And if the plant's key stakeholders could not then provide an acceptable accounting of the transactions . . .
which Ewie knew would be nearly impossible given their

flagrant violation of Scottish and international regulations . . .

If, if, *if* . . .

Ewie reached the end of his private lane, where a holly hedge screened his lawn from the narrow country road rolling past, the brightness of its berries muted now in the crepuscular light. Stepping onto the shoulder of the road, he turned left against whatever traffic might happen by at this early hour, and strolled toward the stone embankment where it was his habit to do some leg stretches before intensifying his pace. The morning was cold but not at all blustery, with just enough bite to be invigorating. Though Ewie was prone to be an abstemious sobriety of temperament, it was the sort of weather that would usually lift his mood like the fine mist curling off the mature Archangel firs that rose a hundred feet into the air on either side of him.

Today he was only wishing the twist in his gut would slacken a bit, so he could summon the appetite for a minimal breakfast.

For if the evidence Ewie had obtained was what it seemed on its face, the apprehension he felt about this evening's meeting was as nothing compared to his dread of its broader consequences. Indeed, his first impulse had been to keep the information to himself until he conducted a quiet personal investigation. But that would have been imprudent. Say word of the alleged goings-on at Cromarty Firth leaked in the meantime? Say his informant grew impatient and brought the hard copies elsewhere—another council member, an Energy Authority constable, some damned English bureaucrat with the Department of Trade of Industry? Lord knows, the man might even rashly trot off to the press. Were his own prior ken revealed, Ewie knew his reputation would be compromised. Or worse. He might well be patsied and have to forfeit his council post. Face civil and criminal prosecution.

It was a mad predicament he'd been tossed into. Absolutely mad.

Ewie had been walking for several minutes, bogged in thought, when he noticed that he'd almost missed the embankment. He frowned at his distraction and stepped off the dirt shoulder for his routine warmup exercises.

Standing close to the rock, he leaned against it with his forearms, rested his head on his hands, then bent his right leg forward and extended the other straight back, holding the stretch until he felt it in his left calf. Then he changed sides. After about a minute, he put one foot up on a projecting ledge and, hands on his hips, bent his knee to relax the hamstring and groin muscles. . . .

Perhaps, Ewie thought, he should have shied away from the plant supervisor. Declined to attend their clandestine meeting at the pub, or at least refused to accept the envelope he was handed under the table. He could then have claimed ignorance with honesty. He was no hero. No warrior chieftain like his namesake Sir Ewen, seventeenth clan chieftain, slayer of the last wild wolf in Scotland, and Jacobite rebel who fought beside Bonnie Dundee at Killiecrankie, where it was said he'd torn the throat out of a ranking English officer with his bare teeth, drinking his blood as it pulsed from the wound. Nor would Ewie compare himself to his great and renowned forebear Major Allan Cameron, founder of the bold 79th Highlanders, which was later renamed the Queen's Own Cameron Highlanders, and then merged with the Seaforths to become the Queen's Own Highlanders.

Ewie was simply Ewie. An estate legatee, resolute bachelor, and minor elected official appointed to the Land and Environment Select Committee, which reported to a policy committee, which in turn was under the higher control of a strategic committee of the district council. His usual issues of concern were sewage improvements, road and bridge repairs, traffic-light placements, and such. Ewie did not pretend he'd inherited the brave disposition of his forebears. Did not share their combative propensities. He was proudly content to have his fabled lineage charted in the social registry, and the family crest and tartan displayed on his mantelpiece.

Finished with his warmups, Ewie tarried by the ledge as the lights of an oncoming vehicle slid over the rise up ahead, on his side of the road. They glanced off the blaze-orange windbreaker he always wore on his morning rambles, a precaution that made it easier for motorists to spot him. The small Citröen that appeared moments later was familiar, belonging to a pretty young woman who owned the bakery just over the Kessock bridge. She slowed as she came closer, pulled out toward the opposite lane to give Ewie a comfortable berth, and exchanged a mannerly wave with him in passing.

Then the road was again empty. Ewie got on with his walk, feeling physically looser, and hoping he'd eased some of his mental tensions as well. But his thoughts soon drifted back to what he'd learned from the plant supervisor, and they were accompanied by unrelieved distress and anxiety.

It would have been easy for Ewie to rebuff the fellow with a smile, a shrug, and a polite tip of his glass before any secrets were divulged. Easy to shut his eyes to the whole scandalous deal. So why on earth hadn't he?

The answer, Ewie knew, was that he was stuck with an inconvenient sense of responsibility. Both as public servant and citizen. The plant at Cromarty Firth employed almost fifteen hundred people from Black Isle down the coast to Inverness, and accounted for perhaps twenty-five million pounds per year in local wages, with millions more filtering into the economy through secondary commerce—a full thirty percent of the Gross District Product. At present the core workforce was involved in decommissioning prototype fast breeder reactors built in the 1950's and '60's. But with the site a top contender for an experimental JET tokamak fusion laboratory, revenues had the potential to double in the next ten years.

If the disclosures were true, however . . .

That word again, Ewie thought.

If.

If they were true, it was not only the expansion that would be threatened, but Cromarty's very license to remain operational. The UK Atomic Energy Authority constabulary would shut down the plant in a blink, sending the area's economic prospects into the deepest of holes.

Ewie started up a moderate incline with brisk strides and rhythmic swings of his arms. He wanted to get his blood circulating, and the oxygen flowing into his lungs. Wanted beyond all else to clear his head.

As he neared the top of the rise, Ewie heard another vehicle coming toward him. A commercial rig, judging from the rumble of its wheels. He reached the downhill side and saw that it was a giant tub of a Unimog. The truck was moving well in excess of the speed limit with its brights on.

Startled, blinking from glare of the headlamps, Ewie stepped further onto the shoulder. The truck kept hauling along as if it were on a speed course. Ewie was sure the driver had his gears in fifth.

Ewie decided to let him go on by before resuming his walk. Probably the driver was some ass who'd fallen behind schedule making a delivery to Inverness, and meant to catch up with the clock by hurtling along this quiet stretch of blacktop with no thought of his or anyone else's safety. Ewie had a mind to memorize his tag number and report him to the police when he got home.

By the time Ewie realized the Unimog had swerved directly toward the shoulder where he was standing, it was too close for him to get out of the way. Blinded by the headlamps, his ears filled with thunder, he reflexively cast his hands front of his face, thrusting his body back toward the wooded area lining the road.

A split second before the front end of the cab mashed into him, Ewie began to shout something that was part question, part curse, and part expression of fear and anger. But the loud roar of the engine drowned out what little of it escaped his lips, and then everything was over for him, all over, his life crushed out, the truck plunging on down the road, away toward the mainland, the blood spatters on its massive fender unnoticeable to anyone who might chance to see it pass in the semidarkness.

They were lying in bed, the husband on his back with the quilt pulled to his bare chest, his wife on her side atop the quilt, facing him, her right hand flat on his stomach. Her nightgown, a flimsy strip of lace-edged silk, revealed far more than it hid. Slung across his body, her right leg was long, toned, the flesh of its thigh smooth and creamy white.

Inspector Frank Gorrie of the Northern Constabulary, Inverness Command Area, was thinking he might be envious of the fellow she was snuggled against, if only his gaze hadn't climbed above the generous swell where the nightie did not quite manage to cover her breasts.

She had a beautiful figure.

Gorrie did not know about the face, would not know until he saw a photograph of her as she'd appeared in life. Most of it was gone, blown away by a .38-caliber bullet, and there was blood all over the rest. The shot that killed the husband was cleaner, a single entry wound in the middle of his forehead. Probably he'd been asleep when it was fired, never knew what hit him. His face was tranquil, eyes closed. There was a dash of foam at the corner of his lips.

Gorrie could see that the pillowcases were soggy and red under their heads, under the pistol clutched in the woman's left hand, her finger curled around the trigger, its short barrel thrust into what remained of her mouth.

Standing at the foot of the bed, Gorrie experienced a brief twinge of guilt that had nothing to do with his appreciation of the dead woman's comely shape. In police work, you noticed what you noticed. The best and worst in people often rubbed up close, and he would not damn himself for being human. But whatever had happened to the couple, or between them, their intimate connection was a strong thing in the room, and Gorrie suspected his discomfort came from the peculiar feeling that he'd somehow intruded upon it.

He turned to the young constable at the door behind him. "What's the crack on Drummond from the Child Protection Unit?"

"On his way. Someone from Social Work's coming with him."

Gorrie motioned to the left, where they'd found the couple's infant son in his nursery adjoining the master bedroom.

"Baby's quiet. You sure he's okay?"

"Aye, sir. We—"

In the outer hallway, the woman who'd discovered the bodies was working up to another fit of teary hysterics. Her name was Christine Gibbon, and she'd identified herself as the best friend of the looker in the tidbit nightie, stressing in the bluntest of terms that she'd held an absolute loathing for the man of the house and gone out of her way to avoid contact with him whenever possible.

"More of a bawler than that little one, she is," Gorrie muttered under his breath. "But let's hear what you were saying. . . ."

"We found some formula in the kitchen. Nappies in a closet near the crib. Robertson gave him a change. And he's got him on the bottle right now."

"Four boys of his own, dabbing the piss off a rashy tossel must be nothing new."

"Aye. I'd suppose."

Gorrie released a sigh.

"All right, you'd best get somebody in here with a camera," he said. "Capture the moment, as they say . . . not that I expect either of these sweethearts'll be sending the other any endearments next Valentine's Day."

The constable smiled feebly, nodded, and left the room. Gorrie noticed he hadn't once glanced at the bed. No great wonder. With the low violent crime rate in Inverness, and this his first year with the Force, he'd most surely never encountered anything comparable to the scene in this room.

Gorrie looked down at his spiral notepad, flipped to a clean page, and was about to add a few words to his notes when Christine Gibbon resumed her emotional narrative to the officer he'd stationed in the hallway. Gorrie perked an ear. No telling whether she'd come out with something he hadn't yet heard.

"I told Claire a hun'red times . . ."

Claire Mackay, the wife, Gorrie thought.

". . . a hun'red time's over 'n *more,* you want to count, that she'd be doin' herself a favor by leavin' the bloody mutt . . ."

Said mongrel dog being Ed Mackay, the husband. Gorrie had needed to coax the Gibbon woman into giving his name in her initial statement, as she'd insisted the very utterance of it would rot her tongue.

". . . to his drinkin' and erse-chasin', but I couldn't get her to listen. See how he provides for me an' the baby, she'd say. If it weren't for him I'd still be in the lands, she'd say. Got to forgive him his weaknesses, and so on, and so forth. Well, *I* say good riddance to the besotted radge, an' keep your sympathy for Claire . . ."

Never mind that it was her mate who appeared to have been the victim in what was shaping up to be a murder-suicide case, Gorrie thought.

". . . poor girl, she'd been better off in that cramped old flat we used to share when we was single. What good's his high job at the plant to her now? Or this high place, in the end tally . . ."

Gorrie frowned at her latest repetition of what had become a tedious song. The "high place" was a suburban bungalow with a nice plot of green here on Eriskay Road, a short jaunt from the city center. The "high job," taking Christine Gibbon's comments backwards, was a supervisory waste-management position at the Cromarty Firth nuclear power plant over on Black Isle.

". . . tell you, officer, I knew it would come to tragedy.

Better they'd gone their separate ways. I'm not one for
dirty talk, but this man was one adulterous *shit*. Always
figured he'd take a hand to Claire when he was in one of
his moods, though I can't claim she declared it out and
open. He'd got her so mousy intimidated, she kept everything bottled inside. And now the bottle's broke. What
she did, she was pushed to do. Pushed, you can be confident. A hun'red times I told the poor girl . . ."

As she dissolved into sobs, Gorrie phased her out,
thinking there wasn't much more of relevance to be gotten
from her. Hearsay aside, Christine Gibbons's account
could be trimmed to a paragraph. She'd come to her
friend's bungalow this morning in her automobile, the two
of them having planned to strap the tyke into a carriage
and go shopping down by the Ness. Because Mr. Mackay
would occasionally take a ride to the plant with one of
the other site-workers, it did not strike Christine as unusual to find his car in the drive. At any rate, she'd
knocked on the door and got no answer. Knocked some
more, no answer. Then she'd rung the bell. Still no one
came to the door. All the while she could hear the child
crying inside the house, which caused her some growing
disturbance. After another ten minutes of knocking and
bell-ringing, Christine let herself in with a spare key
Claire had given her to use in a pinch, and called out from
the entry hall, again without response. With her opinion
of Mr. Mackay being what it was, and no sign of Claire,
and the baby shrieking its lungs out, Christine's concern
led her toward the nursery, at which point she passed the
open bedroom door, was confronted with the sight of the
two dead bodies, and rushed to phone the police, something she could not afterward recall having done in her
trauma.

The rest was distraught babble, and a free-flowing ti-
rade of slurs and accusations against the deceased Mr.
Mackay.

Now Gorrie clicked the tip back into his pen and
glanced out the bedside window. A newly arrived trio of

official vehicles had joined the line of police cars that had preceded them into the front drive. A patrol cruiser led the pack. It was followed by a forensics van, and an ambulance. None of them had its flasher or siren on. The damage was done, they were in no hurry, why stir up the entire neighborhood?

Gorrie watched the patrol car's driver and passenger doors swing open to break the horizontal orange stripes painted across both sides. Watched Robertson and a female social worker exit the car and start toward the house. Then he shifted his eyes to the ambulance at the rear, and watched the emergency medical technicians leave their vehicle for what was no longer an emergency at all, but rather a nasty cleanup job.

Gorrie frowned again. The evidence would be collected and examined, the bodies taken to the morgue for autopsy, and the child passed on to relatives or foster care, depending on who was or wasn't out there in the world for him. Gorrie and his constables would conduct their follow-up inquiries of family, friends, and acquaintances. And when the case report was filed, his instincts told him it would be written up as an explosive domestic incident, the tale of a marriage gone as bad as they got, its last act an eternal mystery to everyone but the two who'd played it out here in the cold, violated intimacy of its setting.

Better they'd gone their separate ways indeed.

Feeling the sudden need for a breath of fresh air, Gorrie turned from the bed and went outside the house onto the lawn.

FOUR

MARC ELATA FOLDED HIS ARMS SO THAT HE HELD HIS
elbows in the palms of each hand. He stood still before
the statue as the American couple and their four-year-old
brat—a four-year-old, at the Louvre!—staggered past him
on the steps. Elata held his breath, willing himself past
the moment, past their babble: "Do you think the Mona
Lisa will smile for us?" said the father, as if the portrait
were a carnival trick. The four-year-old whined about
wanting more French fries, and when were they going to
see a train?

A tour group swelled up on the landing behind him,
chattering in Swedish or something Nordic; Elata pushed
himself to move on, following the Americans in their
quest for the undying smile. If it weren't for the fact that
he wanted to see several paintings—several *master-
pieces*—displayed in the same room as the Mona Lisa, he
might have pointed them in the proper direction as they
continued up the stairs. This way he would have known
where they were, making them easy to avoid.

A thick knot formed in front of da Vinci's most famous

COLD WAR   41

painting; the crowd was a permanent feature of the room.
Elata walked past it, glancing at the equally beautiful
though far less famous da Vincis alongside, but not wanting to go near the rabble to admire them. He had Ucello
and Pierro in mind; he had not thought about the Renaissance masters lately, and wanted to consider their problems of shade and perspective as an antidote to Picasso,
whom he'd had so much of over the past seven days.

An exceedingly fat French woman brushed against him
as he walked. Elata stopped, gave her a nasty look—but
she was oblivious, chattering to her almost equally rotund
companion about the uselessness—*inutile*—of art. Elata
spoke little French, and that word specifically might be
interpreted as edging toward "vanity" rather than uselessness, but he had an ear for such conversations. He had
heard them all his life, beginning at his own dinner table
when he'd expressed his desire at age eight to become an
artist.

Which, despite everything, he had become. If a forger
might be considered an artist.

The human brain's ability to draw fine distinctions cannot be overstated, especially in the gray realm of morality
and ethics. Elata's mind was particularly supple; it had no
great difficulty justifying his actions. First and foremost,
there was the need to survive; he had to eat. If he had
come quite a distance from the days when he was truly
starving—as the Rolex and privately tailored sports coat
he wore over his jeans attested—that distance was not so
great as to dim the memory.

His second justification was that he was actually an
artist. As such, he not only understood what the masters
he imitated were doing, he extended it. Copying them had
become part of his art, part of the great tradition of master
and student that many of them had followed during their
own apprenticeship. He learned their style and technique,
then addressed himself to subjects as they would have. He
did not copy paintings directly. If, when he was finished,
others believed that the work on his easel had been done

by the master himself, that was irrelevant to him. Elata himself never passed the paintings off as anything other than his own. And as far as he *knew,* those who sold them did not either.

That this knowledge was a product of willful ignorance made no difference to him morally, even if it might make such baubles as the Rolex possible.

And then there was the final justification, the grand and undebatable one—art itself. For art transcended all. It transcended da Vinci as surely as it transcended Marc Elata. It transcended Picasso, it transcended Elata's present employer and greatest patron, Gabriel Morgan. It endured and would endure, even if every work in this museum were burned tomorrow.

Elata shuddered and turned abruptly, afraid that he had somehow inadvertently shared his thoughts with the rest of the room. But he had not. The tourists continued to wander through like cows grazing in a field.

He glanced at his watch. Still another three hours to kill.

Elata had not come to Paris to prepare himself for another round of paintings. His job was quite different— Morgan had hired him to detect a forgery rather than produce one.

Elata had done this sort of thing before. He had examined a Giotto supposedly passed down from the Nazis, steering Morgan away because of a tint under one of the eyes—a careless trick in an otherwise competent job. He had stuck to his opinion despite the arguments of two academic authenticators; in the end, Morgan had listened to him and passed on the painting, though not without regret. The painting had subsequently surfaced in an Australian collection, where a fresh and rather destructive laboratory analysis of it had denounced it as a fake—a careless piece of priming gave it away.

From that point on, Morgan insisted on Elata viewing every important piece he bought. Or so Morgan claimed, though Elata suspected that he did not. But the fact that he said so increased the pressure; the forger turned authenticator feared greatly making a mistake. Morgan no doubt considered this as big an incentive as his sizable fees.

Morgan did not rely on psychology or money alone. He made sure his expert was supplied with the proper tools to aid his judgment. In this case, he had arranged for Elata to receive a small piece of paper containing a sketch and swatch of paint. The fact that this piece of paper—a letter by Picasso, exceedingly rare because it contained a description and rough sketch as well as a dab of paint—belonged not to Morgan but to the Musée Picasso was of no consequence to Elata's conscience, though it necessitated certain physical arrangements, this trip to Paris the primary one.

Elata folded and unfolded his arms, moving through the Louvre gallery. He had hoped looking at the paintings would consume some of his nervous energy, but it was no use. He was due at the Musée Picasso at precisely 2:10; he did not wish to arrive early and inadvertently draw attention to himself, but he had difficulty throttling his energy. He was not a patient man. He could not pretend to be a patient man. As a painter he attacked, he sprinted, he moved at the speed of thought; it could be an asset in art, but in life it made for rising blood pressure and insatiable boredom. It took his attention from the de Vries sculpture of Mercury and Psyche as he passed down the steps and out through the halls into the courtyard and park, helplessly propelled by his surging adrenaline.

"Deux," said the voice in her ear. Then it repeated itself in English for her benefit. "Two in position."

Nessa Lear watched from across the street, her vision partly obscured by wandering crowds, as their subject continued through the Tuileries garden toward Avenue du Gl. Lemonier. The American was tall, and the dark, well-cut jacket he habitually wore over a gray T-shirt and acid-washed jeans made him easy to keep track of. The fact that he seemed not to know he was being followed or even suspect it made things even easier.

Of course, it was also possible he was not planning on doing anything worth being followed for. "*Doigts*," the French teammates on her Interpol task force called him. "Fingers." They had given the name to Monsieur Elata for the incredible adroitness and adaptability of his painting strokes, for they believed he was responsible for forgeries ranging from a Rembrandt sketch to an early Matisse study. But the American had never been positively linked to the works—many of which were not even positively identified as forgeries. Elata had arrived in Paris yesterday afternoon, and had so far done nothing any other tourist would have done. He had sped through D'Orsay in the day yesterday, and Notre Dame in the evening, just as he had rushed through the Louvre today. Assuming the French had no law demanding that museum visits be of a certain duration (they might), he had done nothing wrong.

"*Un moment. Merde,*" cursed one of the team members. Nessa leaned around a stopped truck and peered toward the park. Elata had stopped at a vendor and was buying a sandwich. The tail had to continue past. Nessa would have to take over.

She moved forward. She'd been on the job officially less than a week, not counting the skimpy orientation period, and so didn't know much of Paris yet, but that made her seem like the perfect tourist; acting lost would not be difficult, and she wouldn't have to work hard at mispronouncing her French.

Elata wolfed the *jambon*—actually, a ham with cheese on a small French roll—then walked down in the direction of the Jardin du Luxembourg. He still had more than two hours to kill. He thought of going up to Montmartre, but had been warned by Morgan, absolutely warned, not to go near the Feu Gallery, where he had deposited several works during his last visit some months before.

So what was he to do? He stopped for a moment in the park, rubbing the heel of his boot against the yellow pebbles. He gave his eye over to the forms and colors passing by him—thick weaves of wool and puffed nylons, blue wedges, and green tweed. It was warm for March, but still it was March; if it had been May perhaps, he might have feasted on the figures. But late winter dulled the forms; there was nothing to divert him.

After this was over—after Zurich, where there were sure to be more delays—he'd reward himself with a trip to Florence and perhaps Rome. He might take a few weeks and do some of his own work, play with a few sketches, before taking up the other projects he'd agreed to.

But how to kill these two hours?

He saw the Metro entrance ahead, and reached into his pocket for the *carnet* of tickets he had purchased upon arriving yesterday. Nothing like the subway for wasting time.

"Buggers," Nessa muttered to herself. Then she raised her voice to read the name of the Metro station, making sure the microphone tacked below her collar could pick it up and broadcast it to her companions.

Plunging down the stairway, she broke into a trot trying to find her subject. Jairdain should be coming down the other side somewhere—she looked for him as she jostled the contents of her purse for a Metro ticket.

They'd foreseen this, talked about it, planned for it, and yet here she was, nearly falling to pieces.

Inside, the place was a maze. Left or right at the tunnel intersection? There were different lines traveling in cross directions.

Jairdain would take one, but which?

"Go right," he said in her ear.

"Oui. Thank you." Nessa turned and trotted onward, craning her neck upward, ducking around a small pack of Korean tourists. A man with a suit was walking about

twenty meters ahead. Music filtered in from the platform
beyond the access, then the soft rush of the rubber-
wheeled train arriving.

"Damn," she said, throwing herself into a run.

Too late. The rush had been of the train leaving, not
arriving.

Nessa was so busy cursing herself she almost bumped
into the tall, thin American standing in front of the ad-
vertisement for the Louvre at the end of the platform. He
held his elbows in his palms like an X across his chest,
and frowned at her severely as she recovered her balance.

Crisscrossing aimlessly on the subway lines, Elata arrived
finally at Sully-Morland with only a half hour more to
kill. He came up from the Metro and walked down the
Rue de Birague, turning toward the Maison de Victor
Hugo, the home of the famous author, which had been
turned into a museum.

He glanced at his watch. Though less than five minutes
had passed since he had emerged from the subway, fear
paralyzed him—he was going to be late. He turned and
began running, streaking across the Place des Vosges,
dodging the strollers like a madman. He ran up Rue de
Turenne, bolting through traffic. Elata ran every day at
home, but rarely this hard; he reached the Musée Picasso
with fifteen minutes to spare.

He was at the far end of the ground floor, studying the
greens of *Woman Reading* when the fire alarm sounded.
By then he had caught his breath. He walked down the
steps deliberately, went straight as directed by the guards,
down another flight, moved back, turned left, and found
the steps.

A woman in her thirties pushed into him. Her strong
perfume caressed his nose. He felt her push the envelope
into his pocket; he slipped it into his breast pocket and
continued to walk, once more following the guards' directions.

There were sirens outside, police and fire trucks arriving, someone yelling that they had seen smoke in the basement, someone else swearing there was smoke in the back gallery of the first floor—both were correct, as it happened, though in neither case would the small devices emit enough agent to damage the museum or its treasures.

Elata ignored the rushing firemen and the crowd gathering on the sidewalk. A taxi was just reaching the curb. He pushed past two tourists who had queued for it, ignoring their protests as he threw open the door and jumped in. The taxi lurched away without pause; its driver knew already where he was to take his passenger.

Jairdain slammed his hands on the trunk of the car as Nessa reached the curb.

"J'suis dans la merde," said the French Interpol agent.

Pierre ran up to him, immediately joining in the coarse denouncing of their fate.

"Calm down," Nessa told them when she arrived.

"To have lost him here," said Jairdain before cursing again.

"Easy now, lads," she said. "Someone in the museum passed him something when the alarm sounded. We've just got to track it down."

"Oui?" said Pierre. "Who?"

"There was a woman on the steps, two guards, and someone who looked like a tourist," she told them. "We'll hunt down the tourist first. She's the only one likely to get away."

Zurich, Switzerland

Gabriel Morgan had seen both great opportunities and great trials in his life, but the torture he faced presently must surely rank among the most acute. For here he was, in one of Zurich's newest and finest restaurants—A, which might stand for America, or the beginning of the alphabet, or anything else one wished—and he could not, or should not, choose from any of the excellent entrees.

Not American wild duck in a blueberry-tarragon sauce, which carried with it unadvertised hints of mustard and sherry. Not the exotic but somehow pleasing foie gras soup peppered with ostrich bits in sake with white bean coulis and red pepper tortillas. Not even the deceptively simple sole in vermouth, which was built from a *beurre blanc* that would have left Escoffier speechless.

Morgan could have none of these dishes. Or rather, he could have any of them, if he was prepared to pay the price. His intestines had plagued him intermittently over the past six or seven months; the doctors offered different theories and countless remedies, though their advice came down to the same thing: eat plainly. No cream sauces, no spices, no exotic meats. They would prefer that he stay out of restaurants entirely, but if he must go, he should order something *simple*—baked capon, with no spices, no sauce, no salt, no pepper, no skin. They might just as well have told him not to have sex.

Perhaps not, for he could exert enough willpower most days to limit his diet. His other appetites, however, were more difficult to curb, as the Mieser twins, sitting across from him at the table in A's exclusive red room, would surely attest.

He glanced at the girls, who had already settled on what they would eat—salmon and turnip daube in a radish-mango sauce for Lucretia, who loved the *cornichons* that came with it; American Cajun-style blackened catfish for Minz, who hungered for all manner of heat. Lucretia met Morgan's gaze with a smile that hinted his hunger might be easily satiated. Minz, always so competitive with her sister, reached her hand beneath the table and raked his leg gently with her fingernails.

Morgan liked to bring the girls here mostly for the scandalous effect they had on the natives who considered themselves daring enough to venture beyond the traditional German-inspired restaurants in the town's exclusive residential sections. Besides their Italian actress mother, the twins' ancestors included three different dukes and an uncrowned German prince. And while the exact content of their father's extensive pharmaceutical holdings were the subject of much local rumor and debate, their own assets were hardly obscured by the sheer blouses they wore above only slightly more modest black skirts. Morgan returned to the menu. He could choose the planked salmon, which was relatively plain and had not upset his stomach in the past. But it bothered him considerably that, rather than being cooked on American northwest cedar, it was prepared on local pine. Whether that made a major difference in its taste, he could not say, but the knowledge that he was eating a dish flavored by ersatz wood reminded him that he was doomed to an existence removed from the real thing, perhaps forever. And the fact that he could not easily return to the States vexed him far more severely than serial indigestion.

Morgan put off the question of the main course to review the salad choices once more, hoping the diversion would take his mind off America. Switzerland was not a horrible prison, certainly, and he suspected that his fondness for the U.S. was rather like that of the fox for the unreachable grapes. His family had made its fortune here. While he had lived abroad most of his adult life, Morgan had been raised in Zurich not far from this very restaurant. His childhood had not been unpleasant, but it had been constrained; his parents were not rigid so much as antiseptic, if one excepted his father's activities to enhance the family fortune. The feeling of constraint came over him like a cloud every time he returned to the city or even the country. He felt it in his mouth every time he formed a word in his native Swiss German—one reason he tried to avoid the language whenever possible.

But really, Zurich, with its tidy streets and marvelous guildhalls, its medieval facades and peerless banks, was the perfect setting for the family businesses. The Morgans had been dealers in art and antiquities for many generations, both in Europe and in America. While it was true that the World War and its aftermath had given the family incredible wealth, it was equally true that they had been both well off and well respected at the turn of the last century. It was then that the Morgans (their name at the time Molerrageneau) had first branched into things other than art and real estate—trains specifically, and from there electric generation and commercial transport.

Different forebears placed different emphasis on the parts of the empire, which itself waxed and waned, metamorphosing with the times. Morgan's great-grandfather had taken the boldest leap when a packet of small Renoirs had come his way via South America; obviously authentic and obviously pilfered by the Nazis, the paintings had been placed at considerable profit with a client known to be outstandingly discreet and willing to pay in gold bars. From there, as his father liked to say, it was but a matter of addition, though a more objective viewer might have likened it to multiplication. Money from the art side of the family empire helped fund the purchase, and in one or two cases the establishment, of concerns that diversified the family holdings even further. Such business were, by necessity, prejudiced toward the future, balancing the necessary prejudice toward the past that the art dealings betrayed. Those prejudices were among the key principles the family had adhered to since they were Molerrageneaus, principles that included direct personal involvement by one and only one Morgan at the helm, discretion, and above all, boldness.

Which led the family's present overseer to throw caution and the prospect of diarrhea to the winds when the waiter appeared—choosing the rabbit and ostrich ragout in a morel mustard sauce, along with the Potatoes Daphne and the vegetable of the night, which happened to be Peruvian asparagus in a caviar coulis.

Morgan ordered for the twins, who nodded gratefully. He felt his stomach rumble, and had regrets as he handed the menu back to the waiter. But he was a Morgan; he would not turn back. As a final stubbornness—and a gesture at least as provocative to discerning neighbors as hosting the twins—he asked for a bottle of 1985 Latour, a Bourdeaux wine that though still comparatively young, would decidedly not go with any of the dishes.

"Ladies, I've got to take care of some business, but go right ahead and enjoy," he said, leaning to accept light pecks and a squeeze of the thigh from Minz before heading toward the room beyond the bar where the lavatory was. En route he stopped to greet Frau Leber, who was looking particularly potted tonight. He did not know her dinner mate, introduced as a retired French general; Morgan nodded attentively and memorized the name—Ambrose Xavier—in case it might become of use.

In the men's room, he locked the door, then leaned against it before removing the small alpha pager from his pocket. Morgan thumbed a hot-button combination on the miniature keyboard, activating the modem; within thirty seconds he had signed onto a wireless message network and initiated a transmission that launched him as an anonymous, encrypted user on the system—not an easy feat actually, and one that required a rather large program on not one but two different servers. Fortunately, placing the programs on the servers had been assisted greatly by Morgan's ownership of the company. Morgan cared little for the exact mechanics of the program, though he had a rudimentary notion of how it worked. In every area but art he tended to focus exclusively on results. Even in art, it took a great deal to interest him.

The matter he had come to the rest room to check on, for example, interested him a great deal.

A line of messages to a Yahoo e-mail account appeared on his screen. Most were products of list-serves, purposely cluttering the account. Several were dummies posted at random to make things difficult for anyone who might be trying to pry into his business. (There were several candidates who might undertake such despicable activities, including three different agencies of the United States government and one international firm that was a continual source of difficulty.) He opened each message, lingering as if actually reading them. Finally, he reached the one he actually wanted.

"Hemingway was a jerk."

Silly and innocuous certainly, and nothing to do with anything.

Except that it meant his man, Elata, the painter, the forger par excellence whom he had turned into a detector of forgeries par excellence, had gotten the document he needed and was en route to Zurich.

Danke, Herr Elata. Ausgezeichnet.

He had expected the message. He had also expected the e-mail three arrows later, though this one he had hoped not to receive.

"The eyes are the gateway to the soul. But sometimes even the soul gets lost."

This had been sent by one of his deputies in Paris. It meant that Interpol—the eyes—had spotted Elata and trailed him, but had lost the scent along the way.

He had feared this contingency, since he wasn't entirely sure of the woman at the museum. That had been the major reason he'd consolidated his exposure and used the painter to pick up the letter. He had planned to burn the painter at the end of the operation anyway—he had long planned, as his American acquaintance in New York delicately put it, to clip him.

Still, it pained him to consider the many works that would now by necessity be lost, the imitation Giotos, Bosches, Donatellos, and countless lesser-knowns, all of whose work could be conjured as if by magic from the talented hands of moody Herr Elata.

His people would transport the painter safely to Switzerland and keep him hidden for now; there would be no chance of his being followed or discovered. They were used to dealing with Interpol and had several well-tested methods of throwing the agents off the trail.

Morgan flipped down through the rest of his messages, disposing of them quickly. He had deleted four or five when his eyes stuck on an unexpected note:

"A twist. He had a girlfriend."

The message did not indicate where it had come from and was not signed, but Morgan knew immediately who had sent it and what it meant. It was disappointing, for it meant that a complication in Scotland—a complication that was actually owned by Miss Constance Burns, not himself—remained unresolved.

A girlfriend privy to secrets she shouldn't be privy to; she would have to be eliminated.

Perhaps, and perhaps not. Morgan leaned both shoulders against the door. There was no indication in the message that the girlfriend knew anything. Indeed, the very fact that the author of the e-mail had decided to raise the point meant that the matter was far from certain. The author had a large portfolio of abilities, and it was their understanding that the obvious decisions would be made in the field and not questioned. That the e-mail had arrived meant the sender was unsure, and wanted to ascertain Morgan's wishes—and willingness to pay—before proceeding.

A girlfriend. Morgan thought of the twins, who might be said to be among his most intimate acquaintances, at least so far as Zurich was concerned. But neither of them knew the least speck of his business. Killing either would be a foolish waste of resources.

On the other hand, an irate girlfriend seeking to avenge a lover's death—grand operas had been built from less substantial stuff.

The operative could eliminate her in the usual, efficient manner. But what if there were an investigator on the trail? Eliminate him as well? All Scotland would meet with unfortunate accidents before every possible connection to the difficulty was erased.

Nonsense. Not worth the effort.

It occurred to Morgan, as he stared at the white tile floor, that this was the inchworm's problem. Constance Burns was gradually but steadily becoming a liability. She remained useful to the Antarctica enterprise—but for how long? He did not think he could trust her if pressure were applied. If, by some far-fetched chance, things went wrong in a manner he had not foreseen, could she be relied on? Would she crumble before a hard-pressing investigator from Her Majesty's Ministry? If she were confronted, would she give Morgan up to save her skin?

It occurred to Morgan that she might. It also occurred to him that he would not allow her the chance to do so. And perhaps this Scottish business allowed him to construct one of his elaborate escape hatches. Certain gestures might be made that allowed, if things were to reach a difficult juncture, the blame to be placed on her for a range of activities. And in that case, the more murders that could be laid at her door the better.

Morgan also had an idea that his favorite international corporation might add its credibility to the operation. Not that, strictly speaking, this was necessary, but there was a certain symmetry that made it all the more attractive— the Bordeaux that tweaked a neighbor's nose.

"Await further instructions," he thumbed in response to the message.

The rest of the notes were, thankfully, mere gibberish. He clicked the T, Z, and K together, then shut the device. As the programs in the servers ten thousand miles away went to work erasing the electronic path he had taken into the e-mail system, he went to the sink and washed his hands.

FIVE

THE DOCUMENTS WERE SCRUPULOUSLY FABRICATED,
which was how they were able to execute the whole un-
scrupulous and illegal operation without interference.

On paper the four shielded casks, essentially welded
steel-and-lead sarcophagi, each contained ten fifty-five-
gallon drums of spent fuel assemblages generated by the
Turm nuclear power facility in Austria, a landlocked
country dependent on foreign ports for its international
marine transport.

The fact of the matter was that the radioactive waste
had originated at Fels-Hauden, a state-run power plant in
central Switzerland.

On paper the casks were brought by freight train to
Trieste in northeastern Italy via the Österreichische Bundesbahn, or Austrian Federal Railway, which interlocked
with the European Transfer Express Freight Train System,
to be forwarded to the Port of Naples on the Mediterra-
nean coast.

The fact was that the Swiss rail system, Schweizerische
Bundesbahn, had picked up the casks at a departure

station in Berne. In Naples, they cleared customs within hours for transshipment aboard the German-flagged tanker *Valkyrie*.

On paper the end point destination of the receptacles was specified as Rokkashi Village, Aomori Prefecture, Japan, where they would be stored for eventual reprocessing into plutonium-uranium mixed oxide—known as MOX— and utilized as fuel by the light-water reactors that provided the nation with a third of its energy demands. As plotted, the *Valkyrie*'s sea route was to take it through the Strait of Gibraltar, down along the Ivory Coast of Africa, then around South Africa into the Indian Ocean, through the Indonesian Archipelago to the Pacific Ocean, and finally to the Japanese shore for delivery.

The fact was that the cargo's end point was nowhere near Aomori. The Swiss and Japanese had abruptly discontinued negotiations for the transfer after records of the clandestine talks were rumored to have been leaked to the American government, which, under exercise of the United States–Switzerland Nuclear Cooperation Agreement, had recently clamped down on the shipment of radioactive materials with a potential to yield the weapons-capable MOX extract. Executives at Fels-Hauden had later discreetly sought out another channel for the waste disposal. And found one.

Thus *Valkyrie* deviated from its charted course beyond the Cape of Good Hope at the southern tip of Africa, and forged on into the Antarctic Ocean rather than heading east to the Pacific Rim.

In the open sea outside South Africa's territorial waters, beneath a black and moonless night sky, the casks were moved by mechanized winch onto an ice-strengthened fishing trawler registered to an import/export firm based in Argentina.

Once aboard the trawler, they were placed in a special rad-insulated storage hold and ferried deeper into the southern latitudes, eventually crossing the Antarctic Convergence.

As it passed the subantarctic islands, the vessel encountered thin sea ice, which its riveted double-steel hull was able to nose through with relative ease. Further into its trip, the trawler used ice-distribution satellite maps composed weekly by the U.S. Navy and National Oceanic and Atmospheric Administration—and made available over the Internet for the safeguard of research vessels in subantarctic and antarctic waters—to locate and weave its way around heavy flocs of pack ice as it circumnavigated the continent to the Ross Ice Shelf, an immense sheet of ice fastened like glue to the coastline and extending over fifty miles outward into the Ross Sea.

On March 4th, the trawler dropped anchor at the edge of this immense ice sheet and off-loaded its hot cargo onto rubber-belted Caterpillar trucks for conveyance to the mainland. It had reached the end of its outbound voyage.

Where in the continental interior the casks eventually wound up was a detail that neither its marine carriers, nor the administrators at Fels-Hauden, sought to learn.

In certain types of dealings, it is not unusual for all participants to agree that there are some questions better left unasked.

Scottish Highlands

More than five hundred stone forts once sat along the northern stretches of the Highland coast and the islands nearby in the north of Scotland, each in its own way the center of the universe. Their remains haunt the hills; besides the better-known attractions, a hundred walls, foundations, and bits of ceremonial markers lie scattered across many a square mile, some hidden by vegetation, others easily seen. Built during the Iron Age, the brochs remain outposts of distant memory, small and variable bits of the past whose worn rocks can be interpreted in endless ways. A row of stones together in a cow field might have seen incredible glory in the days after they were first chiseled and stacked; or perhaps they witnessed only cowardice and evil. A tourist touching them for the first time might feel his or her breath taken away, the mind recreating battles of kilt-clad warriors wrestling in the morning mist as pipers urged them together. A local growing up nearby might view the rocks as an apt patch for a tryst or a sip of something away from the folks.

All interpretations might be valid in their own way, all shapes, all ghosts. The past, ancient and near, is a country as varied and changeable as Scotland herself. To reconstruct it in a useful way is an act not of imagination but restraint—the possibilities must be winnowed, the ghosts held firmly in their places.

Frank Gorrie had found this true in every case he had ever investigated, from the traffic scrapes to the twelve murders he had seen since becoming a detective. It was not simply a matter of pushing the lies to one side and the truth to another; the lies were most often easy to spot. But the truth—there was a nub of a different matter.

The truth in the case of Ed and Claire Mackay was this: Edward Cailean Mackay had been an arse-chasin' shit, from a good line of them. He'd been gone from Inverness with his wife for several years, working in Wales and England, the neighbors thought, but his reputation remained. He had picked up where he left off upon his return some two or three months ago, as the loquacious Christine Gibbon claimed. Many would testify to it, though they seemed curiously short on names of current girlfriends.

What they wouldn't testify to, or maybe just could not admit, was the likelihood that Claire would put out his roving eye with a bullet. Especially with the wee babe in the next room. Most especially that.

Gorrie didn't have children himself, and he guessed he ran toward overromanticizing the connection between mother and child, tending to view it wrapped in tender rose petals though he had ample evidence from his work to tell him different. It was on exactly this sort of matter that he missed his former detective sergeant and sometime partner most acutely. Nessa Lear had a fine compass for reality. Gorrie liked to say he'd raised her from a pup, picked her from the pool of detective constables and made her into a true solver of crimes. But he'd done too good a job—Nessa had been snatched away for a job with Interpol some months back. Never mind that she had asked for the job herself for several years—to Gorrie's mind she had been wrestled from him, and the loss hurt all the more as no replacement had been forthcoming due to "budgetary considerations."

The deputy area commander, Nab Russell, had promised a successor in the hazy distant future. For the meantime, DI Gorrie and the rest of CID were expected to make do by using "pooled resources"—Russell's personal euphemism for the detective constables. An eager bunch, mostly overworked, in several cases very rough about the edges, they were good at running down the odd leads, but not for bouncing ideas with, as he had often done with DS Lear.

Nessa would have been excellent probing the neighbors, much better than DC Andrews, whose monotone voice tended to make him sound more like a footballer than a policeman. He'd been too quick with the interviews; Gorrie had to take him by the hand.

Did Claire strike you as a killer?

No, sir.

Good enough then.

No, detective, we do it like this:

Had Mrs. Mackay seemed depressed? Drawn out? At the end of her wits, would you say? Was she an angry person? More frustrated than normal?

No matter the phrasing, no was always the answer. Oh, she could yell at Eddie, put him in his place. But murder him? Should have maybe, but until it happened not a one of her friends or family would have predicted it. She had not seemed to suffer postpartum depression; she'd gained her shape back after the birth with a mum-and-child program, where the instructor—a looker herself—said she had a special closeness with the child. Her sister said that she had worked at a bank as a teller but had no plans to go back; it wasn't the sort of job you'd worry into a career.

So that was her story, rounded up with the help of Andrews in about a day and a half's worth of work. A large question remained—where had she gotten the gun? It was not her husband's, or at least there was no indication yet that it was her husband's, and no one, not even Christine Gibbon, could remember any hint of it before.

Having reached a suitable impasse regarding the presumed killer, today Gorrie would turn his attention back to the victim, making his inquiries at the man's employers and rounding up a few lost ends. But as he spotted Cromarty Firth's domelike reactor building looming ahead in the early morning fog, an ungodly, un-Scottish creature wading in from the surf, he thought not of Edward Mackay but his son, christened Luthias Edward. It was one thing to grow up without a ma or a da, and quite another to grow up knowing your ma killed your da and then herself, with you in the other room.

What a legacy to leave a child. Gorrie could do nothing for the lad except his job, and while he regretted that his job might well mean pain for the boy in years to come, he endeavored to do his best to remove any question in the young man's mind of what had happened. He would have done so no matter what the circumstance, but if his patience or stamina flagged at any point, he could gently prod it by recalling the infant in the crib, and imagining him fifteen years on.

A small valley ran between the plant and the road, making the access road seem as if it ran over a moat. Cement obstructions forced approaching vehicles to take a zigging path, and razor wire lined the double row of fences at the entrance; two guards manned the gate and demanded positive proof that DI Gorrie was indeed DI Gorrie.

"Aye, didna' you know me well enough to borrow five

pounds last Saturday, James?" Gorrie told one of the guards as he held out his badge.

"Procedure, Inspector," responded the man, adding in a somewhat softer voice, "I'll be payin' you back next Friday, I'm sure."

Gorrie was met at the door to the plant by a young woman tall and broad enough to play for the local football team; she showed him directly to the plant manager's office, not pausing for pleasantries. Gorrie found his pace slowing with each step, resisting the rush. With white walls sandwiched between white acoustic tile and white linoleum, the hallway reminded the inspector of a hospital corridor, except that it smelled of wood polish rather than antiseptic.

There was no wood to polish in the halls, nor was there any in the manager's office, where the paper-strewn desk, file cabinets, and two movable carts holding computers were all made of metal. John Horace sat behind the desk, his owl eyes blinking once as they entered.

"Come," he said sharply, though they were already inside.

"My name—"

"Inspector Gorrie, yes. Well?"

Gorrie sat down in the chair across from the manager's desk. "I am investigating the death of one of your people here."

"Ed Mackay. Efficient, good at his job."

The manager's manner might be common in London where, judging from his accent, he had been raised, but here it was grating enough to be suspicious as well as borderline insulting.

"What exactly was his job?" Gorrie asked.

"Supervised the removal of waste. We follow the Basel Convention in spirit and letter, Inspector. I'm sure that if you check with UKAE—"

"The atomic commission?"

"Quite. We are regulated—heavily regulated. Nothing moves from here without intricate planning. Even the odd hankie tossed in my basket there will be suitably accounted for. We don't go polluting the environs, Inspector. We have precautions. Our record is exemplary."

"I see," said Gorrie. Under other circumstances, he might have been inclined to skip the lecture—he already knew a bit about Mackay's job. But he generally found it useful to let a man speak, even when he didn't feel an immediate need for the information. And so Gorrie folded his arms and leaned back as the plant manager began citing safety statistics. In three decades there had been over seven thousand shipments of spent fuel worldwide without an incident; the spent fuel had a better transport record than the average loaf of bread.

It struck Gorrie as Horace continued that the shape of his skull was not unlike the shape of the reactor dome.

"Interesting," Gorrie said finally. "Did you know Mr. Mackay well?"

"Yes, of course. Not well, as you put it. But of course I knew him. He was staff."

"He had only been here a few months?"

"Six weeks, two days." The owl eyes blinked. "He had worked here in the early nineties, before moving on to Numberland Power. There were then a series of jobs of increasing importance. His wife wanted to return to the area, I believe, because they were due to have a child and she wanted to be near friends and family. He was very qualified."

"I'd like a look at his resume, if that is possible."

"What is this, Inspector? I read that his wife shot him."

"We try not to draw hasty conclusions." Gorrie rose, but then softened his tone, thinking to add to the manager's willingness to cooperate. "The evidence leans in that direction, certainly. But we must make our inquiries. We have our procedures, as you do."

Horace nodded almost sympathetically.

"I'd like to speak to some of his workmates," said Gorrie.

"That can be arranged." Horace pushed a button on his

speakerphone. The woman who had shown Gorrie here reappeared. "Krista will assist you with whatever you need."

The deceased's staff members had little information about Mackay, responding to Gorrie's suggestions that he might have had a randy appetite with shrugs rather than winks. His secretary, however, seemed to have formed a mild attachment. Tora Grant called her boss "charming" and "very able," but as Gorrie continued with his questions, her answers dribbled down to bare yeses and noes. Finally, the inspector put it to her directly.

"Did you have sex with him?"

Her face turned so red it could have been mistaken for a traffic light.

She started to say something, but quickly stopped. Gorrie waited a bit before gently prompting. "He seemed quite an attractive man."

"A hug 'n a kiss, a little flirting 's all we ever did." She took a hard breath, which made it seem to the inspector that she was lying. "I dina', but might have, I'll admit it."

Her skin color returned to normal with the admission. She looked slightly angry, but gave no hint that she was going to cry, or say anything else. Gorrie waited a moment, then fell back to a few routine questions, circling around.

"Did you know if he had a gun?" he asked.

"Never heard."

"Was he acting strange in the past week or so?"

"Not so's I could tell."

"Meet his wife?"

"Ne'er. Ne'er. Not."

"Very definitive on that." Gorrie made a show of folding his notebook away, a well-practiced trick—he was setting up to lob the seemingly casual question on the way out the door. "If anything occurs to you, please call me," he said, handing over a card.

"Yes."

He took a step, then canted his head to the side as if inspiration had just beamed in from Scotland Yard. "Anyone else?"

"Else?"

"Do you know of other girlfriends?"

She turned scarlet again. "I—"

The secretary had overheard several conversations, as it turned out, but one woman in particular stood out, Cardha Duff. And she should stand out, Gorrie decided when he saw the department phone records: Mr. Mackay had called her two or three times a day for the past three weeks.

From the time Cardha Duff was a young girl, she had hated drugs of all kinds, even aspirin. And yet now at the age of twenty-six, she needed drugs to survive—to be precise, 150 milligrams of Synthroid every day. Cardha Duff needed to take this drug because her body no longer manufactured thyroid hormones, due to the fact that she no longer had a thyroid.

The doctors had removed it six weeks before, after discovering a gray, roundish mass on the right anterior lobe. The mass, about the size of an old farthing, proved to be cancerous; the lab report classified it as medulary thyroid carcinoma, a relatively rare form of cancer that was often hereditary and more often caused by radiation. The origin in her case was not known; she hadn't bothered taking the genetic test because she had no siblings or offspring to warn and decided, quite sensibly, that the cause made little difference to her. There was no treatment or cure beyond surgery. Her prognosis could be estimated from the two different survival charts included with the material she received while preparing for surgery. Depending on which graph one preferred to consult, either 78 or 91 percent of patients in similar circumstances lived five years after the discovery of their disease; ten-year survival was either 61 or 75 percent. Given her young age, Cardha was more likely to fall in the positive end of either curve; there was much reason for optimism. But numbers and percentages told you nothing about your future, and much less about yourself. They told you nothing about fear, and failed miserably to track the daily ironies of "getting on with things," as the pamphlets implored.

Such as the daily irony of the small blue pill. Without it, she became depressed and couldn't concentrate. Taking it made her head buzz, but forget to take it and she felt as if her skin were made of tissue paper. She slid a pill out from the bottle and pressed it onto her tongue, washing it down with two sips of grapefruit juice.

Cardha had barely swallowed when she sneezed. It was a scratchy sort of sneeze, the kind that presaged a cold.

Not what she needed this week. She had a job interview tomorrow at the Playhouse. It was a small position as assistant house manager, but she wanted it badly, part of her campaign for a new start, a fresh go, propelled by her cancer and the realization that she might very well die soon.

The phone rang. As Cardha reached for it she had a premonition that it was about Ed and his wife, the ghastly murderess. So she wasn't surprised when the inspector introduced himself.

"Of course, Inspector Gorrie, I'll tell you everything I know," she said. "I have a doctor's appointment in a half hour. Could you stop by after that?"

The inspector consulted his appointment book. He had a few other matters to attend to. First thing tomorrow morning?

Before the operation, she would have agreed, risking the job interview or even rearranging her plans to meet the inspector. But now she felt stubborn—nothing, not even Ed Mackay, God rest his soul but damn him at the same time, would take her off course.

"The next day perhaps?" she asked.

The inspector agreed and rang off after receiving directions.

Cardha sneezed again. She hated drugs, but she'd have

to get something for her cold. She poured another glass of juice, lost track of herself for a moment—had she taken the thyroid pill or not?

Cardha decided that she had, and resolved to get one of those multicompartment pillboxes with the days of the week inscribed outside. Then she put up her tea and went to see if the morning paper had arrived.

Amid the long clutter of innuendo spewed by Christine Gibbon about Ed Mackay's sins were the names of a few locales where his sinning took place. She was only slightly more selective than the telephone book, but here at least DC Andrews had done a good job narrowing down the list. He had already visited six of the establishments, returning with nothing to report. Inspector Gorrie took the last three himself, visiting them in succession after lunch.

The verdict at all three was similar: "An eye for the lasses" or "a real oinker," depending on whether he'd bought rounds lately.

At Lion's Bridge the owner winced as they were speaking, seeing a customer come in. Gorrie immediately guessed the reason.

"Cuckold?" he said.

"I wouldn't, uh, put it that way," said the owner, who also worked as bartender during the day. Gorrie asked a few more perfunctory questions, then went over to see the party in question.

"Hate the bloody bastard, always winkin' at me. Not a person deserved dyin' more'n him, I don't mind sayin'." Fraser Payton pulled up his whiskey, shooting it down his throat. "I had a mind once to wring his neck with my own hands, and still to God I wish I'd done it some nights. I might still, mind."

"Hardly worth the effort now," said Gorrie.

"Aye." Payton pushed the glass along in the direction of the bar, catching the owner's attention.

It was not hard to guess why Payton hadn't assaulted

Mackay while he was alive—he stood perhaps five-two, a good head and a half shorter than Mackay. He looked to weigh less than half the man.

Still, the short types often had nasty tempers; it occurred to Gorrie that someone with such a deep hate might have killed the wife to cover up the murder, then staged it as a suicide.

"The man was a bad one, Inspector. My Margie was a ripe fool. With her mother now. Run along home to Mom, she did."

A string of synonyms for the lower reaches of the female anatomy spewed from Payton's mouth. Gorrie looked at the man's hands on the table—slender fingers, almost delicate. You could judge much by a man's hands, but you couldn't decide whether he was a murderer or not—too much variety.

"When did your wife leave?" Gorrie asked.

"Seven years this September. Right 'fore he left Inverness."

"Seven years?"

"He was scared o' me, I'll tell you that," said Payton.

The bartender approached to refill the drink. "Steady, lad," he told Payton.

"Scared o' you?" asked Gorrie.

"You're dreamin', lad," said the owner.

"Aye, he was. I heard he'd come back. I'd seen him sulking around. And didn't he see me three days ago, up in Rosmarkie? Aye, was him, as if he were someone more than a shit, meeting with the council member—hid when he saw me. He did." Payton turned to the bartender and raised his finger. "Hid. Hid."

"What council member would that be?" said Gorrie.

"Cameron," said Payton triumphantly. "Ewie B. Cameron, on the land council, among others. A gentleman. Had the sewer in front of my house fixed two years ago. I don't hold him any ill will, Inspector—a fair man and for the people, as were his ancestors."

"Are you sure it was Cameron?" asked Gorrie.

"Oh, yes. And Mackay, the slog. Saw me come in and turned away. Scared o' me. What he didna' know, as far as I'm concerned, he could ha'e her. Would ha'e served her right. Could have been my old wife there in that bed, pulled the trigger."

"Three nights ago," said Gorrie, his tone light, "would have been the day before Mackay died."

"The wife killed him," said the bartender.

"Inquiry will decide that," said Gorrie.

Payton reached toward the bottle in the bartender's hand, tipping down the neck to refill his glass again.

"You're sure it was Cameron?" asked Gorrie.

"It was him."

Gorrie leaned back in his seat, considering the coincidence of the thing. For if his memory was correct, Ewie B. Cameron, latest in a clan of noble and semi-noble Scots, had been killed in a traffic accident the same night Mackay and his wife had died.

An odd coincidence, to be sure.

SIX

FRANK GORRIE SAT NEAR THE WINDOW IN HIS OLD platform rocker and watched the lights of a car out on the street slide across the dark bedroom walls. It was chilly, quiet, his wife dead to the world under the heavy quilts, her breathing soft and regular.

Gorrie couldn't sleep. He was wearing his flannel robe and wool socks and had put one of Nan's hand-knitted throw blankets over his lap. The chair was comfortable, though it creaked when he went rocking back too far. The springs, Gorrie thought. They needed to be oiled. He'd given it a tick on his mental list of waiting house chores. The list was long, and there were many things on it that deserved priority. But oiling the springs wouldn't take much time. Maybe he'd find a spare moment over the weekend. He ought to anyway. Easier than fixing that runny tap in the loo. He'd try to make a point of getting it done. Next weekend seemed a reasonable target. Meanwhile, Gorrie was trying not to rock too far back in his chair. It was late. The stillness exaggerated every sound. He did not want to disturb Nan. Five nights now since he'd been able to get a decent bit of rest. Or was it six?

He counted backward. Outside, the car moved unhurriedly along the street. He could hear its motor running, and the low *shush* of its tires as it drew to a halt by the traffic signal at the corner intersection. Then its lights froze on the wall above his bed. Gorrie noticed the diffuse red glow of the stop signal through the frosty windowpane. A law-abiding driver. Commendable. It was getting on two o'clock, stub end of the night. There were only 130 officers to police the sixty thousand civilians in the Inverness Command Area. Scant odds one of them would be around to cite some luckless sod for running a stop signal. Besides Gorrie himself, of course. And he surely wasn't about to leave the plump, worn-in cushions of his favorite chair.

The signal turned green and the car rounded the corner. Its lights grazed the window, fluttered from wall to wall, then slid across the ceiling. Gorrie counted backward. Five nights, aye, sitting here awake and wide-eyed with a throw over his legs. Wasn't until a full day after answering the call to Eriskay Road that he'd gotten himself into a twist about it. Gorrie did not know the reason for his delayed reaction. But his mind had been making up for it ever since.

He sat there thinking. Nan shifted under the pile of quilts. He couldn't tell whether she had moved from her side onto her back, her back to her side, or from one side to the other. The room was very dark. In the winter she had a habit of pulling the quilts up over her head. Slept like a rock under all that fabric and filling. When the cat came pawing at the footboard for her morning meal, you could rely on Nan to be oblivious. Or pretend to be oblivious. It irritated him, obliging that cat's whims. Sometimes Gorrie would thumb his chest grumpily and protest. Last into bed, first out, he'd say. How's that for a rule? Where's the equity? Who rates higher in this household, me or the bloody fur ball? Nan scarcely heeded him, except perhaps to give him a wry little smile.

Gorrie realized he'd almost leaned back too far, gotten the chair to where its rickety springs would squeak. He carefully eased it down. His rocker was different from the cat. The tiniest noise out of it was enough to disturb Nan through her blankets. She'd heard him rocking last night, and the night before. Leave it to Nan. She had peeked an eye out from the thick folds of her covers, asked Gorrie what was bothering him. Not that she didn't already have an inkling. Or better. Edward and Claire Mackay's deaths had given a fair boost in popularity to the local papers and telly news broadcasts. Certainly it was meatier dish than the traffic watch, daily stats, or a piece about drunk and disorderly teens setting a brush fire in some city park. And Claire's former flatmate, Christine Gibbon, had been generous to reporters with every appalling detail of the sight she'd come upon at the bungalow. Nan had his number, all right. Leave it to her.

Gorrie stared at the quilts gathered up in a mound over his wife's sleeping body. She was a big woman. Even twenty-five years ago, when he had dropped down on his knee to propose to her, it couldn't have been said that she had a waifish figure. But he hadn't wanted to marry a nudie-magazine centerfold. Nan knew her best attributes and put herself together in a way that accented them. And when she got that certain randy look her eyes . . . in spite of his occasional grumbling, Gorrie had no cause to be envious of any man with regard to his conjugal pleasures. Give him his choice of rides, he'd always pick a luxury-model sedan over a Fiat. Not that he didn't appreciate the latter's strong appeal.

Another car approached his house, rolled past. Its headlights swept the walls. Shadows scattered from them like black butterflies, then regrouped. Gorrie thought about the deceased Claire Mackay, and how she had looked in the abattoir that was once her bedroom. Claire Mackay lying in that dash of a baby-doll nightie, her leg half wrapped around her husband's corpse, one hand spread on his naked chest, the other around the gun she'd used to kill him before ending her own life as well. Gorrie could attest that she had been a woman with eye-catching physical attributes. A shape like hers took maintenance. Probably she'd stuck to a regular exercise routine. No doubt she had watched her calories. There had been enough of her exposed for Gorrie to know she'd had no leftover padding from her recent maternity.

He wished it were possible to wash away his recollection of the gruesome sight she'd made of herself above the neck.

Gorrie frowned. *Made of herself* . . .

Claire Mackay. Five nights now he'd been thinking about her final act, and the way she had apparently committed it. A bullet in the mouth, its trajectory blasting through the palate into her brain. That method had the surest results in gun suicides involving a head wound. Took some effort, though. It would have required Claire to turn the firing hand toward herself at an awkward angle, most likely gripping its wrist with her opposite hand to steady the barrel. It would also have meant she would be able to *see* the barrel as she thrust it into her mouth. Well, unless she'd closed her eyes the entire time. They'd been open when he found her, but their lids could have raised postmortem. At any rate, a shot to the temple was more common. Only one hand was needed to grip the gun. It was easier, and usually cleaner. Less blood and tissue splatter. Usually. But it had a downside too. A nervous jitter would cause the bullet to glance off the scalp, inflict nonfatal damage, and leave the person crippled or a dribbling vegetable.

Gorrie supposed the messiness of the scene was another of the things that had niggled at him these past nights. In his experience, women tended to avoid ruining their faces when they did away with themselves. They swallowed pills or poison, slit their wrists in the bath, went to sleep breathing automobile exhaust. If they used a pistol, the fatal shot was most often pointed at their chests. You couldn't state it hard and fast, naturally. But neat was the

preference. A fit specimen like Claire Mackay, who cared
about her looks . . . Gorrie wouldn't have thought she was
one who'd leave herself to be found mutilated. And then
there was her racy wear. It wasn't what she'd have put
on before polishing the nails, setting the hair in rollers,
and going off to dreamland. A woman didn't slip into a
provocative nightie like that, make an irresistible package
of herself, unless she was in what you'd call a romantic
mood. Yet Claire's passion for Ed had gone into a sudden
tailspin, hit some jagged divide in the moments before it
would have brought them to an act of love.

Gorrie shifted in his chair, his frown deepening. What
had her husband done to turn things bad?

Gorrie stared at his sleeping wife in the silence. Shadows crowded him. There hadn't been a passing car for a
while, and the corner traffic signal flashed meaninglessly
at an empty street. He had wondered at the absence of a
suicide note. In the bungalow, he'd noticed that the
wee'un had been fine attended. His room was small but
tidy, his pajamas and linens freshly washed, the closet
shelves stocked with nappies, cotton bobs, and the like.
There were toys and stuffed animals in his crib, bright-
colored mobiles hanging above it. Fine attended. Yet in
the time between Claire's putting a shot in her husband's
head and turning the gun on herself, she'd seemingly
given no thought to what the consequences would be for
the child. Not even to snatching up a piece of paper and
scribbling the name of a family member, godparent,
friend, some preferred or appointed guardian who would
see to his welfare. Instead, she had abandoned her responsibility, left the state to decide what was to become
of him.

Gorrie had seen a lot in his twenty-five years on the
job. More than he wanted. He knew better than to make
assumptions. Still, this affair seemed curious. And there
were some further peculiarities he wanted to straighten out
in his head when the forensic reports arrived from the lab.
That wouldn't be for another couple of weeks, he'd been

told . . . but Gorrie knew how to put on the hustle.

He meshed the fingers of his hands, stretched his arms above his head, heard vertebrae popping along his neck and spine. The illuminated clock on his nightstand told him it was almost 3 A.M. Och, well. Gorrie had hoped he might get tired enough to catch a nod before the kitty sprang from her basket alongside the bed. But it wouldn't be long now till the troublesome bugger started a rumpus. He would sit cozily another few minutes, then go into the kitchen, open a can of Felix, put the teapot on the burner. . . .

"Frank? You in that creakin' monstrosity again? Woke me from a fast asleep."

Gorrie looked at the bed. Nan had flipped the blankets from her head and propped herself up slightly on her elbows. He couldn't see her features in the dark, but knew she was scowling at him just the same. He was certain he hadn't made a sound with the chair.

"Sorry," he said. "I was about to get up and prepare a small bit 'a breakfast. . . ."

She leaned toward the bedside clock. "Breakfast? Are you real? It's not yet three in the *morn*."

"Couldn't sleep much," he said.

"Losh! Frank, this can na' go on. Sittin' up night after night, *all* the night, then takin' yourself off to work. I thought you said you'd try'n get some rest. . . ."

"I tried."

"You're no youngster, d'you ken?"

"Sure enough."

"Then what of it? What's the *matter?*"

"I don't know," he said. It was mostly a truthful answer.

"Frank, if it's that business on Eriskay got you gutted, we should bring it out in the open. . . ."

"Steady on," Gorrie interrupted. He got up from his rocker, ignoring the loud complaint of its springs, and went over to crouch at Nan's side of the bed. "Look, Nan. Suppose I give staying under the blankets a better effort after I come home tonight. Ought to be a breeze with some wifely inspiration," he said, then abruptly bent forward, cupped her chin in his hand, and planted a long, full kiss on her lips.

She sighed. Up this close, Gorrie had no problem whatsoever making out her features. They were crinkled with surprise, exasperation, and affection.

"What was *that* show of tenderness about?" She gave him a soft nudge on the chest. "Lookin' to keep me quiet, are you?"

"Maybe I am, sweets," he said, still crouching over her. "And maybe it just struck me that it's good to be among the lucky ones."

The tall firs lining the path to the estate house watched Gorrie come up the drive with the resolute solidity of guards protecting the approach to a castle, pikes and swords at the ready. The tires of the inspector's Ford Mondeo plowed through the thick bed of stones as he circled the drive to the large house, the path designed to give the visitor a clear impression not so much of the house but the owner's good taste in having it built. The structure dated from the eighteenth century, a time of relative peace if not absolute prosperity for the Cameron who had first occupied it. Had DI Gorrie cared to inquire, he would have been quickly supplied a thick pamphlet with small type documenting the exploits of the Highland Camerons. The booklet was available at several places in the nearby town; several copies were on the shelves of the local library as well as in all the churches and schools, though in the latter case the edition omitted a few of the more questionable stories from the past.

The place's ancient history was of no interest to Gorrie; to be truthful, he wasn't entirely sure that its more recent history was of interest either. The report on Ewie B. Cameron's death was rather clear and precise: hit by a medium-to-large-sized truck in the early morning hours. Death almost instantaneous from a selection of internal and external wounds. The fog and winding, narrow road would have made it difficult to see the victim, who habitually took the walk as part of his daily exercise. The investigation was open as no one had come forward to claim responsibility; it was possible that the driver hadn't seen what he had hit, and thought the noise an animal such as a dog, or even one of the deer that wandered the nearby woods.

Not likely, thought Gorrie, but the driver's solicitor would undoubtedly make the claim if it came to that. A good number of juries might agree, if things were handled just right. Not even the frown of the magistrate would sway them if the accused looked downtrodden and had wife and kiddies in tow.

The stone steps to the front door had slight indentations, scuffed down by three centuries' worth of soles. Ewie had lived here alone, without even live-in help. A cook came to do his meals, and two maids to keep the place tidy; a gardening service trimmed the grass and attended to the hedges. But at nights the place was empty except for Mr. Cameron; there was no Mrs. Ewie Cameron.

There was, however, a sister, Miss Ellie Cameron, who had come up from Edinburgh to attend to matters after her brother's demise. And it was she who came to the door as Gorrie approached.

"Inspector Gorrie?"

"Yes."

"Please." She turned at the door and headed down a long hallway at the right. Gorrie pulled the door closed behind him, then followed. Ms. Cameron's heels clicked on the stones, her pace steady. In some homes the entrance hallways were festooned with historical mementos, some pertaining to the family, many not. But these corridors were bare. No thick Oriental carpet covered the floors, and the walls were plaster, not paneled. Somehow that made him feel more at ease, and even respectful.

Family history notwithstanding, Ewie Cameron had not

cut a large swath in life, even according to the obituary Gorrie had read. He was a relatively modest and quiet man, keen on doing his duty and otherwise remaining private. He observed the unwritten code of conduct applying to all well-born Highlanders, and most certainly descendants of such noble men as Sir Ewen, seventeenth clan chieftain, Major Allan Cameron, founder of the bold 79th Highlanders, and Air Captain "Hick" Cameron, double ace and hero of the Battle of Britain. He contributed to the proper charities, was unfailingly sober when in public, and golfed twice a week, weather permitting.

Ms. Cameron stopped at the doorway on the plastered side of the hall, extending her arm and trying a smile. She wore thick wool pants and a heavy, severe coat; despite the smile, she reminded Gorrie of the woman in charge of payroll and expenses at the Constabulary area, a grouchy and disagreeable woman who was suspected to routinely apply fingerprint and DNA tests to chits that came across her desk.

"I apologize for the dust," said Ms. Cameron, following him into the sitting room. He guessed she was about thirty, though her pudding complexion and heavy eyes could easily belong to someone ten years older. "My brother's maids—you understand."

Two couches faced each other in the center of the room, each flanking a pair of elaborately carved mahogany tables. Various pieces of furniture were arrayed around the outer edges. All seemed very old, but none looked the least bit dusty.

"There's news?" asked Ms. Cameron.

"Ah, no news about your brother, I'm afraid." Gorrie hadn't explained the reason for his visit when he called. "I'm here on another matter. To my ken at the moment it is unrelated, though I may revise my opinion. It is a coincidence to be investigated, you understand."

"I'm afraid I don't, Chief Inspector."

"It's just Inspector, miss," said Gorrie.

A slight young woman appeared at the door with a tray

of tea and store-bought cookies. Her red hair flowed down her shoulders; she wore a white sweater that stopped about an inch above the waistband of a long, blue skirt. She seemed to glide into the room, moving as no servant would ever move in a house.

"Inspector Gorrie," said Miss Cameron, emphasizing his title. "This is my friend, Melanie Pierce."

"Hello," said the woman. Even when she spoke the single word, it was obvious she was a Yank. "Tea?"

"Aye," said Gorrie.

As Melanie poured the tea, Miss Cameron raised her hand gently to the young woman's side, and suddenly Gorrie understood.

Well, to each his own, or her own, as the case may be, he thought. Nessa would have had something to say about this, were she still his partner. Certainly the American was a beauty, with a face that would shine for decades before fading to a soft, misty glow. A more poetic mind would compare her to a fairy goddess come down from the hills.

Aye, and Nessa would have snorted at that, for all her talk of artists and paintings.

"I am working on another case, a murder and suicide," said Gorrie after a sip of the tea. "A sad one. Left a baby."

He told them about the Mackays, running out the main details and then getting to the meeting Payton had mentioned.

"A drink in the pub?" said Miss Cameron. "My brother?"

"It seemed odd, their gettin' together," said Gorrie. "It's a wee bit out of the way for Mr. Mackay to come up here. They were not chums, were they?"

"*Chums,* Inspector?"

"I would nae think they were acquaintances," offered Gorrie.

The dead man's sister obviously didn't know her brother well enough to account for all of his friends. The thought occurred to Gorrie that perhaps homosexuality ran in the family, but he dismissed it; there seemed no chance of that on Mackay's account. The man was hetero to a fault.

"Your brother was never married?" Gorrie asked.

"No. There were some, a few women, but gradually I think Ewie came to decide he liked the single life." Miss Cameron slipped her hand onto the couch, lacing it over her friend's.

"Perhaps there's an address book?" Gorrie prompted. "Or if it was on official business of some sort—"

"We can look in his study," said Miss Cameron, rising. "My brother was very organized, Inspector, so if it was a formal contact, I'm sure it will be recorded in his appointment book."

It was not; the book indicated his night was free. Edward Mackay's name was not in the large Rolodex of contacts on Ewie Cameron's Victorian-era desk, nor could any reference to him be found in the collection of white pads in the top right-hand drawer where the council member apparently kept notes on current business.

"Maybe this man ran into him in the pub and asked about getting a traffic sign or something," suggested the American.

"He's not a constituent," said Gorrie. "Different district."

"Maybe for the power plant," said Miss Cameron.

"Very possible," said Gorrie. He looked over the white pads. The notes were rather cryptic, perhaps taken in response to phone conversations. The top pad, for example, had something to do with lights:

> Lts. 3x
> Fifty yards- 100.
> No budg
> Croddle Firth

Gorrie guessed it had to do with a request to add lights along a roadway in a small village about a quarter mile from here—a guess aided by his memory of a recent news item to that effect.

The second pad down had a phone number from London above the words "Lin Firth Brdge." Halfway down the pages was another line, a question. "Hgh Spec Trprt?"

A small, stone structure that stretched the definition of bridge, Lin Firth Bridge had been repaired six or seven months before. It had been the subject of several news items itself, as the delays there had managed to snarl traffic considerably. The roadway had been completely closed off. Drivers traveling from Black Island south or west had to first go north and east, adding in most cases a good hour if not more to their travels. A headache that, and sure to have caused the poor council member assigned to the oversight committee a fair sight of grief.

Another pad had a note about an upcoming fair. The last two were blank. Gorrie returned the pads to the drawer. He looked through some of Cameron's files and the rest of the desk without finding anything of note. There was no obvious connection between Cameron and Mackay, save for the alleged sighting in an obscure pub by a man who under other circumstances might be judged a suspect in the murder.

Miss Cameron had left Gorrie to explore the study on his own. He closed the desk, glancing around the room at the bookcases with their neatly aligned leather-clad volumes. Here and there a framed photograph stood in front of the books—Ewie with his parents, Ewie with a dog, Ewie receiving a certificate of some sort from a local vicar. Unlike the sitting room, here there truly was dust; obviously the maids were not allowed to enter.

A man's life ran to this—dusty photographs, odd notes on a pad, an empty house. Gorrie made sure he had closed the desk drawers, then went to say good-bye to Miss Cameron and her friend.

Inverness, Scotland

Running late to his appointment with Cardha Duff, Inspector Gorrie stopped at a pub near Walder Street to ring her and tell her of the delay. The phone rang and rang, which made him uneasy; he hadn't thought she'd supply much in the way of information, but wouldn't know what to think if she skipped the interview. Maybe the whole thing would be too much for her, he thought—cause of the murder and suicide, all that—but she hadn't sounded particularly distraught on the phone the other day.

The coroner wouldn't be preparing his report on the deaths for another few days yet, but the head of CID had left a note on Gorrie's desk asking when the case might be wrapped up. The tabloid chaps had come up from London as well as Glasgow and Edinburgh, and now were calling him every few hours to see if there were new developments. At least he shielded Gorrie from the rabble.

Gorrie wended his way from Rosmarkie through Inverness, off toward Clava Cairns and the hamlet where Cardha's flat lay. He turned off the main road into a small set of apartment buildings, then took another turn and found his way blocked by an ambulance.

"Inspector—we were just sending for you," yelled a voice from the other side of the ambulance.

It belonged to Robertson, the constable who had changed the nappies on the Mackay child.

"What's going on here, Sergeant?" he asked the constable.

"Another suicide, looks like, Inspector, according to the ambulance people. Been dead since sometime last night, they think." Robertson frowned deeply and shook his head. Handling three deaths in less than a week might rate as a record for a constable in the Inverness Command Area as far back as the war.

"Wouldn't be at 212?" said Gorrie.

"It is, sir. A Cardha Duff, going by the license. Not a good photo."

"Rarely are," Gorrie told him, walking up toward the building.

The thing that struck Gorrie immediately was that Cardha Duff could in no way be considered beautiful, especially in comparison to Claire Mackay. Few people looked good in death, and this woman looked especially bad, her nose and eyes swollen red, her mouth frozen in what might have been an agonized shout for help. But even allowing for all that, it was clear that she offered no challenge to Ed Mackay's wife in the looks department. The most attractive thing about her was her red hair, which even Gorrie, no expert, could tell spent most of the week frizzed into unmanageable odds and ends.

Just now the hair lay matted to one side of her head, a twisted dirty tangle that pointed away from her ghost-white face. Cardha Duff's body sprawled face-up in front of a TV, a few feet from the couch. Her left arm lay out as if in supplication. She had a bandage at the inside joint of the elbow; she'd obviously given blood the day before she died.

A final act of charity before death.

"Has forensics been called?" Gorrie asked the constable who'd been watching the door.

"On the way, sir. Sergeant Robertson took care of it straightaway."

The ambulance people stood at the side of the room, waiting to hear what they should do. Gorrie wanted to know how the body was when they found it; they assured him they'd only moved it a little, ascertaining she was dead.

"The neighbor, she saw us," volunteered the driver.

"Which neighbor was that, son?"

"Gray-haired woman, Mrs. Peters. 213. She thought something was amiss because she didn't answer to the knock. Came in with us."

Gorrie nodded. "Now tell me why you think it's a suicide."

"Pills on the floor, one near the radiator and another under the sink," said the other attendant quickly. She had a stud in her nose and spoke with a Lowlands accent—Gorrie wasn't sure which prejudiced his mind worse.

"And how d'you know that, lass?"

"I'm not your lass now, am I?" She'd flushed, though, and Gorrie waited her out. "I went to use the john and I saw it. I didn't touch a thing. Not a thing," she said finally.

"How long have you been on the job?" he asked her.

"A few weeks. What is it to you?"

Gorrie went to the bathroom. Though the scene was now obviously contaminated, he used a pencil to flick on the light, peered in a moment, then lowered himself to his knees and looked around. He could see a small capsule below the edge of the towel rack, near the molding and radiator. Another sat below the baseboard casing.

Cold capsules, he thought, but the lads at the lab would be able to tell. Best to leave them to be photographed for position.

If they were cold medicine, most likely they would match the bottle at the bottom of the empty waste bin—Talisniff. Wife used to give him that for the sniffles. There was another bottle of tiny pills that seemed to be for a thyroid condition, along with the usual feminine paraphernalia.

"Wait in the ambulance would you, both of you," the inspector told the attendants. "Don't go until I release you—myself, no one else."

They would end up staying well past dinner, and Gorrie would feel sorry for being so peevish.

SEVEN

PETE NIMEC FELT A HAND TOUCH HIS SHOULDER, AND
came awake at once. In his home, always within quick
reach of a weapon, he could succeed at something more
than light sleep. Now he straightened up with a start that
jostled his sling seat on its rail.

He blinked away scraps of a horrendous dream brought
on by fatigue: Gordian dead on a concrete floor, the killer
who'd butchered four of Tom Ricci's men in the Ontario
raid standing over him.

In his dream, the killer had again done his bloody work
like a precision machine, but the savage pride in his eyes
was all too human.

Nimec tried to imagine how Ricci had been affected by
Ontario, imagine what private anguish it had left him to
wrestle down in the depths of night.

He took a breath to relax and settled into the canvas
webbing of his seat. Master Sergeant Barry, a loadmaster
with the Air National Guard's 109th Airlift Wing—and
more specifically, its flying component, the 139th Tactical
Squadron—stood before him in the cabin of the Hercules

ski bird. He was mouthing words Nimec couldn't hear.

Nimec held up a finger to indicate he needed a second, then popped out the foam earplugs he was given at the Clothing Distribution Center in Christchurch.

The ceaseless noise and vibration of the engines throbbed into his auditory canals.

Barry leaned forward, cranking his voice above the racket. "Sorry to disturb you, Mr. Nimec. Captain Evers is a huge booster of UpLink International, and he'd like to show you the view from the flight deck. This close to touchdown it's really impressive."

Nimec was relieved. He'd been ready to learn they'd boomeranged again. Air travel from New Zealand to Antarctica took eight hours by turboprop, slightly under that if you caught a nice tailwind. The previous day a heavy fog over the continent had forced his flight to double back just short of the point of safe return—about sixty degrees south, two thirds of the way there—resulting in seven wasted hours in the sky. The day before that one wasn't quite as bad; his plane had returned to Cheech only an hour out.

Nimec looked up at the young loadie. The Herc's cargo hold was a crude, bare space designed for maximum tonnage rather than comfort, windowless except for a few small portholes at the front and rear. He felt as if he'd gotten stuffed into the barrel of a rumbling cement mixer.

"Tell me the deck's got soundproofing," he said. "Please."

"New acoustical panels, sir—"

"Lead the way."

Nimec rose stiffly in his cold-weather gear. The red wind parka, jump suit, goggles, mittens, bunny boots, and thermal undergarments were his own, as were the extras in his packs. At the terminal prior to departure, loaners had been issued to passengers whose clothing and equipment hadn't met the emergency survival specs mandated by the CDC under the United States Antarctic Program's rule book.

The same guidelines had required Nimec to be physically qualified before leaving San Jose. This meant a complete medical checkup, which included bending over an examining table for a latex-gloved finger probe, that truest and most humbling of equalizers. He'd also needed to visit the dentist, who'd replaced a loose filling and informed him he was charmed to have already gotten his wisdom teeth yanked, since no one could be PQ'd with any still rooted in his mouth. Because medical facilities on the continent were thinly spread—and pharmaceutical stores limited—a minor health problem like an impacted molar or gum infection could easily become the sort of crisis that required an evac in perilous weather. It was a dreaded scenario that USAP took great pains to avoid.

As Barry led him to the forward bulkhead, Nimec saw that several of the twenty-five men and women who shared the hold with him were stretched out against the supply pallets jamming the aisle, their duffels and bedrolls tossed loosely atop the wooden planks. The majority were American researchers and support workers traveling to MacTown. There were also some drillers headed for Scott-Edmondson at the Pole, an Italian biological team on their way to Terra Nova Station, and a group of boisterous Russians hitching a partial ride to Vostok, located deep in the continent's interior at the coldest spot on earth . . . which seemed curiously appropriate given their national origin. The rest were extreme skiers from Australia who'd somehow arranged for slots aboard the flight and had occupied five consecutive seats to his right at takeoff.

Out to make the first traverse of some polar mountain range, the Aussies annoyed Nimec despite their attempts to hobnob. He had trouble with people who took frivolous risks with life, as if its loss could be recouped like money gambled away at a casino. He understood the competitive impulses that drove them, but had seen too many men and women put themselves in jeopardy—and sometimes die unlauded—for better reasons than seeking thrills and trophies.

Barry ushered him into the cockpit and then ducked out the bulkhead door. Occupied by a pilot, copilot, flight engineer, and navigator, the compartment was lined with analog display consoles that showed the true age of the plane, although they'd been gussied with some racked digital avionics. As promised, its sound insulation dampened the roar of the Allisons, and the field of view offered by the front and side windows was magnificent.

The pilot turned from his instrument panel to glance at Nimec.

"Greetings," he said. "I'm Captain Rich Evers. Enjoy the scenery, we've got ideal approach conditions."

"Thanks," Nimec said. "I appreciate the invite."

The pilot nodded, turned back to his panel.

"Wouldn't want you to think I'm trying to sway anybody about my niece's job ap with your company . . . it'd be at that new satellite radio station UpLink just launched," he said innocently. "Her name's Patricia Miller, super kid, graduated college with honors. A communications major. Her friends call her Trish."

Nimec looked at the back of his head.

"Trish."

"Uh-huh."

"I'm sure she'll get a square evaluation."

Evers nodded again.

Nimec moved to a window as they descended through wisps of scattered, patchy clouds. Soon the ocean came into sight beneath the Herc's nose, its calm ice-speckled surface resembling a glass tabletop covered with flaked and broken sugar cubes.

"Looks like a dense ice pack down there," Nimec said. "That how it is the whole way to the coast?"

"Depends," Evers said. "In summer months the floes tend to cluster around the mainland in a circular belt, then give way to open water. What you're seeing's actually a moderate distribution. The big, flat blocks are tabular bergs that have broken away from the ice shelf. They're very buoyant, lots of air trapped inside them, which is why they reflect so white. An iceberg with darker blotches and an irregular form is usually a hunk of a glacier that's migrated from inland and rafting mineral sediment."

Nimec kept studying the ice-clogged water. "How big is 'big'?"

"An average tab is from fifty to a hundred fifty feet tall, and between two and four hundred feet long. Take a look out to starboard, though, and you can see one I'd estimate goes up over three hundred feet."

Nimec spotted the iceberg out the window, surprised by its illusory appearance.

"Wow," he said. "I wouldn't have guessed."

"Bear in mind the visible mass of a berg is maybe a third of what's below the water. That's by conservative measure. Sometimes the base is nine times as deep as the upper portion is high."

"Tip of the iceberg."

"Exactly," Evers said. "I'll tell you something . . . it's been a little over three years since my Air Guard unit took over Antarctic support ops from the Navy's Squadron Six. The Ice Pirates. They'd been hauling supplies and personnel to the continent for a half century, got disestablished because of spending cutbacks. About a year later I'm transferred to Cheech from our home base in Schenectady, New York. The twenty-first day of March, 2000. That very day NOAA polar sats pick up the largest iceberg in recorded history calving off the Ross Ice Shelf. A hundred and eighty-three *miles* long, twenty-three wide. Twice the size of Delaware. And of the previous record holder."

Nimec released a low whistle. "And you've been hoping it was just a coincidence ever since."

"Rather than figure it was a Western Union express to me from the Man Upstairs?" Evers turned to him again, rolled his eyes heavenward. "Got that right, my friend."

Nimec smiled, went back to looking out the window. He was still trying to adjust his sense of scale.

Evers noted his expression.

"The sprinkles of white around the bergs are mostly pancake ice mixed in with growlers . . . slabs the size of cars," he said. "Proportions are deceptive from this altitude in the best of circumstances, and impossible to judge in poor weather. It's why fog and overcast concern us as much as flying snow. When the sunlight's refracted between a low cloud ceiling and snow or ice cover on the ground, everything blends together, and there's no sight horizon."

"Zero visibility," Nimec said. "I've gotten stuck driving in blizzards more than once. Feels like there's a white blanket across the windshield."

At his station, the navigator shifted toward Nimec. The blue laminate name tag on his breast identified him as Lieutenant Halloran.

"It isn't quite the same," he said. "Any flier will tell you there's no worse pain in the ass than getting stuck in a fog whiteout."

Nimec looked at him, thinking his tone was a bit too purposefully casual.

"If there's a heavy snow alert, you know to stay wheels-down until the storm passes," Halloran said. "But say you're airborne over the ice and hit a fog bank. Around the pole it can happen just like that." He snapped his fingers. "The way our eyes and brains are wired, we use shadows to judge the distance of things on a uniformly white field—and in a whiteout you lose shadows. So even if the air's dry under the clouds and you're able to see an object, the perspective may be false. No, scratch that . . . it *will be* false. With winter around the bend, you have to be especially careful because the sun's inclination isn't very high regardless of the time of day."

"Meaning it won't cast much shadow."

"That's right. Unless you're keeping a close check on your instruments—and sometimes even then—you can get disoriented, fly upside down without realizing it, smash into the ground while you think you're still a mile up. Or drop off the edge of a cliff if you're on foot. Happened to some of Scott's men. Around the turn of the last century, wasn't it, Chief?"

Evers nodded. "The *Discovery* expedition."

Halloran looked pleased with himself.

"And isn't just humans that are affected," he went on. "You know what a skua is?"

Nimec shook his head.

"Think of a seagull, but smarter, wilder, and mean as the devil. Those birds can dive from midair, snatch a tiny piece of food out of your hand without nicking a finger, swoop in on the tits of a nursing elephant seal to drink her milk. But for all their sharp instincts and reflexes, I once saw hundreds of them, a whole flock, splattered over an area of a quarter mile after a whiteout lifted."

Nimec gazed out the windows in silence. The transition to clear water was as abrupt as Evers had described. For a while he could see nothing but the thick crowd of bergs floating below him in apparently motionless suspension, and then the plane was past the ice belt and over the open sound.

Looking ahead into the near distance, Nimec was struck by a long, solid border of white that rose up against the calm blue-gray sea and then swept back and away to the furthest range of his vision.

He recalled the briefs he'd studied in preparation for his mission, and instantly knew they were nearing the forward edge of the Ross Ice Shelf.

"We enter our final approach pattern in a couple of minutes," Evers said. "There'll be an unloading and refueling stop at MacTown. Ought to be fairly short. Then we take off for Cold Corners."

"I assume it's back to coach class for me."

Evers nodded. "Sorry. They do a nice job grooming the ski way at Willy, but it can be bumpy." He paused. "I'm banking to port in just a second. You might want to take a peek out the right-hand windows before you go aft and buckle up."

Nimec felt the aircraft tilt gently, and looked.

Below them now, the ice shelf was a continuous sheet of whiteness that gleamed so brightly in the sun it made his eyes smart. A stepped ridge of glaciers sat atop it, extending seaward from the interior like a wide, rough tongue questing for water. At the far end of this glacial wave, two frozen mountain peaks reared thousands of feet above a great hump in the otherwise flat plain of ice. A plume of smoke flowed from the summit of the larger mountain, tailing into the wind.

Evers glanced over his shoulder at Nimec.

"That area where the ice looks like it bulges up is Ross Island. Home to Mount Erebus, his baby brother Mount Terror, and the fifteen hundred Americans at McMurdo Station," Evers said. "Terror's the quiet one. As you can tell, Erebus is something of a hothead."

Nimec kept looking out the window.

"I knew MacTown wasn't too far from a volcano," he said. "Didn't have any idea the volcano was active."

"You bet it is," Evers said. "Regular with its tantrums too. Erebus has been in a constant state of eruption for almost three decades now . . . what amounts to a slow boil. It vents six times a day, sometimes with a rumble you can hear for miles. Sends bullets of molten lava and ash over the rim of the crater. The past couple of years those discharges have gotten more intense, and there've been some significant seismic tremors on the island."

Nimec turned to face him.

"Fire and ice," Nimec said. "I've been around a little, seen some unusual places. None of them were anything like this."

Evers briefly met his gaze.

"Terra Australis Incognita," Evers said. " 'Unknown to the sons of Adam, having nothing which belongs to our race.' That's what the legend says about Antarctica on a map by one of those Benedictine monks who tried to keep the gears of civilization turning in the Dark Ages. His name was Lambert of Saint Olmer."

Nimec grunted. "You know your local history."

"I read between flights . . . helps me cope with the end-less holdups," Evers said. "You know what, though? Old Lambert was right on. This is a different world. Or may as well be. Nobody will really ever belong here. Not a single one of us."

"Just visitors, huh," Nimec said.

"*Unwanted* visitors." Evers's face was serious. "Here's another piece of information to stuff in your hip pocket. You know the satellite photos I mentioned? Look at any aerial views of the continent and you'll notice it's shaped like a giant manta ray." He paused, shrugged. "Call me crazy, but there are days when I'd swear it's a reminder. Mother Nature's way of telling us something important about this place."

Nimec was still looking at him.

"Namely?" Nimec said.

Evers moved his shoulders up and down again.

"Its sting can be fatal to humans," he said, and got to work landing the plane in silence.

McMurdo Station
(77°84' S, 166°67' E)

"Willy" was Williams Field, a prepared airstrip on the fast ice eight miles from McMurdo Station proper. As the Herc taxied to a halt, flight directors in hooded red-issue ECW outfits used hand signals to guide it into position.

A fleet of different vehicles hemmed the fringes of the ski way. Immediately alongside it were bulldozers and other equipment for clearing, raking, and compacting the snow pile. An enormous 4X4 shuttle raised on six-foot-high balloon tires—Ivan the Terrabus, said the lettering on its flank—stood ready to cart deplaned passengers to the station's main receiving center. There were forklifts for off-loading the cargo pallets, fire trucks in case of a landing emergency, scattered vans, tractors, and motor sleds.

Willy's operational facilities were identical to those of

an ordinary small airfield in so many respects, it almost blunted one's appreciation of the fact that the whole thing had been constructed on a plate of floating sea ice. It had air-traffic control towers and a considerable number of maintenance and supply buildings with corrugated metal sides. But each of these structures rested on skids, and had been towed from the main field six miles closer to the station, a seven-thousand-foot strip that could be used by aircraft with standard wheeled landing gear until sometime in December, the middle of the polar summer, when the ice runways there began to give in and melt to slush.

Nimec had learned much of this from his files, and seen more with his own eyes upon touchdown. He had adequate time to hear about the rest from Halloran and two other members of the aircrew as they sat together in a heated visitors' lounge near the apron, sipped passably decent coffee, and watched the Herc being emptied of freight as it took fuel through the lines.

The stop was lasting longer than he'd expected. Almost two hours after the plane's arrival at McMurdo it remained parked on the ice, the activity around it ongoing without any hint of a letup, its engines running because the minus-50° Fahrenheit temperature was just eight degrees above the danger threshold at which its hydraulics would begin to fail—the rubber hoses, gaskets, and valve seals getting brittle enough to crack, the JP8 fuel that powered the Allisons becoming too viscous to flow freely despite its special cold-weather formulation.

Draining his paper cup, Nimec glanced at his watch, then at the busy airstrip outside the window to his left. He let out a grumbling sound and stretched his arms.

"You have to get in sync," Halloran said, eyeballing him from across the cafeteria table.

Nimec shook his head, turned his wrist to display the watch's face.

"I switched to New Zealand time at Christchurch," he said.

Halloran looked sideways at his fellow Guardsmen. Then all three laughed.

Nimec bristled. "Didn't realize I said something funny."

Halloran fought in vain to stifle a chuckle. "Sorry, no offense intended. I meant you should synchronize the clock in *here*." He tapped his forehead. "This place, the sun doesn't rise or set, but kind of crawls around you in a circle like a snail on a basketball hoop for about six months. Then it hibernates for the winter."

His explanation, such as it was, only made Nimec grumpier.

"I don't care if the sun balances on the tip of my nose for half the year," he said. "Things need to get done."

"Sure. I'm just saying to remember where you are."

"So your advice is, what, that we check our schedules on arrival?"

Halloran frowned.

"Listen," he said, motioning his chin toward the window. "You have any idea how long it takes to plot and cut an ice runway?"

Nimec shook his head, shrugging, uncertain whether he cared at that particular moment. He'd spent the better part of his week hurtling through transoceanic airspace, spent much of the week before getting poked, prodded, and pissing into paper cups in an accelerated barrage of medical examinations. He was annoyed by his own crabbiness. And he missed his sweetheart Corvette.

"At least sixty, seventy hours," Halloran was saying in answer to his own question. "Think about it. The field groomers get through with all their snow-moving and grading, then a storm plasters the area and they're back to square one. That happens so often—with a vengeance— nobody even thinks to rag. It's just business as usual."

"Your point being . . . ?"

"Exactly what it was when we started this conversation," Halloran said. "Adjust. Don't try to impose yourself on this place. Even most governments acknowledge it's ungovernable."

Nimec looked at him. *This place*. Nothing at all out of the ordinary about the phrase. But he somehow found Halloran's repetition of it interesting . . . and hadn't Evers also used it at least once rather than having named the continent?

"Take things as they come," Nimec said, putting aside the thought. "Does that sound about right?"

Halloran continued to disregard the obvious pique in his tone.

"About."

"You have a very Zen attitude for a military man," Nimec said.

Halloran smiled, touched the circular ANG 139th TAS shoulder patch on the blouse of his flight suit. A nose-on view of a Hercules ski transport against a blue background, with the polar ice caps embroidered in white at the top and bottom, it was designed to be symbolic of a compass: the wings of the plane crossing east and west to the edges of the patch, the tail rudder similarly pointing due north, the skis lowered toward the southern cap.

"Very Zen," Halloran said to the Guardsman beside him, a fellow lieutenant named Mathews. "Maybe we should have that stitched right here above the plane, make it our official motto. How about it?"

Mathews grinned and told him it sounded like a good idea. Then all three members of the aircrew were laughing again.

Nimec sighed, rapped the table with his fingers, listened to the engines of the plane humming outside the lounge.

Something told him he was at the hard rock bottom of what would be a steep and difficult learning curve.

Cold Corners Research Base
(21°88' S, 144°72' E)

Topped with fuel, the Herc finally got back under way some three hours after alighting at Williams Field. Its de-

parture commenced with a jarring bounce as its wheels
dropped to crack the ice that had melted around its skis
from the friction of landing, and then had frozen over
again to hold the plane steadily in position. After the
wheels were retracted, it was a swift, smooth slide over
the ski way to takeoff.

Cold Corners was four hundred odd miles south on the
coastline, an aerial sprint of just about an hour. Nimec
stuck it out in the webbing of the aft compartment, which
he found much less disagreeable now that the bulk of its
freight and over half its passengers—including the loud
Russians and Australian adrenaline junkies—had gone on
to their various destinations. The hold space freed up by
their departure also gave Nimec a pretty well unrestricted
choice of seating, and he grabbed a spot by a porthole
that afforded good bird's-eye views of both McMurdo and
Cold Corners.

The contrast between them was striking. Seen from
above, MacTown resembled an industrial park, or maybe
a mining town that had sprung up without systematic
planning over a span of many decades. Nimec guessed
there were probably between a hundred and two hundred
separate structures—multistory barracks-style units, rows
of arched canvas Jamesway huts, smaller blue-skinned
metal Quonsets, warehouse buildings, and upwards of a
dozen massive, rust-blighted steel fuel-storage tanks
strung out on the surrounding hillsides. Tucked among
them were a couple of appreciably more modern com-
plexes that Sergeant Barry identified as NSF headquarters
and the Crary Science and Engineering Center, but Nimec's overall impression of the station was one of rambling, indiscriminate sprawl and exceeding ugliness.

Very much on the other hand, Cold Corners looked like
the working model for a future space colony . . . and by
no accident. Roger Gordian's innovative flair and pen-
chant for cost efficiency made him an almost compulsive
multitasker. Cold Corners was envisioned as an all-in-one
satellite ground station, new space technology center, and

human habitability and performance lab for long-term interplanetary settlements, and the heart of the base was configured of six sleek, linked rectangular pods on jackable stilts that allowed it to be elevated above the rising snow drifts that eventually inundated most Antarctic stations. In his oversight of the installation's security analysis, Nimec had stayed abreast of its development from conception to construction, and knew the few outlying buildings included a solar-paneled housing for its supplementary electrical generator, a desalinization plant to convert seawater beneath the ice crust into drinkable water, a garage for the vehicles, a trio of side-by-side satcom radomes, and of course the airfield facility that was its lifeline to civilization. The main energy, environmental-control, and waste-disposal systems were in utility corridors—or utilidors—beneath the permanent ice strata.

Minutes after Sergeant Barry announced the Herc was coming up on Cold Corners, Nimec felt its skis deploy with a thump. Then it made a sharp left turn, and the level white spread of the airfield swelled into his window.

On the ground at last, Nimec unbuckled, zipped into his parka, shouldered his bags, and went about exchanging farewells with the airmen.

The wind was staggering as he descended the exit ramp to the field. A downscaled version of Willy, it had a more modest complement of personnel shuttles and freight haulers waiting to meet the plane. Also present was a small welcoming committee clad in the ubiquitous cardinal-red survival gear. It seemed colder here than at McMurdo, and the party's members wore full rubber face masks that rendered them indistinguishable from each other. Nimec saw somebody he guessed was its leader step toward the plane ahead of the rest.

Nimec had taken about two steps toward the shuttle bus when that same person rushed over and swept him into a tight, eager embrace.

"Pete." A woman's voice through the mask, muffled

but familiar. And close against his face. "God, I've missed you something awful."

Nimec's surprise dissolved in a flash of happiness. He smiled openly for the first time in hours, ignoring the raw sting of the wind on his lips.

"Same here, Meg," he said, wrapping his arms around her.

EIGHT

SCOTTISH HIGHLANDS

GORRIE WAS STOPPED AT A RUSTY OLD PUMP AT A little service station south of Newtonmore, working its hose toward the rear of his hatchback, when another driver pulled up on the opposite side of the island, exited his Vectra, and went around to stand alongside him.

"You'll want to let me piss in your tank before filling it from that pump," the man said. "Healthier for the engine, guaranteed to be more economical."

Gorrie waved the fuel nozzle at a paper coffee cup on his trunk.

"No, thanks," he said. "But you ought to make that bloke in the convenience shop a like offer before he puts up another pot of spew."

"Really?" The man broke into a grin. "Well, I've got news, it's already done. What else you think you've been sipping right there?"

Gorrie grinned back at him.

"How've you been, Conall?"

"You mean before or *after* motoring fifty kilometers through the fog?"

"Och, you're reminding me of Nan," Gorrie said. "I'd expect you'd be grateful, consider it a holiday to be rescued from your shoebox office in Dundee."

Conall snorted. "Got me on that," he said.

They extended their hands, shook vigorously.

Gorrie opened his gas tank door, unscrewed its cap, inserted the fuel nozzle, and squeezed the handle, feeling in vain for a lock to hold it in the "on" position. It would have been nice if his coffee were drinkable, he thought. Conall hadn't griped for nothing. The weather was indeed drearily foul, with occasional plops of rain and soft hail coming out of the smoky gray mist.

The pump's sluggish dial readouts were turning behind a scuffed, grime-smeared glass panel.

"All right," Gorrie said. "What have you brought to make me happy?"

"And violate enough of the Procurator Fiscal's rules to get me fired from my job several times over?"

"That too."

Conall reached into an inside pocket of his leather car coat. He took out a cardboard floppy-disc mailer.

"Here you go," he said, passing it to Gorrie. "Preliminary lab results on your fallen peach and her husband."

Gorrie nodded, stuffing the mailer into his own topcoat.

"Appreciate it," he said. "Don't suppose you had a chance to give the files a look."

Conall shook his head.

"Afraid not," he said. "But I hear the coroner's ready to confirm the deaths a murder-suicide, issue a report that'll put the inquiry to a fast and easy rest."

Gorrie considered that a moment, then shrugged.

"We'll see, brother-in-law," he said, and finished gassing up.

"What about my redhead?" asked Gorrie.

"Aye, that's where you have yourself a piece of something to match the weather," said Conall. He took the gas pump and held it out like a pointer. "An interesting case."

"And?"

"Report is nae finished."

"Conall—come now. Not a hint?"

His brother-in-law leaned back on the blue fender of his car and shined an idiot grin. Then he began pumping fuel into his Vectra.

"I suppose this will cost me a pint or two around Easter," offered Gorrie finally.

"I was thinking of those fine cigars ye had at Christmas."

"That was Fennel had 'em, not me."

"Fennel and you are close as stones in a castle wall."

"I'll send my sergeant after the report."

"The sergeant you complained had flown off to Paris for a job hunting art thieves? The lass who has not been replaced despite your crying buckets of tears to the superintendent."

"Not to the superintendent."

His brother-in-law smiled. "Ten cigars."

"Two. They're five pounds apiece."

"I suppose you'll find out soon enough through official channels."

"Three."

Conall returned the nozzle to the pump. "Truth is, the lab report won't tell you anything, save the T4 is more than a wee bit high, above 37 ug/dLs. Very high, that. She had a great deal of phenylephrine hydrochloride in her stomach as well. Now, if you cared to get technical—"

"Conall, you're irritating my nerves," said Gorrie. "What does it mean?"

"Five cigars?"

"I'll see what I can do about the cigars, lad. I'll do my best."

"She had no thyroid. She was taking artificial thyroid hormone because she'd just had her thyroid taken out. Cancer, I suspect."

"And?"

"Well, she took too much of it, you understand. The

hormone. That's the T4. You'll have to fish out the medical records, but the thinking is she forgot what she was doing and took two pills a day instead of one, two or three times. And then she took the cold medicine and it gave her a stroke. Far too much of that too. Small dose together might even have killed her, but here there was no chance. Some people have no sense when they're medicating themselves."

"Stroke?"

"Aye. Bad luck. Sort of thing they warn you about at the chemist. It could also be suicide, I guess. But it'd be a very clever way to do it—too clever. Easier to get a gun like the Mackay woman."

"Getting a gun is not that easy for most of us," noted Gorrie. They hadn't been able to trace the weapon, though he'd put DC Andrews back on it three days before.

Conall shrugged. "More than likely it was an accident. Medicine was taken off the market a year or two ago."

"Matched the type on the floor?"

"I believe that will be the report."

"Do you ha'e anything else for me, laddie?"

"Not a thing. Arm nick was the sort of thing you would get giving blood. Nice work on the thyroid incision, I'm told. Takes a real artist to sew it up."

"Her face was puffed up."

"Aye. The sinuses. She had a cold, remember?"

"Aye."

"There was a bruise on her chest, probably bumped herself falling."

"Can you give blood when you have a cold?" Gorrie asked.

"Why not? Five cigars," added Conall. "And I'd like the disc back when you're done."

"Aye," Gorrie grunted.

An accident then, like council member Ewie Cameron's accident. A coincidence, random and unconnected. The sort of thing that happened all the time.

●　●　●

A walrus waited for Gorrie in his office, polishing its tusks on a large piece of pastry supplied by one of the girls down the hall. He sat behind Gorrie's desk, brushing crumbs away with his stubby fins, every so often touching his enormous mustache to see if any had strayed there.

The walrus was the deputy area commander, whose arrival at the Inverness Command Area's CID section could bode no good at all.

"Sir," said Gorrie, who had been warned by scurrying comrades before he approached.

"Inspector Gorrie, I'm pleased you could make it this morning," said the deputy commander, Nab Russell.

"I've been nosin' around," answered Gorrie. "What brings you here, Chief?"

"There are rumors, Inspector, that your methods of detection are not proceeding with the snap and polish expected of the Northern Constabulary," said Russell.

From another man, the words would have been meant to elicit a laugh. But another man was not the deputy commander. In a minute, Gorrie knew, he would begin to cite the Constabulary's unprecedented detection rate—62 percent, up four percentage points from the year before and, more importantly, four points higher than that of the Central Constabulary. Not that there was competition, mind.

"I believe a review of my methods will pass any muster," said Gorrie.

"You're trying to connect a traffic accident involving a respected council member—a legate holder, a man descended from heroes, Frank—an unfortunate accident to a tawdry suicide?"

"At least one was murder," said Gorrie.

"Cameron slept with the wife?"

"No evidence of that. I didnae even think it has been suggested."

"Where's the connection then?"

"It would be premature to connect them, sir. Inquiries are being made."

"Inquiries, lad! I'm not the bleeding press. What is it you have?"

"The dead men met together the night they were murdered," said Gorrie. "That's it."

The walrus pounced. "One was murdered by his wife. The other died in an accident."

"Manslaughter, at the least."

"Pending an investigation—and that is not your case," Russell reminded him.

"I didna ask to be assigned it, sir."

"You made hints."

"I followed strict procedure when I met with the detective sergeant in charge," said Gorrie sharply.

He had. The hints were made in a pub later on.

"Frank." The walrus leaned to one side, then slid back in the desk chair. With appropriate adjustment for specifics of geographic locale, the speech that followed could have been given by nearly any police supervisor in the islands of Great Britain since the Romans. Crimes to be solved, yes, but flights of fancy not to be indulged. Connections sought, but fantasies nipped in the bud. Investigation to be pursued, but wild-goose chases to be foreclosed.

In some cases, the obvious was the obvious. And there was the detection rate to consider.

Finally, Gorrie couldn't take any more of it. "Her hand was at the wrong angle," he said. "I didnae think it could be suicide."

"What?" asked the walrus.

"She was holding the gun the wrong way to have killed herself. If she were a man, perhaps, or stronger, but to have fired it the way she did, the bullet would have traveled further to the right of her head. To fire it the way she had"—Gorrie held his own hand to demonstrate—"her arm would have had to have been twisted."

"The autopsy says that?"

"The report only notes the angle of the wound."

"And the body might not have been moved? Or the arm jerk back as a reflex?"

"You'll have to trust me on this, Nab. My instincts—"

"Frank, instincts?"

"I helped you out of the traffic division—"

"For twenty years you've held that over my head. Twenty years, lad."

"And I'll hold it twenty more, God willing."

The walrus had no argument for that. More importantly, he was finished with his Danish. He rose.

"You have to close these cases out, Frank. The London papers are having a field day with us."

"I wouldnae thought you cared about a London tabloid, Nab."

The phone interrupted a recapitulation of the earlier lecture. Gorrie reached over and picked it up.

It was the detective in charge of the Cameron traffic accident case. They'd just found the truck they thought had hit the council member.

Gorrie caught a glimpse of an ancient stone house on his right as he turned down the road near Loch Ness where the truck had been found. Fifteen years before, the stone house had been the residence of Kevin and Mary Mac-Millan; it had been the scene of the first murder he'd ever investigated. Tidy case that—wife on the floor with her head bashed in, husband holding the hammer he'd done it with when the constables rushed in. Sergeant Gorrie spent more time typing up the report with his two-fingered typing than he did interviewing the suspect.

The truck was a year-old Ford, registered to and stolen from Highland Specialty Transport the night Cameron had been killed. It was a large diesel tractor, its front fender scratched slightly, one of its headlights smashed, and on its fender a small speckle of "something red and dried, foreign, not part of the finish"—the young detective's exact words in his preliminary report—had been found.

"Tip came in directing us here on the hot line," said Lewis. "Newspapers good for something, at least."

The two investigators stood near the cab as one of the forensics people ran a small, battery-powered vacuum cleaner across the floorboards. The exterior of the truck seemed fairly clean, not what you'd expect if it had sat on the side of the road gathering dust for a week.

"Cleanest lorry I ever saw, inside and out," said Lewis. "You could eat off the floor."

"Vacuumed?"

"Maybe."

"But that's likely blood on the fender. And the glass."

"Aye."

They could do a DNA test on the fender, and attempt to match the headlamp glass with glass at the scene. If this truck had killed Cameron, they would know it.

"We're under five minutes from the spot where Cameron was found," said Lewis. He pushed back the hair on his forehead. He seemed to be combing it down to hide a bald spot, except that he had no bald spot. "If it was here the morning after the accident, two dozen constables missed it, along with myself at least twice."

"When do you think it was left here?" Gorrie asked.

Lewis shrugged. "We'll set up a barricade and ask people who pass this way going from work."

Gorrie stood back a few feet and surveyed the scene. The shoulder across the way was wide enough for a waiting car, easily parked in the shadow of the pines.

Hadn't the words Specialty Transport been on one of Cameron's pads?

Gorrie reached into his pocket for his notebook, though even before he opened it he realized he hadn't written down what the council member's pads had said.

Bad detective work, that. What would the walrus say?

"Sergeant, have you a phone I could borrow?" he asked Lewis.

"It's my personal phone, Inspector."

Gorrie held out his hand.

Melanie, the sister's American friend, answered on the second ring. Ms. Cameron was out, but she volunteered to check the pad. Gorrie listened as she pulled open the drawers.

"Right or left?" she asked, and his heart sank.

"Left, I think."

"Nothing here. Wait, I'll try the right."

It was there. Halfway down the page of the second pad was the note: "Hgh Spec Trprt?"

Highland Specialty Transport. Or highly special transportation. Or Hugh Spectre Transport.

"There was a phone number, wasn't there?" asked Gorrie. "Read it to me, would you?"

He punched the number into the sergeant's phone, even though it meant breaking his promise to the sergeant that he would only call the nearby number. A very correct though very young bureaucratic voice answered on the other end.

"UKAE Nuclear Waste Regulation, Transport Division."

"Transport Division?"

"Sir, can I help you?"

"What precisely is it you do, son?"

"I hang up the phone if I don't have an explanation as to why this is not a crank call," said the man.

Gorrie explained who he was and why, more or less, he was calling. The young man became considerably more helpful. He believed he had spoken to Cameron, who sat on the area Land and Environment Select Committee. The council member had inquired about forms and regulations governing transport of spent nuclear fuel. The conversation had not lasted long; Cameron had been referred to Constance Burns. The head of the UKAE Waste Division liked to deal with elected representatives personally.

"She takes all VIPs," said the young man. "I'm not sure if she spoke to the committee member or not, just that he would have been referred."

"Could you tell her that I'd like a word?" said Gorrie,

who wasn't sure if he qualified as a VIP or not.

"Afraid she's out of the country on vacation in Switzerland. She calls in every morning and evening. Shall I give her your number?"

"Why don't you give me hers instead?"

"Well, sir, our privacy policy—"

"Come now, be a good lad," said Gorrie.

"Well."

"You never know when you might need a favor," suggested the inspector.

"As a matter of fact, if it was convenient, I could use one. There's a matter of a speeding ticket."

"Speeding? And when were you in the Highlands?"

"My girlfriend, Inspector, she suggested a holiday and, well, you know how it is. . . ."

"You're going to fix a ticket?" asked Lewis as Gorrie punched in the number for Ms. Burns's mobile phone.

"I was hoping you would," said Gorrie.

The phone was off-line. Gorrie left a message, then dialed the hotel next. He had the clerk ring the room, but received no answer.

The plant manager at Cromarty Firth had emphasized how safe transporting spent uranium was. Gorrie decided to drive over to the plant and find out why the matter had been on his mind.

Caught unawares, reception took a few minutes to find a suitable minder to escort DI Gorrie to Horace's office. When he arrived, he noted that the pile of papers had grown a bit, as had the smell of furniture polish. Horace himself remained unchanged, not quite dismissive, yet not what one might call polite either.

"I can't recall Ewie Cameron calling me. You can check the diary with my secretary," Horace told him. He held a fountain pen in his hand, and every time he answered a question he glanced down at the paper at the top of his desk, applying another check.

"Perhaps I will do that," said Gorrie.

"Mackay called him concerning the plant?"

"I didnae know that he did."

"He didn't bring anything to me," said Horace. "No problem was reported."

Gorrie nodded. There might be many reasons Mackay wouldn't talk to Horace about a problem, starting with the fact that he thought Horace was involved.

"I might talk to your secretary then, and Mackay's," said Gorrie.

"Please," said Horace, who now put his head down practically onto the desk, checking off a succession of blanks on the paper in a wild flurry.

The secretary had not recorded any meeting with Mackay during the week before his death, and according to the records they hadn't spoken outside of regular staff meetings since he had come on. Gorrie formed no judgment of that, just as he did not hold Tora Grant's frown against her when he appeared at her doorway. Mackay had not been replaced and she was obviously overworked trying to help handle some of the paperwork. Gorrie's first request—for a roster of the department—was met with an even deeper frown.

"Addie at Personnel," she said, digging her fingernails into her folded arms.

Gorrie nodded. "Miss Grant, what is the procedure for removing waste from the reactor?"

"I'm sure I wouldn't know all the steps. The procedure—you'd have to talk to the men. It's not like taking out the trash, Inspector. Spent fuel has to be carefully handled. The regulations are enormous. It has to be cooled in one of the ponds near the reactor. The spent rods stay quite long—years."

"Had there been a removal since Mr. Mackay arrived?"

"I can check the records, but I believe the last was eight months. There's no set schedule. You see, there are so few places for it to be reprocessed, and transport is quite a procedure. The spent rods have to travel in special containers, and can only be taken aboard a special ship."

"Who owns the ship?"

Grant frowned, but pulled over the keyboard to her computer. Punching a few keys, she brought up an address book.

"BNFL. British Nuclear Fuels plc. The amount of material is very small, you understand; it's the way it has to be transported that complicates things. Sellafield is typically where it would be sent."

"What happened to the man who held Mr. Mackay's job before his arrival?"

"Matthew Franklin transferred to UKAE—the energy commission."

"Hard worker?"

"I couldn't say. I came on with Mr. Mackay."

Gorrie paused, considering how to proceed. The secretary pushed a piece of hair up at the side of her head behind her ear, her whole body heaving with a sigh. She seemed a good sort, slightly bewildered by the job and loss of her boss, he thought. She had a round, attractive face, but in five years, maybe less, her looks would muddle into a sort of plainness as her hips rounded and her legs grew thick. Gorrie thought of his own wife, which made him sympathetic toward the girl.

"Do you know who Ewie Cameron is?" he asked.

She shook her head.

"Did Mr. Mackay speak of any government official?"

Another shake.

"Would he have?"

"The plant manager would generally handle any important matter, I believe," said Miss Grant.

Mackay had not kept an appointment book, and a look back at the department phone records did not turn up Cameron's number, nor any besides Cardha Duff's that seemed extraordinary. The secretary's sighs grew as she showed Gorrie through the forms and papers Mackay had been working on before he died. To Gorrie, nothing was amiss—or everything was; he couldn't tell.

"Specialty Transport," he said finally, "does the name mean anything?"

"Trucking firm that handles the spent fuel and some of the items that are bulky," said the secretary.

"Are there reports here that pertain to it?"

"The traffic file," she said, going to the files and thumbing through.

Gorrie took the folder and opened it on the desk. Four sheets sat at the top of the folder, out of order; they had been photocopied from other reports, which themselves were copies of thicker filings. The pages documented pickup times, routes, transmittals; all had blanks in the areas for "Incidents" and "Comments."

"They record when the waste was picked up and when it was transferred to the next shipper," said the secretary. "The main copies are filed with the commission."

"UKAE."

"Yes."

"Why would Mr. Mackay be looking through them?" Gorrie asked.

"To help plan for another shipment of spent waste, if he was. Would you mind terribly, Inspector, if I went back to work?"

Gorrie nodded, but the secretary hesitated. "I heard—the woman Ed . . ."

"Aye, Cardha Duff. I wouldn't call it suicide," he added. "Probably an accident due to medication."

She pursed her lips and shook her head, then turned away quickly to her desk to have a cry.

Gorrie went back to the documents. Except for the dates and some slight variation in the waste amounts, they could have been identical. The pickups were always made around the same time, late at night, moved by the same route, and were presented at the dock loading area roughly sixty minutes later.

Gorrie took out his notebook. Cameron's pad had mentioned Lin Firth Bridge. The bridge wasn't noted here—

it wasn't much of a landmark—but the truck would have crossed over it.

So that's what Mackay had found.

Gorrie took down the dates of the transport, knowing even before he checked that one would include the few days the bridge was closed.

NINE

MARKED AGAINST THE SUN'S 4.5 BILLION YEARS OF existence, the coming event was nothing truly anomalous, but a result of the natural interplay between its atmospheric and orbital processes.

A body of seething gas and plasma, the solar sphere does not rotate on its axis in the same coherent way as the solid globe we inhabit. Rather, its rotation is fluid, the radiative and convective zones that compose its outer layers—and 85 percent of its radius—turning faster at the equator than at its poles. This causes its lines of magnetic force, which run longitudinally from positive north to negative south, to stretch and twist.

The phenomenon is easily understood with this model:

Imagine a ball sliced into three crosswise sections. Now imagine rubber bands attached to it, top to bottom, with pins inserted into each section. Give the middle slice of the ball a faster spin than the others, and the rubber bands are stretched along with its movement. Continue spinning it faster and the rubber bands coil tightly around the ball, eventually tangling and kinking up in places . . . assuming they have sufficient elasticity not to snap first.

As the sun turns in its differential rotation, the lines of force running through its gaseous outer layers stretch and intertwine until they develop similar kinks—wide, swirling magnetic fields that most often occur in leader-follower pairs that are bonded by their opposite polarities and drift across the surface in unison with smaller fields strung out between them like ships in a flotilla. Attenuated lines of force bulge up from the positively charged leader fields, and are pulled back to the negative followers, forming closed bipolar loops that reach many thousands of miles outward toward the sun's corona. Pressure exerted on the solar atmosphere by the intense magnetic fields dampens the upward flow of hot gas from the interior. The regions covered by the fields are, therefore, about two thousand degrees cooler than those surrounding them and appear as dark blemishes to observers on earth.

These we call sunspots, and their number rises from minimum to maximum levels in eleven-to-twelve-year cycles. A typical sunspot grows in size over a period of days or sometimes months, and then shrinks after the cycle peaks and the bands of magnetic force unwind. A spot moving across the sun as it rotates on its axis will take twenty-seven days to complete a journey around the equator and thirty-five days to circle the upper and lower hemispheres.

Like rubber bands, the lines of force extending upward from sunspots *do* occasionally snap. This happens when they stretch past a critical height 250,000 miles above the surface of the sun and break through its corona, releasing their stored energy in a fiery maelstrom of subatomic particles that lashes into outer space and goes sweeping across the entire electromagnetic spectrum.

We call these solar flares, and their emissions will bombard Earth within days if angled toward it. Major flares have been known to cover eighty thousand square miles of the sun—an area ten times larger than our planet—and equal millions of hundred-megaton hydrogen bomb blasts in strength, triggering worldwide disturbances in Earth's magnetic field. They cannot be forecast with absolute certainty, though any significant increase of sunspot activity is considered to be a possible indicator of solar flares in generation.

On the third day of March, during a peak in the sunspot cycle, a group of frecklelike spots that seemed the very definition of unremarkable to astronomers who routinely track them moved to the far side of the sun in their orbital course. There over the next two weeks, beyond the range of visual observation, they began to enlarge, multiply, and align in long, close-grouped strings. By the twelfth of the month the spots had become highly asymmetric; their heavy concentration resembled a spreading, blotchy rash on the hidden face of the sun. The escalated growth and proliferation would continue for several days to come.

Again, in the long view, this outbreak was a blip. A millennial tickle in the life of the sun.

Nothing extraordinary.

As the time line of human history goes, it was without documented scientific precedent.

Later, debate would arise over a suggestion by some scholars that the last comparable episode occurred in the summer of 480 B.C., a year for which Chinese, Korean, Babylonian, Celtic, and Mesoamerican records—including glyph-dated early Mayan stelae—present what has been interpreted as correlative evidence of rapidly changing sunspot patterns, and brilliant, tempestuous displays of the northern and southern lights many thousands of miles from the poles. That is the same summer King Leonidas I and his three hundred Spartan warriors made their heroic resistance against thousands of invading Persians at the Hot Gates, a narrow mountain pass between the Aegean coast and central Greece, only to be undone by a local betrayer, who showed the Persian force a route that led them over the mountains to a rear assault upon the defenders, killing them almost to a man.

A coincidence? Likely so. Although the oracle Leonidas consulted before deciding to hold the pass is said to have been influenced by his interpretation of some obscure cosmic portent.

Such speculation aside, it remains doubtful that a magnetic storm of even the greatest severity would have had a consequential impact on affairs in Greece or elsewhere in that ancient era.

This was, after all, many centuries before civilization became dependent on the telecommunications networks and electrical power grids that would be thrown into utter chaos by its shock waves.

Cold Corners Base, Antarctica

In more than one sense, Pete Nimec's trip to the hallway rest room was another step up the learning curve he'd foreseen at McMurdo.

Nimec supposed it was partly his own fault. The three or four cups of coffee he'd drunk in Willy's passenger lounge had worked their way through him soon after the Herc was off-deck, but a peek behind the shower curtain enclosing its cargo section's makeshift latrine—a fifty-five-gallon steel drum with an attached funnel for a urinal, and a loathsome, sloshing plastic honey bucket—persuaded him to try to hold out until after he reached Cold Corners. And he'd succeeded, asking Megan to show him where he could make a pit stop on the way to her office.

Inside the unisex rest room's single stall, Nimec had found tugging himself out from under his boxers, long johns, flannel-lined blue jeans, and various overlapped shirts an uncomfortable exercise in patience and control. But he managed to get his business done without embarrassment.

Now he filled the sink, soaped his hands under the automatic dispenser, and washed them in the plugged basin, complying with a sign above the sink that said its taps weren't to be left running while you cleaned up. Nimec was about to splash his face with some fresh, cold water when he read the second item on the extensive list of dos and don'ts, and discovered the limit was one basinful per person. *So much for that.*

He dried his hands with a paper towel, tossed it in the trash receptacle, went to the door. A coin-operated condom machine was on the wall beside it. He paused and checked the sign. Unsurprisingly, the machine's contents weren't rationed.

Nimec emerged from the rest room. A small group of men and women looked askance at him as they walked past. Puzzled, he turned to where Megan was waiting for him down the hall.

He asked her about the plainly disagreeable glances once the two of them were seated in her office.

"I followed the rules," he said, making the Scout's-honor sign with his right hand. "Not that I can see how they'd know if I didn't."

She regarded him with amusement from across her desk.

"That bunch was mostly OAEs," she said.

He pulled a face. "Mostly what?"

"Old Antarctic Explorers . . . longtimers on the ice," she said. "Sorry. The lingo here gets contagious after a while."

"And exactly how's *that* supposed to have something to do with their attitude?"

"Isolation breeds a clannish mentality. The crew can be prickly toward outsiders. Or perceived outsiders. Their consumption of water is one of the things that raises spines."

"Gracious," Nimec said. "I hope they're better hosts to those politicos who're due for a visit."

Megan Breen smiled her smile. It was always real. And always measured. Over the years Nimec had found that people either got the combination or they didn't. The ones who did were usually charmed to helplessness. The ones who didn't thought her calculating and manipulative. In the predominantly male world in which she functioned as Roger Gordian's next-in-line, the split was close to even.

He got the smile completely.

"Our desalinization plant turns out fifteen thousand gallons of usable water on a good day," she said. "That's for cooking, cleaning, machine and vehicle use, hydroponics . . . the whole show. I know that may sound like a considerable amount, Pete. But it takes two gallons to wash your hands under a running tap, as opposed to one gallon washing in a filled basin. I could rattle off the comparative stats for high-versus-low-efficiency showers—"

"And toilets, I'm sure," he said.

"One and a half gallons for ultra-low flush. Three to five for standard models."

"You had that notice posted, didn't you?"

"Worded it myself."

"Then I won't beat the issue of my lousy reception to death."

They were both smiling now.

"Just wait till we get you a name patch," she said. "When those malcontents find out who they offended, they'll want to go scampering under a rug."

Nimec sat a moment, glancing around the office. It was a small, well-ordered cubicle with bluish soundproof paneling and recessed overhead fluorescents. No windows. No decorative touches to enliven it. Two big maps covered nearly the entire wall to Megan's right. One was a satellite image of the Antarctic continent. *Shaped like a giant manta ray.* The other showed the rugged topography of the Dry Valleys. There were three colored pins—red, yellow, blue—marking different points in the latter.

Nimec turned back to Megan. The last time he'd seen her, she had been the embodiment of corporate chic, letting the world know she was playing to win with a pricey designer suit and a smart wedge-cut hairstyle that just brushed the tops of her shoulders. Now her hair went tumbling loosely down over bib overalls and a maroon twill shirt, framing her face with thick auburn waves, highlighting her large emerald eyes like the deepest of sunsets over a wood of Irish pines. Nimec supposed she could dress herself in sackcloth and still be as lovely as ever.

He sat there a while, looking at her. He could think of a dozen matters they had to discuss, every one of them pressing, every one relating to the incidents that had brought him so far from home. But he was uncertain how to approach the subject he really wanted to talk about first.

"So," he said. "How've you been?"

She shrugged, her hands on the desk.

"Cold," she said. "And generally busy."

"How about when you aren't busy?"

"Cold and lonely."

Nimec gave her a little nod. There had been photographs in her San Jose office. Vases with fresh flowers from the shop down the street. And abundant sunlight.

"I hear people come to Antarctica to find themselves," he said. "Or reinvent themselves. It's being away from everything they know. And the emptiness. I suppose they must feel like they're filling it in. Writing their lives over on a blank page."

Megan shrugged again.

"That may be true for some," she said.

"And you?"

She paused a beat, but otherwise did a good job of seeming unaffected by the question.

"There's no place else like this on earth. It's magnificent. Beautiful in its way. It gives you the room and time to contemplate. But I'm doing this because Gord needed me here to get our operations off the ground."

"So if not for his asking you to stay . . ."

"I'd scoot back to California like a kitten jumping onto a warm lap," she replied, looking directly at him. No hesitation this time.

Nimec considered asking her what was actually on his mind. Instead he decided to change the topic. He cocked his head toward the map of the Dry Valleys.

"I figure those pins have got something to do with the missing search team," he said.

"You figure right, Pete." Meg swiveled in her chair,

faced the map, and pointed. "The yellow one shows where they struck camp. It's where McKelvey Valley crosses the northern mouth of Bull Pass. See?"

He nodded.

"The red pin would be about four miles from the campsite, straight down into the pass," she said. "That's where they were last sighted."

"By whom?"

"A chopper pilot named Russ Granger. He's been at McMurdo forever, makes regular air runs to its research bases in the valley system."

"He have any contact with the team?"

"No," she said, and then thought a moment. "Well, let me revise that. They *did* exchange hellos. But it was just a fluke that Russ passed over Scarborough and the others at all." She paused. "He says they seemed perfectly fine to him."

"When would that have been? The time of day, I mean."

"Ordinarily we'd be entering vague territory. But I think I know where you're heading, so let me put my answer in context," she said. "Time measurement becomes almost arbitrary when the whole year's roughly divided into six months of daylight, and six months of darkness. Most stations set their clocks to match up with a time zone in their home countries for ease of communications . . . though that can lead to chaos when they have to make arrangements with other bases. Here at Cold Corners we've opted for Greenwich time simply because that's what they use at MacTown, and there's considerable interaction between us."

"Then whatever time it was for Scarborough's group would've corresponded with the pilot's."

"Yes," Megan said. "Russ was heading to Marble Point." She gestured toward its position on the Dry Valleys map. "That's a little refueling facility at the foot of the Wilson Piedmont Glacier, about fifty miles northwest of McMurdo. He'd made the first two stops of his shift, and thinks it was about seven A.M. when he saw our party."

"And your best guess about how long they'd been out on foot . . . ?"

"Two hours at most. The area they covered had some tedious rocky patches, but Scarborough would have left camp early."

"Old military habit?"

She nodded. "He isn't the type to waste a minute."

Nimec contemplated that, peering at the map.

"They were just getting started," he said.

"Yes."

"What about after the pilot saw them that morning? They report in to Cold Corners at any point?"

Meg was shaking her head now.

"That would have been largely at their discretion. Of course we'd have expected to hear from them if they located the rover. Obviously if they needed assistance. But we never received a Mayday. It's the part that drives me crazy, Pete . . . trying to understand why Scar wouldn't have let us know he was in trouble."

"Had me and the boss wondering too." Nimec rubbed his chin. "Any chance I could talk to the pilot myself?"

"It should be easy to arrange. Russ drops by to help us often enough."

Nimec nodded, pleased. He was still looking at the map.

"I assume the blue pin marks the spot where Scout's transmissions zilched."

"Yes," she said. "It's at the opposite end of the pass from our recovery team's camp. A span of twelve miles."

"How come they didn't pitch their tents closer to it?"

"The only way into the valleys is by chopper, and landing one in Bull Pass is a dangerous proposition. It's narrow in places, and winds are fickle. That leaves us having to choose between drop zones at McKelvey to the north and Wright to the south. And the approach from Wright

Valley on foot is full of obstacles. There are ridges, hills, all kinds of steep elevations."

Nimec was silent, thinking. Then he turned from the wall map to look at Megan.

"How soon can you have a helicopter ready so I can check out the area for myself?"

She faced him across the desk, a wan smile tugging at the corner of her mouth.

"What's on your mind?" he said.

"Pete, if anybody else had spoken those words, I'd be positive he was kidding. You arrived less than an *hour* ago. Get some food into your stomach. Rest up. Then we can start to talk about making plans."

"I caught a few winks on the plane," he said.

She pursed her lips. The smile did not quite leave them.

"How about we strike a compromise," she said. "Grab a bite together in the cafeteria."

"I'm not hungry—"

"Today's special is a hot turkey breast sandwich on homemade club. You won't believe our greenhouse to-matoes. And the coffee. We have a selection of lattes and mochas. Cappuccino too. And espresso. Also four or five blends of ordinary roast if your taste leans toward the pedestrian side."

He looked at her.

"Lattes in Antarctica," he said.

She nodded. "This is an UpLink base. Moreover, it's *my* base. And despite these ghastly earth-mother clothes, I'm still Megan Breen."

Nimec suddenly couldn't help but crack a smile of his own.

"Okay, princess," he said. "Let's eat."

One million miles from Earth

The satellite glided through deep space like a solitary night bird, its keen electronic sensors picking up signs of the coming storm as they were swept toward it on the solar wind.

The Solar and Heliospheric Observatory—or SOHO—was a joint space probe conceived by NASA and the European Space Agency in the 1990's for gathering a wealth of scientific information about the sun and its atmospheric emissions. In early March 1996, fourteen months after its liftoff from Cape Canaveral aboard the upper stage of an Atlas IIAS (Atlas/Centaur) launch vehicle, the satellite was injected into a counterclockwise halo orbit around the sun at what is known as the L1 Lagrangian point—named after the eighteenth-century French astronomer Joseph-Louis Lagrange, who theorized there were calculable distances at which a small object in space could remain in fixed orbital positions between two larger bodies exerting strong gravitational pulls upon it.

The mathematical formulations must be precise. Should an object in the middle of this interplanetary tug of war wander from its position by more than a few degrees, the delicate equilibrium becomes upset and its orbit will rapidly degrade.

In SOHO's case the L1 point equaled four times the distance from our world to the moon, with any significant deviation from that point certain to result in an uncontrolled plunge toward either the earth or sun. One complication the observatory's development team had to address, however, was that their preferred orbital position for SOHO was slightly *off* the L1 point, since the radio interference that would occur when it was in direct line between the two opposing spheres was bound to corrupt its data transmissions with static. A second problem was that other bodies in the solar system—distant planets, moons, asteroids—had their own weaker attractions that could jiggle SOHO's path a little bit this way or that to ultimately disastrous effect.

The team's solution to both these problems was to equip SOHO with an onboard propulsion system for periodic orbital adjustments, knowing this imposed an inherent limitation on its mission life. For once it exhausted the hydrazine fuel that powered its thrusters, SOHO would slip from its desired Lagrangian station and go tumbling off through space beyond recovery.

Original projections were that the billion-dollar spacecraft would be able to conduct its observations and experiments for from two to five years before the propellent reserves went dry and its mission reached an end.

Six years later and counting, it was still plugging away.

Some things are still built to last, and every so often they last longer than expected.

In March 2002, SOHO's SWAN and MDI/SOI instruments, two of a dozen scientific devices in its payload module, sniffed the astrophysical equivalent of what American prairie farmers once would have called a locust wind.

An acronym for Solar Wind Anisotropies, SWAN is an ultraviolet survey of the dispersed hydrogen cloud around our planetary system that can detect glowing hot spots in space caused by fluctuations of solar radiation. To the SWAN's wide-angle eye, which charts the full sky around the sun three times each week, a surge in the emissions striking these areas will cause them to light up like flashes from warning beacons even if the surge originates beyond the sun's visible face, outside the range of earthbound telescopes.

MDI/SOI—short for Michelson Doppler Imager/Solar Oscillations Investigation—is more direct in its approach, measuring wave motions that vibrate through the convective layer of the sun. Depending on their amplitude, deviations from the wavelengths commonly registered by MDI/SOI can put scientists on the lookout for helioseismological events that are roughly analogous to earthquakes and may be indicators of impending solar flare activity.

Relayed to earth by its telemetry arrays in near-real time, SOHO's information about the flurry of concurrent beacon flashes and solar tremors did not take long to create a stir of excitement in its command-and-control center in Maryland.

Two men in particular got the headline-making jump on the rest of the pack.

Cold Corners Base, Antarctica

Nimec ate the last bit of his turkey sandwich and set the empty plate onto a cafeteria tray beside him. Then he lifted his demitasse off the table and sipped.

"Well?" Megan said. "I await your verdict."

"Mmm-mm," he said.

"I may be a princess," she said. "But I'm known for my benevolence, truthfulness, and good taste."

He grunted. "About arranging for that helicopter . . ."

She made a preemptive gesture. "After we've had our coffee."

He sat with the steaming espresso in his hand, watching her drink from her cup. It contained a double something-or-other with caffeine, flavored syrup, and a light head of froth.

Several minutes passed in silence that way.

"Okay, Pete," she said at last, dabbing her upper lip with a napkin. "The chopper aside, what's on your mind?"

"That line sounds very familiar," he said.

She nodded. "It does. It also got a straight answer out of me."

He looked at her without comment.

"Come on," she said. "I didn't miss your backpacker's travel guide remarks about hearing how people find spiritual cleansing, harmony, and oneness among the king penguins. Or your question about whether I've joined that righteous crowd. Or most of all your long looks. Something's bothering you. I think we should get it out in the open."

Nimec kept looking at her, then finally expelled a breath.

"You told me you came to Antarctica because the boss

asked," he said. "Or at least you implied that. But I hear you volunteered."

Megan lowered her cup into its saucer, waited as someone came moving past on his way from the service counter to another table.

"It seems you've been hearing a lot of things," she said when he'd gone.

"Not from you," he said. "That's the problem. We never consulted about your reassignment."

"You're being unfair. I let you know a month beforehand."

"After the decision was already made."

"Pete—"

"I'd just like you to tell me why I wasn't advised sooner," he said. "All the years we've worked together, depended on each other, you never left me hanging. And then you did."

"Pete, I'm sorry. Honestly. I didn't realize that was how you felt."

"Then tell me. Straight answer."

Their eyes met. And held.

"It's sort of complicated," she said. "Gord wanting me here is the truth, but he's the one to give you his reasons. As for myself, there were personal issues."

"They involve Bob Lang?"

"Yes," she said. "I preferred not to share them at the time."

He nodded. Their eyes remained locked.

"And now?"

"I'd still rather not."

"You change your mind, I'll be ready to listen."

"I know, Pete," she said. "And thank you."

He nodded again and sat there quietly finishing his espresso.

She reached out, touched his arm.

"Are we okay, Pete? Settled, I mean."

"Settled."

They were silent another minute, her hand still on his arm, squeezing it gently.

"All right," he said then. "Coffee's done. We should discuss the helicopter."

She nodded, reached down into the kangaroo pocket of her bib-alls, and extracted a connected Palm computer.

"All the luxuries of home," he commented.

Megan slipped the computer's stylus out of its silo and tapped its "on" button.

"We try to be with it," she said with a shrug. "Now hush, I need to jot out an e-mail. We're presently short-handed as far as pilots go, but I'll explain that later. Meanwhile, I think I've figured out how to kill two birds with one electronic stone."

NASA Goddard Space Flight Center
Greenbelt, Maryland

The men were known as Ketchup and Fries.

These were of course not their given names.

Ketchup was really Jonathan *Ketchum,* a sixty-year-old project scientist at the Experimenters' Operations Facility in Goddard's Building 26, the operational nucleus of the SOHO project. He had been with the EOF's permanent MDI/SOI team since its establishment in the mid-nineties, and was considered one of its top men by the principal investigator.

Fries was Richard *Frye,* another member of the MDI/SOI team. At twenty-six, he was its most recent addition, regarded as a babe in the woods by senior group members. This is the embedded reflex of those with tenure who are protective of their own status. Ketchum saw in Frye an inquisitiveness and joy of discovery that was like a bright reflection of himself as a young man. He knew Frye was already a better scientist than most, and had potential to be the best by far.

Ketchum had taken Frye under his wing from the start of the young man's NASA employment, but their student-mentor relationship soon grew into an intellectually stimulating bond of equals. Ketchum imparted a maturity of understanding to Frye; Frye helped recharge Ketchum's sense of wonderment daily.

Together they had become a team within a team.

Ketchup and Fries.

Nobody could say with any certainty who had cooked up the nickname. Because its ingredients included a heaping measure of disparagement, and perhaps a pinch of envy, credit went unclaimed and unassigned.

In the beginning they found the label vexatious. Eventually, however, they came to bear it with a certain defiant fondness. At some point their feelings became almost proprietary. Ketchup. Fries. What would one be without the other?

Besides, just look at the crap the visiting observers regularly threw at them.

The Auslanders, as they'd been tagged (again without attribution), were a group of scientists from institutions in France, Switzerland, Germany, the U.K., and a handful of other European Space Agency nations who had either contributed to the design and construction of SOHO's gadgetry or were involved in studying its returns. All SOHO's participants could retrieve this information from an archived, indexed, easily searchable electronic database without ever leaving their respective countries, but guest committees from abroad would sometimes show up at Goddard during research campaigns that engaged several of the observatory's instruments at once.

Ostensibly their motivation was pure and unselfish, springing from a desire to help foster a spirit of international collaboration and share in the immediacy and excitement of these campaigns. The real, dirty scrub was that the Web curators of "collaborating" institutions often delayed inputting e-base updates about major discoveries, while their employers raced to contact news organizations and grab the glory—and subsequent funding windfalls—for themselves. It was a good bet that every principal investigator had a number that would provide fast access to a local CNN bureau chief programmed into his phone's memory.

A joint operation to examine the current cyclical peak of sunspot activity had been under way for over two years now without the EOF group's foreign colleagues showing any inclination whatsoever to pay them a house call. Then, lo and behold, with the recent evidence from SWAN and MDI/SOI that the sun had developed an acute case of the measles on its far side, they had come pouring into Goddard from astrophysics labs around the world, arriving with effervescent camaraderie, *bon jour, gutten tag,* and cheerio. And though the NASA scientists *did* acknowledge that both solar observation devices primarily responsible for the new findings were European in origin, they were resentfully convinced their co-investigators— a.k.a. unwanted party crashers, a.k.a. the Auslanders— were pushing and bumping their way through the door for one reason, and one alone: to make sure nobody at NASA beat them to the flash-dial button.

Today Frye had made it his godly mission to get to the EOF well ahead of the polyglot horde, and was probably at his workstation hours before they had begun to yawn, blink, and stretch through their morning wake-up routines. He himself had been unable to catch any sleep after bringing home printouts of the previous evening's final MDI/ SOI data logs, and using them as the basis for an intricate series of equations prepared with what remained his three favorite computational tools—a #3 pencil, a legal pad, and his own scrupulously logical brain. All the observables told him that the sun's helioseismologic agitation had increased by tremendous—in fact, nearly exponential— leaps and bounds in the last twenty-four hour period, and he'd been eager to do two things: check the overnight logs for further changes, and see how his data and math jibed with the latest information from SWAN, whose nonresident Auslander monitoring area just happened to be on the other side of a glass partition from his own true-blue *resident* project scientist area . . . and, well, well, wouldn't you know, it also just happened to be unoccupied at that early hour.

Now he sat at a bank of display terminals, pondering SWAN's most recent full-sky maps of the sun . . . or more accurately, the sun's hydrogen envelope. Each spectroscopic image had been composed over a regular three-day interval, and was color-graded to profile the radiation intensities—"hot" and "cool" spots—of different coordinates on the envelope. Because the probe was in an almost stationary position relative to earth, following its elliptical revolutions around the sun, the equatorial solar plane showed up as elongated, and each map resembled an Easter egg splashed with various shades of purple, orange, green, and yellow.

Soon Frye's heart was pounding. He got out his cellular phone and rang his complementary half at home.

"Hello?"

"Ketch, what're you doing?"

"Dripping shower water on my bedroom carpet at the moment," Ketchum said. "Do you know what *time* it is?"

"Time for you to get your ass over here to the center."

"What've you turned up?" Ketchum's tone had abruptly swung from mild annoyance to sharpest curiosity.

"Look, you remember that bullet we dodged last April . . . the solar flare that would've been all hell if it hadn't missed Earth?"

"Of course," Ketchum said. "The X-17 . . ."

"Well, I think we're about to find ourselves downstream from a roarer that'll make our X-17 look like a cap gun popping off."

"Are you certain you're not overestimating—"

"This one looks like the beast, Ketch. I mean it. The fucking *beast*. And it'll be charging right at us once it's hatched."

Ketchum took an audible breath at the other end of the line.

"I'm on my way," he said.

Marble Point, Antarctica
(77°25' S, 163°49' E)

"Hey, Russ, you're back in right the nick. Got an e-mail inside from that unbelievable redhead over at Cold Corners."

Russ Granger jumped from the Bell's cockpit onto the helipad, his boots mashing down on thumbnail ripples of white powdery snow, a coat he figured had to be close to a foot deep. When he'd left two hours earlier to fly a sling-load of food rations out to the Lake Hoare camp in Taylor Valley, the landing area was clear, its markings visible from a good altitude. But that was how it was in this place. Sastrugi, as the wavy drifts of snow were called, formed quickly parallel to a rising wind, and it had picked up a great deal since his departure.

He looked at the parka-clad station manager. Though the sky was still showing a lot of blue, snowflakes were blowing through the air from some widely spaced cloud scuds that had come in over the ice shelf.

"Megan Breen?" Granger said.

The station manager's hooded head bobbed up and down. "You heard me say 'unbelievable,' right? Should I have added the word 'hot'?"

Granger pulled up his own fleece-trimmed hood against the stinging flurries.

"That woman's a hundred percent business, Chuck," he said. "Take my word for it, there's nothing in that message to make either of us sweaty."

Chuck Trewillen motioned to his rear. Beyond the depot's fuel lines stood three orange Quonset huts and a couple of old dozers, their shovels heaped with snow. Beyond them was another small building that had served as Trewillen's isolated home for the half decade he'd held his job at Marble Point. Beyond that building there was only the great sawtoothed jut of the Wilson Piedmont Glacier.

"You ought to hear the noises that glacier makes when

it's calving bergs," Trewillen said. "It sort of pants and moans. I'm talking loud, deep moooooans." He shrugged. "Sometimes *they're* enough to get me worked up."

Granger smiled, clapped Trewillen on the shoulder.

"You've been out here alone way too long, man," he said, and started toward the computer hut.

Granger paused in the entrance to the air-heated Quonset, stamped caked snow off his boots, and unzipped his jacket. Then he sat at the desktop and tapped a key to erase its screen-saver—flamingos on a tropical beach, lush palms and turquoise water in the background.

The beach scene gave way to an e-mail application's opening window. Granger dragged and clicked to the Inbox, and saw Megan Breen's message at the top of its queue—the single new one. Its title was simply his first name in caps followed by a string of exclamation marks.

Typical Megan, he thought.

The message itself was also characteristically brief and straight to the point:

> Russ,
>   A colleague from San Jose has come down to find our missing people and he needs your assist ASAP. Hopes to borrow you from Mac for a flyby of B. Pass. Let me know when you can make it.
> Best/MB

Granger fished a hard pack of Marlboros from his open jacket, put a smoke in his mouth, and fired it up with his disposable lighter. Given the extreme urgency of Megan's request, he knew that clearing it with his bosses at McMurdo wasn't anything to worry about.

He frowned, dragging on the cigarette.

No, it definitely wouldn't be a problem.

The real problem was this "colleague" she'd mentioned, and the complications his arrival could bring about for the people who really padded Granger's bankroll enough to make living in this stinking, abominable icebox worthwhile . . . and further down the line, the serious mess it could churn up for Granger himself.

He took another deep hit off the cig and its tip flared.

It wouldn't be much fun springing the bad news on the Consortium, but he'd have to get in touch with them, see how they wanted him to handle the situation.

Yeah, he thought. The thing was to contact Zurich directly, let the kingfish have it in front of him.

ASAP.

Inverness, Scotland

Nan Gorrie looked again at her watch and once more at the stove, where a fine piece of mutton sat in a soup of juice and rapidly coagulating fat. Her husband usually rang ahead the few times a year he might be late; he'd been awfully distracted this past week, and she preferred to hope that he had forgotten, rather than worrying something had happened to him. There had been a few occasions as a constable that he'd gotten into scrapes, but none that had risen to the level of what she might call actual danger. As a detective, his days ran at an even pace. His nature helped pour oil on the seas, smoothing the swells; if he felt apprehension, she had rarely known it.

But the way he'd been going lately, rising in the middle of the night, pacing and rocking, rocking and pacing . . . Frank Gorrie was not a pensive man—not a fool nor shallow by any means, but no brooder. Some men—James Fitz came to mind, the Irishman who lived in the next house but one—spent their time staring into space, contemplating the whys and wherefores of the universe. Frank was more a solid sort—a piece of mutton who knew what he was about, which had been a large part of their attraction.

She suspected the wee child at Eriskay had distracted him. The social worker had called him twice now to report on the infant's progress.

She too had sympathy for the infant, but the matter

went beyond that. They were well past their inability to have a child. She was. It had struck her hard but she had come to accept it, a decree from God. Artificial measures were not so commonplace fifteen years ago, and even now the idea seemed foreign.

The doorbell rang. Nan took a towel in her hands, wiping them though they weren't wet as she walked through the front room to the door. As her hand reached the doorknob she felt her breathing grow quite sharp.

"Sorry to bother you, mum," said a thin young man in a blue jumpsuit. He had a small box in his hand, an instrument of some sort. "Report of gas in the neighborhood."

"Here?" she said, rubbing her hands together as her breathing relaxed.

"Trying to trace it," he said. "Have you smelled anything?"

"Afraid not."

"Well that's a good thing then," said the man, already heading next door.

The phone rang as she closed the door.

"I hadn't realized the time, sweets," said her husband when she picked up.

"Losh, Frank—where are ya now?"

"At the office. I have some calls to make—would you eat without me?"

"Well of course, if I'm hungry." She glanced back at the stove.

He was quiet for a moment. Nan thought of saying something about the child, but couldn't find the words.

"I may be here a bit," Frank told her. "Some calls to make."

"Well, be here by eight, would you? We have a guest coming round."

"Not your brother, I hope—he'll be asking for cigars."

"Don't you go encouraging him to smoke now."

"Who's the guest?"

"An American teacher. She's been on holiday and today she came to the school to see our methods. Head-mistress brought her over. Very nice Yank."

"You should have invited her for dinner."

"And that would have been sweet, wouldn't it, with you standing us up."

Actually, she had, but the American had said she had another engagement. She had seemed charming, however. A little too enthusiastic—but that was a good fault to have when you were young.

"By eight," she reminded her husband.

"Count on it, Sweets."

In the red-lit room at UpLink's satellite recording center in Glasgow, Glyn Lowry banged the space bar on his keyboard in frustration. For the past three nights, an intruder had been attempting to hack his way into one of the UpLink e-mail servers. The attempt seemed to be the work of an amateur, but that didn't mean it couldn't do considerable damage. Nor could it be allowed to continue. UpLink's security programs easily kept the intruder at bay—but for some reason the powerful sniffers that Lowry launched to track him down had failed miserably.

It looked like the same story tonight. The sniffer pretended to allow access to the UpLink system, downloading a large graphic file. As the file loaded on the hacker's computer, it activated a Trojan horse. That program would then give Lowry a complete rundown of the route back to the hacker. It would also give Lowry access to the hard drives on the hacker's computer.

But as the seconds ticked away, it became increasingly clear that it had failed again. They were obviously being attacked by someone more sophisticated than the average thirteen-year-old.

Had to be fourteen at least.

His computer appeared to have hung, just as it had last night. Lowry picked up his cola and reached to reboot. Just as his fingers touched the keyboard, the cursor began running across the top of the screen.

Access achieved. Dumping drives c:, d:, e:.

"No shit," said Lowry. He leaned back in his swivel chair and gulped the last bit of the soda. Then he tossed the can and slid back the keyboard. "Let's have a look at our sweetheart's life, eh?"

Besides the normal systems programs—Windows ME, *definitely* an amateur—and office suites, the hacker chap had a good store of perv pix-nudie shots that confirmed for Lowry that he was indeed dealing with a teenage boy. There were a number of word-processing files that looked like German to his admittedly unfamiliar eye. He flipped through a few, took a look at some more of the porn, and then found a directory of the standard plug-and-play hacker scripts that allowed so many idiot brats to pretend they were true geeks.

But it was when he started to examine the contents of the lad's D: drive that things got interesting.

The chap liked to break into e-mail systems. He had accessed a Fleet Street newspaper, which included quite a few off-color remarks about the Queen. He'd also gotten into UKAE, the regulatory agency for British nuclear power. Lowry glanced through the texts, which were run together with the headers indicating when they had been sent. He was on the second page and giving thought to returning to the nudies when a message in the middle of the page caught his attention.

"Eliminate Ewie Cameron. Set up as an accident. L (POUNDS) 100,000. CB."

The Highland Camerons were not the most renowned family in northern Scotland, but they were well known enough to have been included in several of the lectures on local history Lowry had attended over the past few months on the days he kept his mom company in Inverness; the Cameron estate was located about a mile from her home.

As Lowry continued to read the messages, he picked up the phone and called his supervisor.

TEN

HIGH ABOVE ROSS ISLAND, THE VOLCANO'S FULMI-
nating lava lake seethed and bubbled and abruptly shot a
dollop of molten rock into the sky with a belch of pressurized gas. Trailing smoke and licks of flame, the red-
hot ejecta hurtled toward the rim of the summit cone, and
over it, and then smacked into the mountainside a mile
away. It was larger than a howitzer round, and its ballistic
impact threw a cloud of ash, snow, and ice crystals up
from the crater's rim.

There the plastery magma bomb hardened in the su-
percooled air to lay among countless other chunks of ig-
neous debris tossed across the slope.

While signs of the eruption traveled across many miles
in this frigid and barren land, they drew only a scattering
of attention.

It was heard clearly by National Science Foundation
vulcanologists working on the mount's upper elevations,
and produced a tremor that rattled the equipment in their
mobile apple huts. Its sonic precursors (vibrational pulses
that signal an impending eruption) and signature oscilla-

tions (harmonic changes that indicate a discrete eruption, or series of eruptions, in progress) were registered by seismometers and broadband microphones that the researchers had installed and maintained with steady diligence throughout the Antarctic summer.

Ten thousand feet below on another corner of the island, the discharge and resultant concussion would be audible as two dull, thudding blurts of sound to McMurdites who took notice. Few did, however. The continuous volcanic output had never inflicted damage on the station, and was for them little more than background noise.

Eastward across the Transantarctic Mountains, the seismic precursors were detected in instantaneous-wave readouts from sensors on Erebus's flank that had been well camouflaged from the NSF research team. As the sound of the explosive outbursts carried to Bull Pass, bouncing faintly between its craggy walls, hidden men and equipment went into clockwork action.

Three thousand feet underground, a boom-mounted drill came alive with a percussive jolt, its tungsten carbide bit boring into solid rock. Protected from its deafening clatter inside their safety cabin, the drill controller and his assistants breathed filtered air behind the face shields of their high-efficiency, closed-circuit respirator helmets.

Two thousand feet underground, a large jaw crusher began grinding and smashing the contents of its mineral fill chamber, the first stage in the yield's multistage separation process.

A thousand feet higher, a pair of specialized trolley-assisted haul trucks, slung low for tunnel clearance, started forward on an inclined concrete ramp. On a stone shelf several levels beneath the surface, their semiprocessed loads would be stored in excavated pockets until ready to be moved into the open and rigged for helicopter airlift to the coast.

Soon after Erebus quieted, the trucks ceased to roll.

The deep drilling continued longer, a departure from the original requirement that it start and stop in tight coordination with Erebus's rumbling expulsions. Once needed to preserve secrecy, the precaution was now followed only when opportune. Methods had changed after a half decade of continuous production. Engineering breakthroughs, advanced sound-baffling techniques, the current depth of excavation, and a shrewd, cavalier willingness to exploit every aspect of the unique environment had all led to terrific progress since the initial investment bore first fruit.

Five years. Expanding markets. Soaring profit margins. Things were going sensationally well. Output had reached an unbridled peak, and further growth was a given provided operations were allowed to keep running smoothly.

Like any other commercial organization, the Consortium was determined to ensure that no obstacles arose to interfere with its success.

Zurich, Switzerland

The broad subject of the meeting was UpLink International, and those in attendance had come with understandable and fairly similar concerns.

His sky-blue eyes astute behind his reading glasses, Gabriel Morgan smiled from the head of the conference table; a great, expansive, vigorous whopper of a smile. Lots of teeth, his fleshy mastiff cheeks drawn up, his wide brow creased under a deliberately uncombed thatch of silver hair. Every facial muscle enlisted to make it the heartiest smile possible.

This was not to say his attitude was light or blasé. Albedo was his brainchild, and he better than anyone else at the table understood that this session had been called to deal with a matter of pressing importance. But a smile could be spirited and serious at the same time, no contradiction. He'd learned that under the tutelage of his father at a very young age, the same way his father had learned from his grandfather. As chairman of the group, Morgan knew one of his fundamental responsibilities was to exude calm authority, soothe jitters, allay undue fears. Reassure his partners that he had a full awareness of the developments in Antarctica, knew their particulars top to bottom, and would by no means allow them to progress into a crisis situation. That they amounted to minor stumbling blocks, bothersome but easily remediable hassles.

Morgan trusted his ability to manage, and knew one of the keystones of his success was a talent for passing his confidence right on down the line. Business executives and government officials from several different countries, the people around him were behind-the-scenes movers, concealed switches embedded deep within the world's political machinery. Men and women who could trip the right circuits and—by virtue of their relative obscurity— initiate activities their nominal superiors either would not or could not authorize. But he was the *prime* mover. The well of encouragement they turned to when their buckets needed replenishing. And his smile was an invaluable, pliable utensil that helped him ladle out the goods.

He shifted his thickset frame in his chair. On his immediate right, Olav Langkafel, a quiet but integral cog in Norway's Energy and Petroleum Ministry, was voicing an anxious hypothetical about the close reconnaissance capabilities UpLink might have out there on the ice. Morgan decided to address it with an example that would also hopefully resolve some of the issues raised by his six other guests. Give them the overview they seemed to be missing.

"Before you go on with that last what-if, let me ask you a question," he said, raising a finger in the air. "Are you by any chance acquainted with the term 'zoo event'?"

Langkafel was momentarily nonplussed. Morgan supposed it wasn't too often that he got interrupted.

"No," he replied. "I am not."

Morgan slid his glasses down the bridge of his nose, regarding the Norwegian over their solid-gold rims. A man of few words, Langkafel. Blond hair and mustache, fair complexion, stern features. In his navy-blue suit, white shirt, and red tie, he gave off an almost regimental air.

Morgan added a dimension of wise understanding to his self-assured smile . . . with just the merest hint of condescension thrown in to keep Langkafel in line. It was a delicate balance. His goal was to communicate that he was far enough ahead of the game to have expected Langkafel's response, but that the expectation signified neither dismissiveness nor a lack of respect.

"The phrase is pretty obscure," he said. "Caught my ear a while back, though, and stuck with me. I like how it's sort of mysterious, but not so dramatic you'd think a Hollywood screenwriter dreamed it up. It refers to something that happened near Bouvetoya Island, right at the edge of the Antarctic Circle, a frigid hunk of rock I'm betting you *have* heard about. Your country's held a territorial claim on it for a while, correct?"

Langkafel nodded rigidly. "Bouvetoya is a designated nature preserve with few natural resources worth mentioning. Its chief value is as a site for satellite weather stations."

Morgan knew that, of course. And he had known Langkafel would know. But he wanted to spread around the verbiage, engage the group, get his points across without appearing to lecture. It was an approach he'd borrowed from trial lawyers: When the goal was to deliver information through someone else's his lips, you never asked a question whose answer wasn't entirely predictable. Whether you were in the courtroom or boardroom, the essential tactic was the same.

Mindful of his digestive problems, Morgan resisted the tray of *biscotti* in front of him, and instead raised a glass of carbonated mineral water to his lips. He drank slowly, watching buds of filtered sunlight shrivel on the burgundy curtains over the room's terrace doors. Two floors below, in the main hall of the restored medieval guild house he had occupied since his lamented flight from the States, the art gallery his family had run for nearly a hundred years was silent, its staff having canceled the day's appointments at his instruction. With dusk, the specialty shops and fashion houses along the right bank of the Limma would be closing as well. Morgan imagined their owners offering courtly good-nights to prosperous clients, the musical tinkle of chimes above their shutting entries, and then their lights blinking out one by one. That was Zurich for him. A city of ritualized decorum and sterile elegance. Of priggish, elitist bankers and financiers.

And, Morgan thought, of ultimately civilized exiles.

He put down his glass, scanning the group around the table, his eyes gliding from person to person. Stored in his mind were two curricula vitae for each of them—the public and private, sanctioned and unsanctioned, licit and illicit details of their personal lives and careers. All were tangled up in invisible strings, pulling some while they themselves got pulled by others.

Take Feodor Nikolin down at the opposite end of the table. On the front of the sheet, Nikolin was an advisor to the elected governor of Russia's Baltic oil and gas pipeline region. Back of the sheet? The election and his civilian appointment had been fixed by the new ultranationalist boss at the Kremlin, President Arkady Pedachenko, whose Honor and Soil Party had crested a populist wave to power . . . Nikolin by no coincidence being Pedachenko's nephew by marriage, and a former colonel from the military's Raketnye voiska strategicheskogonaznacheniya, or Strategic Rocket Forces, which oversaw Russia's nuclear arsenals.

Take Azzone Spero, the Italian Treasury and Economic Planning Minister. King of the kickback, he'd violated a slew of legal bidding procedures to award government waste-collection licenses to front companies run by the LaCana crime syndicate, known to earn billions annually from the illegal dumping of hazardous wastes throughout Europe.

Or take Sebastian Alcala, the squat, dark man seated opposite Nikolin. His open résumé showed him to be a mid-level administrator with the Argentinian mining exploration secretariat. But Morgan's secret file tied him to everything from embezzlement of state funds to facilitation of illegal arms traffic for the black marketeer and narco-terrorist El Tio, who'd recently slipped into limbo like a vanishing ghost.

The book was similar for the rest. There was Jonas Papp from Hungary, an entrepreneur in the transitional market economy with several legitimate upstart software firms and a flourishing underground income stream from his money-laundering enterprises. There was Constance Burns, Morgan's UKAE inchworm. And there was the South African foreign trade deputy with a perpetually outheld palm, Jak Selebi. . . .

"I'm wondering if you can explain the incident to everyone, Jak?" Morgan said at length. His eyes had come to rest on Selebi. "I realize this Bouvetoya thing was long before your government's time, but maybe it'd be best that way."

Selebi looked back at him. "In a sense you've answered your own question," he replied, speaking with a mannered British accent. "When the change came, our predecessors took much of the information about their relinquished nuclear weapons program with them. They did not want it available to us. We may assume they judged that the development of such capabilities was to be exclusively reserved for civilized races." He paused a moment, his brown face expressionless, devoid of the cutting irony in his voice. "I can tell you this. Throughout the nineteen-sixties, America launched a dozen orbital satellites for the detection of atmospheric nuclear explosions. This program was named Vela. A Spanish word, I believe . . ."

"Meaning 'Watchmen,' " said Alcala.

"Thank you." Selebi exchanged glances with him. "The crude optical sensors on the Velas could not fix locations with anything close to the exactitude of modern satellites. Otherwise, their reliability was unchallenged . . . until one of them, Vela 6911, registered a double flash scientists associated with an atomic blast of between three and four kilotons."

"These matched other signals the U.S. Naval Research Laboratory picked up here on earth," Morgan said. "Acoustic waves around the Scotia Ridge, a chain of mountains between Antarctica and Africa that's mostly underwater. Except where it *isn't* underwater and the mountaintops poking out above the ocean's surface form islands. Bouvetoya's one of them." Another smile. "Sorry to break in after asking you to tell the tale, but I felt it was important for everyone to be aware of that little nugget."

Selebi's nod showed flat acceptance.

"The consensus of military, intelligence, and government nuclear research scientists responsible for analyzing the Vela evidence was that an atomic detonation had occurred at or below sea level," he continued. "But when these findings were presented to the Carter Administration, it ordered a second panel of academics from outside the government to conduct a separate review. Their assessment refuted the original determination. It stated the indications were unverifiable and may have been based on false signals caused by sensor malfunction or a meteor collision. The dispute it sparked between the two panels led to animosities that I understand linger to this day." He looked at Morgan. "That is the extent of what I can say about the affair with confidence."

"Then let me put in some footnotes," Morgan said. "One of the scientists in that first group was a top-notch man with the Los Alamos think tank. Knew his stuff inside out, helped develop the Vela program. When their report got the presidential blow-off, he made some testy comments, said they were all zoo animals coming out with idiotic theories to discredit his panel's conclusions. Talk is that the White House was gun-shy about a confrontation with the South Africans, whom it damn well knew were manufacturing atomics, and maybe doing it with Israeli participation."

He shrugged. "You got to sympathize with Jimmy's predicament. With the gas crunch fresh in people's minds, and Khomeini swift-kicking the Shah out of Iran, the poor guy was deep in the moat. Sharks closing in around him. Another domestic or foreign affairs boondoggle and any chance he had of swimming his way out was finished. The press, political opponents, average citizens, everybody wanted a pound of his flesh. Jimmy, well, the last thing *he* would've wanted was to out two long-standing allies for their complicity in banned nuclear-bomb testing. What was he supposed to do? Impose trade embargoes? Ask the U.N. Security Council to censure them? Neither option would've been to America's advantage. So the sats, Navy, CIA, and Defense Intelligence Agency people became wrong, and the ivory-tower professors became right. In my opinion, Jimmy managed to *convince* himself of their rightness, and the nuke turned into an unexplained occurrence. Better for everyone that way."

Constance Burns was nodding her head.

"A zoo event," she said.

The affirmative smile Morgan directed at her was as gentle as a pat on the back.

"There you go," he said. "Now, as our good friend Jak more or less implied, there's a dash of supposition in what we've been talking about. Over the past couple of decades South African officials have admitted to the test, then backed off their admissions, then acknowledged them again, then qualified their acknowledgments, then shut up altogether. Same with the Israelis. Their newspapers printed articles quoting Knesset members about their government's exchange of nuclear weapons blueprints for uranium from South Africa's mines, then got those quotes retracted on them. But I believe the story of the zoo event's been written. A nuclear detonation took place near Bouvetoya Island in September 1977. Low yield, about a third of a Hiroshima. Maybe subsurface, maybe an airburst. It took place. And the leader of the Western world covered his ears, and closed his eyes, and claimed to be

deaf and blind to the incident. Because dealing with it
wasn't advantageous to him. And for one other major reason."

Langkafel looked at him. "Which would be . . . ?"

"It happened within the Antarctic Circle." Morgan
swiveled around to face the Norwegian and pushed his
glasses lower down his nose with his finger, perching
them on his nose's tip. "Where else on earth would it have
been so easy to chalk the whole thing up to a quirk of
nature? Where else does every country that's got a flag-
pole stuck in the ice want to pretend it's given up strategic
interests for some high-flown scientific principle? They all
want to tap the continent's resources. They all want bases
where they can deploy armed forces. But they keep skating around each other, none of them wanting to make the
first move. If the time ever comes when one of them does,
their loops, spins, and figure-eights will stop, the blades
will come off, and they'll have to use their edges to carve
out real territorial borderlines. This is my wedge of the
snow pie. This is yours. You say no? Well, we got ourselves a *scrap* here. Power replaces principles. The coldest
spot on the planet becomes its biggest geopolitical hot
spot. That's the reality nobody's set to confront. For now
they'd rather leave it to the polies and penguins."

"And us," Constance Burns said.

"That's right." Morgan's eyes swept the table. "Us."

The group sat quietly for a while. Morgan sipped his
water, feeling tiny bubbles bursting on the back of his
tongue. There were no remaining traces of sunlight on the
curtains. He was eager to adjourn the meeting. Get out
alone, walk the dark twisting streets of the city's old town.
Take a shot at scraping some dirt from between its pristine
cobblestones.

It disappointed him when Nikolin broke the silence to
voice his concerns. "As far as everything you've mentioned, Gabriel . . . the information is enlightening, yes.
Fascinating. And I'm sure we all understand the points it
exemplifies. Its general bearing upon the UpLink problem.

But the issues Olav raised—I still would like them addressed with greater specificity. UpLink is a transcontinental firm, not a national entity. Like our own alliance, it enjoys an independent status that relieves it from certain conventions . . . and constraints . . . to which governments must adhere. To what extent in the present context, we cannot be certain. But its resources, should they be marshaled against us, would be a serious threat. That I *do* know." He paused. "UpLink's support of my chief of state's predecessor, Vladimir Starinov, kept him in office years longer than would have been the case had it not lobbied NATO to give him economic assistance."

Morgan was careful to screen his impatience behind a polite, attentive expression. He linked his hands across his chest and leaned toward Nikolin.

"Think about it," he said. "Think *practically*. It isn't hard to get a read on UpLink's limitations out there. The ice station is small. Isolated. Contained. What's the lid on its sustainable personnel? Let's estimate two, maybe three hundred. Ninety-eight percent of them would be technical engineers, researchers, and support people. No chance they could run the works when it comes to the security operations we've all heard tales about. It would be logistically impossible to carry anything like a full detail. And they wouldn't feel the pressing imperative anyway. On one hand, the continent's a fortress. On the other, remember, it's the big rink. Nobody for us to worry about there but Boy Scouts and Girl Scouts at a skating party. So now we learn they got this ace—you use that same word in Russia, right?—they got this ace out of San Jose investigating their own zoo event. I say, don't let it faze you. The situation's manageable. Look at how we did it in Scotland. Now think Antarctica. Last year, midwinter, that party of ten, eleven researchers and staffers got evacuated out of McMurdo. Biggest incident of its kind ever. USAP was a little vague with its explanations, don't ask me why. Maybe the beakers came down with cabin fever, went a little crazy, got into an old-fashioned punch-out, and were embarrassed to admit it. Or maybe the caginess was just a typical bureaucratic reflex. Next thing you know, though, you got thousands of conspiracy theorists on the Internet posting bulletins that they made first contact with flying saucer people. *There's* Antarctica for you. Ace and his skeleton crew want to start grubbing around us? What we do is complicate their lives. Create distractions. Diversions. We know the playing field, and we're in place to capitalize on its eccentricities. Things can happen. Freak accidents. Unexplained occurrences. Zoo events that will keep them too busy to get close to us. And the long night's coming on them soon enough. Then they've either got to leave for where the skies are blue, or ball up in their hole for the duration."

There was an extended silence. Morgan watched his company at the table. They were looking at one another, nodding.

"Your words are encouraging," Langkafel said then. "I believe that I speak for the entire group in that regard."

More nods around the table.

"But," Langkafel said, "I do have one further question."

Morgan looked at him. Waited. His smile gone now.

"Our pursuits in Antarctica require long-term stability," Langkafel said. "What will we do when those at the UpLink station awake from their hibernation to probe our affairs again?"

Morgan thought a moment before he answered. He took off his reading glasses, folded their stems, and put them carefully beside the thin report binder in front of him. Then he fastened his eyes on the Norwegian's thin, dour face.

"They won't awake," he said. "Trust me, Olav, things are already in motion. UpLink's about to be touched by us. They'll think it's a disaster, but that's all it'll be—a touch, a prelude to the real action. Before we're through, I intend to give them a zoo event to remember. This is going to be their final night. Just trust me. *Their final night.*"

•   •   •

Gabriel Morgan's bodyguard slid from the alcove in the hallway as his boss left the office, discreetly trailing as Morgan descended the steps of the Zurich guild house toward his black S55 AMG Mercedes. Another of his men stood at the landing; Morgan was not generally given to such ostentatious shows of protection, but today's matters called for certain realistic precautions. Not that he expected the Italian to ambush him—it had been made quite clear by all concerned that nothing of value would be brought to the meeting by either side—but being an Italian, the man was likely to be careless, and thus might have provoked the attention of unwanted guests. Interpol already had its hounds out.

As his man opened the door to the street, Morgan felt a wave of paranoia sweep in with the cold air of the street. It did not come, however, from his present mission, but from what had to be considered diversions. Important, certainly, but not of the moment. Nonetheless, they percolated inside his chest, making him hesitate as his bodyguards scanned a street he already knew instinctively would be safe.

The latest update on Uplink International and its Antarctic operations included information that, while in no way directly challenging Morgan's plans, nonetheless indicated an accelerating and disturbing trend. His own timetable for dealing with them was proceeding as scheduled; he had seen the threat as he saw all threats and taken the necessary steps months ago. But Mr. Gordian and his hired do-gooders would have to be watched very closely.

Some years earlier in his quest to acquire cutting-edge enterprises, Morgan had made certain overtures to the esteemed American entrepreneur; the response he had received still rankled. Their parallel presence in Antarctica now was truly coincidental, an accident of ambition on all sides—but Morgan would not deny that closure at the pole would provide a sense of satisfaction in many ways.

And then there was Constance Burns, his UK associate

in the Antarctic venture. In yet another display of stunningly bad judgment, Miss Burns had taken it upon herself this morning to call with news that she was coming to Zurich a few days before their arranged conference with the other members of the Consortium. This was, she hinted during their brief conversation, a ploy to establish the visit as a vacation. She had apparently taken the precaution of calling from a pay phone, and there was in any event no reason to suspect that her calls would be monitored or even observed, but it was the sort of indiscretion that boded poorly, representing a severely flawed judgment that would inevitably lead to great difficulty.

Morgan sensed that the inchworm—she not only thought like one, but had she green hair she would have passed for a human relative of the species—intended to wring an accounting from him of the Scotland matters, which he had handled on her behalf. But at least she'd had the good sense not to bring it up on the telephone. He had graciously promised a driver and car to meet her at the airport and take her to all the important sights. They would also keep her from being a problem until the meeting. After that, further arrangements would have to be made.

The Scotland matter itself remained unresolved, though hopeful. His agent had been instructed to stay at her post indefinitely, but she had not been easily convinced. Like so many excellent killers, she was American, and impatient by nature. Fortunately, being American, her patience could be bought, and a price was finally arranged after considerable haggling. In the meantime, she had decided to go ahead and eliminate the girlfriend gratis—a tidy touch that made Morgan regret that when the time came to eliminate Constance Burns, he would have to give up the agent in the process.

But not a hair of any of these problems had anything to do with today's business. They were distractions, diversions, needless anxieties. As his men on the street nodded, Morgan stepped out from the door and filled his lungs with the cool air. He embraced it, flinging open his coat, taking another long breath, gliding toward his car. He must live for the moment; everything else would sort itself out in time.

Morgan slid into the rear seat of the sedan, settling in as Hans and Jacques got in on the other side. Wilhelm put the car into gear and they moved gracefully away, heading for Luzern.

Out of habit, Morgan reached for his alpha pager to check for messages. But then he remembered his resolution. There would be time to think of Miss Burns, of Scotland, of the inestimable Mr. Gordian, he reminded himself. For now, his mind must be clear; he must prepare himself for the Italian. He settled back against the thick leather seat, listening as the tenor warmed up to Verdi's "Brindisi" in the opening act of *La Traviata*.

On April 26, 1937, aircraft belonging to Nazi Germany destroyed the city of Guernica, Spain. They acted on behalf of General Francisco Franco and the right-wing Nationalists, fighting in a war that would eventually claim the lives of at least one million people, many of them civilians. The target's status as a holy city for the Basque people was the sole reason for the attack; the length of the raid and the fact that civilians were hunted down by the attacking aircraft gives the lie to any claim that this was anything other that a deliberate massacre designed to both intimidate and desecrate. For three hours, the German Luftwaffe dropped incendiary devices and explosives, strafed women and children who had run into nearby fields, and otherwise worked hard to obliterate every trace of life in the town. In an ugly era, it was a particularly ugly deed.

And yet, strange, dark beauty blossomed from it. In January 1937, Pablo Picasso received a commission from the Spanish Republican government: a painting to occupy one wall of the Spanish pavilion at Paris's Universal Exposition scheduled for later that year. He had struggled

with what to portray. On April 30th, he saw photographs
of the German attack at Guernica in the evening newspaper *Ce Soir*. The photographs provoked one of the
twentieth century's most important works, a monument to
man's inhumanity and at the same time a testimony to the
power of art—*Guernica*.

The construction of the painting was documented by
Dora Maar, whose photographs reveal the various per-
mutations and stages it underwent as the master created.
These helped it become not only one of the most famous
large-scale paintings of the twentieth century, but also one
of the most studied.

More obscure, indeed for all practical purposes unknown, were fourteen small works intended—*perhaps*—
as companion pieces in the exhibit. Each elaborated in a
different way on elements of the masterwork—the bull,
the lantern, the warrior, the dead child. And each related,
in ways at times obscure and at other times obvious, to
the Catholic Stations of the Cross—of which there are
also fourteen.

Morgan's heart raced as he slowly slid color laser prints
of the paintings through his fingers. *Guernica* had been
rendered mostly in shades of black and white, as if it were
a newspaper documenting the horror. The accompanying
works were color, exquisite pieces with shades like
stained glass somewhat brighter than, say, *Weeping
Woman*, painted in October 1937 and traditionally linked
to the time and style of *Guernica*. Their style echoed the
geometry of *Guernica*, and yet had the feeling, the softness of expression, the depth of such works as *The Dream*
of 1932. Bizarre yet familiar, violent yet loving, they were
works without peer in the Western world.

Morgan felt his tongue heavy in his mouth. His enthusiasm was a weapon that could easily be turned against
him—how many times had he used such enthusiasm in
others as his own tool in negotiations? The beauty of the
paintings was nothing. Art was merely a statement of desire; a forger worked the equation backwards, intensifying

the latter to provoke the former. A lover was very easily cuckolded.

He was a true lover now. Sitting at the small cafe table across from the blue-green waters of Lake Lucerne, he was as emphatically in love as any fifteen-year-old who had lost his cherry a half hour before. His hands were sweaty. He couldn't speak. He tried to hide his enthusiasm with a frown, but knew it appeared phony.

And he didn't care.

"I can deliver within a few days, a week at most," said the Italian. "Once the financial arrangements are made."

Morgan folded the photocopies as deliberately as he could manage, then slowly placed them into the pocket of his jacket. He fixed his gaze on a swan in the lake's cold water about thirty meters away.

The terror of the bull—the sharp line and bold color—the perception of soul . . .

Before such genius, what was he? What was anyone?

"The possessors realize that there are difficulties involved with pieces of such magnitude," ventured the Italian, attempting to open negotiations.

"Mmmm, yes," Morgan said, continuing to gaze at the water. He had spent considerable resources examining the possibility that the paintings were indeed valid. The governing rumor was that they had been given by Picasso to a friend of Dora's soon after the exhibit closed; the reason was obscure and varied according to the teller, although the favorite was that they were used to buy the freedom of fourteen Jews—a romantic tale that Morgan necessarily discounted. In any event, all agreed the works had been spirited off to Bavaria by an art-loving colonel, then sold in 1945 to a Russian general, who met with an unfortunate accident in Hungary during the 1950's. At that point, the rumors ceased completely.

Morgan had hired a private detective from Bonn with certain heartfelt beliefs that solidified important connections to the past. After considerable effort, the detective produced two letters mentioning the paintings. A historical consultant had found hints in other documentary evidence, including two unpublished photos that seemed to show portions of them at the sides of *Guernica* as it was being completed. The consultant had also supplied certain hints that could be used to authenticate them, including the letter found in the Musée Picasso in Paris. But even if this sketchy evidence, taken together, convinced him that the paintings had indeed been done, nothing he had found so far meant that the works in the Italian's possession were the paintings. Even if the Italian was not known to deal in forgeries, even he could be fooled.

Two art historians had been retained for their opinion. They would examine the works before any deal was consummated. Elata would be the pièce de résistance—the master forger's eye looking for signs of his craft.

But first, a price had to be settled on. Morgan reached into his pocket and took out his reading glasses, fitting them deliberately around his ears as a sign that he was now negotiating.

"The price," he told the Italian gently.

"The figure fifty million has been suggested."

Morgan folded his arms and sat back in his seat. The Swiss waiter, as discreet as any in the breed, caught his eye across the tables and ducked back into the restaurant for another bottle of mineral water.

"But of course, thirty might be more realistic," said the Italian.

At an open auction, with documentation proving they were real, it was conceivable that bidding on each work alone would begin at ten million and quickly escalate; as a set their worth was simply incalculable. But there would be no open auction, at least not in Morgan's lifetime.

He almost didn't want to buy them, for if he did he would inevitably have to part with them; he was a businessman, after all.

He could indulge himself. He might indulge himself. If he sold them off individually, he could keep one or two.

The bull?

Perhaps the infant. The light blue streak underlying the eyes—pure innocence.

Did it exist anywhere in the world outside of art?

The waiter appeared. There was no one else outside on this cold day, and he walked quickly to his customers. As the man poured the water into the glass, Morgan glanced toward his bodyguard at the edge of the railing in front of the lake. He looked a little bored, which Morgan took as a good sign.

"The works will be impossible to sell," said Morgan after the waiter had gone.

"Not for a man of great reach."

He must make a bid, and yet he did not wish to. It was sacrilege, an insult.

He had not thought that when he put a number on the Renoir ink. A ridiculously low number—ten thousand American dollars. He had ended buying it from the Russian *mafya* official for fifteen, then selling it for half a million three months later.

But the child's innocence could not be bought. The bull's fear—what price?

A dollar, a billion.

"One million per painting, the usual method, upon verification," said Morgan.

"An insult," said the Italian. *"Pazzo. Pazzo."*

Pazzo meant "crazy" and was among the mildest epithets available. They were very close.

Morgan resisted the temptation to pull the photocopies from his pocket. Instead, he turned back toward the lake. The white swan had been joined by a black one. He watched for quite a while before the Italian spoke.

"Twenty for all."

"Fifteen," said Morgan, deciding on his price. He rose, removing his glasses and placing them back in his breast pocket. "Make the arrangements. A single word in the usual manner when you are ready; use 'innocent.' It has a nice ring."

He rose swiftly, giving his companion no chance to protest.

Paris, France

Nessa studied the carrot stick before biting into it. Since joining Interpol, she had gained nearly five pounds. She couldn't be called overweight, but if this pace continued her body would soon resemble one of those delightful rum cakes that seemed to lie in wait at every corner. At least the food was contributing to her language skills; "Châteaubriand" fairly rolled off her tongue.

She turned her attention back to the transcript of the interrogation of Mme. Diles, the low-level research assistant at the Musée Picasso who had passed the letter to Elata. The woman claimed she did not know why she had been offered ten thousand dollars for that particular document, nor by whom, nor why only the original would do.

Because his works were so well known, Picasso was not a good candidate for high-level forgery. Stolen pieces of his were somewhat common on the black market, but Elata could probably do far better mimicking other artists.

Jairdain pressed his forefinger to his lips, holding the tip against his nose.

"Most likely he's still in Paris," said the French investigator.

"Yes," she said.

"Perhaps he wants to forge letters now."

"It's the daub of paint, I think," said Nessa, glancing at the photocopy on her desk. "It's the only thing unique about the letter."

"The ink."

"Could have asked for any letter. They wanted this one specifically. June 3, 1937. He wrote it while he was working on *Guernica*."

Nessa's concentration in art history was the Renaissance, but she had taken several courses on modern art, including one that combined the study of Picasso with

Matisse. *Guernica* had taken up about a week's worth of lectures, thanks largely to the photos that had been taken of its evolution. She remembered an afternoon's discussion of studies for the painting; there had been six at the very beginning, a rush of ideas the first day. Possibilities had evolved on the canvas itself. One of the students— Karl, long hair, glasses—had suggested Picasso was considering companion pieces or even variations. The professor said there had been rumors of such pieces, but none had surfaced after the war.

Was Elata seeking to create those pieces? It was the sort of grand, bold artistic gesture he was known for— Doigts was unintimidated in the face of genius. He was, after all, a genius himself.

"Why the paint, though?" she asked aloud. "To get the color right? One color?"

And then she realized they had looked at things backwards.

"He *has* a Picasso," she told her partner. "From this period. He's trying to authenticate it."

"C'e?"

"Who else but a master forger would know all the tricks? It must be." She jumped up from her desk. "An unknown Picasso, painted around the time of *Guernica*— perhaps even intended as a companion. It would be worth millions. Many millions."

"Magnifique," said Jairdain. "Now all we have to do is find the bastard, and we will both be the most famous Interpol detectives of all time."

Nessa frowned and picked up another carrot.

Bull Pass, Antarctica

She had been alone in the blackness for hours, or what seemed like hours, before she heard the scream.

Her hands cuffed in front of her, she'd sunk down in a corner after they took him, her knees pulled to her chest, welded rivets pressing into her spine. Hunkered in that angle between two walls, she'd listened numbly to the pounding of machinery somewhere outside the cage. The noise and blackness seemed one, merged. A grinding, shapeless thing wrapped around her, confining her as surely as the walls of the cage itself.

After a while she had slipped into a faded, bottomed-out semblance of sleep, only to be awakened by the scream, startling as a rocket flare inside her head. But when she came back to full alertness, she heard nothing. Nothing but the machines grating away out there.

Out there in the black.

She felt her heart bumping in her chest now, felt her temples throbbing, pulled in a breath of stale air. It helped a little, but not much. *God, God.* That single, piercing scream. Maybe she'd imagined it. She'd been woozy with fatigue before she nodded off. Very possibly she'd imagined it.

She thought about the beatings they'd given him, tears swelling into her eyes. She didn't want to think about the beatings, hated to think about the beatings, but couldn't keep her mind from turning back to them. He was a strong man. Physically and mentally. Stronger than she ever could be. But it was hard to see how anyone would be able to withstand much more of their vicious, unforgiving abuse.

She sat there gathered into a ball. The blackness was absolute. She could have held her hand directly in front of her face and not seen the vaguest hint of its outline. Absolute. Only the noises beyond the cage had variation.

She listened to them, trying to take note of the changes.

Time passed.

The drumming rhythms quickened and slowed. There were periods when everything switched off. Beneath the sound of the machines, and in the occasional lulls, she could hear the quiet susurrus of air blowing through unseen ventilation grilles.

She prayed to God the scream had been something she'd imagined, dreamed, whatever.

She listened intently to the machine noises. She wasn't sure what compelled her. Perhaps it was ingrained habit, a mind used to filing and sorting information. Perhaps it was only to give her moments shape, definition, a sense of onward movement. Or perhaps the reason was simpler, and she just needed to try and focus on something besides what those men had done to him. What they might be doing to him right now.

She hoped she hadn't actually heard that scream.

The beatings had been awful.

He couldn't take much more.

Alone, trapped, the cuffs digging into her wrists, she slumped against the walls of the cage. The air hissing in from the shaft was not exactly warm, but it had raised the temperature enough to keep her from freezing, keep her alive down here, keep both of them alive before they took him away.

She wished she knew where he was, *how* he was.

The beatings.

Her thoughts insisted on doubling back to the beatings.

Like those that came afterward, the first assault had been sudden and brutal. The men who'd burst into the cage wore hard-shell helmets with lamp assemblies, and she'd flinched from their piercing bright beams, blinded for several horrible seconds. But when her eyes recovered from their shock, the part of her that was trained at observation had amazingly kicked in. She'd noticed their coveralls, and their safety vests with luminous yellow stripes, and the card-shaped dosimeter badges on their chests, a type worn in laboratories where ionizing radiation hazards were present. Laboratories in which she herself had worked. She'd noticed that the lights rapidly intensified without manual adjustment, and that each was composed of multiple lenses, like the compound eyes of an insect . . . state-of-the-art, probably white LEDs controlled by a microcomputer. All six or seven of them were carrying firearms. Submachine guns, she believed, although such weapons were beyond her realm of experi-

ence. Or had been. Her training and background were in
science, but recent events had dealt her a harshly different
kind of education.

It had felt planned out to her, almost staged. The men
went silently about their appalling work, a couple of them
grabbing her arms, pushing her back against the wall, re-
straining her. Two others pointed their weapons at him,
gestured him toward the middle of the cage. When he
refused, scuffled with them, the rest of them closed in
around him. They pounded him mercilessly. They used
their fists, kicked him with steel-reinforced boots. They
made no attempt at interrogation. They did not respond
when she begged to know what they wanted. They just
kept hitting him, the beams of their helmet lights jostling
from the furious motion, leaping about the walls of the
cage.

She screamed for them to stop, pleaded with them to
stop, but they continued to ignore her. And during it all
the man with the strange birthmark on his left cheek—it
was melanocytic, a perfect crescent, like the shadow of a
sliver moon—had watched from off to the side, looking
frequently in her direction. If the whole torturous episode
was indeed choreographed, she had no doubt in her head
that he'd been the one to arrange its lockstep savagery.

The beating had seemed to go on endlessly before they
were finished. And then he was writhing on the floor in
agony, gasping for breath, his lips cut and swollen, his
nose bleeding, his face a mass of bruises. The man who
had been watching from the side turned toward her, strode
to where the others held her pinned to the wall, and stood
there regarding her with eyes that showed neither hostility
nor conscience. They were like camera lenses in their
level objectivity. In a way that was his most frightening
aspect. He was as lacking in malice as pity. A man doing
his job. His quiet dispassion had unbraced her.

She'd shuddered through her entire body as the others
held her immobile against the wall.

He waited a moment, leaned close.

"Later," he had said softly.

Nothing else.

And then he'd turned, and his men had released their grip on her, and followed him out the solid metal door of the cage, passing into the black.

That was the first visit.

They had come back often since. Sometimes it was to measure out more violence against him. Sometimes they left trays of bland, greasy stew and water. When they brought the food, it was always without the man she'd assumed to be their leader. He would just arrive for the beatings. None of them ever asked any questions. None of them spoke. It was always the same.

They ate their tasteless food in the blackness, ate to stay alive for however much longer they could. Two prisoners holed away without explanation, without knowing when their sentence would reach its end, or what would happen to them afterward. It was difficult for him to chew or swallow. She'd had to help him take down the unsavory mush, slip little clots of it past his swollen lips with her fingers. After the third round of severe punishment he'd vomited, been unable to hold the food in his stomach for quite a while. Talk of escape arose between them, but neither had any idea how it might be accomplished. They had wondered aloud why they were being held, could only guess that sooner or later their captors meant to question them about the base. There was no way to be sure what they expected to learn, what motives they might have, it was all so baffling. But he told her he'd promised himself not to give anything up to them. Not unless they began to direct their violence at her would he give anything up.

She wasn't surprised. He was a brave man. She wished she felt that kind of courage on her own.

The beatings continued to alternate with the crude, bare-sustenance meals.

Time after time it was the same.

Until the last time.

That last time they returned, it was to take him away.

By then he'd been in desperate shape and could barely stay up on his legs. She remembered panicking as they dragged him off the floor, into the blackness beyond the cage. She had verged on crying out that she'd tell them whatever they needed to know, anything, if they only let him be. But then she'd thought of his vow to defy interrogation, his resolute, unsubmitting *heart,* and checked herself. She hadn't wanted to fail him, to fall short, and had bitten down on the words, watching them take him away, watching the door of the cage slam shut behind him—

Another scream suddenly bayoneted her thoughts now, and she jerked bolt upright as if slapped, the chain of her handcuffs clinking coldly between her trapped, chafed wrists.

The screaming continued to slash the blackness; shrill, tormented. There was no wishing it away anymore. No telling herself it wasn't real. That wouldn't work, wouldn't help, not now. . . .

She heard footsteps outside the cage, several sets of them, approaching with that familiar martial cadence. Then the cage door opened, lights glaring inside, dazzling her. She cowered back, squinting, shielding her eyes with both hands as they adjusted to the brightness.

The marked man entered, the rest of her jailers hanging behind him, positioned to either side of the entrance with their weapons at their hips. He crossed the floor of the cage, stood very still before her, framed in that terrible blaze of light.

Shevaun Bradley waited.

Trembling, cringing against the cage's metal wall, she waited.

At last the marked man bent low over her.

"Now," he said, "we talk."

And outside in the black, Scarborough's screams strung on and on above the heavy clashing roar of great machines.

ELEVEN

HAVING WORKED OUT THE SOLUTION TO A SEEMINGLY insoluble problem, the mind longs for verification. It is not simply enough to know intuitively that something is correct; humans desire external confirmation. A math student wants the proof to be convincing and communicable. A police officer making an arrest wants the satisfaction of a conviction in a court of law.

Nessa wanted the Picasso, or more likely, the series of Picassos. She had consulted experts on her theory of a painting from the time of *Guernica*; there had been no firm consensus, but to her mind that made it even more convincing. Even more convincing was the buzz from certain quarters that she was not the first to make such inquiries. A Japanese collector had approached a professor in Barcelona, a curator in Los Angeles had been queried by a Belgian entrepreneur—there were questions in the air.

If she could find Elata, Nessa figured she would know within a half hour if she was right or not. She would charge him with theft and threaten him with a jail term of several years for stealing the letter from the museum. She would find out about the Picassos—as well as many other paintings. For he was a nervous man, haughty but on the edge and easily broken; she'd seen it in his eyes on the platform.

She could have grabbed him then. But at that moment there had been nothing to charge him with.

Nessa stared at a list of the men and two women who were suspected of having employed Elata over the last decade; it was not a long list, but every name was a prominent member of the art community and the world at large. Two had net worths that topped that of several countries. To say that their wealth and power protected them was an understatement—though with the right evidence, such as a sworn confession from the master forger himself, even the difficult might be attempted.

Others had tried to take Elata down. To fantasize like this was dangerous.

Her boss wanted him. More—he wanted the Picassos. He salivated over them—phony or real made little difference. Find them, and his career would be made; the French government would undoubtedly issue a medal.

Her boss wasn't kidding. He'd authorized her to go "anywhere in pursuit of tangible leads." Whatever resource she wanted, she could have.

As long as she succeeded.

Nessa pushed the thick pile of papers into the case folder. It was late, far past quitting time; the other offices were dark. She shoved the printouts and her notes into the top drawer of her desk, locked it, and went to leave.

The phone rang. She nearly blew it off, but then decided to pick it up—sometimes her ma called her here when she couldn't reach her at the apartment.

Then again, her mother was sure to ask her whether she had a boyfriend for the umpteenth time. Perhaps she should just let it ring.

Nessa grabbed it a half second before the voice-mail system would have taken over.

"Nessa Lear," she said.

"Put more snap into it, lass. You want 'em tremblin' before they start talking to you."

"Gorrie!"

"I won't argue with you," said her old partner. "It's too good to hear your voice."

"How are you?"

"Up to the kilt in muck n' mire."

"You're drivin' roun' Inverness in a kilt these days? Do you carry your bagpipes with you?"

" 'Neath the kilt." His voice suddenly downshifted. "Ness, dearie, I need a favor."

"Favor?"

"I have a string of accidents that add into something more than accidents, if you know what I mean. Murder, I think."

"In Inverness?"

"It's been known to happen."

"How can I help?"

Gorrie told her about the records involving the nuclear plant's waste. Interpol had a database of international terrorists, and he wondered if he might have her check the names against them. He also had the name of the transport company that moved the waste.

"This isn't an Interpol matter," she told him.

"I know," said her old partner. "But I'm beginning to think the woman at UKAE is involved. Constance Burns. Ever hear of her?"

"Not at all. You want me to run her name too?"

"Couldn't hurt. She's in Switzerland on vacation, or at least supposed to be. Hasn't returned my calls yet, an' I was just settin' here wonderin' why."

"Technically, you're supposed to be dealing through MI5," she said. "Or at least—"

"I called to London and there's no one can help me till the morning," he said. "You would have liked this case, Nessa. Deputy Chief Constable is in a twit over his detection rate."

She typed in her password and entered the data bank. She hadn't been here long enough to know what the bosses might think of helping out a fellow police officer; she imagined the reaction could run from awarding her a commendation to kicking her back to Scotland.

"Nothing on any of your hits. Transport company again?"

"Highland Specialty Transport. I have done some checkin' on my own. Seems to be a subsidiary of a Yank concern: Aesthetic Transfers."

"Aesthetic Transfers?"

"Aesthetic Transfers Inc. I have the address here."

"Hold on, Gorrie." Nessa pulled open the drawer. Her fingers trembled as she clawed at the file.

Aesthetic Transfers—an international transportation firm specializing in international art and antique shipments and used by several museums. Sole stockholders—Morgan Family Trust (II).

Part of the Morgan empire controlled by Gabriel Morgan—a suspected dealer of fraudulent and black-market artworks and current tax scofflaw wanted by the U.S. Treasury Department. A suspected associate and possible employer of Marc Elata. Holed up in Zurich, Switzerland, where he had successfully fought off extradition by U.S. authorities.

"Frank," she said, picking up the phone again. "Tell me everything again, very slowly. No, wait—give me your number. I'll call you back on my mobile phone."

"Department will pay for the call."

"That's not it—I want to get going. I'll talk to you on the way."

"Where are you going?"

"Switzerland. Give me your number."

Inverness, Scotland

When he hung up with Nessa, Gorrie glanced at the clock. Though he had told his wife he'd be home by eight, he realized there was little sense making it there on the dot; she'd be talking schoolteacher talk with the visitor for hours and he'd only end up brooding in the corner. Better to take the time to work on this tangled knot.

Talking to Nessa made things no clearer, though it was good to hear her voice again. She seemed to be making a splash.

Gorrie's thoughts returned to Cardha Duff. If the murder had anything to do with the power plant and its waste, the lass didn't fit—unless Mackay had told her about the goings-on there.

Possible.

He drew out the file on the murder, looking over the report on her belongings. Nothing unusual, but then they hadn't bothered with an extensive inventory, given the circumstances of death. The apartment hadn't appeared ransacked. He could go back there and hunt around, but wouldn't a murderer have done the same?

If it was murder. The lab report leaned heavily toward accident.

If someone intended on killing her—if someone really wanted to do her in—why wait for several days after the others?

Maybe they didn't know about her until then.

Gorrie went back through his notes to make sure that Christine Gibbon hadn't given the name during their initial interview. It didn't appear there—but DC Andrews had conducted the actual interview, and he had not as yet typed his notes for the file.

A week late at least. Nessa would not have been so tardy, even as one of the unwashed.

Gorrie picked up the phone and called the young detective constable at home. Andrews's wife answered, giving a timid hello.

"Hello, Marge," Gorrie told her. "I just need a word with your husband. I won't keep him, I promise."

"Inspector Gorrie, how are you," she said loudly, undoubtedly intending her husband nearby to hear and decide whether he wanted to be bothered or not. Their two-year-old cried in the background.

"A quick question's all," promised Gorrie again.

"Here, Inspector," she said as the babe's cry crescendoed.

Andrews came on the phone with his husky voice. "Inspector?"

"When you spoke to Christine Gibbon, did she mention any of Mackay's alleged girlfriends?"

"You mean the Duff tart?"

Gorrie didn't answer.

"She may have," said Andrews. "Timing blurs a bit."

"Can you check your notes?"

"Haven't got 'em, sir," said Andrews, turning from the phone a moment as the baby continued to cry. "Can you shush 'em?" he asked his wife.

"Never mind, Andrews."

"That's it, sir?"

"Good night."

Gorrie dialed Gibbon's number, but got only her answering machine; he left a message asking her to call back. Finally he opened another of the files on his desk and fished out the news items on the case. Christine Gibbon had given more interviews after the murder than a movie star promoting a new film. He glanced through the stories, but none included Ms. Duff's name, only hints that there was "another woman."

One story declared that the interview had taken place in the "historic taproom of Brown Glen Hall, where the interviewee is a well-regarded raconteur."

The phone on his desk rang. He picked it up, thinking it was Gibbon returning his call.

Instead, it was a man who identified himself as Phil Hernandez, an executive with UpLink International.

"What precisely is that?" Gorrie asked the man, who had an American accent.

"We're an international communications concern," said the man, adding that he was in the security division, filling in for another person Gorrie had never heard of. "One of our people at Glasgow intercepted a hacker trying to break into our e-mail system."

"Computer crimes are a bit out of my expertise," Gorrie told him. "And Glasgow—"

"It's rather complicated." Hernandez explained that in investigating the attempted hack, they had uncovered possible evidence of another crime. They were alerting Scotland Yard's computer branch, but some of the e-mail they encountered seemed to pertain to Inverness and they had been referred to the local CID.

It appeared from the e-mail that the owner of an estate there named Cameron had been targeted for murder.

Until Ewie Cameron's name was mentioned, Gorrie paid scant attention. Now he pulled over a pad and began taking careful notes. The man read four e-mails; only one was directly incriminating—it mentioned Cameron by name and gave a price for his death. But there was another one referring to a "trashman," and still another advising that the job would not be considered complete until all complications were eliminated.

That one was dated two days ago. All were signed "CB," and all had come from the UKAE computer system.

"I don't know that these are authentic," said Hernandez, "but we can help you find out. Scotland Yard will undoubtedly be in touch."

"I'll arrange for a detective to go to your Glasgow office," said Gorrie. He wrote down the contact information, unsure who he could send who might actually understand how they had managed to come up with the information.

CB—Constance Burns, of course.

It was all suspiciously easy, just like finding the truck with a spot of blood still on the fender.

Gorrie hung up—then hit *69, which on their phone system redialed the number that had just been connected. On the third ring, a Yank picked up the phone.

"UpLink International," he said. "How can I direct your call?"

"Is there a Mr. Hernandez who works there?"

"Hold on and I'll connect you."

"Thank you, but it won't be necessary now," Gorrie said, hanging up. He started a new folder for the UpLink information, then put it on top of the others at the side of his desk. The large clock on the wall read five minutes to eight.

He must not show up at home too late, he decided. This new business would hold off the higher-ups for some days, perhaps even win him more men. Russell would bristle when he heard Scotland Yard had been contacted.

Still, there was time to stop by Brown Glen Hall and see if he could find Christine Gibbon there.

She was not there, which didn't surprise him terribly. And no one remembered anyone odd hanging around who might have overheard her running her mouth.

"Tourist types this time of year? Not many," said the regular bar girl, Sallie, as she delivered a few Guinnesses to a pair of regulars near the dart board. "Haven't had but a one these past few weeks. No monsters in our parking lot."

"We've got a ghost," said the bartender, as if making a pitch. "Two."

"Aye, but you don't advertise him, that's your problem," Sallie told him. "What we need is a good sighting or two."

"Nice American girl a week or so ago, about the time you're talking," said the bartender. "Good-lookin', if she'd put on a little weight up top. Needs titties. Wouldn't kick her outta bed, though."

"Nice arse, you ask me," said an older man standing at the bar nearby.

"Christine Gibbon bent her ear that one night," said Sallie. "Maybe she's the one you're looking for, Inspector."

"I didnae say I'm looking for anyone," said Gorrie.

"I don't know that Chrissie bent her ear," said the bartender. "The Yank paid for the drinks."

"What's happened to the wee boy, Inspector?" asked Sallie.

"They're hoping a sister will take him."

"Best thing for it."

"Did anyone else listen to Christine Gibbon?" Gorrie asked.

"Only five of us ever here most nights, Frank," Sallie said. "Until the winter ends."

"And school lets out," added the bartender. "That's when business picks up."

"You serving kiddies now?" said Gorrie.

"What I mean is, that's when the tourists come up," said the bartender.

"No one else unusual?" Gorrie asked Sallie.

"We're not unusual enough for you?"

Gorrie hunched his shoulders and considered ordering a drink. But then he remembered his wife and her schoolteacher friend.

A schoolteacher in Scotland in March, the middle of the school year.

"Did Miss Gibbon mention a Cardha Duff?" he asked them.

"She might have," said Sallie. "One of the girlfriends?"

"Describe the tourist, would you?" Gorrie said, instead of answering.

"Five-eight, curly auburn hair not very long, no tits as I told you."

"Dark clothes, large purse. Has money, though she tries to hide it," added Sallie.

"How so?"

"Leather bag, very nice shoes. Drove a common Ford, blue little thing, type anyone would rent."

"Did she use a credit card?" Gorrie asked.

"Cash. No trouble with the money like some Yanks," said Sallie.

"Where was she staying?"

"Didn't say."

"Still around," said the man who had spoken before. "Saw 'er at Grant's using the telephone one day. Chemist's the next."

"Couldn't've been her," said Sallie. "She had a mobile phone—I saw it poking from the top of the bag."

"I wouldn't forget an arse like 'ers." The man went back to his beer.

Paranoia tickled Gorrie's senses as he left the pub. The coincidence of the killer seeking out his wife was just too great—and yet, if someone had come to town so skilled as to make four related murders seem completely unrelated, wasn't it just possible that he would seek out the one person trying to tie them together and prove they were murders, not accidents?

He, not she. A woman couldn't have committed these crimes, or wouldn't.

Why not? Held down Cardha Duff while she injected her? Duff was a wee lass, and if sleeping, might have been easily overwhelmed. The small chest bruise at her ribs might have come from a knee or an arm.

Losh, as Nan would say. You'll be seeing pipers in the mist next, and soldiers manning castles that haven't existed in five hundred years.

A schoolteacher in March. Two schoolteachers in Inverness.

Maybe the Yanks all had mid-winter holiday.

Gorrie saw the blue Ford in his driveway and kept going, continuing down the block to Peterson's house. He put the car in their driveway, then got out and walked back, feeling foolish. A small lorry approached from the opposite direction; he tensed as it slowed, then saw it was only the local gas service.

"Excuse me, sir," said the driver, leaning out the window. "We've had some phone calls of gas smell in the neighborhood this afternoon and evening. Have you smelled anything?"

"No," said Gorrie.

The man nodded solemnly. "Probably a disturbed person but we're required to check it out. Missed my dinner over this."

The man drove on. Gorrie crossed the street and stopped in the front yard next to his house, trying to see past the curtains into the sitting room. He could just make out Nan on the couch. Her visitor sat in the armchair at the corner, back to him.

Nan rose and went to the kitchen. The visitor got up as well, took a look after her, then went to the window. She had short, curly hair and a thin, attractive face.

Why would she look out the window?

Any of a million reasons, Gorrie thought.

Nan returned to the room with a fresh pot of tea. The visitor turned back, gesturing out at the window. They began laughing.

What a fool I'm being, Gorrie told himself. He went back to Peterson's, got his car, and went around the block as if just coming in.

"Hello there," he said, stomping his feet at the front door. "Good evening, miss."

"Hello," said the Yank, rising as Nan came and took his coat. The visitor held out her hand. "Stephanie Plower."

"A pleasure," he said, shaking her hand and looking into her face. She was of the right height to match the lass Sallie and the others had described; her hair was right as well. But she seemed heavier than their description, a bulky, loose-knit sweater camouflaging what he imagined was a fullish top.

A sweater that hid a bullet-proof vest?

He wasn't merely paranoid but delusional, he thought to himself.

"You're a schoolteacher?" said Gorrie, taking a cup from his wife.

"Oh yes. In the States. I was just telling your wife, we're on vacation. Holiday, I think you would say."

"You've seen Loch Ness, I expect."

"Of course—but no monster, I'm sorry to say." Miss Plower rattled off a full itinerary. She had been to the ruins of Fortrose Cathedral, Chanory Point, Fair Glen (though the cherry trees were dormant), and two dozen other local highlights.

A lot of time in Inverness, Gorrie thought. And a lot of visiting in the area where Cameron was found.

"Have you tried our pubs?" he asked.

"Doesn't drink," said Nan, with a hint that perhaps others might take the example.

"A visit to Scotland without stopping in a pub?"

"I expect I'll visit one soon," answered Miss Plower. "Your wife said you were a detective."

"An inspector, yes."

"You must have interesting cases."

"The odd sort, now and again."

She smiled. Gorrie noticed that her bag wasn't nearby— Nan would have put it in the closet straightaway.

If she had a gun, she'd have it there, he thought. And if she was a killer, she would have a gun.

A simple thing to make an excuse, get up, and check.

"Frank has been with the police twenty-five years," said Nan. "Tell her the story of the boat rescue. That's a favorite."

"Wasn't much."

"A boat rescue on land," Nan told Miss Powers. "Some wee lads were havin' a bit of fun—"

"I saw some police up on the highway near Rosmarkie yesterday afternoon," said Miss Powers. "Must have been an accident."

"Wouldn't know," said Gorrie. "Traffic constables, I expect."

The American sipped her tea.

"She's heard about that business on Eriskay," said Nan.

"Terrible," said the American.

"Oh, yes."

"Jealous wife? That's what the paper said."

Gorrie got up. "I've forgotten to put out the garbage.

Let me take care of that before it slips my mind again."

"Frank," hissed his wife. "The garbage now? Manners," she added in a stage whisper.

He ignored her, walking quickly to the closet. He reached inside, past his jacket, looking toward the floor for the American's bag.

"Now, Inspector, do you think I would be so foolish as to leave my weapon in the bag?" said the American behind him. "Back out now, with the pocketbook please, and keep your hands high. Stay where you are, Nan."

Gorrie thought of taking the umbrella near the corner of the closet and smashing her with it, but he couldn't tell how far she was away from him. There was also Nan to consider. So he complied slowly.

"What sort of accident will you dress this up as?" he asked, still facing away from her.

"Something will occur to me, I'm sure," she said. "Slide the bag on the floor."

"And if I don't?"

Instead of answering, she reached forward and grabbed it from his hand.

His chance—he'd missed it.

"There have been reports of gas in the neighborhood," she said, sliding something from the bag and placing it on the floor. "I don't suppose they've found the leak yet."

"They've already checked here," said Nan.

"Incompetence is rife," said the American.

"I wouldn't think even my detective constable would accept the coincidence of six accidents so close together," said Gorrie. He turned halfway toward her, about six feet away in the small room.

Not quite enough for a lunge.

"Into the kitchen now, both of you."

Gorrie glanced toward his wife. The teapot was near her; if she could just pick it up, it might catch the American off guard.

Surely the woman's reflexes were quick enough to kill both of them before the water even scalded her.

She'd kill them soon anyway.

But she wouldn't shoot them if she didn't have to. She wanted this to look like an accident, and the bullets might be found.

"The kitchen, Inspector," said the American, sidling past him toward the door.

She wanted to lock it. She could just barely reach it and still cover them.

Not both at the same time. He had to do something quickly.

"Nan, the kitchen!" he shouted.

As the killer jerked her head toward his wife, Gorrie twisted around and sprung at Plower. The gun went off near his face, but he heard it as if from a vast distance away, muffled by his surging adrenaline. She was stronger than he'd guessed, far stronger, and the bulk at her chest had come from a special vest; he felt the hard panel with the first punch. He slammed his skull against her chin, felt a sharp pang at the back of his neck, pushed himself against her with everything he had, hoping Nan had the sense to run and save herself.

She didn't. But it was quite likely the smash she gave the American with the hammer from their tool drawer was the blow that rendered her unconscious.

TWELVE

A STORM WAS COMING, AND THE PETRELS AND SKUAS were its outriders, brawling up from the bare sea cliffs in wild sprays of gray-white wings.

Above their Bellany Island rock colonies a moist, restless warm front from New Zealand had bumped against the outer bounds of an Antarctic air mass. Cold and dry, heavy as the breath of a slumbering frost giant, it presented a resistant barrier.

In collision, the two fronts took on a clockwise rotation, generating great eddies of wind around a central area of low pressure. Rising above the dense mass of cold air, the buoyant warm flow pulled its moisture higher into the atmosphere to be cooled and condensed into radiating bands of clouds.

As the fronts continued to spin in conflict, their winds gained speed and intensity, sucking up more water vapor from the low-pressure trough, pushing the clouds further toward its edges, evolving into a potent cyclonic cell that whirled southward across the Antarctic Circle, racing over archipelagoes, open sea, and pack ice toward the continental landmass.

A storm was coming.

Streaming from their bleak slopes, the rousted seabirds were first to know its aggressive force.

Soon many others would as well.

South Victoria Land, Antarctica
(Approx: 74°50' S, 164°00' E)

They tramped over the snow berm ferrying a pair of cargo-laden banana sleds toward the first of their widely separated destinations.

The team consisted of ten men. Their parkas, wind pants, and duffels were white. White too were the ski bags they carried over their shoulders on padded nylon web slings, their lightweight fiberglass sleds, and the canvas tarpaulins over the large, sealed crates that had been left at the drop-off point some three quarters of a mile back. This was a heavily crevassed area, and Granger had refused to land his helicopter any closer to the depot.

At the rear of the small column, two men hauled their freight of equipment on sturdy polyfiber tow cords, harnesses buckled around their chests and waists.

They marched along the north side of the trench with a kind of slow wariness, the lead walker probing the untracked snow ahead with a telescopic avalanche pole, its shaft locked at its maximum six-foot extension. Far from any known camp, their chances of being detected by ground or aerial recon were slight. Their clothes and equipment were furthermore designed to blend with the terrain, and the sun's prolonged descent toward austral winter had butted it increasingly low toward the horizon, leaving no appreciable shadows to betray their movement.

The wind blew hard and cold. They moved on toward their goal, their leader repeatedly thrusting his probe into the rumpled snow, locating a masked drop, and then steering them around it. The depot's location had been programmed into their GPS units, and they would reach it soon enough if they stuck close to the berm line. Their main interest right now was getting safely past the crevasse field, past those fissures waiting beneath the snow, their open, icy mouths filled with darkness. Often hidden under fragile snow bridges—corniced drifts that sweep across their openings and become obliterated from sight as surrounding accumulations overspread their peaks—they might be a few feet in depth, or two hundred feet. One did not learn which until the misstep was already taken and the bottom fell out from underfoot.

After a while the lead man stopped, planted his avalanche pole in the snow, and slipped his binoculars from their case. Beside him along the slope, the others stood with the crampons of their mountaineer boots biting into the hardpack. The dry wind nagged at them, flapping the ruffs of their parkas, clotting the fibers of their balaclavas with their own frozen breath. Out beyond the opposite embankment, sastrugi flowed away northward in wild, swirling patterns.

Glasses held up to his eyes, the team leader looked carefully down into the trench. The entrance hatch was buried in snow, but he could see the reflective strip at the top of its marker wand projecting above a nearby drift.

He signaled to his men, and all but the load carriers began preparing for their run. They zipped open their ski bags, extracted their boards and poles, mounted rigid alpine touring bindings onto the skis, and slipped their booted feet into them.

The leader moved to the edge of the depression on his skis. Behind him, the carriers unharnessed. There would be no need for their assistance below; better they rested here and stayed with the sleds and crates.

"Gehen Meir!" he ordered in throaty Schwyzerdüsch. Then he leaned into the fall line, bent low at the knees, pushed off with his sticks, and went slicing downhill.

The rest whipped after him, poles swung out and back, powder flying from the tails of their skis in wide sweeping sprays. The floor of the trench came upon them in a rush, and they wedged their tips and edges to check their descent, turning parallel to the grade, plowing snow into the air as they braked.

Near the marker wand down at the base of the slope, the leader inspected a high undulation in the surface cover, gave his men a confirmatory nod, and crouched to remove his skis. They quickly followed suit, then got to work digging at the mound with foldable snow shovels from their duffels.

Soon they had exposed most of a circular stainless-steel hatch, its frame almost flush with the rock of the hillside. There was no lock. Intruder prevention depended on effective concealment rather than access control, for mechanical rods and electromagnetics were prone to climatic damage and might very well fail to release.

It took fifteen minutes before the manhole-sized entry hatch was completely dug out. The leader stood to one side and waved for a couple of the men to pull it open. Then he took an electric krypton lantern out of his bag and strode through the passageway, the lantern held forward, the rest of the group filing in at his heels.

The small, cavelike storage depot measured five yards in depth, somewhat less in width. Shielded from wind chill, insulated from outside temperature extremes by the snow and ice cover, its corrugated steel liner was cold enough to patch with frost from the vapor of their exhalations, but still perhaps twenty degrees warmer than ground level.

The leader paused a few feet past the entry, swept his lantern from side to side, and steadied it to his right as his men hastened to pull a large protective covering from over a low wooden platform that spanned the length of the shallow tunnel.

Within moments the covering lay crumpled around the skis and treads of a half-dozen white snowmobiles. Dressed with flared aerodynamic windshields, cargo

racks, and saddle bags, the swift, agile little vehicles sat
atop the platform in a neat row.

The leader turned to the opposite side of the tunnel and
saw a wooden skid stacked with rubber fuel bladders by
the bright glow of his lamp. These, he knew, contained a
premixture of high-octane gasoline and two-stroke oil for-
mulated for cold-weather running.

He grunted. *Ja, gut. Alles ist burzüglich.*

Everything was indeed as he'd been told it would be.

Satisfied, he looked back at his men, then used the
torch's bright shafting beam to point toward the snowmobiles. They had a long distance to travel across the ice
plate, and no time at all to waste.

"Bring them down and put some fuel in their tanks—
hurry!" he said, still speaking Swiss German. "I want to
return to the others, unpack the weapons and explosives,
and strike out for our target within the hour."

Cold Corners Base, Antarctica

"Diamond dust," Megan Breen said. "Something to see,
isn't it?"

Nimec looked where she was pointing. Arcs of irides-
cent color chased across a glittery veil of ice crystals wa-
vering above the helipad despite a total absence of clouds.
In the far distance, sun dogs teased the horizon at opposite
sides of a solar halo, the circle's violet inner rim bleeding
away into faint rainbow bands of green, yellow, tangerine,
and primary red.

"It's easy to appreciate," he said. "Harder to enjoy under the circumstances."

Megan turned to face him. She was in minimal ECW
gear, her parka's hood down, snow goggles raised above
her brow, no balaclava. The comm tech had notified her
of the arrivals just ten minutes ago, but she could already
hear the choppers rumbling in, and expected to be out of
the cold before too long.

"And wood sprites in the gloom weave magic secrets," she said.

"Nice line. Yours or borrowed?"

"You know I'm not that poetic."

"Nice anyway," Nimec said. "What's the message?"

Megan gave him a shrug.

"Our astronomers and field photographers throw conniptions when diamond dust settles on their optics," she said. "They spend weeks preparing to observe an event of some sort or another, use the finest equipment available, and a little ice shoots the works. It wastes time, effort, and lots of money. People get upset, accuse each other of negligence, incompetence, all sorts of idiotic things. And naturally I wind up having to referee. It's worse than a nuisance. But the *sky*. That's the other side of it for me."

Nimec frowned. "This time it isn't about telescopes," he said. "It's about three missing human beings."

Megan was quiet for several moments.

"I don't need to be reminded of that," she said then.

Nimec instantly regretted his snappiness. He studied her features. Her gaze was direct, penetrating, but showed no sign of anger. Somehow that made him even more regretful.

"Guess that wasn't one of my smartest remarks," he said.

Another pause. "Probably not." She took in a slow breath. "Pete . . . one thing I've learned from my stay on the ice is that there can be magic secrets in the gloom. Don't close your eyes to them. They help you learn how to *live*."

He was silent. They both were. Colors slipped and tailed through the suspended ice motes overhead. Still out of sight, the two approaching helicopters knocked away at the air.

Nimec supposed he really was on edge. Some of it a carryover from those tumbling boomerangs aboard the Herc. Some of it was his impatience to get going with his search for Scarborough and the two scientists. But there

was more besides, and he knew it involved Annie Caulfield's imminent landing aboard one of the choppers. The
news that Annie was already in Antarctica with the Senatorial delegation had made him feel nothing less than
ambushed.

He rubbed his face with a gloved hand, thinking. How
had Meg originally alluded to their presence? *We're short-
handed as far as pilots go, but I'll explain that later.* Just
a passing comment as she'd tapped a number into her cell
phone. It had gone right by Nimec. But when she got
around to her promised explanation, he had learned that
one of the base's three chopper pilots was grounded because his bird was in for repairs, that another was on
emergency loan to a French station because their only
resident pilot had shipped out for civilization due to illness, and that the third had been to assigned to give the
distinguished visitors—DVs, as she called them—a lift
from Amundsen-Scott station, the first stop on their tour
of the continent. *It's the storm that's being predicted,
Pete. Bad weather's nothing abnormal around here, but
once it hits, there's a chance it can last for days. The
Senators pushed up their schedule to get here before it
grounded them at the South Pole, and we were obliged to
make accommodations, go ahead with our hosting duties.
Incidentally, did Gord happen to mention that Annie
Caulfield's been nannying them?*

Ambushed, Nimec thought. Why feel that way, though?
Why should the prospect of seeing Annie again have so
much guilt attached to it? They'd made an effective team
in Florida, but that was in connection with the Orion
probe. It was a working relationship. Well, mostly. There
was that movie afterward. Dinner and a movie. A nice
evening. Annie had introduced him to her kids when he'd
picked her up . . . Chris and Linda. Nice. But their date,
say you wanted to call it that for lack of a better term,
their date was collegial. More or less. At best they were
casual friends unwinding after a tough shared assignment.

And once it was over they'd gone their different ways. Again, more or less.

Nimec wasn't denying he'd felt an attraction to Annie at the time—who wouldn't, after all?—but he'd known there had been no sense pursuing anything even if she were the least bit interested in him. Which was itself an unrealistic thought. She'd been widowed only a year or so before. Lost her husband to cancer. She wasn't ready. Also, he had his responsibilities in San Jose, and Annie had her own at NASA's Houston space center. *Texas*. Things wouldn't have worked out long-distance. Yes, he'd phoned her a few times, just to see how she was doing. And sure, they'd talked about getting together in indefinite terms, the way people often did. But nothing firm was ever discussed. The last time they'd spoken was last October or thereabouts, and it was true she'd mentioned that he was welcome to visit if he had any time off around the holidays, stay in a spare bedroom at her place, but he'd considered it one of those polite gestures rather than a serious invitation. And say he *had* made the blunder of taking her offer at face value? It would have been asinine. An awful imposition. He'd meant to get back to her anyway, but those weeks before Thanksgiving had turned into hell. Pure hell. With Gord in danger everything else had fallen by the wayside. And there had been so much catching up to do since. . . .

Annie had no reason to be insulted. Why club himself over the head with irrational guilt?

Nimec stood there outside the base, steam coiling from his nose and mouth. His cheeks had started to burn and he made himself stop rubbing them. Five degrees above zero out here, and Meg had described today's weather conditions as mild, a calm before the storm. Since when was five above *mild*?

The thump of the copters grew louder. Nimec searched the sky, spotted one of them to the west, flying fast, the UpLink logo becoming visible on its flank. That would be the DVs, he thought. Not the first bird he would have liked to see. But the good thing was that he'd get the formalities with those pols out of the way. Plus his foolish nervousness about Annie. His main focus now was making arrangements with Granger. Seeing if he could take him out over Bull Pass ahead of the snow.

The helicopter came in, reduced speed, landed about a hundred feet from him, the downwash of its rotors stirring a cloud of snow off the ground. Then its blades stopped turning, its cabin door slid back, and its passengers came hopping out.

Megan glanced at her wristwatch.

"Right on schedule," she said. "Special delivery from Washington by way of the Geographic Pole."

Nimec didn't comment. There were three Senators in the delegation: Dianne Wertz, Todd Palmer, and Bernard Raines from the Appropriations Committee. Obviously unaware of Meg's affirmative characterization of the weather, they were wrapped head-to-toe in CDC orange bag garb. Still, it wasn't hard to tell them apart. A former basketball pro, Palmer towered above the rest, and had reflexively hunched as he emerged from beneath the chopper's slowing rotors. Wertz would be the one scrambling to keep pace at his side—Nimec had met the Senator from Delaware at an UpLink function, and remembered her as kind of slight. That left Raines to bring up the rear. Almost seventy-five years old, the committee chairman carried himself like a man whose senior rank qualified him as beyond having to match strides with anyone, almost diverting attention from the fact that in many instances he no longer could. The fourth member of the party had stayed back to help him across the snow, a tactful hand on his elbow.

Nimec took a quick glance at Raines's companion, unwillingly tightening up inside.

Annie.

Megan leaned close, interrupting his thoughts.

"Time to officiate, Pete," she whispered, and then hurried to greet their visitors.

Nimec followed a step behind her, suddenly aware of the NSF copter clattering toward the landing zone. About a quarter mile away, it would be touching down in minutes.

Megan whizzed through the obligatory formalities.

"Senator Palmer, I'd like you to meet our head of corporate security, Pete Nimec . . . Pete, I'm sure you recognize Senator Todd Palmer . . . Senator Wertz, it's a great pleasure . . . Chairman Raines, we feel so deeply *privileged* . . . Annie, I know you and Pete don't need any introduction. . . ."

Nimec stared as she came close. Hooded, bundled up, Annie nevertheless managed to look fantastic. Fresh. She might have arrived after a half hour's drive from her home in Houston rather than a long tossing helicopter ride out of South Pole station.

He hesitated.

"Annie, hello—"

"Nice to see you again, Pete," she said with an entirely pleasant, equally impersonal smile. Then she turned to Raines, escorting him on toward a waiting shuttle. "Sir, I'm sure you'll be interested in seeing our scientific facilities. . . ."

And that was that. They were gone in a flash.

Nimec watched them climb aboard the balloon-tired vehicle. He didn't know what he'd expected from Annie. But being left to feel inconsequential wasn't it.

Confused, he waited as the second chopper made its descent, its skids gently alighting on the plowed, tamped snowfield.

Moments later the pilot jumped from his cockpit and crossed the landing area to where Megan, Wertz, and Palmer were about to start for the shuttle. Megan briefly freed herself from the DVs and led him toward Nimec.

"Pete, this is our friend Russ Granger from MacTown," she told him. Then she turned to the pilot. "Come on, let's scoot you out of the cold. Pete's anxious to discuss a few things about our current search plans. We're hoping you can fly him into the Valleys as soon as possible."

Granger smiled and tapped Nimec's shoulder with a gloved hand. At least *he* seemed interested in talking to him.

"Whatever I can do to help," Granger said.

New York City

Of all the types of on-air interviews Rick Woods had to conduct, the scientific stuff was his biggest pain. And these geniuses from NASA, Ketchum and Frye, whom he was guessing might be a little fruity, and whom he knew were duller than Sunday morning sermons, talking about solar flames in endless multisyllabic strings . . .

Flares, Woods thought. The correct term was solar *flares*. As his twit of a director, Todd Bennett, had already reminded him a dozen times from his seat back in the control room . . .

These space brains on the remote feed from Goddard were making him work his balls off trying to keep things from tanking. The only bigger duds Woods could recall having as guests were the mathematicians who'd come on to discuss chaos theory; *their* incomprehensible rambling had gotten him dizzy. A flying ant gets gulped by a toad in Guangdong, China, and somehow that causes a gondola with two lovers in it to capsize in Venice, which eventually leads to a fucking earthquake in San Francisco. And then the quarks, leptons, muons, and gluons enter the picture, zipping around in ways that make it impossible to predict whether New Year's Day would follow Christmas next year. Ridiculous.

"Ketchum's losing us with the jargon, Rick." Bennett's voice was in his earpiece again. "Get him to explain what he means by an X-class flare."

Woods cleared his throat. Maybe adding some humor to their discussion would pick up the pace.

"Uh, Doctor," he said. "For average minds like myself,

would you explain the difference between X-class and *business-class*?"

Ketchum nodded from the Maryland sister station's newsroom, seeming to miss the pun.

"The X classification system measures a flare's power, and aids our ability to forecast how it will impact on our planet," he said. "We use a simple numerical table based on *X-ray* emissions from the region of the sun where the flare occurs."

Simple my ass, Woods thought. "And this latest one you've detected, can you help us understand why we should be concerned about it?"

"Yes," Ketchum said. "I should first emphasize that we haven't actually observed a flare, but unusual sunspots and other indicators on the far side of the sun that are distinctive signs of impending flare activity. It would roughly correspond to tracking tropical hurricane seed-lings on radar. . . ."

Woods tried to keep his mind from wandering. Even school shootings were easier than this. Distraught as the interviewees might be, you came to know which questions to ask by rote. *Can you recall Timmy displaying hostile or antisocial behavior before the tragedy? Resentment to-ward his classmates? An ethnic group? Is it true none of your school's teachers or guidance counselors ever asked him about that swastika tattoo on his forehead? And what about reports that he had a habit of firing an illegal M-16 at neighborhood dogs and cats from his front porch?*

Woods suddenly felt indecent, but things got to him. It wasn't that he didn't appreciate his good luck. This was major-market cable TV, twenty-four-hour news, and he co-anchored the afternoon weekday slot. He would be the first guy to say there weren't many more enviable gigs in the business. Before landing it, he'd hosted a live enter-tainment segment for the network, thirty minutes daily right before prime time. Some of that was fun. Meeting famous actors, actresses, and film directors. The Oscars and Grammys. Those awards presentations always gave him a kick. But six years at it was much too long. No one took Hollywood beat reporters seriously. Hard-news people considered you one step above a gossip monger, a paparazzi. The glamor wore thin after a while. The beautiful people started looking uglier and uglier. And when boob-job-and-baby-fat teenaged pop singers treated you like a microphone sock, it could be the absolute pits.

Woods had grown tired of it.

Getting offered the co-anchor post had been a break. A *huge* break. His predecessor had been old-school, started out his career in print journalism, spent almost twenty years as a political field correspondent. With their cable channel's daytime numbers trailing CNN, Fox, and MSNBC by several percentage points, its programming executives had studied the audience comp and decided they wanted new blood, a face with youth appeal, someone more comfortable engaging in peppy cross talk with Marsie Randall, the female half of their anchor team. Woods was offered the spot on a trial basis, given an ironclad contractual guarantee that he could return to star-chasing if things didn't work out. Shit, never mind huge, it was the break of a *lifetime*. He had jumped at it, relocated from the left to right coast. And at the request of his producers, he'd started wearing a pair of glasses with plain lenses over his 20/20 peepers for a brainier look. Now, six months later, ratings for the time period had almost doubled, and he'd re-upped for two more years with a substantial pay increase and built-in elevator clauses that would continue to boost his salary if the Nielsens kept improving.

Overall Rick Woods was pleased. He felt appreciated, gratified, financially stable. But nothing was ever perfect. On this network, one to five P.M. weekdays was early fringe. The demographic was mainly post-boomer housewives with at least a couple of years of college—the ones who stayed away from Mountain Dew and pink polyester stretch pants, and who wanted an alternative to the soaps, courtroom reality shows, and trailer-trash clown antics.

They were a tricky audience. Moving targets. You had to strike just the right balance with content, give them something that was not quite a morning magazine format, and not quite Jim Lehrer. Give them *infotainment*. That meant filling the spaces between lead and breaking stories with background pieces, analysis, talk, a little fluffy human interest to round out the blend.

The science stuff worked its way into the lineup maybe once, twice a week. Woods found it endurable when the stories related to ordinary people's lives. Child-development studies, medical breakthroughs, home computing, these things he understood. But he hated when his producers got too smart for their own good, booked guests who'd start running off at the mouth with complicated theories . . . or when they bought into one of the stunts NASA regularly pulled to grab attention and justify its existence to taxpayers, such as the big load of crap it was currently dishing out—

"Rick, pay attention!" Bennett yipped over their IFB line. "Ketchum's got a bad case of eye bounce, makes him look evasive. Bring in the young one, try to nail him down on the flare's severity. Ask what consequences it will have for earth."

None, Woods felt like telling him. *Nugatory, Todd. This segment's not only pointless, it's duller than dead air.*

"Dr. Frye, let's bring you into the conversation," he said. "To use your colleague's weather analogy, the solar storm system that's brewing would be exactly *how* severe . . . ?"

"I think Jonathan was trying to explain that we can't be exact at this stage," Frye said. "My belief is we're going to experience a series of X-20's or higher, which would be very energetic. Putting it in perspective, a flare that's categorized below an X-9 generally has few noticeable implications for us. As its power climbs the scale, though, increasing geomagnetic disturbances may result. . . ."

"And can you please tell our viewers around the world

how they should expect these, uh, X-20 solar flames—"

"Flares!" Bennett said.

"—solar *flares* to affect them?"

"Again, it's tough to be certain. We can only look back at what's happened in the past, and use that as the basis for informed guesses," Frye said. "About thirty years back, a group of flares in the X-15 range interrupted satellite transmissions, and resulted in serious power-line voltage swings in at least two of our Western and Midwestern states. It also caused the explosion of a 230,000-volt transformer in British Columbia—"

"Well, thirty years is a long time," Woods said, wanting to be quick with his follow-up. "I'd assume that with, ah, modern technologies we won't have to worry too much about the lights going out nowadays."

"Unfortunately, it's just the opposite. In the nineteen-seventies power companies hadn't really computerized their operations. Very *few* computers were used by private or government offices. The Internet didn't exist. There were no PCs. No public wireless-telephone networks. But society's become dependent on sophisticated electronics over the past three decades. It's integral to our economy. Our national security. While some equipment's been shielded against high-level discharges of cosmic radiation, we can find plenty of room for improvement. As a NASA employee I'm concerned about the sensitive equipment on our orbital platforms, and more fundamentally about the exposure of astronauts aboard the International Space Station to harmful dosages of radiation. I've also wondered about the vulnerability of satellite communications linking us to the more remote parts of the globe. Parts of the Far East, for example. Or the poles . . ."

Where the polar bears would have to make do without their fucking cell phones and downloadable porn, Woods thought. Christ Almighty. This guy was going to start a mass panic if he went on with his horseshit about cosmic rays.

"It sounds as if you're scripting a Doomsday scenario,

which of course isn't the case," he said. "We should pause to reassure everyone that there's little risk of solar flames producing the whole range of disturbances you mention—"

"Flares!" The director yowled again. "They're called *flares*!"

Woods was getting aggravated. If Bennett wanted to be such a goddamn stickler for terminology, he could come out of the control room and finish the interview himself.

"By the way," Woods said. "Aren't solar *flares* accompanied by *flames?*"

Frye looked a bit thrown by the seeming non sequitur. "Well, sure, they'd be associated with eruptions of flaming gases in the heliosphere—"

"Thanks for making that clear, Dr. Frye," he said.

"And fuck *you* for being a spiteful prick, Mr. Woods," Bennett said out of sight.

"Returning to the point I raised a moment ago," Woods said. "Is it fair to state that you gentlemen don't, foresee any, uh—"

He faltered, unable to think of the word. This happened to him sometimes. Mostly when he was doing the science stuff, which was another reason he despised it. The word just got stuck in traffic somewhere between his brain and mouth. Goddamn. Goddamn. Where was Bennett when you needed him, why was he letting him dangle here, what the hell was the word . . . ?

"Catastrophes, you spiteful, *unappreciative* prick," Bennett said.

Woods fought back a sigh of relief.

"*Catastrophes* over the horizon," he resumed, "but are rather just sketching out the problems that should be addressed as our knowledge of flares increases? Giving us some, uh . . ."

"Cautionary advice," Bennett said.

"Cautionary advice, that is?"

This time it was Ketchum who answered. "Yes and no. We're certainly not trying to scare anyone watching your program. But it does look as if there's an impressive event in store for us, and we should all do our best to prepare. That's why we've come on your program to talk about it."

"I see . . . and, uh, when did you say it's going to happen?"

"Richard and I think we're looking at a window of somewhere within the next two to three weeks, but we don't have enough data to tell you precisely," Ketchum replied. "That's another area where my meteorological comparison might be useful. Storm systems stall or pick up speed, change course, collide with other building low-pressure centers . . . as complex as the variables can be when we're trying to forecast movement in our own atmosphere, it's important to remember much less is understood about the sun's."

Woods noticed his cue blinker. Thirty seconds until the commercial. Thank God. He was still recovering from his momentary bobble of the tongue. And had a sick feeling that Ketchum was about to start in about flying ants and Chinese toads.

"Okay," Bennett said. "Ask them something personal, then cut to the break."

Woods paused a tick. Did these flat tires even *have* personalities?

"Ah, gentlemen, our conversation's been fascinating, and I'm sure we'll be hearing much more from you in the days to come," he said. "We're running low on time, but in our last few moments, could you, uh, talk a little about how you earned your unusual nicknames at Goddard . . . Ketchup and Fries, is it?"

Both men nodded, smiling.

Ketchum said, "I'll defer to Richard on that."

Frye said, "I think somebody just cooked them up because we get along well as a team."

Woods smiled back at them, wondered again if they were gay.

"Well, that's it, fellows, thank you for coming together this afternoon," he said.

"Any time," Ketchum said.

"Our pleasure," Frye said.

I bet, Woods thought.

And that was finally a wrap.

Victoria Land, Antarctica

They had made camp in a saddle between two immense glaciers, pitching their dome tents against the eastern slope, camouflaging their snowmobiles with the drop taken from the storage depot.

Perched on a lower ledge, a group of skuas had watched them with black unblinking eyes.

Five hours later the birds still had not moved. The team leader glanced at them as he emerged from his tent, stepping through its door flap into the cold.

They merely stared back.

He zipped the flap shut and strode away from the ledge in his insulated boots, then stopped with his binoculars raised to the southwestern sky.

He did not like what he saw. A fleet of saucer-shaped lenticular clouds had appeared in the distance, climbing over the polar plateau on a turbulent wave of air. Their bases were shaded deep blue, their curved foaming tops a lighter grayish color.

He angled the glasses toward the ground. Far down the narrow cleft through which his men had ridden, the world was vague, without contrast, its outlines melting into hazy softness.

He rubbed the steam from his breath off their lenses, but nothing changed.

Soft, he thought. *Too soft.*

He didn't like it at all. Before leaving his tent, he had checked the latest meteorological data on his rugged handheld field computer, accessing it over the terminal's wireless Internet connection, comparing the information from several portal sites—base forecasts, infrared maps from orbiting hemispheric satellites, NOAA synoptic charts, scattered automatic weather stations. Updated at intervals of between ten and thirty minutes, the readings were consistently ominous. A severe gale was whipping toward the coast of Victoria Land, accreting momentum as it neared the Ross Sea and ice shelf. McMurdo had already assigned it a Condition II classification: winds in excess of 50 knots, a chill factor of at least minus-60F, visibility no better than a quarter of a mile, and perhaps as low as a hundred yards.

Affairs were about to pass largely out of his control, but he would press on with the mission regardless. It was his responsibility, no more, no less.

He lowered his binoculars and started back toward the tents. Though he'd raised his neck gaiter to the bridge of his nose, the crescent birthmark on his cheek already burned from the extreme cold. It was a constant bother to him here, as it had been during his alpine training with the Stern unit of the Swiss Militärpolizei. For a man who had spent most of his life in places where warmth was scarce, this was an absurdity of sorts, a strange and uncommon jest that matched the rareness of his stigma. Yet he had long since come to abide it. In the Jura Mountain farming village of his boyhood, he had suffered merciless slashes of pain throughout the endless winter stretches. Only his shame over the freak blemish to his appearance had brought a harsher sting.

Kind des Mondes, his mother had called him as far back as he could remember. A child of the moon. It had not been a name kindly used. There had been precious little kindness in any of his mother's words, but he had finally taught himself that didn't matter. Emotions always betrayed. Better to steel the backbone and toughen the gut than be distracted by them.

At his orders now, the men were quick to break camp and stow their bedrolls and folded tents aboard their snowmobiles. The gathering of birds continued to study them from their perch, barely curious, simply watching because of their nearness. He looked at the creatures as he waited, lifted a chunk of ice off the ground, and suddenly snapped it at them with a hard overhand throw.

It struck the ledge with a crack, breaking to pieces. The birds jumped and fluttered in surprise, scolded him indignantly, but did not take flight.

He gave them a slight nod of appreciation.

"Eine gute Gesellschaft," he said, turning from the ledge.

They had been good enough company in their way.

Minutes later he mounted his snowmobile, throttled up its engine, and went speeding on across the ice toward his goal, the rest of his band traveling close behind him.

Cold Corners Base, Antarctica

"What I need is to get down low into the pass," Nimec was saying. Soon after returning to base from the helipad, he'd steered Russ Granger to a partitioned workstation where a downscaled, black-and-white version of Megan's Dry Valley contour map was spread across the desk, circles drawn with colored pencils substituting for the pins she'd used to mark its key sites. "I want to see it with my own eyes."

Granger nodded from the chair beside him.

"Understood," he said. "I can take us pretty far in at its wider sections."

Nimec's forefinger bull's-eyed the circle indicating the coordinates of Scout IV's final transmission, and the presumable outer limit of the recovery team's search area. "What about here?"

Granger shook his head.

"Your map doesn't convey how rough it is around the notch," he said. That much was absolutely true. "The terrain's bad enough. But our real problem is katabatic wind pouring straight down the notch's lee sides. The lower it gets, the harder gravity presses on it, and the faster it

blows. You fly near ground level, it's suicidal. Like riding
a toy raft through heavy rapids."

"What's the best you can do, as far as that goes?"

Granger traced a path with his hand. "We'll swing
around the notch, dip into Wright Valley just to its south."

Nimec thought a moment, then grunted his acceptance.

"A couple of things, though," Granger said. "It's obvious we have to work around this storm that's on the
way. I don't think it'll be bad enough to force evacs out
of any NSF field camps. But I'll have to make some trips
over to them, check that the personnel are stockpiled to
last it out."

"Any reason why I can't come along? We could shoot
right over Bull Pass after your last hop."

Granger had anticipated the question. He pretended to
think through an answer that had been readied well beforehand.

"It'd be fine with me," he said. "But we'd need to head
out together right away, so I can have time for everything.
Figure you'd be gone from here at least twenty-four hours.
It's either that or wait until the blow's over—"

Nimec waved an abortive hand in the air.

"Then we go now," he said. "Otherwise, we could be
talking about a holdup of almost a week. We couldn't
afford that kind of delay under any circumstances. But the
bad weather puts us in a vise. If our people are still alive
out there, they need to be pulled out."

Granger nodded again. That was definitely what he'd
figured the UpLink security chief would say. It was also
very much what he had *wanted* Nimec to say. The sooner
they were up and out of Cold Corners, the better. He
couldn't know precisely when the sabotage squad would
show, or how their progress would be affected by the
storm. He was, however, positive that Burkhart wouldn't
quit on his mission. It just wasn't in his hardwiring.

"Okay," Nimec said. "You mentioned there was something else on your mind."

"Right." Granger set for his payoff pitch. "Say we visit

all the field camps and maybe have to deliver some canned food, meds, equipment, and so on. It would mean a few refuelings at Marble Point, plus back-and-forth loops to McMurdo for the requested supplies. That gives us a full slate right off the top. And like you said, we're cutting it close. Working against the storm."

"The bottom line being . . . ?"

"I can promise we'll get to Bull Pass. But that twenty-four-hour timetable was just a guess. Depending on how many resupply drops I have to make, and when the blow hits, we might wind up having to stick around MacTown a few days before I can bring you back here. And I want to make sure you don't have any problems with that."

Nimec was quietly thoughtful. Megan had told him that Annie Caulfield and her small bundle of Senators had opted to cut their stay at Cold Corners to a few hours, overnight at the longest, and arrange for a return to Cheech before they found themselves snowbound. Meaning it was almost certain that he wouldn't have the chance to see Annie again before she departed. Which was likely for the best anyway.

"No," he said after a moment. "I've got no problem at all."

THIRTEEN

COLD CORNERS BASE, ANTARCTICA
MARCH 13, 2002

THE SQUAWK CAME OVER THEIR HEADSETS JUST AS Granger was about to release the chopper's main rotor brake.

"Abort takeoff, Macbird," the comm tech radioed over the base freq. "I say again, it's all fliers down. Over."

Nimec looked at Granger from the passenger's seat.

"What the hell's going on?" he asked.

Granger shrugged uncertainly, pushed his helmet microphone's "talk" button. At the edge of the landing zone, a flight director was slicing his right hand across his neck in a throat-cutting motion. Granger watched him through the Plexiglas windscreen and felt a sudden crick of tension in his back.

"Rob, we got clearance from you not three minutes ago," he said into his mouthpiece.

"I know," the comm tech said. "And I'm sorry. This is an all-points travel advisory out of your home nest. NOAA synoptics show the storm's accelerated on a northeasterly track. Present movement has it heading straight toward us over the Ross Shelf, and McMurdo says there's been more strengthening to the system. We're looking at a possible upgrade from Condition II. Over."

Both men were silent in the chopper's cabin. Its engines kept running. After a few moments Granger reached toward the instrument panel to cut them, then leaned back in his seat staring outward as the twin-turbine whine died away.

Nimec was still looking at him with a sunken expression.

"I don't believe this," Nimec said. His hand was balled into a fist against the metal frame of his window. "There anything we can do?"

Granger took a deep breath. This was about the worst foul-up he could imagine. The fucking worst.

"Nothing besides wait," he said at last, and started unbuckling his harness.

Victoria Land

They raced ahead of the storm, the wind hard at their backs, streaking cross-country over miles of snow and ice.

The sky pressed down on them, a low flat deck of clouds. Whiteout had cut visibility to thirty yards, and each rider kept his eyes on the trail of the vehicle before him to avoid separation from the group, their headlights and reflectors of no use in the stirring mist.

In the lead position, Burkhart rode with his thumb heavy on the throttle, squeezing every last bit of speed out of it, his determination a red-hot knife stabbing a passage through the soft barrier emptiness.

He leaned forward as he straddled his seat, knees locked around its leather, gloved fingers tightly gripping its handlebars. The 'mobile dipped, then nosed up, pitching with the terrain's rise and fall. Powder sprayed from its track in flying ramps, shredding across the curved surface of his windshield. He porpoised down into a steep trench, shot along its bottom, and topped its opposite bank at a full tear, skis springing over the snow.

He could feel the storm at his neck, tumid, angry, coursing overland with unexpected swiftness. Some of his men had wished to suspend travel, find a protected spot where they could hunker down until it lifted. Their tents were designed to withstand the force of the gale. But he'd insisted they bear on at a constant pace.

Let their targets be stationary captives of the elements. His team would be a moving force.

The storm was like a rushing stallion, and they could either stay in front of the charge or be trampled.

Cold Corners Base

Ten minutes after exiting the chopper, Nimec was in Megan's square, monotone-blue office, still wearing the wind parka he'd donned for his scratched departure.

"They think they can ground us, they're wrong," he fumed, standing in front of her desk. "McMurdo doesn't have any right butting into our affairs. They've got no authority."

She regarded him from her chair. "Pete, calm down, this is just as frustrating for me. . . ."

"Then get on the phone with somebody over there. Explain that we appreciate their concern for our safety, but have decided to do what's necessary to find our people."

"I can't for a lot of reasons. Russ is one of their pilots—"

"Okay, then we'll use our own. The guy who was jockeying the pols around is back, why not him? I know he isn't as familiar with the Valleys. But it's not like he's *green*. . . ."

"I told you, Russ is only part of it. Cold Corners operates under special arrangement with USAP. We receive direct sponsorship from the American government. In a sense, we represent an extension of its foreign policy interests here. Though we've never locked horns over anything, McMurdo Station is an official United States base, and we're arguably subject to its auspices."

Nimec leaned forward over the desk, knuckling its edge with both hands.

"And you know, and I know, and these walls know we've bent the rules before," he said.

Megan sighed. "The air-travel restrictions were called with good reason. You've never been through a Condition II Antarctic storm. I have. And trust me, MacTown's alert is absolutely nothing to disregard."

"Who's doing that? I checked the weather outlook. The storm's still miles to our southwest. Even further from Bull Pass. And Granger told me we'd need an hour at most to fly from here to there. I'm not thinking to go ahead with the kind of thorough search I wanted, but if I can accomplish anything at all it's worth a try. Give me three, four hours and I'll be back in plenty of time."

Megan shook her head. "You're still missing the point," she said. "Maybe a little intentionally. You know how forecasting works. Anyone who's ever gotten drenched in the rain because the local weatherman predicted a sunny beach day knows. It's a matter of estimates. Especially in this place. The situation could deteriorate faster than anyone thinks. Look at how the storm's motion has already shifted from the original forecast."

Nimec stared at her. He could see where this was leading. "Antarctica. *It* controls the show. Like mighty Olympus. Have I got that right in my head yet? Or do I have to hear it from one more person?"

Megan looked at him.

"Listen," she said. "My decision has to be about the good of the whole base. If you wind up in a bad situation, getting you out of it becomes a priority. Which would mean putting more of our people at risk. I can't allow it."

"And how about Alan Scarborough and those scientists? Since when have *they* stopped being a priority?"

Megan sat in silence for perhaps thirty seconds, her gaze suddenly sharp.

"Alan wouldn't want anyone doing something as unwise as what you've suggested," she said in a tight voice.

There was another long interval of silence. Nimec straightened, lifted his hands off her desk, and stepped back from it.

"So we're done, that it?" he said at last. "*This place* makes the call."

Megan shook her head slowly.

"No, Pete," she said. "I do."

Their eyes momentarily clashed.

"Appreciate you telling me," Nimec said, and abruptly turned away from her, leaving the office without another word.

Near Cold Corners Base, Victoria Land

Burkhart stood in an ice-sheathed elbow of rock and gazed through his binoculars as the rising, snarling gusts blew around him.

There, he thought. *There it is.*

He could see UpLink's ice station in the basin below, perhaps a half mile to the north, its modular core elevated above the snowdrifts on mechanical stilts. Much closer to his position was the geodesic dome housing the critical life-support facility that had been marked for destruction.

Unseen beneath the neoprene face mask he'd donned in the worsening cold, a touch of a smile. He had emerged from the senses-numbing vacancy of the whiteout, reached his destination with the gale well at his rear.

He turned to the man who'd accompanied him onto the bluff.

"Go back to the others," he said. "You're to make camp in the lee slope, wherever its best shelter can be found. Shovel plenty of snow over the ground flaps of our tents. Be sure the flies are also secure."

The man's eyes widened behind his goggles, but he remained quiet.

"What's on your mind?" Burkhart said.

The man hesitated.

"Tell me," Burkhart said. "I'll reserve my bite."

The man shook his head.

"I don't understand why we'd wait," he said. "We've driven ourselves without halt to outpace the storm."

Burkhart looked at him, wind clapping the sides of his hood.

"Langern, you're mistaken," he said. "We're *meeting* the storm. Joining its attack. There's actually much it can help us take care of, can you see?"

Langern stood a moment.

"Yes, I think," he said. "But there's danger in it—"

"No worse than in immobility." Burkhart made a dismissive gesture. "Is anything else bothering you?"

Langern just shook his head.

"Then get moving," Burhkart said. "I'll be along shortly."

Langern started across the snow, walking downhill to where the rest of the men had waited with the snowmobiles and equipment.

Alone on the escarpment, Burkhart lifted the binoculars back to his eyes and resumed studying the base.

There was much yet that he wished to observe.

Cold Corners Base

"I really feel responsible for you being stranded," Megan said. "Sorry, Russ."

Granger was careful not to show his uneasiness.

"You didn't call in the storm," he said.

"No, but I did call you, even knowing it was on the way." She shook her head, her shoulders moving up and down. "Guess I'd been anxious for Pete to make it to the pass and take a look-see."

"Don't worry about it." Granger coerced an accepting smile out of himself. "There isn't much difference whether I'm wheels-down at Cold Corners or MacTown. And from what they told me over the radio, our field camps are in fair enough shape for the duration. So it's not as if my detour caused any harm."

Megan looked at him a moment, then nodded.

"Let's just keep our fingers crossed that the weather blows over fast," she said. "Meanwhile, you should be okay using this bunk. There weren't any others available with our delegation from the States needing accommodations." She paused, glanced down at the neatly made bed to her right, and settled herself. "It's Alan Scarborough's, you know. Sam Cruz here is his roommate."

Granger turned to the man beside them in the little dorm and shook his hand. In fact, he wouldn't feel remotely okay sleeping in that bed. Knowing what happened to the rover's S&R team, the idea of it gave him the horrors.

"This must be a tough spell for you," he said to Cruz. "Hope I'm not being too much of an imposition."

"No, no, please," Cruz replied. He was darkcomplected, wavy-haired, with a strong grip. "It'll be good for me to have some company."

Granger had noticed the humorous marker-inked rendering on the closet door across the room. He glanced at the words above it.

"Prisoners of Fashion," he read aloud.

"Blame me for that one," Cruz said. "Megan lets us juvies amuse ourselves by making a mess of our quarters. It's sort of an in-joke I'll explain to you later."

Granger manufactured another smile and plucked at his synthetic thermal vest.

"Think I already get it," he said.

A half hour after stalking out of Megan's office, Nimec beckoned the manager of base security over to the same paneled workstation he'd seized for his ultimately wasted planning session with Granger.

"I want to conduct a site security check while there's an opportunity," he told him. "Tour the installation so I can get a close-up sense of things."

And feel like I'm doing something marginally constructive with my time, he thought but did not say.

The Sword base chief nodded. He was a burly guy named Ron Waylon, with a thick walrus mustache and a head that was shaved smooth except for a gladiatorial nape lock reaching to the middle of his back. The lock of hair was bound with a leather cord down its full length. Some sort of body tattoo peeked above his shirt collar on the right side of his neck. The silver earrings he wore on both sides were shaped like long swords, an interesting but questionably appropriate variation on the organizational badge. Or maybe they were supposed to be daggers and Nimec was reading too much symbolism into them.

Whether or not that was the case, he'd found dress and appearance codes to be pretty damn lacking at Cold Corners. Hadn't the base chief been clean-cut when he was hired? Or was his recollection about that also off the mark?

"Yes, sir," Waylon replied now. His road-warrior appearance belied a disarming mild-manneredness. "I'm thinking I should mention CC's probably different from other locations, where the emphasis would be to harden it against corporate spies, armed intruders . . . *human* threats to property and employees. Here we try to prepare for emergencies shaping out of natural events. Like, say, the storm that's headed toward us. If any of our personnel become sick or injured when we're snowbound, it could be a long spell before relief arrives. So we push real heavy on self-sufficiency, and drill a crisis-and-escalation checklist into everybody's minds. We try not to ignore perimeter defense. But rescue transport, triage, stopgap equipment repair . . . I guess they'd be stressed over it."

Nimec nodded, itching to make himself useful.

"Understood," he said. "How soon can we do this?"

"Be ready in a jiff, sir. We just need to suit up."

Nimec rose from his chair. He gave the big man an after-you gesture.

"Lead the way and I shall follow," he said.

•   •   •

Megan Breen stared at her computer screen feeling strangely under assault from the e-mail messages in her queue. Turn on the machine, and there they were demanding attention, zipped through electronic space from scattered points of origin around the world. Amsterdam, Johore, Tokyo, New Delhi, San Jose, Washington, D.C. . . .

There were two, no, three, waiting to be answered from Bob Lang in Washington, D.C.

She sighed. It was stupid, she knew. An armadillo's reflex to roll up behind its head and tail shields. But when the boss had first requested that she do a stint in Antarctica, its isolation—and separateness—*had* appealed to her. In fact, his proposition had come at just the right stage in her life, filling a definite need to time-out from the Cuisinart grind of corporate affairs, the relationships with men that seemed like listless dances around a circle broken and faded from too many retracings of her own footsteps. . . .

She didn't immediately acknowledge it. In fact, she'd been too knocked for a loop at the time to know exactly what to think.

"We've been through a lot of wear and tear lately, Meg," Gord had said when he'd broached the idea. "A change of scenery might be good for you. Something dramatic. Along with the chance to captain your own ship." And then he'd given her the look that might have almost convinced her she'd been struck by a thunderbolt. "I know it could only help you prepare for the day you inherit mine."

Boom.

Megan's automatic reaction had been a kind of befuddled astonishment. *Inherit mine.* The thought had never occurred to her. Not consciously, at any rate. The boss had been her vertical constant for too long. Her Kilimanjaro towering at an unmatched height. Turn her eyes to their loftiest reach and he'd be there. Even when he was hospitalized, part of her had denied admittance to the prospect that she could lose him. Somebody take his place one day? *Her?* It seemed inconceivable. . . .

Gordian had asked her to wait a bit before giving her answer, let the idea sink in, and she'd agreed out of deference alone, or told herself that was the reason, figuring she'd put the whole crazy thing out of her mind, wait a respectable week or so, and courteously decline.

Surprise, surprise. She'd found herself thinking about his proposition, really thinking about it, at odd instances throughout that day. And the next day. And the next. The thoughts had sneaked up on her during morning workouts, business conferences, lunches, cocktail parties. They had slipped between lines of office memoranda, the paragraphs of a novel she was reading, song lyrics on her car stereo. And they'd struck her often when she was with Bob, much too often . . . once, finally, while they were thrashing toward the climax of an ardent scene on his living-room rug.

It was fairly crass as turning points went, but you weren't often able to choose their times of arrival, and she supposed you just had to be grateful when you recognized them. That hers had coincided with a moment of intense physical pleasure, some emotional connection to Bob clicking off even as her body aggressively pursued its own independent gratification, was fitting and probably necessary in its way. Action plus conflict equaled change, wasn't that how it went?

Megan didn't fault Bob for not noticing; she was almost sure she hadn't shown any outward signs, and there had been enough happening to distract him if she had. But the episode had been privately embarrassing. And worse, terribly depressing as she stood in his shower the morning after, wishing she could stay under its stream until the pipes ran dry. She'd always believed she wanted loose romantic ties, easygoing friendships with sizzle. Now, suddenly and unforeseeably, Megan had realized that she needed more rather than less . . . and wondered how she could have been so dissatisfied without knowing it.

The first thing at work that same morning, she had gone

to the boss's office and told him she was taking him up on his offer. She did it without stopping at her own desk, not wanting to give herself pause to reconsider. Not wanting to *overthink*. Seeing at last that her greatest fear in life wore the shape of her own heart, she had refused to back away from coming to terms with it.

Three weeks or so afterward, Megan had swapped her Cole Haan city heels for mukluks and was riding a plane toward the southern polar cap. And she hadn't regretted it for a second. Little about being in Antarctica was easy. But her choice, its *timing,* couldn't have been righter. . . .

Megan was still thinking in front of the computer when she heard a light knock on the door, told whoever it was to come on in, and saw that it was Annie Caulfield.

"Hi," Annie said, entering. "This an okay time?"

"Actually, you're rescuing me from a screen full of e-mail I'd prefer to neglect." Meg rose to show her inside, pulled a chair up to her desk. "I was sort of expecting Pete Nimec anyway."

"Oh." Annie sat, cleared her throat. "How's Pete doing? I heard he came out of San Jose in a hurry."

"That he did. As a huge favor to me," Megan said. "To be honest, we've had some differences that need to be ironed out . . . but you got that strictly on the QT." She shrugged. "I'm sure my minor waves with Pete can't be more trying than playing travel guide to the Capitol Hill Gang."

"That's probably not understating the case. They're so used to being coddled by aides and interns, motherhood's starting to seem like a breeze by comparison." Annie smiled. "Seems we both needed a break, huh?"

"No understatement there either."

They looked at each other across the desk.

"Annie Caulfield, you're about the best visitor I could have wished for right now," Megan said. "I'm just sorry the storm's messing with your schedule."

Annie flapped a hand in the air.

"Houston can survive without me a few extra days,"

she said, and then was quiet a moment. "You know, Meg, the main reason I dropped by was to thank you for the open reception my group's gotten in light of everything else that's going on. And I don't mean some bad weather." Another pause. "Having been Chief of Astronauts for a lot of years . . . and especially after Orion . . . well, I understand how it feels to be hijacked by outside circumstances. What you and the rest of the base staff must be going through with your people lost out on the ice. Yet you've all bent over backwards to make us welcome."

Megan nodded a little.

"Glad things are working out," she said. "The kids going to be okay with your extended absence?"

"Are you kidding? When they hear I'm stuck in the snow they'll think it's an answer to their prayers," Annie said. "My mom's staying with them, poor woman . . . *she's* the one I worry about."

Megan smiled. She clicked in on Annie's expression, realized there was more on her mind, and waited.

"I don't mean to be nosy," Annie said after a companionable silence. "But since you've mentioned it . . . what's bothering Pete? He seemed so great to work with in Florida. We became friends . . . and then, well, kind of lost touch . . ."

"Between us again?"

Annie nodded.

"Pete's a gem," Megan said. "He means everything to me. There's no one in the world I'd rather have at my side in a crunch. But I guess certain adjustments are hard for him." Her eyes made contact with Annie's. "People in general have trouble changing direction. And *men* . . . they're the worst. Quick to move when they know it's wrong, slow when they know it's absolutely right. I'm sure I don't have to tell you. Put a guy at a crossroads, and you've got a real problem. He'll stand there with his feet planted forever unless somebody gives him a push."

Annie chuckled a little.

"Meg," she said. "it's been really super talking to you."

"Same at this end." Meg was smiling again. "How about we do some more once we're through with today's business? We have a bar here . . . the Meat Locker, hardy-har. I guarantee you'll be impressed at how well it's stocked."

"Promise to drag me out before the last call and you're on."

Megan looked at her and winked.

"Dear girl," she said, "one of the beauties of living in Antarctica is that last call's whenever you want it to be."

Pete Nimec pushed open the high-mounted 4x4's passenger door, then frowned as gusting wind slammed it back hard against his shoulder. He gave it more oomph and jumped out into shin-deep snow.

Waylon came around from the driver's side of the truck. He'd left the engine running.

"Storm's really on the move now," he said.

Nimec couldn't make out his comment. It was difficult enough to hear through his hood and face mask without the wind batting the words off into space.

"What was that you said?" he almost shouted, moving closer.

Waylon pointed overhead to the south, his arm at ten o'clock. "Check out the space invaders."

Nimec gazed up at a huge floating armada of vaporish flying saucers and took an involuntary breath of raw air. It ranked as one of the eeriest sights that he'd ever seen.

"They snow clouds?"

"More of an advance escort," Waylon said. Steam puffed from his mouth and froze into little pearlets of ice on his mustache, causing it to droop further down the sides of his chin. "Those are lenticular hogbacks. If this storm fits the regular pattern, we'll see some shreddy cirrus clouds made up of ice crystals stream in behind them and then get low and thick and cover the sky. That's whiteout time, and it's no fun. The cumulus clouds come last, bring the main front. You know them right away because they've got these ugly anvil tops. The higher their tops, the harder they slam down on you."

Nimec looked at him. "Sounds like you know your stuff."

Waylon shrugged. "A bug in the jungle *better* know when an elephant stampede's on the way."

"Your antennas tell you how long before it reaches us?"

"I'm guessing an hour till snow starts falling, four or five before we feel the real brunt. But don't hold me to that," he said. "The on-line sat voodoo says it'll be closer to six, which just seems way outside the mark."

Nimec stood looking at him in the face of the wind.

"I'll go ahead and bet my money on you," he said.

Waylon didn't comment. After a moment he nodded his head toward the long, ribbed metal structure to their right, where a group of men had formed a human conveyor belt from the entrance to a Caterpillar parked outside, stacking its flatbed high with crates.

"Anyway, sir, I've got a couple of reasons for showing you this arch first," he said. "One, it's our outermost building, a warehouse where we store contingency provisions. I figured we'd start here and work our way back to the main compound."

He paused, watching the big tracked vehicle get loaded up.

"And two?" Nimec said.

"What you see is a perfect example of a Sword operation, Antarctic style," he said. "It's obviously not very exciting. The crates are filled with canned food and bottled water. We're shifting them to the utilidors in case of a pinch, which is SOP before any Class II storm."

Nimec was perusing the arch from where he stood. Although a wide path had been dozed in front of the entrance, its roof and sides were inundated with a thick caking of snow.

He searched his recollection.

"Just curious," he said. "Maybe there aren't any marauding hill tribes about to come after your soup and jerky sticks, but you ever get any security systems functional out here?"

Waylon shook his head. "We considered all kinds of monitoring and access-control equipment to stay in line with normal UpLink requirements. Experimented with swipe-card scanners, biometrics, even robot hedgehogs . . . didn't have much luck in these conditions."

"Yeah, now that you mention it, I remember the requisitions totaling up to a fortune," Nimec said. "The techies kept trying to modify the stuff. Weather-harden it."

"And every one of those req slips probably had my name on them," Waylon said. "No matter what we did to enhance their shieldings, the electronics would go down as fast as we got them fixed." He pointed a gloved hand at a spot above the arch's open entry door. "There're some surveillance cams hidden up top. IR thermography, one-eighty-degree rotation, recessed so they're protected from *some* of the elements. On a good day they work all right. But it takes constant maintenance to keep frozen precip off the gimbals and lenses."

Nimec grunted. The wind boomed around him, a gust almost lifting him off his feet. He was starting to desperately miss the 4x4's heated interior.

"Okay," he said in a loud voice. "What's next?"

Waylon shrugged.

"Your call, sir," he said. "I can walk you inside the arch for a look around, or drive us on over to the water-desalinization and treatment dome."

Nimec looked at their waiting vehicle, decided in about a second.

"Let's roll," he said.

Near Cold Corners Base, Victoria Land

Burkhart crouched under the tent fly as he entered from outside and quickly zippered shut the double door flaps. Here in the upper elevations, the pregnant clouds had begun to spill their frozen moisture, flinging drops of sleet and snow hard into the wind.

Squatted over their open crates of weapons, his men turned to look at him, the cloth sides of the tent thumping and rattling around them.

He flipped off his balaclava, pressed a warm hand against the searing birthmark on his cheek.

"Get ready," he said. "It's time to strike."

Elata paced the length of the small room, trying to contain his energy. He'd been here, in this room, in this small stinking village near the Italian border, for five days now, five overlong and crushing days, waiting. He needed this to end, and soon.

Pages from three sketchbooks littered the floor. He'd tried to draw, but it had deepened his frustration. Lines of other artists intruded into his work. A sketch of the bed became an early Van Gogh; the scene from his window a study by Titian. The masters swirled around him like ghosts. He was losing his sanity as well as his sense of himself.

It was Morgan's fault. Morgan had put him here. Morgan had sucked him into his orbit, jailed Elata as he himself was jailed in exile.

Elata dropped to the floor and did a set of pushups, trying to stifle his paranoia. Then he folded himself back up and crossed his legs, trying to meditate.

This would end in an hour, a day. He was free to walk around the village if he wished; he would be shadowed, but that was for his own protection—Interpol had issued a bulletin for his arrest.

Morgan would pay him and supply him with a different passport. He would be off to nearby Milan, then down to Florence. He could see friends there; they would let him stay for as long as he wished, even forever.

He'd give up forgery completely. There would be objections—Morgan would complain bitterly. Worse, he would tempt him. Money was to be made. But Elata had enough money.

If anyone objected, he would threaten to tell all to Interpol. He had only to make a phone call—one phone call—and hundreds of art collections would be called into question.

He could make the call now. He was tempted. He wouldn't even have to say anything himself—there was a list in a safety-deposit box in the States that could keep the wolves at Interpol busy for decades.

If he did that, Morgan and the others would be very, very angry. They would kill him. He would have to expect that.

A heavy set of footsteps ascended the steps. It was Morgan's minion, Peter. The thug never bothered to knock before opening the door.

"Time to go," he said. "We're not coming back."

"Fine with me," said Elata, grabbing his knapsack but leaving the sketches on the floor. He went down the stairs quickly; a small yellow Fiat waited nearby, the same car that had brought him here. Belting himself in, he felt paranoia steal over him again. Peter pushed the seat forward harshly as he climbed past into the back; the forger pushed back with a shove.

They could kill him now and he would have no way of avenging himself.

The snow-topped Italian Alps glittered above them as they drove down toward Lake Maggiore. A man in a small boat worked a set of nets near the shore, taking in a meager catch of *lavarelli* or whitefish, undoubtedly doing a job taught to him by his father, who'd learned from his father and so on back through time. A small speedboat sat half-beached on the shore, an old man sitting cross-legged on its bow. As they drew parallel to the speedboat, the Fiat driver yanked the wheel hard to the left, sending Elata against the door despite his seat belt; the wheels screeched and gravel spat as they came to a halt next to the boat.

Elata unfolded himself from the car slowly, ignoring Peter's idiotic grunts that he should hurry. He got into the speedboat deliberately, choosing the front seat next to the wheel. The others took the back. The old man stood on the shore and pushed the prow up with his left hand; his arms seemed no thicker than cornstalks, but the push was strong enough to send the boat bobbing backward into the lake. The old man took a step and sprang up, his agility belying the deep wrinkles of age on his face. He jumped over the windscreen, landing square in the seat. The motor revved to life and the boat curled backward and then sped off, foam coursing away and the wake upsetting the fisher's nets nearby.

A stone building seemed to appear from the middle of the lake a few miles ahead, rising from the shadows of the mountains.

"Ecco," said the driver. He pointed to the castle, apparently their destination.

"Che è?" asked Elata in Italian. "What is it?"

"Castello Dinelli," said the old man. The Castle of the Nello Family. He began telling a tale of *banditi* who had built it during the fifteenth century, men richer than the Borgias and several times as cruel, robber barons who had done what they wanted to the world.

"What became of them?"

"What happens to all of us? The bottom of the lake to feed the fish," said the old man in Italian.

It's true, thought Elata. *"É vero."*

The island fortress was built straight up from the sheer, chiseled rock; the water lapped against the walls. The only spot to land was a small ramp of mossy rocks flanked on both sides by walls, which made it easily defended. It was impossible to see what might be behind those walls, in the castle beyond, from the water.

The driver reversed the propeller as they approached, slowing to a bare crawl; he turned gingerly, stopping parallel to the rocks, but still a good three or four feet from the island. Elata bent and took off his shoes, rolling his pant legs up; he guessed the water would come to his knees. He reached for his bag, but Peter grabbed hold of it, nearly throwing him off balance.

"What's the story?" Elata said.

"We're not allowed on the island. Just you. They're watching."

"I can't have my bag?"

"They're very nervous, and they're calling the shots."

"Well, I need something from it."

"So take it."

Elata reached into the knapsack and took out the letter he had been given at the Musée Picasso. He palmed his alphanumeric pager as well, putting both into the inside pocket of his wool suit coat.

"We'll be here, painter," said Peter. "Just don't do anything stupid. They're not very forgiving."

Elata threw his shoes and socks to shore and got out of the boat. The water was deeper and the rocks more slippery than he'd thought; he slid backward, stopped only by the side of the craft. His pants were wet well up to his thighs.

If the letter got wet, the daub of paint it contained would be useless. He took off his jacket and held it high above his head, not even daring to throw it ashore for fear he might miss. He walked forward slowly, waddling more than walking. Finally, he reached the dry rocks and could put on his shoes and walk up the ramp.

Elata expected to hear the motorboat rev back up behind him. He expected bullets to glance off the rocks. He expected to die any second, the victim of an elaborate setup.

"Signor Elata?" asked a voice from behind the rock wall on the left.

"Yes."

"Buon giorno, signore. Come sta."

"Sto bene," he said, trying to take a breath.

"I much admire your work. You are a genius," said a short, thin man with close-cropped hair who stepped out from behind the rock. A small sapphire earring sat in his left lobe. He reached out eagerly and shook Elata's hand. "I have long wanted to meet you."

"Okay."

"You are the third expert Signor Morgan has sent, you understand. But the others—they were clerks. Academics. Schoolteachers." The small man practically spat as he spoke. "You will understand this. You—it is a pleasure to meet you. Truly."

Elata started forward. The man caught him.

"I must warn you, my associates, they are very, very suspicious. There are video cameras. One right there, you see?" He pointed toward the yellow wall of the castle where there was, indeed, a video camera. "They hover nearby in a helicopter. Anything bad that you do, anything even suspicious—I'm afraid that it will not go well for you."

Elata nodded.

"I would not like you hurt. That would be a terrible thing. You have much more to accomplish, eh? The world should not lose you." The Italian could not have been more sincere. "You may leave when your inspection is done, but the others must stay," added the man.

"Why?"

He shrugged. "Until the transfer is complete. Simply a precaution. These exchanges are always difficult to arrange. It is a dance. My partner wanted you to stay as well, but I persuaded him that you would be insulted. We would not want you insulted." The man smiled and nodded. "A small boat will pick you up. Signor Morgan will not object, I am sure."

"Can I see the paintings, please?"

"This way," said the man, springing forward.

Elata followed him up the ramp to a narrow corridor behind the wall, and then around a sharp corner that led to the castle interior. A large wooden door stood open. The Italian entered; two men in creased jeans sat glumly on a small bench just inside. Elata guessed they were the other experts Morgan had sent; he wondered what their opinion had been.

This was too elaborate to be a trick, but perhaps the sellers would simply kill anyone who thought the paintings were fraudulent.

Morgan was supposed to protect him, the bastard. How could he give his true opinion under these conditions? He had the letter—but what good was it? How could he compare the paint? He trusted his eye better than any laboratory, but still—this was a job for a team of scientists, not an artist.

The short Italian pushed open a small rectangular wall at the side, its thick iron hinges creaking harshly. Elata had to stoop to step through.

Light flooded into his eyes. He'd stepped into a small courtyard.

Fourteen paintings, each approximately eighteen by twenty-six inches, stood on easels before him. He looked at the first and his lungs ceased working; his eyes turned to the second and his heart stopped. By the third he knew he would never himself pick up a paintbrush, either to make a forgery or do something of his own.

There was no point. These fourteen paintings held all possibilities of art—not merely agony but joy, not simply sorrow but triumph. Beyond this there was nothing.

"You may use this phone," said the Italian, pressing a cell phone into his hand. "Take your time. I will leave you." He retreated, then paused at the door. "Of course, if you think they are fake—"

"They're not fake," said Elata. There was no sense bothering to compare the paint.

"You'll want to study them carefully before your conclusion. There are X-rays, whatever you want."

Elata said nothing.

"I'll leave you," said the Italian, slipping away.

The phone rang just as Morgan pushed himself back from Lucretia on the divan. Minz, her head resting on her sister's leg, reached for him lazily.

At other times, most other times, he would not have bothered to answer the phone, but he was waiting for this call. He reached back and took the handset; as he brought it to his ear he felt a sharp pain in his chest, a difficult feeling of remorse—what if the Picassos were fake?

The Italian and his partner would be eliminated, but that would be no consolation, none at all.

"Yes," said Elata. His voice was hushed, the syllables of the word drawn out.

Morgan said nothing, reaching back and hanging up the phone instead. He slid one hand beneath the oversized divan, reaching for the alphanumeric pager so he could set the exchange in motion.

His other hand slipped onto Minz.

"Be with you in a moment, hon," he said, turning his full attention to the pager's miniature keyboard. "But we'll have to make it quick; I have to meet a helicopter at the airport in ten minutes."

FOURTEEN

THE SNOWMOBILES DESCENDED TOWARD COLD COR-
ners through razor bends in the slope, tacking between
rock falls, ramparts of drifted and avalanche-piled snow,
blue ice pinnacles that soared hundreds of feet into the
dusky hanging clouds.

Out front, Burkhart again coaxed the team to speed, his
engine greedily pulling fuel from the tank. The wind
bragged in the faces of his riders, pelted them with freezing precipitation. Spiral blooms of snow and hail exploded
in the beams of their headlamps. Bullets of electrically
charged graupel smacked their helmets, flattened out with
little coughs of static that went rasping up and down their
encrypted radio communications link.

If his task went off as Burkhart intended, the storm
would be their only resistance. But in matters like this
there could be sudden and unexpected turns, and he had
done all he could to prepare his men for a change in plans.

Their firearms had been an easy choice. Lightweight,
compact, field-tested after hours sheathed in ice at minus-
300°F cold-chamber temperatures, the Sig Sturmgewehr

552's were optimally designed for extreme-weather commando action. Their hinged trigger guards could be
moved to the left or right to facilitate firing with alpine-
gloved hands. The variable-magnification optics were
frost-resistant and reticulated with luminous tritium
markings, their foresights hooded against glare and snow.
Each of the transparent three-stack magazines under their
barrels held thirty rounds of 5.56×45mm NATO ball ammunition. Attached side by side for rapid open-bolt reload,
they effectively gave the guns a ninety-round capacity.

The riders carried these assault weapons on their backs
in biathlon harnesses, as Burkhart had done on ski-patrol
drills with the Swiss special forces, where he'd had to
unclip his weapon from its straps and zero in on a line of
numbered targets from both prone and standing positions,
firing after rapid downhill runs, his performance measured
to a rigorous standard of time and accuracy.

In his elite unit, Burkhart's skills had leaped above the
highest bar. It was as if he were born possessing them.
But he'd accepted recognition from his superiors and
comrades with indifference. His competitiveness came
from old angers of the soul, and he'd worn his decorations
as emblems of a secret spite. For the child of the moon,
every medal pinned to his chest was a reminder of some
beautiful shining face that had once looked scornfully at
him under the sun, left further in the past as he flogged
himself toward new levels of accomplishment.

At last, though, it was restlessness as much as anything
else that had sent him along the path of the mercenary.
His prowess had seemed wasted against cardboard soldiers. What pluck was there in mock combat against an
enemy that bled red dye? Games had not demanded
enough of him. And so he had moved on to find a prof-
itable and satisfying alternative.

Since then Burkhart had only improved upon his innate
abilities, refining his tactical know-how, his situational
adaptability. He had actualized a vision of his own poten-

tial, made it hard as steel, and found a kind of chambered peace within it.

Now Burkhart took a sinuous curve around a glacial edge and urged his bike over a series of jarring bumps into the downhill channel he had reconnoitered before the storm. A final glissading run, his flaps threshing up a wake of powder, gravity squeezing the ribs around his heart, and then he was on a smooth flat field of ice, headed across the basin between the mountains and frozen shore.

Dimly visible through the snow, just a handful of miles seaward, lay the UpLink base.

Cold Corners Base

"Pete."

Nimec turned his head from the window in the empty corridor. It was oval and not much larger than a porthole, its fixed pane reinforced with a shatter-resistant polymer coating. He had stood there alone staring at the thick pulsing snow outside, listening to the freight-train roar of the wind, once pressing his hand against the glass to feel its buffet. He could see neither land nor sky, only the close, incursive whiteness.

"Meg," he said. He had not noticed her approaching. "Figured I'd take a look at the thousand-pound giant."

"And maybe stare him down?"

"Maybe."

She stood beside him awhile.

"I've been trying to find you," she said. "Ron Waylon told me he'd taken you on the grand tour, then left you at your workstation after you two went poking around the utilidors."

"How'd you know I'd be here?"

"I didn't exactly. Just had a hunch you might be where everyone else wasn't, and wandered around until I hit the spot."

"It would've been faster and easier to have me paged."

"But absent the intimate touch for which we strive at this lodge."

Nimec looked at her another moment, then moved his somber eyes back to the window.

"I know what you're thinking and feeling, Pete," she said.

"Never occurred to me you didn't."

"One thing to keep in mind is that the storm won't reach the Valleys. None of them do. The mountains form a barrier. And any snow that does get over them is dried by the katabatic effect before it hits the ground."

He kept staring out the window.

"Our people have been missing eleven days," he said.

"Yes."

"Maybe no one's been able to get to Bull Pass on foot since they were lost. Or obviously down in a chopper. But the boss told me MacTown sent out pilots in Twin Ospreys. And we've used Hawkeye III. State-of-the-art satellite recon that can practically image a mole on somebody's chin."

"Pete, you know air and orbital sat searches are hampered by the terrain no matter how sophisticated the tech. There are recesses, cliff overhangs . . . too many blind spots."

Nimec turned to her again.

"Eleven days," he said. "And counting. We have to be honest. Let's believe they found food and water caches. Give them that. How long before they'd all succumb to the cold? When do we stop talking rescue, and admit anything we do is about recovering bodies?"

Another silence.

"I won't offer false encouragement," Megan said. "Not to you or myself. But neither will I stop hoping. You'd have to know Scar. He'd try to find places where they could shelter, and the same ground features that make hunting for his group difficult might very well provide it."

Nimec didn't reply. He was conscious of the wind barreling outside.

Megan studied his face.

"There's more on your mind," she said.

He waited a moment, then nodded.

"Working with Tom Ricci these past couple of years . . . I suppose the way he thinks outside the box has started to rub off on me. Something about the rover disappearing, and then those people who went looking for it, makes me suspicious. Or maybe that's going too far, using too strong a word. It makes me *wonder*. I'm not sure about what. I figure the reason I'm not sure is there's probably nothing to it. But I've been on my job so long, I can't stop wondering. It's instinct. Doesn't matter where I am. Doesn't matter that it's pretty hard to imagine who'd want to make trouble for us here, interfere with what we're doing. Or how they could. I'm looking for answers when I can't even decide if there are any logical questions." He paused, moved his shoulders. "I wish I could put it to you straighter."

"You've been straight enough," Megan said. "I never disregard your instincts, Pete. We need to talk more about this."

"Yeah," he said. "But it's late, and I want to sit on my thoughts a little longer, give them a chance to work themselves out." He paused. "That's why I waited to bring them up."

Megan looked at him. The blowing wind and snow slammed aggressively against the window.

"I'm supposed to meet Annie for drinks," she said. "You can join us if you like. It might make the waiting easier. For you and me."

Nimec was quiet.

"Better not," he said then. "Don't think I'd be very good company."

She stood looking at him a few seconds, nodded.

"We'll be at the bar if you change your mind. You know where it is?"

"I can find it."

She nodded again, and started away down the silent corridor.

"Meg?"

She paused, half turned toward Nimec.

"I almost forgot to mention you run one hell of a lodge," he said.

Megan smiled warmly at him.

"Appreciated," she said.

Burkhart heard a cannonade in the southern distance: long rolling rumbles, a bellowy roar, then a rending crash. Someone less familiar with Antarctica might have mistaken the din for thunder, but that was an infrequent occurrence on the continent. Instead he knew it to be a berg calving from the ice sheet, its great tortured mass breaking off into the sea, the stresses of its division accelerated by the storm.

As the sounds continued rocketing across the sky, he set his full attention on the dome some eighty or ninety feet up ahead. His men waited at his sides, snow whipping around them, their snowmobiles left a short distance back. The vehicles would have made this final stretch of ground easier to cross, and Burkhart was convinced the wind would have muted the buzzing of their engines even if they had ridden straight into the center of the compound. Still, he'd taken no chances and ordered his group to dismount.

Given a choice, Burkhart would have vastly preferred the storm's assault had not coincided with their mission. But he had refused to be stopped by caprices of the weather, and decided what couldn't be helped might be turned to his advantage. For one thing, it reduced the likelihood of his men encountering base personnel—almost certainly they would shelter in until conditions improved. It was also just as well he would not have to worry about the observation cameras mounted high on the desalinization plant's dome. To his knowledge, no other Antarctic research base had *any* real perimeter surveillance, a measure believed pointless in an environment that gave natural safe haven from attack . . . and unworkable besides. Nor did the rest of the installations maintain defensive forces. While UpLink had broken with convention and done what it could on both accounts, the cameras were little more than token reminders. Scarecrows to frighten the birds away from the crop field. Having learned about them independently from Granger and the captive scientist, Burkhart had originally planned to steal past blind spots in their placement and motion patterns, and if necessary knock out those that presented the most serious threat of detection. He had been bothered by the thought that disabling them could trip an alarm and alert the facility's security contingent to his team's presence nonetheless, but that too had ceased to be a meaningful consideration.

Once he'd learned of the storm's approach, Burkhart had become sure it would incapacitate the cameras, and what he saw now supported his confidence. Cataracted with snow, their lenses stared outward from the roof of the dome like blank, blind eyes.

There would be nothing to come in the way of his entry.

His submachine gun held at the ready, he led his men forward through the battering wind. He estimated its speed at close to forty knots, strong enough to rock him on his heels—and the worst of the storm was still many miles and hours to the south. When its brunt finally struck, Burkhart realized travel of any kind would be out of the question.

His team reached the dome, circled to its slatted rolldown door, and gathered before it. Ever cautious, Burkhart paused a moment to glance up at a security camera, noting its white-filmed lens with reassurance. Then he bent, unfastened the door's wind locks with a gloved hand, grasped its handle, and raised it.

Recessed overhead lighting bathed the structure's interior in a soft, even glow. Burkhart entered with a quick step, Langern and three of the other men following closely, lowering the door behind them, the rest of his team taking watch positions outside the dome. After all he had led them through, knowing the dangerous return journey they faced, it was odd to consider they would only need minutes to execute their job. But something would have to go very wrong for it to take longer.

He scanned the enclosure from behind his goggles, listening to the continuous hum of working machinery. On a large steel platform, an array of three water-distillation, treatment, and storage tanks—their respective functions stencil-painted on their exteriors—was connected to an intricate mesh of pumps, intake and outlet valves, hoses, PVC pressure lines, and electronic metering and control consoles. A pair of wide main pipelines curved downward from the distillation tank through the platform and then deep into the ice underneath. These, in turn, led outward to branching feed ducts, where seawater melted by recaptured exhaust heat from the base's power generators was forced up through reverse-osmosis filters into the tanks.

It was a clean and energy efficient system, Burkhart mused. An *impressive* system. That he would have to cripple it gave him a strange twinge he'd experienced on occasion throughout his career as a soldier of fortune. Perceived but unidentified, the feeling would brush past him like a stray, vagabond brother who'd been missing since childhood, his existence nearly faded from memory.

And then, as always, it was gone. Burkhart stepped up onto the platform and called for one of the men to join him. An Austrian named Koenig, he approached briskly, well prepared for his role in the operation.

"Place the TH3 under here." Burkhart moved to the distillation tank's inflow pump, touched a hand to the metal plate over its motor. He thought a moment, then indicated the valve where the seawater pipeline connected to the pump. "And here. On these plastic lines as well. It will simply look as if the fire spread to them from the motor housing. *"Du seist das?"* He paused. "Be sure to give the charges a five-minute delay."

Koenig nodded, waiting to see if there was more.

Burkhart thought again, but decided to leave his instructions at that. There were bound to be heat sensors, an alarm of some kind, and his band would have to be away from here before anyone responded. They also needed time to see that their tracks were scattered as they retraced them, though much of what had been underfoot as they approached was blue ice, and he believed the wind would take care of the light imprints they'd made. The trick was to be careful of overkill, balance his objectives against the risk of discovery, cause sufficient damage to take the plant out of commission while making it appear accidental. As it was, the fire's rapid ignition and intensity would bring about considerable flooding beyond the initial destructive burst, even if automatic cutoff occurred when the pump went down—an interrupt mechanism Burkhart had no doubt would be in place.

Prompting Koenig to get to work, he watched him remove the pump motor's cover plate, then slip off his outer glove and reach into a belt pouch for a laminate squeeze tube of the type that might contain toothpaste or pharmaceutical ointment.

Koenig unscrewed its cap, pulled off its airtight nozzle seal, then ran the nozzle slowly over the motor's exposed wiring and components, pinching the tube between his thumb and forefinger to dispense a spare, smooth coating of its glutinous contents. Within seconds he'd moved on to the connector valve.

Although Gabriel Morgan had never said where he'd procured the incendiary material, Burkhart's independent sources had rumored that it was engineered in a now-defunct Canadian laboratory operated by El Tio, the head of a transnational underworld combine who was alternately rumored to be dead or in hiding. Wherever it came from, Burkhart knew the pyrotechnic solgel nanocomposite was a product of far-boundary chemical technologies.

Standard military-grade thermate—or TH3—was a fine granular mixture of iron oxide, aluminum, and barium that generated temperatures of between 5,500° and 7000° Fahrenheit when ignited, sufficient heat to melt through a one-half-inch-thick steel sheet, its combustive reaction producing a molten iron slag that could do further, extensive damage to metal surfaces and equipment. There were, however, quantitative and qualitative limitations to its precision usage. It required slightly over twenty-five ounces of TH3 powder to generate a forty-second burn of significant destructive yield, and conventional mixing processes resulted in somewhat heterogeneous and volatile compounds that could have inconsistent results. Because the distribution of ordinary thermate's constituents was uneven, a small amount was less reliable than a larger amount—much as a pinch of mixed salt and pepper might be noticeably short one or the other ingredient, while chances were an entire shakerful would not.

The solgel process synthesized—in essence, *grew*—thermate's molecular chemical components within a matrix of crystallized silica gel, encasing them in beadlike particles a thousandth of a meter in size. So uniform and energetic were the beads that each was like a microscopic incendiary grenade. For Burkhart's purposes, they had been implanted within a pH-neutral material that resembled soft putty and contained an ethylene glycol additive to lower its freezing point to minus-30°F, allowing it to retain its malleable consistency in ECW conditions.

Burkhart wondered how many infinitesimal thermatic particles were contained in a single drop of the material. Thousands, by fast estimate. Perhaps *tens* of thousands. The desalinization plant was going down, and even returning it to partial functionality would be no small feat.

Now he stood quietly as Langern climbed onto the platform and got a spool of timed initiator cord and clippers from one of his packs. When he finished applying the thermate putty, Koening helped him set the lengths of cord, snapped the plate back over the pump's motor, then looked over his shoulder at Burkhart.

"*Fertig,*" he said in German. "We're ready to ignite the material."

Burkhart looked at him, nodded.

"Do it," he said.

Zurich, Switzerland

The woman was taller than Nessa had thought she would be, slightly younger, but unmistakably English. She crossed the breakfast room of the hotel with the air of someone who knew her place in the world—at its pinnacle.

Nessa waited for her to pick up the menu before going over to the table. The corners of the detective's eyes scratched and her mouth was parched, but she knew those annoyances would vanish as soon as she opened her mouth.

"I beg your pardon," said Constance Burns.

"Yes, I suppose you do," Nessa told her. "My name is Nessa Lear and I'm with Interpol. No, thank you, sit here a wee bit, please," she told the woman, grabbing her arm firmly and pinning it to the table.

Burns's eyes seemed as if they might pop out and strike her in the face. Nessa flattened her right hand against the underside of the table, ready to overturn it if the bitch tried to get away.

Not that she would get very far. The building was surrounded by the Swiss police.

"My friends at the door there, the very handsome lads in the suits, are with the national police force," Nessa told Burns. "I'm afraid I've forgotten the German name for it, which they seem to use here; I was never very good with languages in school, and now going from French to German with English in between has gotten my brain in a twist. Plus I've had no sleep, tracking you down."

"Miss—"

"In a few minutes, my friends over there will take you away. You're wanted in connection with an inquiry in Scotland. Some accidents. Or murders. Definitely murders. But questions have been raised concerning shipments of depleted uranium, and I suspect they will be looking to you for answers."

Burns jerked her arm, but Nessa held it down firmly. She really was tired; she could feel the burning sensation in her muscle as she pressed against the table.

"Don't be in such a hurry," Nessa said. "I was hoping you might help me so that I could help you in your future life, such as it is. I'm seeking Marc Elata."

"Who is he?"

"A forger. A very good one."

Burns made a dismissive sound.

"Gabriel Morgan?" Nessa asked.

"The bastard. The bloody, sodding bastard!" Burns screamed, and pounded the table with her free hand. "He's left me to take the blame for everything, hasn't he?"

"Everything?"

Burns went silent. Nessa waited nearly half a minute before asking, "Nothing else?"

She waited a few more seconds, then waved over the Swiss detectives. Burns pulled her hand away as Nessa let go, holding it to her chest as if it had been hurt.

Maybe it had. It did look quite red. But perhaps because the two policemen who prodded her shoulders did not appear terribly sympathetic, Burns made no comment as she rose and walked from the room under their escort.

John Theiber, the Swiss liaison—a tall, wide-shouldered man with gorgeous blond hair—came over as they left, saying something in clipped German to the men before turning toward Nessa.

"Your office in Paris wishes you to call," he said in an English so perfect the Queen would have assumed he was one of her subjects. "A Mr. Jairdain."

"Thank you, Captain."

Nessa punched the number as Captain Theiber took a few steps away to accord her privacy.

Such manners.

"Jairdain."

"What's up?" she asked.

"About a half hour ago, we received a strange e-mail, *beaucoup* strange, sent to our public e-mail address," said the Frenchman. "It was from Elata."

"Elata?"

" 'Picassos at Castello Dinelli now. Quickly. Elata.' That's the message."

"That's it?"

"There's also a bank name and address, along with a number in America. We believe—I don't know if I have it correct, but the FBI liaison believes it is a safety-deposit box—a safe in a bank there. They are getting an order to have it seized. Louis is taking care of it."

Nessa looked over at the gorgeous Swiss. "Castello Dinelli?"

"An island castle in Lake Maggiore, at the Italian border. Near the border. In the fourteenth century—"

"We need to get there now," she said, jumping up. "That helicopter you promised—where is it?"

Hal Pruitt had thought landing Pedro Martinez in the pre-season draft to be the deal of a lifetime until it was finally cut, at which point he'd realized he couldn't live with himself for having gone ahead with it. As Captain Ahab had screamed from the *Pequod*'s bow moments before he went under with a long sucking sound, his topmost greatness lay in his topmost grief.

Pruitt sighed and leaned back in his seat, hands linked behind his head, elbows winged out to either side. He was alone at a computer console on the lower level of Cold Corners' main facility, only thirty minutes into his four-hour security/communications shift. In the heat of the chase, Martinez had seemed a bargain at any price. Still did, looking at it purely from the standpoint of what the

guy brought to his team's pitching roster. This *was* Pedro
here. Multiple Cy Young Award winner. A career earned
run average of two bucks, two and change. Maybe the
best arm since Koufax. Arguably the most dominating
modern-day pitcher in the game, though it was Pruitt's
steadfast opinion that Roger Clemens edged him out as
king of the hill by virtue of his stare-you-in-the-eye guts-
iness, ability to bear down in tight situations, and of
course his longevity. With eighteen major league seasons
under his belt and a zillion broken strikeout records, the
Rocket's critics could wet their diapers about his high-
and-ins all they wanted. He had *stuff* in humongous abun-
dance. That, and a plush red carpet waiting to be rolled
out for him at the door to Cooperstown.

Hal Pruitt guessed he liked Clemens better than anybody who'd ever fastballed a batter at the plate, which
was why he'd outbid the McMurdo Skuas by nineteen
dollars to pick him up for his own fantasy team, the Cold
Corners Herbies, this year . . . five dollars over and above
what he'd laid on the auction block for him the year before. Of course it didn't hurt that Clemens had been wearing a New York Yankee uniform in real-world baseball
since the '99 season, but that was another story. Sort of.
Anyway, Pedro was the issue right now. Pedro, whom
Pruitt had gone after like obsessed old Ahab stalking the
White Whale—*towards thee I roll!* Pedro, the final jewel
in his crowning lineup of starters, guaranteed to put his
team in position to outstrip the competition. Pedro Martinez, who also happened to be a star player with the real-
life Red Sox, hated arch-rivals of Pruitt's beloved Bronx
Bombers since the earliest hominid species emerged from
the steaming veldts of Africa to club stones at each other
across diamond-shaped patches of turf.

Pruitt leaned forward on his chair, his hands poised
over his computer keyboard like those of a master pianist
about to launch into some intricate concerto, thinking he
needed a nimble, delicate touch for the e-mail he was
writing to Darren Codegan, GM of the Palmer Base Pole-

cats, in an effort to make himself right with some kind of trade before the April 1st season kickoff. As he listened to the lunatic wind rattle outside the building walls, it was hard to imagine spring training was almost at an end within the neatly demarcated borders of civilization, where the sun went up and down rather than around and around in hanging circles. But the final exhibition games were in fact being played in Florida and Arizona, with home stadium groundskeepers getting their gorgeous green grasses groomed and ready for opening day. Pruitt knew he very definitely had to move fast.

He chose to believe that he looked at baseball with a capitalistic, pragmatic eye, treating it as a business that was more or less the same as any other. It was not without good reason that his Herbies, which he'd named after an Antarctic slang word for the very sort of hurricane/blizzard crossbreed that was now roughing up Cold Corners and the rest of his neighborhood, had won three consecutive on-line Ice League championships. If the other GMs in the league wanted to criticize him for raising the bar on individual salaries, fine. If they wanted to scoff at his handing over a quarter of his team's capped payroll to a single player, let them go ahead. Pedro was a unique talent. Well worth $65, plus Shane Spencer and a couple of AAA infield prospects from the Yankees farm system.

Pragmatically speaking, Pruitt thought.

The problem with this latest deal was that it had suddenly banged him up hard against the limits of that pragmatism. It was true some had called his attitude into prior question because of his tendency to stack his team with players who either wore, or had once worn, the midnight-blue pinstripes and interlocking NY on their caps—*see ya*, Kay and Sterling, oh, exalted voices of the New York airwaves—but again Pruitt knew this was because they possessed duller entrepreneurial minds than himself. These were the Bombers they were talking about here. Winners of almost thirty World Series titles they were talking about here. You wanted the best in the big leagues, you picked from the top of the heap, so of course his franchise was going to be something like ninety-five-percent Yanks. And what about his first baseman, Jason Giambi? Or Kenny Lofton in his outfield? Neither of *them* had ever called the hallowed Stadium home.

Pruitt released another deep exhalation. All would have been fine and dandy if Pedro hurled for Baltimore, Kansas City, maybe Toronto. Better yet if the Devil Rays or Tigers had been the ones to steal him from Montreal back in '98. But the fact was that Pedro Martinez pitched for Boston, the Evil Nemesis. And since a GM's victory in fantasy baseball was determined by his players' average rankings at season's end, Pruitt had put himself on a torturer's rack by acquiring him. Who was he now supposed to root for when the Yanks and Bosox had a Bronx blast or Fenway face-off? What if they were in a neck-and-neck pennant race come September? Despite Pruitt's quest to win that Ice League pot—which came to a sweet two grand—the pull between commerce and loyalty had gotten well nigh unbearable for him weeks before the first regular season crack of home-run wood even went echoing into the blue American sky. It was a sure thing six more *months* of it would sap his very will to live . . . especially because he'd been forced to give Shane Spencer, the Yank utility man who'd heroically worked his way back to the majors after suffering a right knee ACL tear, to GM John Ikegami's Snow Petrels over at Amundsen-Scott in exchange for the finances he'd required to close on the Pedro deal with Cadogan's thin-benched, low-slugging Polecats.

There was no way around it, he thought. Pedro had to be ditched. Spence had to be reacquired. A transaction had to be transacted. And Pruitt had the Machiavellian makings of one very clearly in mind.

Ichiro was the linchpin of his scheme. John Ikegami had dropped out of the frantic Suzuki auction in a frustrated snit, surrendering him to the Petrels after he'd emptied the last of his $260 purse on Hideo Nomo, Kozuhiro

Sasaki, and Tomo Ohka for reasons he adamantly denied had anything to do with matters of ethnic pride. Pruitt really didn't care about Ikegami's reasons for coveting Suzuki, who would be a valuable asset to any team in the league. It was enough just to know he *did* want him with a passion. Because now Pruitt was thinking he would dangle Pedro Martinez and the heavyweight bat Jason Giambi in front of Cadogan, provided Cadogan was willing to give Ichiro to Ikegami for Spencer, the two Yank minor leaguers, and a large handful of cash, all of which Pruitt would then get in *return* from Cadogan as part of a three-way swap. His purchasing power recharged, Pruitt would be able to go after a replacement starting arm to fill the hole left by Pedro. Maybe Andy Pettite. With Mike Stanton to strengthen his bullpen if there were some leftover funds. Either that, or he could see what the Air Guard Herkybirds over in Christchurch were asking for Jose Visciano.

Pruitt skimmed over the language of his message again. It could use some minor refinements, one more quick but careful pass before it was ready to go.

He lowered his fingers back onto his keyboard, and was about to make the first of his changes when a loud electronic warning tone grated from the console beside him, a row of color-coded chicklet lights to one side of his console blinked on in startling sequence, and the e-mail on his display screen was displaced by the base security program's automatic pop-up window.

Pruitt's response was practiced and immediate, his mind cleared of everything except for a task list that would need to be executed in a hurry. Bolt-erect at his station, he palmed his computer mouse, clicked to zoom, clicked again to recall and isolate an image, his eyes wide with rapidly building shock and astonishment as they confirmed what they were seeing was no bogie.

Less than fifteen seconds after the alert sounded, he flipped the redline radio switch on the panel beside him and got hold of Ron Waylon.

• • •

"It's the desalinization plant," Waylon told Nimec. He was breathless from his urgent hustle to the security station. "The images are from those FLIR thermacams behind the ceiling panels . . . ones we installed to replace the outside cameras when they went inoperational."

Nimec nodded tensely. He recalled Waylon showing him their locations during their base tour just hours ago, while explaining that his people hadn't yet gotten around to removing the weather-damaged external units. Both men were standing behind Pruitt as the thermal infrared pictures on his monitor shifted through their color palette. They could see four intruders—actually the spectral radiant heat signatures of four intruders—moving about inside the dome, heading toward the door. And Nimec knew that wasn't the worst of it.

"Look." He indicated three bright red streaks on the image, matching them against assigned colors on a horizontal measurement bar at the bottom of the screen. "Something's burning in there."

"Fires," Waylon said. "They have to be fires. And they're damned hot." He breathed, pointed. "Jesus Christ, looks like one's on an inflow pump . . . and over here, this is the seawater pipeline . . . I don't know what the hell's going on. . . ."

Nimec looked at him, his heart pounding.

"We're being hit," he said. "Pull together some men, we have to get out there *now*."

A long, narrow room on the main building's upper level, the Meat Lockers had metallic walls, bar, tables, and chairs that were washed with a reflective tungsten-blue radiance from overhead truss lighting to create a decor and ambience that wryly suited its name.

The crowd of off-duty ice people assembled inside was subdued but not altogether cheerless. Their awareness of the missing three was weighable as they marked the passage of the storm, but these were men and women whose rigorous living conditions demanded a unique spirit and adaptability, and it was understood that brooding would do nothing to help the situation. Morale was bolstered in different ways. During work rotations their stresses were redirected toward productive effort, a conscientious attendance to shared and individual responsibilities. And while it had been some days since anyone commandeered the small corner stage where they would showcase variable degrees of musical talent on better night/rec cycles—and sing karaoke when the prospects for diversion were lean— it seemed out of the question to concede that the fate of Scarborough's team had been decided. Hence, many of them continued to gather here in their downtime, drinking together, making small talk, amusing themselves, determined to carry on as well as possible in spite of their common fears.

Annie Caulfield sensed all this as she gazed across the room and watched a group of CC's staffers shoot their own idiosyncratic version of darts. With each successive round a moveable bull's-eye, striped red and white like the Geographic South Pole's traditional marker, was peeled off the board and reaffixed slightly further below center, mirroring the annual thirty-three-foot movement of the polar marker as it shifted with the ice cap. Eventually, Megan Breen had explained, the bull's-eye would meet the scoring ring and get stuck back in the middle of the dartboard.

Annie noted the game's out-of-whack humor with an appreciative smile, then turned back toward Megan to resume their meandering conversation.

"So I've told you how much it hurt when Pete backed off from me, and you've told me how much it hurt your FBI director when you backed off from *him*," she said. "Does that about cover things?"

Megan looked at her across the barroom table.

"The story thus far," she said. "Sounds simple."

"Mm-hmm," Annie said. "But *feels* complicated."

Megan nodded.

"I'll drink to that," she said.

"Here, here," Annie said.

The women raised their tumblers of Barbayannis Aphrodite ouzo, clinked, and took long sips.

Loose, glassy-eyed, they sat quietly at the table, picking away at plates of olives, sliced hydroponic tomatoes, and cheese to moderate the ouzo's strong licorice flavor and absorb enough alcohol to keep their heads barely afloat. At somewhere around eighty or ninety proof, the liqueur was CC's recreational drink of choice, perfect for shaking off the cold and remedying cabin fever.

"Anyway, here's a question. Well, actually two questions." Annie had snatched at a drifting thread of thought. "You've been at Cold Corners . . . how long now? Three months?"

"Three months, twelve days"—Megan paused, checked her wristwatch—"fourteen hours."

"Three months plus then." Annie said. "I'm curious . . . what's the one thing you miss most about home?"

Megan shrugged.

"Easy," she said. "My kitchen."

Annie flapped a dismissive hand in the air.

"Come on, be serious," she urged. "I'm asking as somebody who had hopes of being the first woman colonist on Mars."

Megan shrugged again.

"I'm completely serious," she said. "I like to cook."

"Cook . . ."

"And bake."

"Bake . . ."

"European pastries, especially croissants," Megan said, gulping more ouzo. Her voice was a little dreamy. "Maybe because making the crusts is such a challenge. About two years ago I had the kitchen professionally remodeled with all commercial appliances. My range is the *best*. It's one of those great big stainless-steel jobs . . . dual-fuel, you know. Six gas burners, an electric oven that keeps the temperature right where you set it."

Annie looked at her a moment. Then she suddenly ducked her head, clapping a hand over her mouth.

Megan leaned forward. *The damn ouzo,* she thought guiltily. There were more than a few staffers who could down it like lemonade without showing any effects, but poor Annie was a vacationer, only a few hours out of a helicopter from Amundsen-Scott. How could Megan have even *considered* suggesting that she order it?

"Annie, what's wrong? If this poison's getting to you—"

Annie shook her head in the negative, keeping it bent, still covering her mouth.

Megan's eyes widened at the stifled sound that escaped Annie's lips.

"My God," she said. "You're *laughing.*"

That was the final straw. Annie giggled helplessly, struggled to compose herself, and laughed even harder.

"I'm sorry," she said. "Really, I hope you aren't insulted—"

It was a no-go. She broke up again.

Meg looked at her.

"Okay," Megan said. "Out with it. What's so funny about my domestic interests?"

Annie waited until she'd managed to catch her breath. "Honestly?"

"Honestly."

"Picturing you in a kitchen apron sort of caught me by surprise." Annie wiped her eyes. "I just had the impression you'd yearn for Bay Area shopping or nightlife or something . . . that you'd prefer to get your desserts from a gourmet shop instead of a cookie sheet."

Megan realized she'd split a grin of her own.

"I'm not sure why, but something tells me I should be offended by that characterization," she said.

"Probably should," Annie said. "*I* would be, come to think of it."

The women faced each other, both of them laughing now.

"Annie," Megan said, "I've told you before and I'll do it again . . . your visit's been a *major* reprieve. This ladies' night out most of all."

Annie nodded, reached for her glass.

"I think we should drink to taking the big step," she said.

"From colleagues to friends?"

"In one drunken toot."

"It's going to be an unholy alliance," Megan said, and was about to lift her own drink off the table when her cell phone bleeped in her pocket—a three-note sequence she'd tagged to Pete Nimec's cellular only hours earlier.

She held up a finger to Annie, took out the phone, and flipped it open against her ear.

"Pete, hi," she said. "If you've changed your mind about joining—"

She fell silent, listening. Annie watched Meg's relaxed expression abruptly transform—the grave, alarmed look that came over it making her very worried.

"Yes . . . yes . . . *how could?* . . . okay, I understand . . ." Megan said. Her eyes snapped to the group at the dartboard. "Wait, I have some extra people with me. Stay where you are, we'll meet you right away."

She shut the phone with one hand, then glanced at Annie with dismay.

"We have a problem," she said, pushing herself up off her chair.

"Meg, I don't see how you expect me to use half these people. . . ."

"They can handle themselves."

"They've been *drinking.*"

"I know. That's just how it is. They weren't on rotation."

"But I need to rely—"

"I'm vouching for every one of them."

Nimec and Megan stood facing each other in silence. They'd linked up in one of the interconnected utilidors bored into the solid ice underneath the station, its hooded lights shining down on a tubular steel liner crusted with frost like the inside of a freezer, the temperature almost forty degrees below zero. Close around them, Sword ops were hastily shrugging, zipping, and snapping into their ECW outfits as they came pouring into the tunnel.

After a moment Nimec nodded.

"All right," he said. "Any suggestions about how to divide the manpower?"

"I've got two of our best with Annie and the Senators. I think we can spare four more to secure the area around the building."

"That's seven men," Nimec said. "Not enough."

"Eight men, counting Hal Pruitt."

"Still won't do."

"Our total force is twenty-nine, Pete. There are only so many places where anyone can gain access to the base, and I can't see anyone trying a full-scale action in this storm. It's not feasible."

"Maybe you're right. But we also didn't expect what we already *know* is happening, and I'm not about to gamble," Nimec said. "I say we double up the perimeter defense into teams, leave four men inside to guard against a breech. That leaves me with thirteen—"

"I'll go along with two men to patrol the building," Megan said. "You'll need the rest with you. And I've got the maintenance and support crew as backup. They're a solid bunch, Pete."

Nimec started to protest, hesitated, then nodded reluctantly.

"Your call again," he said. "Make sure Pruitt stays at the monitors. We need him to direct traffic."

"I understand." Megan thought a second. "How do you feel about informing MacTown of our status?"

Nimec adjusted a velcro strap at the collar of his parka, then got his gloves and outer gauntlets out of a pocket.

"I can't see how they can help us right now," he said.

"And I'm not sure I like involving outsiders until we have a better idea what our status *is*."

Megan sighed. "I don't know. We can't stand around doping this out. But there's an argument for contacting them. In case anything happens to us—"

"Do either of you want my take?"

This was from Ron Waylon, who had stepped up behind Nimec, his balaclava pulled over his head, the hood of his coat already raised.

Nimec glanced over his shoulder.

"Let's hear it," he said.

"There's no 911 help in Antarctica," Waylon said. "If we can't stand on our own, then by the time somebody responds, it'll be to bury us. Seems to me there's nothing wrong with holding off unless things start to look bad. No matter what, we'll have our chances to reevaluate."

They looked at him. Looked at each other. Both were nodding.

"Issue decided," Nimec said. His eyes steadied on Megan's. "You gonna be okay?"

"Yes," she said. And suddenly grasped his wrist. "Try not to let anyone get hurt."

He squeezed the back of her hand, pulled up his hood.

"That's the plan," he said.

Burkhart halted in the snow as he led his team toward their snowmobiles.

"Wait," he ordered, using his headset to communicate with them. Even raised to a shout, his unaided voice would have been overpowered by the wind. Yet he thought he'd heard a sound beneath its leviathan roar.

He wiped his goggles, peering back in the direction from which they had trod.

Someone other than Burkhart might have barely discerned the inverted bowl of the dome through blowing sheaves of whiteness. His keen eyes noticed a vague scintillation *behind* the dome . . . a paper-thin skim of light that seemed to be sliding toward him along the ground like a wide, flattened wavelet over the surf.

He thought briefly of the woman scientist.

There had been more backbone in her than he'd suspected.

He turned to his men.

"They know we're here," he said.

FIFTEEN

ELATA WALKED ONTO THE DOCK AS A DEAD MAN MUST walk—with great purpose and deliberation. The Italian's boat had taken him back to Astona, still in Switzerland. But the location did not matter. Morgan undoubtedly had people to trail him; this might even be part of his plan, not the Italian's. Elata would not get away, and did not intend to. He had already sent the e-mail to Interpol, using their public address obtained off the Web clipper service. He trusted that the note would find its way to the proper person; if it did not, a second one to the FBI in the U.S. was bound to.

The man guiding the Zodiac rubberized craft hadn't minded him using the pager as they sped toward shore, nor had he reacted when Elata threw the device into the water.

What became of the notes and what the police did in reaction to them no longer concerned him. He had a few Swiss francs in his pocket, enough to buy a small note-book and a pen from the stationer he found two blocks away from the dock. There was enough change for a large coffee at the cafe next door. Wanting privacy and feeling somewhat considerate—surely Morgan's men would be here at any minute, and he didn't want to trouble the patrons—he decided to sit outside despite the brisk breeze. Elata took a long sip of the strong, black liquid, then began to write.

"Today, God has proven to me that he does exist," he wrote on his pad. He labored over the words; he was a painter, not a writer, and even if he was merely writing the truth, he had difficulty letting it flow.

"He has shown how petty man is. Or no, how petty and evil *some* men are. I must include myself among them. For until today I did not fully understand the potential man has, or what he should truly aspire to. I did not understand how good and evil coexist and do battle always, nor the importance of—"

Elata looked up. A man in a hooded blue sweatsuit stood a few feet from him. A newspaper was folded over his hand; beneath the newspaper, a slim, silenced .22 pistol.

Elata nodded. The paper jerked upward and he heard the sound of a bee swarming around his head. The buzz turned into the drone of a Junker Ju 86; as he slid forward against the table, his eyes were filled with tears, not because of his pain or regret at the way he had lived his life, but because he saw the images Picasso had drawn once more as he died.

The old castle sat in a gray circle of water roughly equidistant from the shores, its large stones a defense against time as well as human enemies. The brigands who had built it used it not so much as a hideout as a depository; they had bought off anyone with power enough to storm or starve the island fortress, and needed only a place that could be secured against fellow thieves.

Morgan's needs were more complex. Eyeing the castle from the forward seat of his Sikorski S-76C, he considered whether it wasn't time to leave Switzerland for an extended period. The latest messages from Antarctica presaged failure there, and even if the Scottish matter unfolded in a suitable manner, there might be unforeseen repercussions.

He had to congratulate himself for being an agreeable three or four steps ahead on both counts. Clearly the Scots were befuddled. The misdirected uranium would be found in a rusting hulk in Glasgow harbor. Not *the* misdirected uranium, of course, not even a portion of what had actually been diverted. But enough to close out any investigation successfully. His agent, meanwhile, would arrange for a last accident as directed; with luck she would be apprehended, implicating Burns, not him—a precaution arranged by the expedience of using the inchworm's identity for all contacts in this business.

As for the inchworm herself: She would meet with a regrettable air mishap en route home this afternoon, when the private aircraft Morgan had supplied her would mysteriously disappear at sea. Suitable portions would be found at a respectable interval several weeks into the future.

Thus would a host of problems be solved even before they became problems. The situation in Antarctica remained considerably more complicated, but he could afford to be hopeful there as well; nothing on the continent directly connected him with the venture, with the exception of the easily disposed of e-mail account.

As a precaution, however, he should leave Switzerland, at least for a while. His money could only purchase so much tolerance. One of the former Soviet Republics would afford safety; he had places in Iran and Peru prepared. But could he live in any of them?

He wanted to return to America, with its free air and ready indulgences. Even to go to a place like Thailand or Malaysia, where he could live like a king—what would be the point? If it meant giving up greater glories, the chances of appreciating moments like the one that lay ahead of him, what would be the sense?

"Boat's clearing," said the pilot.

"Very good."

His men in the speedboat, carrying off the professors. He had actually considered keeping them alive—he did owe them a debt of gratitude—but in the end, he judged that this treasure was simply too valuable to jeopardize. The two men would not reach the shore.

The fact that Elata had been treated differently by the Italian bothered Morgan. His men, of course, would find him, but it raised the possibility—distant but distinct—that this was an elaborate fraud and that Elata was involved in it. It would be foolish to try to cheat Morgan, but men did foolish things all the time.

The Italian was no doubt halfway to Milan by now. He might as well go to Antarctica, for all the good that would do him if the Picassos proved to be fake.

The helicopter pitched its nose downward, passing over the fortress twice. Morgan's men had already searched it using IR sensors; they'd swept it for booby traps and neutralized the electronic surveillance system. What they hadn't done was establish a suitable place for a helicopter to land. The castle covered the entire island; while there were two courtyards, neither was particularly large, and the pilot feared he'd damage the rotors on the side wall even of the biggest.

"I can take you back to the shore and meet the speedboat," suggested the pilot.

"Not viable," said Morgan. "I'll climb down."

"Long way to go, even if we had a ladder," said the pilot. "Which we do not."

"The boat landing then."

"I can't get in with those rocks."

Morgan considered waiting for his people to finish with the professors. But every night—and every morning, and every afternoon—since meeting the Italian, he had taken out the photocopies and reexamined them. He had decided beyond question to keep the bull and the infant; he suspected, in fact, that he might eventually decide to keep them all. Fifteen million dollars was a minuscule amount of his fortune. Compared to the true worth of the paintings, it was laughable.

If they were real. Elata and the others had said they were, but he had to see himself.

"Get as close as you can and I'll jump. Hover over the boat landing."

When he was younger, Morgan had been a good enough athlete to play first string soccer through college. He still worked out every day and, largely because of his stomach problems, was not horribly overweight. But the wash from the helicopter blades and the craft's jittery approach nearly unnerved him as it hovered near the wall. The Sikorsky's stowed landing gear made it impossible for him to climb down, and while the pilot was able to get closer than he'd thought to the wall, there was still a considerable distance between Morgan's legs and the stones as he lowered himself out the doorway.

But he remembered the face of the child. Holding his breath, he let go.

Morgan landed on the smooth stone ramp, a good two feet from the edge of the water. He tottered forward, but easily regained his balance. There was more room here than it seemed from the air, he decided. Ignoring the pain in his ankle, he walked up the ramp into the empty castle.

The paintings were in the small courtyard, ahead on the left. His heart began pounding heavily, his feet slipped, his head buzzed.

Smaller than he imagined, though he had pored over every detail beforehand, the paintings stood on cheap wooden easels in staggered rows at the middle of the twenty-by-ten-foot atrium. His glimpse of the first left him disappointed; the perpendicular outline of the lantern outline in the teeth of the horse played poorly against the boldness of the flaming background.

But his next step took him in view of the child. Morgan felt the mother's hand clawing with despair, grasping for the last breath draining the infant's lungs. The baby's eyes—top closed, bottom fixed upward—took hold of his skull. Morgan took another step and felt his senses implode.

Who could have faked such work? No one, not even Elata.

He walked to each canvas as if in a dream. He touched each in succession, running his fingers around the edges of the canvas, tracing the edge of the stretcher at the back.

My God, he thought—war provoked this. Violence begat such awesome beauty.

The helicopter revved outside. Morgan remained fixed, lost in a trance. Finally, after he had seen each painting again, after he had absorbed each one's beauty and ugliness—yes, of course they contained ugliness, they had to, as man possessed good and evil—he took each with great care and placed them in the vinyl cases the Italian had left. Then he made seven stacks, and carried two out toward the helicopter.

The pilot had put out his landing wheels and managed to perch at the edge of the ramp. The rotor continued to turn, albeit slowly.

"Help me!" Morgan yelled as he struggled with the door.

"I've got to hold the aircraft," shouted the pilot. "We'll slide into the water if I don't."

Morgan carefully slid the paintings into the rear of the craft.

"There are twelve more," said Morgan.

"Wait!" the pilot yelled as he started to go back. "You have a message—a radio message."

"What?"

"Here." The pilot handed him the headset and then fiddled with the radio control. Morgan, leaning into the helicopter, put it on.

"What?" demanded Morgan.

"The Swiss have arrested Constance Burns," said Peter. He must still be aboard the boat—Morgan could hear the motor's drone in the background. Of course—they would be running south for Italy, having panicked and initiated the backup plan.

So be it. They were small insects who could be dealt with at a more convenient time.

"Danke schön," said Morgan simply. "Thank you very much." He reached to pull the headset off.

"Interpol was involved," said Peter, flustered by his employer's nonchalance. "The Kommando der Flieger has been alerted."

"Danke," repeated Morgan, removing the headset. Swiss Air Force or no, he would take every Picasso from the castle. He clambered back across the ramp, losing his footing because the spray from the helicopter made the rocks slippery. He dropped one of the paintings on the way back, held his breath as it careened toward the water, propelled by the wind. It smacked against the wall, pinned there until he retrieved it.

"Turn off the rotors," he told the pilot when he reached the helicopter.

"We'll slide into the water."

"I'll take the chance," he told him.

"We may not be able to take off."

"Turn them off," said Morgan in a voice so strong it could have killed the engine on its own.

The heavy drone of the Aérospatiale Alouette III's Turboméca made it nearly impossible for Nessa to hear the transmission, so even if she had spoken German and could have deciphered the heavy Swiss accent, she would have had trouble understanding what was being said.

The ever-helpful Captain Theiber, sitting in the rear compartment behind her, had no difficulty, however. In his calm baritone voice, he supplied a concise interpretation when the transmission was complete.

"Two jets from Fleigerstaffel 8 have taken off from Meriringen," he said. "That's north of us. A pair of trainers from Magadino are airborne as well. They are propeller-driven, but they should match a helicopter. And a liaison is contacting NATO. Herr Morgan will not escape."

"I'm confident," said Nessa, though she felt anything but. Having rallied such vast resources, she had better end up with something in her net besides the gorgeous scenery.

And a case of airsickness, which had started to creep up her esophagus.

"The lake," said the pilot.

The edge of a blue-green bowl opened in the white and gray ahead. A town, two towns, lay to the right. The pilot had the throttle full bore—they whipped forward at just over two hundred kilometers an hour.

"Ten minutes," predicted Theiber. "Less."

"The PC-7's will approach from the west," said the pilot, pointing in the distance. "Castello Dinelli will be straight ahead."

Nessa leaned straight ahead, willing it to appear.

Morgan's ankle had started to swell and his knees were deeply bruised from his falls by the time he slid the last painting into the helicopter. He had to shove his chest to the side awkwardly to get into the craft, which was listing and had its left forward wheel underwater. The pilot's frown did not lift as the rotors whipped into action; he wrestled with the controls as the aircraft began bucking violently.

"Go!" commanded Morgan.

"I'm trying," growled the pilot.

Morgan buckled his seat belt and leaned against the seat as the helicopter pitched upward. Falling on the rocks had temporarily fatigued him, but as he thought of the paintings he now possessed, his characteristic bonhomie returned. "Now, now," he told the pilot. "Come—you'll be richly rewarded. Let us fly back to Zurich now."

The helicopter trembled for a few moments more, but began gradually to lift steadily. The pilot's frown faded.

Then a dark cross appeared a bare meter from the windshield and the Sikorsky lurched sideways to duck it.

"Shit! Don't ram them!" shouted Nessa. "Tell them not to ram him!"

The two Pilatus PC-7's buzzed in front of the Sikorsky so close, it seemed as if one of the wings would clip the rotor.

"It's under control, I'm sure," said Captain Theiber. He leaned forward and put his hand on her shoulder.

A few minutes before, Nessa would have reached up and touched his hand with her fingers. But the captain's tone suddenly felt patronizing.

"Can you reach them on the radio?" she asked the pilot, ignoring Theiber.

"That switch," he said. "The international emergency band." His own hands were busy—he ducked the Alouette to the right as the Sikorsky began skittering away from the two orange-red Swiss Air Force planes.

"Helicopter leaving Castello Dinelli, this is Interpol," said Nessa. "You are ordered to follow the directions of the Commando Fliers."

"Kommando der Flieger," corrected Captain Theiber over the circuit.

"Yeah, thanks." Nessa flicked his hand off her shoulder. "Follow our directions and you won't get hurt. You are to follow us back to the Magadino airport."

The Sikorsky began powering away southward. It was a civilian version of the American Blackhawk combat helicopter, and its twin turboshafts could propel the helicopter more than twice as fast as the Alouette—and in fact could give the two small trainers a decent run if its maneuverability was used correctly.

It was not, however, in any way a match for the F-5E's the Swiss Air Force had scrambled, which chose this moment to close from the rear.

"You're surrounded. Give up," said Nessa. "Mr. Morgan can't possibly pay you enough to die for. We can arrange a deal, I'm sure."

Morgan punched the radio with his fist. Interpol? How in God's name had the inept bastards traced him here?

"We have to land," said the pilot.

A silvery-gray object whizzed down from overhead, whipping across the lake in front of him. The helicopter pilot threw the Sikorsky around, heading back toward the castle. Another helicopter, probably the one with the woman who had been speaking to them over the UHF band, was heading for them.

"We have to land," repeated the pilot.

There were always contingencies; there were always escape routes. When the Americans had closed in on him for that tax nonsense, he had found a way to get out. There would be an escape now.

Morgan thought of the eyes of the child in the painting. One closed, one open.

"The jets are firing at us," said the pilot.

"Fly into the helicopter," said Morgan, pointing ahead. "Into it! You're insane."

"They'll veer off," he said. "The jets will back off."

"And then?"

"Then we will think of what to do next."

"He's heading right for us!" Nessa shouted as the Sikorsky came on.

They were low to begin with. The pilot veered to get out of the way, and the aircraft's doors and rotor blades practically touched the lake.

"Get the sodding buggers!" said Nessa, clenching her teeth against the rising bile.

For three hours, the German bombers attacked Guernica. First they hit it with explosives and firebombs. The people of the town fled into the nearby fields, seeking shelter. The planes followed them there, strafing victim after victim, the aircrews laughing as the bullets danced into the bodies. Red blood pooled everywhere. There was no escape.

Morgan would not be captured. It was not a matter of spending time in prison, or being paraded around as an international prize. He would not give up the Picassos.

"Where do you want me to go?" asked the pilot calmly as the other helicopter veered away. Castello Dinelli sat in the water about a half kilometer away. "Should we land back near the speedboat dock, or follow them all the way to Magadino?"

"Neither," said Morgan softly. "Go for the castle."

"It's fifty meters away. Then what?"

In answer, Morgan slipped the small Glock from his belt and shot the pilot twice in the head. His body slumped forward, but the aircraft continued ahead, its trajectory edging slightly downward but still aimed at the stone walls.

It was not the contingency he had wanted, but there was the consolation of having owned the Picassos, if only for an hour.

Nessa watched the Sikorsky slow as it approached Castello Dinelli.

"I think they're going to try to land on the castle island, maybe in one of the courtyards," she said.

The Sikorsky glided toward the yellow stone rampart, its nose tipping lower. It seemed to hesitate, then slide to the left, then crumple into a red burst of flames as it smacked into the wall.

"No!" shouted Nessa. "No, no, no!"

The only answer was a spray of black and red as the Sikorsky's fuel tank exploded.

SIXTEEN

COLD CORNERS BASE, ANTARCTICA
MARCH 13, 2002

NIMEC HAD OWNED A MOTORCYCLE WHEN HE WAS IN his twenties, and had rented a snowmobile on two separate winter vacations with his ex-wife and son. Riding them was similar, but it could be dangerous to think they were exactly alike. A snowbike's lower center of gravity demanded a light touch when you leaned and cornered. There were differences in surface traction speeding across snow and ice. And you had to keep your feet on a snowmobile's running boards, avoiding the habit of kicking one of them out for balance. That was bad enough on a cycle because it could easily hit a road obstruction; it was worse when deep snow might drag hold of you, tearing up an ankle or knee.

He was not a man to make foolhardy mistakes.

Waylon's experience qualified him for the lead position, and Nimec had jumped his machine out of the util-idor's exit ramp right at his back, the others following in single file as Cold Corners One vanished behind them in a swirling curtain of snow.

Nimec thought about their next move as they approached the dome. He couldn't make assumptions about his opposition's force size or resources. He didn't have time to worry about their reasons for striking at the base. But their strike's *intent* was clear; they'd stuck it to one of the CC's critical life-sustaining functions, and the immediate question was what they would do next. Whether they would break for it, or wait to ensure that the bleeding they'd inflicted wasn't stopped.

He gripped his handlebars, plunging directly into the teeth of the wind, his knees bent against the snowmobile's metal flanks, its powerful engine vibrating underneath him. The best he could manage was a guess, and that guess would determine his tactics. Meaning it had damned well better be a good one. So what *did* he know about the men who'd hit the water-treatment plant?

The important things weren't hard to deduce. He didn't know where they'd come from, but there was only cold desolation for miles around. Since they hadn't popped out of a hole in the sky, he presumed they must have traveled a very long distance. Someone would need extensive skill and knowledge of the terrain to manage that under the best of circumstances, and in this storm it would be incredibly rough going by any means. In fact, it would have seemed unthinkable to Nimec just a small packet of minutes ago.

Whoever these people were, they had already demonstrated themselves to be capable, selective about their target, and committed to taking it out. Above all, they had shown they had moxie to spare. They would count on the weather getting worse before it got better, know it would be impossible to remount their strike, know they only had one real shot. Nimec thought it apparent that they'd hoped to accomplish their mission on the sneak—but say they had a notion they'd been discovered. They definitely would've had to contemplate it. Would men of their caliber and determination withdraw before they were positive of success?

Nimec wondered about it a second. Would *he*?

"Waylon, you reading me?" he said into the voice-activated radio headset under his hood.

"Loud and clear."

"How far to the dome?"

"Close," he said. "Under a thousand yards."

Nimec was taken by surprise. That was much *too* close. He couldn't see anything past Waylon's tail, and had no intention of rushing in blind.

"Okay," he said. "Listen up. Here's how I want to do this. . . ."

Snow splayed around Burkhart's bike as he brought it to a stop. The dome was just ten or fifteen yards to his left, its tetrahedral planes and angles smeary in his vision.

Straightening in his seat, he listened to his men move into position around the dome and then abruptly cut their engines. He thought he could see gray scribbles of smoke issue into the flying whiteness from the hair-thin spaces between the dome's lowered door and doorframe.

Burkhart stared out toward the base. The low wave of light he'd spotted before had fragmented, but that did not mean it had ceased advancing. His eyes narrow behind his helmet shield, he looked over his right shoulder. Was that a faint, rippling trace of it out there?

He believed so. As Musashi had written in his *Book of Five Rings,* it was better to move strong things from the corners than to push at them straight on. From what Burkhart had learned about the enemy through his intelligence sources, they would know this as well as he did.

His Sturmgewehr across his chest, Burkhart watched, listened, waited. The mission had strayed far from his intentions. He had wanted to get in, deliver a clean blow, and get out. That he was now heading toward an engagement meant he'd very seriously stumbled. No good could come of it—but there was also no retreat.

Burkhart waited in the rampant storm. Then, suddenly, he once again became aware of the swelling, pulsing sound of engines under the wind's louder clamor . . . this time coming from all around him.

The corners were closing in.

The dark smudges of smoke Burkhart noticed outside the dome were no trick of the eye.

Behind its roll-down door, his solgel incendiaries had ignited with brilliant, white-hot slashes of flame, instantly reducing the desalinization unit's flow-pump motor to a tarry mire of fused steel and plastic. The pump quit with a shudder, chuffing out acrid, concentrated fumes that bleared the dials and alarm lights on its control panel as they floated past. Bristling vines of fire circled its butterfly inlet valve and coiled over the meshwork of low-pressure PVC pipes around the water tanks. They seared, sagged, and blistered, their melted plastic segments springing distorted fish-mouthed leaks, showering the dome's instrumentation with jets of distilled water. Raw seawater began flushing from the main pipeline, pouring down onto the tank platform, running over its sides. The smoke rose, spread, seeking fresh air. It eddied against the door, slipping through its weather seals in thready wisps.

Out in the wind and snow, Burkhart continued his waiting game.

Further away, Pete Nimec and his men pushed their snowmobiles toward the dome as quickly as they could. Nimec did not think getting inside would be easy, but still he hoped they might have time to somehow prevent the machinery that produced Cold Corners' entire usable water supply from becoming severely maimed.

He didn't have a shot.

The moment Burkhart had put his combustive charges in place, time had run out.

"Sir—I've spotted some of them."

"Where? I can't see a thing."

"A little ways ahead of us," Ron Waylon said. "I'd guess maybe forty, fifty yards. At about ten o'clock."

Nimec kept Waylon's blaze-orange parka in his head-lights as he whirred along behind him. He had mostly gotten the hang of the snow bike, but the bare ice patches that would come up on it without warning kept threaten-ing to rob its skis of traction and wrench the handlebars out of his grasp.

He squinted through his goggles.

"You said *some?*"

"Right—"

"How many? Still can't see anything . . ."

"I'm not sure. There could've been three, four. They were on bikes. Moving. Wearing winter camouflage." Waylon paused. "The bikes were white too," he added.

Nimec thought a moment. His instincts had been right.

"We made *more* than three of them inside the dome," he said over the com-link. "Looks like it's how I figured. They've deployed around it."

"Looks like," Waylon said.

Nimec swooped on toward the dome, a guy named Mitchell pacing at his rear, the rest having split off at his direction.

"Okay, both of you reading me?"

He received two affirmatives in his earpiece.

"This is it," he said, then let go of his right handgrip to reach for the weapon strapped over his shoulder.

The dome to his near left, Burkhart was still poised to throttle his snowmobile into action when one of his float-ing patrols hailed him over their radio link.

"Kommandant, ich sehe sie."

It was Langern, at the opposite side of the water-treatment facility.

"Wie viele?" Burkhart replied.

"Mindestens drei Männer. Sind auf rotes Schneemobi-len."

Burkhart clicked his teeth. At least three men had been sighted. On red snowmobiles.

As he'd suspected, the enemy had broken up into harrier teams.

"*Schätzen?*" he asked.

"*Ungefähr fünfzig meter östlich.*"

Burkhart tasted adrenaline at the back of his tongue. The machines Koenig had reported were approaching from fifty meters to the east.

His alertness notched to its utmost level, Burkhart looked over his right shoulder, glimpsed the noses of two more snowmobiles through the snow—these speeding toward him from a westerly direction.

It further confirmed his assessment of the enemy's diversionary tactics. But he had no doubt their main thrust still would be reserved for the dome's entrance.

"*Lass keinen näher kommen,*" he ordered, thinking that they had gotten close enough.

Much about Antarctica was alien to Nimec, but he would have recognized the sound of automatic gunfire anyplace on earth.

The initial burst came from approximately where Waylon had seen the snow bikes, its distinctive crackle carrying across the distance even in the high, wild wind.

His opponents were throwing themselves into an outright confrontation, forfeiting stealth to delay his Sword ops from reaching the dome.

The nasty little cold war they'd initiated had just gotten very hot.

Nimec mentally bold-faced a decision that he'd known had to be. Sword was a civilian security outfit whose international presence was licensed through a clutter of separate arrangements with UpLink's host governments, most of them skittish about having armed foreigners on their real estate. Nonlethal threat response was Sword's option of first choice, and its techies had developed a collection of ingenious suppressive tools toward that end. Nimec's operatives were not cowboys on horses riding the range in search of desperados. But he had never allowed them to be victims-in-waiting either. Their rules of engagement were right in line with those followed almost universally by police and military forces. Deadly fire was to be returned in kind.

It made things stickier in theory that Antarctica was a piece of real estate unlike any other, *demilitarized* by global pact, everybody here supposedly living a harmonious coexistence, one big happy human family, their baser impulses and ambitions renounced. But in practice it didn't change a thing.

Nimec's people were under attack, taking *fire,* and getting killed by a bullet was the same the world over.

Gordian's words surfaced from recent memory: *They can't always be protected from violence. But we have to keep our watch.*

"Guns on max settings," Nimec told his men over their comlink.

He pressed a stud over the trigger guard of his own compact variable-velocity rifle-system assault weapon, an action more than slightly hampered by his thick cold-weather gauntlet. The baby VVRS, as Tom Ricci called it, used embedded microelectromechanical circuitry to switch the gun's muzzle speed between less-than-lethal and deadly-fire modes with a touch. At the low-speed setting, its subsonic rounds would remain enclosed within plastic sabots designed to blunt their penetrating capacity. Shot from the barrel at a higher pressure, the frangible sabots petaled off to release 5.56mm tungsten-alloy cores that struck with the murderous force of standard submachine-gun ammunition.

Now there was another spatter of fire, closer than before, barely up ahead.

Nimec heard a gaining whoosh from over to his left, and snapped his eyes in that direction, but saw nothing except dense, whipping white fans of snow.

And then, suddenly, the whiteness bulged out at him.

"Everybody, heads up—"

That was all Nimec had time to say.

His semiautomatic rifle raised, spitting angrily, Burkhart's storm-rider made his pass.

The half-dozen men Nimec had chosen for the fire-suppression team advanced on the dome, their bikes pushed to top speed against the wind, treads slinging up snow in rapidly collapsing arcs. Strapped to their backs were eighteen-pound canisters of FM-200 and inert-gas flame extinguishant. As instructed, they'd locked their VVRS rifles into man-killer mode.

They'd expected a fight, knowing their access to the dome would be blocked regardless of whether their cover teams managed to draw off the opposition. What they did *not* yet know was how much resistance they would have to tackle . . . but that was certain to become evident in short order.

They glided on, the curve of the dome rising before them, tendrils of smoke scratching into the white around it.

Then they saw snowmobiles crossing the flat, open span of ground between themselves and the water-treatment plant, a row of machines spreading out to the left and right in bow-wing formation.

The fire-out team's designated leader, a veteran of Operation Politika named Mark Rice, knew the score the instant he observed their widening pattern of movement.

"Scatter!" he shouted into his mike. "They're trying to outflank us!"

Nimec had a chance to register the bike coming on fast from his left, darting out of the snow, its rider a blur as he triggered his first rounds, then sharpening in his vision like a wraith assuming form and substance.

The Sturmgewehr rattled out a second volley, and Nimec banked sharply off to elude its fire, leaning hard into the turn—almost too hard. He overbalanced, keeling his snowmobile sideways, but somehow managed to recover an instant before the bike would have leaped out from under him, spilling him from his seat as its handlebars wrenched free of his grasp.

Nimec heard the whine of his pursuer's engine from behind now, and glanced over his shoulder, wind slapping his masked, goggled face. The rider had stayed at his right rear flank, his sleek helmet visible behind fluttering tapers of whiteness. His throttle was wide open, and smoke spewed from his exhaust into the sheering wind.

Nimec swung evasively again as his pursuer's gun barrel emitted a third staccato burst, staying looser, trying not to fight the machine.

This time he held it in control. Gliding clear of the gunfire, he saw sugary powder gout upward where the bullets intended for him pecked the ground, felt what he thought might have been flying, splintered chips of ice lash across his coat sleeve.

His eye caught a flash of orange ahead of him—Ron Waylon's coat—and then glimpsed the streaky white uniform of another apparitional rider hurtling at Waylon, the two of them engaging, maneuvering around each other, dueling in snow-spraying, cat-and-mouse circles.

Several yards to Nimec's left, the figure of a third attacker had swung toward Mitchell at a full tear. Mitchell launched his bike's front end off the ground like a motorcyclist pulling a wheelie, one hand on its rubber grip, then started firing VVRS rounds over the top of the rider's windshield. The rider sprawled from his seat, his helmet visor shattered and bloody.

Nimec raced on straightaway, trying to put some distance between himself and the man at his back. Then he heard a prolonged exchange of fire between Waylon and his opponent stitch rhythmically through the wind. For an interminable moment both were lost from sight, surrounded by a spreading, churning cloud of kicked-up snow.

A shrill scream. Plucked away by the cheating gusts.

The gunfire stopped.

"Waylon, you all right?" Nimec exclaimed into his mouthpiece.

Silence over his radio. The snow cloud drifted milkily in the unsettled air.

"Waylon, do you copy . . . ?"

Nimec was still moving rapidly on his own bike, no more than fifteen seconds having elapsed since the riders launched their attack. He turned back to see the one on his tail accelerate and pull alongside him to the right, staring at him through his tinted visor, the bore of his Steyr rifle practically in Nimec's face.

His heart knocking, his fingers easy on the bike's left handlebar grip, Nimec flicked up the baby VVRS with his right hand, leveled it, released a tight spurt of ammunition. Blood boiled from the rider's chest and he flew from his seat, landing spread-eagled in the snow cover, his bike careening off in a skidding, plowing, crazily weaving run.

Nimec returned his attention to where he'd last seen Waylon just as a white cammo snowmobile came shredding out of the cloud of raised snow, riderless, its headlights blown out, its chassis studded with bullet holes. It plunged ahead for the barest of moments, then flipped over twice to land on its cowling and handlebars, the wraparound windshield breaking away, its upended skis pointed skyward on their extended struts.

Waylon in his headphone: "Okay here, sir."

Then Mitchell: "Check."

Nimec breathed hard, and took hold of both handlebars again, his weapon hanging from its shoulder strap.

"We better get on over to the dome, see what help we can be there," he said.

"I'm sorry everyone's been inconvenienced, and realize most of you were pulled out of bed," Megan Breen was saying. "But as you know, we've received a fire alert from one of the outbuildings. It's our normal practice to gather all non-base personnel into a single area during occurrences of this sort. Having you in one place benefits our ability to coordinate a response."

Annie Caulfield, Russ Granger, and the entire Senatorial gang of three looked at her from their respective chairs in the small, pleasantly furnished common room provided to guests sharing Cold Corners' DV accommodations.

It was now fifteen minutes since Pete and his men had gone out into the storm to face God only knows what kind of threat, and Megan was thinking that if she could somehow get this next piece of business done without revealing her agitation, she could probably keep a grip on herself through anything.

Still in his robe and slippers, Bernard Raines wrinkled his face, snuffling as if he'd gotten a whiff of something foul.

"You say a fire," he said. "I hope it isn't serious. For the sake of your people's well-being, of course." He cleared his throat. "It seems to me getting outside assistance in the storm would be difficult."

Megan responded to the fear in his eyes.

"I appreciate your concern, Senator," she said. "But a strong point of pride throughout UpLink International's entire organization is that we're very good at avoiding disruptions to our operations in any environment. That's especially true for those of us stationed at Cold Corners— our contingency planning staff takes its responsibilities very seriously."

Bravo, Meg, Annie thought, listening to the exchange. *Couldn't have finessed that one better myself. It even might've topped my interview performance on the McCauley Stokes Show.*

Raines had almost reassembled his poise.

"Why, yes," he said. "I see what you mean. And we have the highest regard for UpLink's capabilities." He looked around at his fellow Senators and waved his hands in an expansive gesture. "That's speaking for everyone in my party, I'm sure."

Both of his colleagues were nodding.

"I suppose bringing us together in here was only prudent," Wertz said. "A sensible precaution." She paused, crossing her arms. "Without making too much of it, though, when do you think the alert condition will be called off?"

Megan looked at her.

"That depends on when we hear from our firefighting team," Megan said. "With a little luck we'll have you safely and comfortably back in your quarters tonight . . . before anyone gets too homesick for civilization. Then we can all relax and can get some sleep."

Across the room, Granger sat quietly in his chair. The redhead was as cool and slick as the block of ice she probably snuggled up to at night. He wasn't sure how much she knew about the fire's cause. But she would at the very least know where it had broken out, and was minimizing its impact to the politicos . . . which made him wonder what else she realized and was keeping to herself.

Granger crossed his arms, feeling a chill in his stomach despite the more than adequate warmth of his surroundings.

He felt neither safe nor comfortable, and sleep was the furthest damn thing from his mind.

Phil Corben wanted to know how he'd gone from a night of beer and darts at the Meat Locker to lying outside in the cold to die.

Thrown face-down off his bike, snow mashed into his eyes, nose, and mouth, halfway burying him where he'd fallen, the flesh under his insulating garments damp with blood from his monstrous gunshot wounds, Corben *wanted to know.*

It wasn't that he was muddled about the events that had brought him to this point. Although his wounds had left him slack and disoriented, he could have recounted what happened in something very close to a coherent, sequential order. There wasn't that much to it . . . he'd sped toward the water-treatment dome with Rice's squad, and the men who'd set fire to it had rushed to meet them, and the shooting had started, and he'd gotten in the way of a burst of bullets.

Easy to follow.

The problem for him was believing it was all *real* as opposed to being part of some grotesquely implausible nightmare.

He didn't understand why this was so. At thirty-two years old, Corben had already taken his disproportionate share of hard knocks. In fact, adversity had fairly well cleaned up on him—his daughter Kim succumbing to childhood leukemia when she was just five years old, the breakup of his marriage afterward, and then, months before he'd retired from his U.S. Naval EOD command and hitched up for a civilian post with UpLink on the ice, losing three of his best friends and teammates to an accidental chopper crash as they were returning home from land-mine-disposal operations in Sierra Leone, a humanitarian United Nations effort that had been a trip to the beach until their MH-47 Chinook troop transport went down due to unexplained engine failure.

While experience had taught Corben the futility of seeking reasons for the calamities that far too often slammed people on their heads, he'd gone on looking for them just the same. Maybe because bad luck didn't seem a good enough explanation for him, or mostly didn't, and he'd needed something else—if not necessarily better—to carry him through his days and nights.

Sprawled deep in snow, choking on his own blood, blown from his bike like a shooting-gallery duck, Corben desperately wanted to know how any of what had happened *could have* happened. How he could be about to perish from an act of brutal aggression here in Antarctica. *Here.* The one place where he'd envisioned finding an outer calm and stillness that might somehow penetrate his troubled heart, and where he was instead leaking blood from a chestful of bullet holes.

Figuring there probably wasn't a chance he'd get his reasons even with another hundred years tacked onto his life, Corben still wanted more damned time to hunt them out . . . and now suddenly wondered with a kind of dazed, stubborn truculence if he had the giddyup to keep his pursuit going maybe, *maybe* just a little while longer.

Blood slicking his trigger-finger mitten shells, Corben tried to raise himself on his elbows and forearms, pushed his chest up out of the snow a few inches, then sank into it again—but not before managing to turn over onto his back. He expelled thick clots of blood, snow, and snot from his nose and mouth, feeling glassy particles of flying snow drill into the weave of his balaclava as they cascaded relentlessly down from the cloud sheet. You gave and you got, he supposed.

He could hear bikes swerving around him, see sparkles of gunfire at the corners of his eyes, see smoke puffing up into the turbulent sky overhead, and knew the white-suited men who'd come out of the storm like mechanized ghosts were continuing to hold Rice and the others off from the dome. The longer they hindered the squad's entry, succeeded in keeping their arson fire burning, the less of the plant's equipment would be salvageable.

Corben rasped in a miserable breath of cold air and turned his head from side to side, trying to locate his fallen VVRS. The pressurized red cylinders of fire-extinguishant and oxygen he'd been lugging on his back rig were bedded together in snow over to his left. Fine and dandy. But what about the weapon? Unable to see it, he reached out his arms, began probing the snow around him with tremulous hands, thinking it might have gotten hidden somewhere under the surface.

It was then that Corben became aware of an engine sound in the gale—the unmistakable buzz of a snow bike.

He lay on his back and groped more urgently for his weapon as the buzzing gained in volume, using his bloodied mitten like a rake, scrubbing it over the snow cover . . . and at last made contact with something thin and hard and smooth.

Corben glided his hand over the object, knew he'd found his VVRS, and brushed away the granular deposit covering it. He was desperate to scoop the weapon out of the snow, get it fully into his grasp. The bike was very close now and he *needed* it in his grasp.

And then he had it. His fist around its stock, he snatched it up with a huge swell of relief, clutching it against his body almost like someone who'd rescued a cherished pet from drowning. But that was only for a moment, and he wasn't about to congratulate himself. Things were moving too fast, the bike approaching with what had now become a roar.

Corben slipped his finger around the sabot gun's trigger, angled its barrel upward. The baby VVRS only weighed something like ten pounds loaded, but felt heavy as a cannon in his weakness. He was sure he didn't have the strength to keep it raised.

Not for very long.

Perhaps ten seconds elapsed before the snow bike finally swept toward him through the blinding whiteness, bumping to a sudden halt just a few feet away.

Staring up past his gunsight, Corben lowered the rifle, once again overtaken by acute relief.

The bike was *red*, its rider wearing a parka shaded a little closer to orange.

He hopped off his seat, knelt, bent close to Corben. All around them guns were still firing

"Phil," the rider said, and looked Corben over carefully. "It's all right, don't worry. Gonna have to get you on my bike, strapped onto my grab-rail. Then we head back to base, okay? Your fighting's done, I'm taking you out of it."

Corben recognized Cruz's voice through his face mask.

"Tie me up, Sam," he said, nodding faintly.

•   •   •

Burkhart was also ready to pull out of the fight.

He raced evasively astride his snowmobile, followed close on by an UpLink rider, wishing only to end the chase and extract his men before any more of them lost their lives. Considering the dimensions of his blunder, they had gotten off cheaply having taken just three casualties. But the dome's entrance had been blocked long enough, and their job here was done. They had struck at the UpLink team's corners, only to be outflanked themselves, a countermove that hadn't surprised or daunted Burkhart. The thick smoke pouring from the dome told him the flames inside would have devastated its crucial desalinization apparatus—and that had been his single objective. He had no interest whatsoever in continued one-upsmanship.

It was time to finish things.

Squeezing fuel into the snowmobile's engine cylinders, he leaned partway from its saddle, swung the Sturmgewehr around in his gun hand, and pressed back its trigger. The gun clapped fire at the red bike behind him. There had been two in pursuit moments ago, but he had been able to shake off one of them, losing it after a pitched, breakneck series of evasive maneuvers.

The rider who'd stayed on top of Burkhart was better than the other by far.

He kept right with him now, surging up from behind, swerving to avoid Burkhart's stream of ammunition, lifting his own weapon above his handlebars to release an answering salvo.

Burkhart heard lead rounds chew at his rear bumper, felt the percussive rattle of their impact. Bits of the snowmobile's pocked, gouged chassis spewed up around him.

Finish things, he thought.

Bent low behind his windshield, he opened the bike's throttle, accelerated with a rush, and then sharply jerked into a full turn, swinging around to face his pursuer, applying the brakes with gentle pumps of his fist, aware he would tailspin if he worked their lever too hard.

Burkhart could feel his suspension rods quiver from stress as the bike hauled to an abrupt stop, its skis swashing up thick billows of snow.

His feet planted on the boards, he straddled his seat and poured a continuous volley out of his submachine gun, his fire cutting through the encompassing whiteness, aimed directly at the snowmobile coming head-on toward him.

The move caught his harrier off guard. The UpLink rider slewed, tilted high onto the edge of his right ski, then was flung from his bike as it suddenly ran away from under him, overbalanced, and tipped sideways into the snow yards from where he'd landed.

Burkhart released his brake lever, launched forward, brought himself to a second jolting halt in front of the thrown rider, and jumped off his bike.

The UpLink man was badly hurt. Dumped onto his right side, his leg bent where it shouldn't have been— broken in at least two places below the knee, Burkhart saw—he struggled to pull himself out of the snow, rolled off his hip, and somehow got into a twisted semblance of a sitting position, his VVRS still in his grip.

Burkhart rushed toward him, kicked the weapon from his hand before he could fully bring it up, retrieved it, and pointed his own gun at the rider.

The men looked at one another in silence, their eyes meeting through their dark goggles for the briefest of moments.

Then Burkhart pivoted away from him, scoured the back of the overturned snowmobile with sustained gunfire, riddling the gas tank with bullets, puncturing the spare fuel container on its rear rack. Mixed gasoline and oil blurted greasily into the snow.

Burkhart flicked a glance back over at the injured rider.

"Man kann nie wissen," he said.

You never know.

A moment later he shouldered his weapon, turned to remount his snowmobile, and radioed out the order to with-draw.

As he approached the dome, Nimec heard the chatter of a baby VVRS to his left, and snapped a look through the flowing whiteness. He saw blood erupt from a storm rider's chest, then saw both bike and rider capsize into the snow. An instant later, the Sword op who'd done the shooting sped over to where one of his teammates had been downed by the storm rider, got off his snowmobile, and crouched beside him, shaking his head in horrified denial.

Nimec braked and sat absolutely motionless, pods of snow bursting in the air around him. He heard a choked-back cry from the kneeling op, and was grateful when the wind pulled it away.

Even from a distance of some yards, he knew it was too late for the guy's partner. His goggles were shattered and most of his forehead was gone.

"I can't believe this." Waylon had slid up beside Nimec and was staring out at the bloody scene. "It's just so hard to *believe* this. . . ."

Nimec said nothing. It was hard, yes. And the decision he needed to make was harder still.

He turned and peered straight ahead at the dome. The smoke lacing from its entrance hadn't abated, but the fire-suppression squad was almost there now, riding toward it unopposed. And although he could hear sporadic bursts of gunfire at their fringes, CC's mounted attackers had vanished from sight.

Nimec unexpectedly thought of the day that he and Meg had first talked to Tom Ricci about joining up with UpLink, on a spring afternoon a year or so back. They had met with him at his place in Maine, and were on his deck overlooking Penobscot Bay when a bald eagle had soared from a nearby tree, prompting every other bird in sight to flutter off into nowhere, all of them dispersing at the same time.

"It'll generally stay quiet for five, ten minutes after she's gone," Ricci had remarked. *"Then you'll see the gulls, terns, and ducks come back, sometimes a few at a time, sometimes hundreds of them at once, like there's been an all-clear."*

Nimec felt an odd twinge. He supposed this was his day for recalling other people's words.

"They scattered," he said. "Just like that."

Waylon glanced out toward the dome, then faced Nimec.

"The men who hit us," he said with understanding.

Nimec nodded.

"They did what they wanted. And now somebody's given them the word to retreat."

Waylon looked at him.

"We have to go after them—"

"No."

"No?"

Nimec gave him a second nod.

"We don't know how many of them are out there, where they came from, or where they might be planning to hole up. Probably don't know a bunch of other things that I haven't thought of, and that we ought to know before flinging ourselves into a manhunt. And our priority's to safeguard the base," he said. "Besides, the storm's getting worse. It'd be craziness to have our people riding blind in it."

Waylon kept looking at him.

"What are we supposed to do?"

Nimec hesitated a moment.

"Call off our troops and put out the fire," he said, then juiced his engine and went racing off toward the dome.

The fire-suppression agents carried into the water-treatment dome by CC's Sword ops shared the capacity to arrest intense flames without leaving a damaging residue on sensitive computer and telecommunications equipment—an almost certain collateral effect of foam or water. Both nonconductive formulations were certified environmentally green, and as such had gained approval for use on the Antarctic continent.

These important similarities apart, each possessed separate and unique properties.

FE-13 was the commercial name for trifluromethane, a cryogenic substitute for Halon, which had been banned from global production in 1989 for its ozone-depleting qualities. Stored as a liquid in an airtight steel container, FE-13's minus-115° Fahrenheit boiling point meant it discharged as a colorless, odorless gas that would lower the temperature of exposed areas to levels that were too cold to sustain a burn.

Inergen was a blend of argon, nitrogen, and carbon dioxide gas that quite literally strangled flames in an enclosed space by depriving them of the oxygen they fed upon, while leaving sufficient O_2 for humans to breathe. Though it had been proven effective in fixed systems where a facility's normal air ventilation could be closed off as Inergen was dispensed—the very sort installed in Cold Corners One—the base's scientists and support personnel had been evaluating its value as a firefighting accessory that could be used on the move, both in conjunction with FE-13 and as a possible backup. The key had been to develop special ultra-high-pressure canisters that held and released the mixture in sufficient concentration to dampen a blaze where airflow *couldn't* be easily inhibited.

Until now their redundant firefighting technique had been successful only in controlled trial conditions.

It performed as well as anyone could have hoped to put out the dome blaze.

The fire-out team converged on the desalinization plant even as their white-clad opposition swept off into the storm, leaving them with unimpeded access to its entrance. Flameproof Nomex cowls pulled over their balaclavas, breathing masks covering their noses and mouths, oxygen tanks on their backs, they rushed into the smoke-

filled space in practiced fashion, holding their extinguishant cylinders in front of them, nozzles hissing out their
gaseous contents.

There were several things going in their favor as they
waded across the dome's flooded interior to the central
platform. Its power generators had kicked into automatic
shutdown, eliminating the threat of electric shock. And
the sickly yellow-gray fumes that filled the dome had
started brimming out into the cold as soon as its door was
raised, sucked away in churning, convection-induced fun-
nels. The enclosure cleared of smoke fast, allowing them
to work their way over to the water-treatment unit in bare
seconds.

The fire they encountered was intense but contained,
and already doused in numerous spots by the water that
had poured in torrents from the seared, ruptured flow
lines. It took just over three minutes to get it under control, another one or two to smother the last of its hot
orange blooms.

Unfortunately, it was obvious to every man present that
the critical harm had been done long before they arrived.

Nimec and Waylon climbed down off their bikes and then
stood in the entry to the dome, staring at the mangled
desalinization equipment within as reeking dregs of
smoke flitted toward them and were skimmed raggedly
away into the wind.

"It's a mess," Waylon said. "A goddamned mess."

Nimec looked at him.

"Where does this leave us?" Nimec said.

Waylon was silent a perceptible while. His gaze did not
move at all from the drenched, smoldering equipment.

"I haven't got any idea," he replied at last.

Darting through the tempest on his snowmobile, leading
the surviving members of his team back toward their sheltered camp, Burkhart weighed his operation's failures

against its successes and tried to determine on which side the balance fell.

His assigned goal had been met; he had ravaged the desalinization plant. Perhaps not irreparably destroyed it, but that was never the plan. His blow to the UpLink base never had been meant to be mortal, just sufficiently forceful to make its tenants concentrate on nursing their open wounds.

That was all on one side of the scale. But what about the other?

He had lost four of his best. He had exposed himself, revealed what was supposed to have looked like an accident to be a manned attack . . . and as a consequence assured that UpLink would have its hounds out in force once the storm relaxed its grip on the coast.

It would be acceptable to Burkhart if they only came after him—he was a professional whose occupation demanded putting his neck on the line. What was more significant, however, was that he had opened a path to their learning the truth about the whole Bull Pass endeavor.

Where did the balance of success and failure fall?

He knew the answer, knew he could not *hide* from it.

Its opprobrious weight hung heavy as a mountain on his back.

SEVENTEEN

PETE NIMEC'S FACE BETRAYED NO EMOTION AS HE looked down at the five zippered white body bags laid out on the floor of the utilidor. The line of four to his right bore no name tags. A fifth, set apart from them, did.

It read: *Sprague, Wm. Sword ID: 45734-CC12.*

Disturbing as it had been for the men to bring their casualties here prior to evac, it had made undeniable, practical sense. And in Antarctica practical considerations were always the last word.

Like all of the base's subsurface tunnels, the utilidor was twice as cold as a morgue refrigerator compartment, which would be typically kept at 40° Fahrenheit. Indeed, its temperature more closely matched that of the super-freezers used in cryogenic preservation banks, making it ideal for its current purpose.

Consistent with USAP and Antarctic Treaty rules, Cold Corners' strict waste-disposal procedures required that all refuse generated by human habitation, including byproducts of laboratory experiments, effused motor oil and gasoline, food scraps, paper wrappers, plastic and metal throwaway containers, bodily excreta, sanitary napkins, condoms, contraceptive sponges, and any other rubbish that could not be recycled on-site, was to be either compacted and baled, or sealed away in large drums for transport off the continent. Some of the retrograde—as prepped waste is called on the ice—was then repositoried near the airfield in rows of milvans, trailerlike metal storage containers manufactured for loading aboard military cargo ships.

Because the flights that carried away the discard arrived with irregular frequency during austral summer—and in winter months arrived not at all—the volume produced by CC's inhabitants often exceeded the storage capacity of the milvans. At such times, all retro except segregated toxic chemical, medical, and biological waste was brought down into designated utilidor chambers, which allowed for its interim cold storage in conditions that prevented decomposition and posed no threat to health or the environment.

In practical terms, frozen human remains met the definition of retrograde to the letter.

Nimec turned to see the strapping figure of Ron Waylon come up beside him. They exchanged a serious glance. "How's it going at the dome?" Nimec asked.

Waylon made an indeterminate gesture with his shoulders.

"It'll be a while before I can tell whether we can get the pump back in action." He offered a bleak smile. "Wish I'd known what was in store when I went and bragged about us being good at patching things up."

"Say we can't get it running," Nimec said. "What then?"

"Good question," Waylon said. "I've ordered a replacement unit, but the whole system's manufactured to spec in California. The components have to be assembled, shipped, installed, and operational before our freshwater reserves run out." He shook his head. "It cuts things awful close."

"Maybe closer than we can stand?"

"Maybe," Waylon said. "And that's with crisis usage restrictions in place. No way around it, sir, we're in a scrape."

Nimec grunted, then stood in quiet thought.

"Okay," he said. "What about those volunteers I wanted?"

"The men should be down here soon," Waylon said. "They're getting a Delta out of the garage to move the bodies out to the airstrip."

"You hear anything from the comm tech . . . Huberman, that his name . . . ?"

Waylon nodded.

"Clay Huberman," he said. "He verified the transport aircraft are on their way. A pair of de Havillands out of Punta Arenas."

Nimec looked at him. "That's Chile. And aren't those planes little eight seaters?"

Waylon nodded again.

"Twin Otters," he said. "They're flown by a private Canadian outfit that specializes in polar aviation, does a lot of contract work for NSF. Everything from ferrying around researchers to rescue operations. The crews really know their stuff. Brought that doctor out of South Pole station last winter—"

"That's not the point. The 109th Guard was supposed to handle this from Christchurch. We were expecting a Herc. I *asked* for Captain Evers . . . he's somebody we can trust."

"I know, sir. But the weather's still spotty around Herbie Alley—that's out on the South Sea between Black Island and White Island—and it doesn't look like anybody's going to be able to take off from Cheech for another couple of days."

Nimec dropped his eyes to the body bags and then raised them back to Waylon's face.

"There's no rush for these men," Nimec said. "And if it's only a short time, we can adjust our drinking water rations so the Senators won't have to worry about getting too thirsty. They'll just have to give up their showers and smell as bad as the rest of us."

Waylon was momentarily silent.

"This isn't a decision we can make here on base, sir," he said then. "When it comes to emergency extractions, it's Air Force, NSF, and Department of Interior who get together for the call." He paused. "They've got other considerations. Besides the weather or even our water plant going down, that is."

Nimec looked at him. "What else is there?"

"Clay tells me it's the solar flare activity NASA's been making a fuss about. National Oceanic and Atmospheric Admin's been consulting with them, thinks it might pan out sometime over the next week. I guess the main concern is that flights could be grounded indefinitely if it's severe enough to foul radio communications. The bottom line is they want the Senators out right away."

Nimec shook his head with displeasure.

"NASA," he muttered. "We've got too many cooks standing over the pot. And I don't like it."

Waylon was quiet again. He appeared to be waiting for something. Nimec couldn't tell what it was, but figured the base chief would get around to letting him know.

Meanwhile, he had his own preoccupations.

"Those twin-props," he said. "How soon they arriving?"

Waylon thought for a moment.

"The trip's got two legs," he said. "It takes about five hours for the planes to cross the Strait of Magellan. Then they stop at Rothera station out at the western tip of the peninsula."

"That'd be the Brits, right?"

"Right," Waylon said. "They're being about as helpful as we could ask. The most accessible place to refuel's a depot outside their base, and Rothera's providing a thousand gallons." He moved his shoulders. "After the layover, I'd figure the second half of the flight to take another dozen hours."

Nimec rubbed his chin.

"Okay," he said. "The situation's what it is, and we'll make the best of it. But I don't want any passed balls. As far's what went down here during the storm, the only thing the Senators know is there was a fire at the dome and we lost one of our men putting it out. And that's all they need to know. When they climb aboard their plane, I don't want them seeing these four"—he indicated the untagged body bags—"loaded onto the other prop. If they do, and ask us about it, we've got no choice except to tell them the truth. UpLink depends on government support. There are relationships we have to protect. If we're seen as not honoring them, we might as well pack our suitcases and go home. Here and everywhere in the world."

Nimec left his explanation at that. Waylon seemed to know the stakes well enough on his own.

He also seemed to be still waiting to say something. And having a hard time getting it out.

"What haven't I covered?" Nimec asked.

Waylon was quiet another few seconds.

"About Sprague," he said then, struggling to control his emotions. "We want to give him some kind of service."

Nimec looked at Waylon. How could that have failed to occur to him?

"Sure," he said. "I mean, *of course.*" He expelled a breath. "Is there a chaplain on base?"

Waylon shook his head.

"MacTown has a fella who tours during the holiday season," he said. "That's about all." He was thoughtful. "A lot of us on the ice, we get to feel religious without observing a particular religion. I don't know why that is. Or maybe I do and can't express it just right. But being here kind of shaves the differences between people. You step outside the buildings and tunnels, look at what's around you, what nature's really *about,* and you realize nobody's any bigger or smaller in the big picture than anyone else."

Waylon swallowed, then looked down the white spun-bonded bag containing his deceased comrade.

"We want a service, but don't know what the hell kind we're supposed to give him."

Nimec was thoughtful in the cold silence of the utilidor chamber.

"We'll figure something out," he said.

Nimec was in Megan Breen's office minutes after arising from the utilidor, his ECW outer garments doffed and stashed in a clothing locker.

"You get a callback from Gord yet?" he said.

Megan regarded him across her desk.

"Yes," she said. "And he's heard from the Secretary of State."

"What's Bowen's reaction to what happened to us?"

"I suppose it falls somewhere between worry and utter astonishment," she said. "But he's conceded that we're best able to deal with it ourselves for now."

"Conceded?"

Megan nodded.

"He isn't happy about it," she said. "In the view of the United States we're a commissioned government outpost that has come under enemy attack. At the same time, Article 1 of the Antarctic Treaty bars, and I quote, 'all military activities, including weapons testing' from the continent. It goes on to make an exception for military personnel and equipment used for scientific purposes, but that's not pertinent. What is, is that the treaty was reinforced by the '91 Madrid Protocol on Environmental Protection . . . and that they combine to put DoS in a logistic and political quandary. The U.S. doesn't have a ready force anywhere close to us that could launch an effective search and counterstrike. And this is so off the board, no one's ever contemplated a straightforward mechanism that would allow America to launch an armed venture."

Nimec grunted.

"Not knowing who came at us makes it more complicated," he said. "You have to wonder whether it's a foreign government or an independent operator. Maybe even the same sons of bitches who put out a hit on the boss."

"Agreed," Megan said. "But let's not jump ahead of ourselves. The outcome of Gord's conversation with State is that we got what we wanted. They're staying out of our way on this. Sword has been given an endorsement to act with broad discretion safeguarding Cold Corners against further threat, and it's come from the highest level of government."

Nimec looked at her.

"Deputy Pete," he said.

Megan smiled thinly. "Something like that."

Nimec nodded.

"I'm going to snag Russ Granger right away," he said. "He had the snow-movers digging out his helicopter even before the wheels-down order was lifted this morning. Looks like he intends on flapping back to McMurdo, but there's no chance he leaves base without taking me out over the Valleys like we planned before the storm."

"However you choose to play it," Megan said. "Under the circumstances—now that there's no question we have enemies here—I thought you might elect to use one of our own pilots."

Nimec shook his head.

"Not for the overflight," he said. "You told me yourself that Granger knows the lay of the land better than anybody. And when I think about where those men in white came from, a big arrow pointing straight to Bull Pass flashes in my brain. If they're down there and a bird with UpLink markings passes, you can bet they're ducking for cover. Better they see one whose feathers they recognize and figure is harmless."

"Which makes Russ's NSF chopper perfect, since he does Dry Valley runs all the time."

"Yeah," Nimec said. "I wouldn't have to tell him anything's changed as far as the reason for our flyby. And it *hasn't* really changed. How it looks to me now, I find the opening to a wolf den out there, I find where Scarborough's team got dragged."

Megan mulled that a bit, then gave him a nod.

"All right," she said. "What's next on our discussion list?"

Nimec hesitated.

"Before I came up here, I was in the utilidor with Waylon. Where we brought the bodies," he said. "Waylon reminded me that we don't have a clergyman to say anything for our man who was killed in the attack. When we send him off on the plane."

Megan looked at him.

"Bill Sprague," she said.

Nimec nodded.

"I promised we'd take care of it," he said. "But I'm no good at words. And I don't know that I'll be back from the Valleys before the flights leave."

Megan sat in quiet thought.

"It's okay," she said. "I'll preside. That's how it should be."

They fell into momentary silence again. Then Nimec gave her a nod.

"I'd better suit up and get hold of the whirlybird man," he said, pushing back his chair.

Megan was watching him as he rose to leave. He noticed her steady attention and paused in front of her desk.

"What is it?" he asked.

"Just thinking," Megan said.

"Uh-huh. I kind of figured."

They looked at each other.

"Well?" he said.

"It's something that's probably none of my business," Megan said.

"Oh," Nimec said. "So whose business is it?"

Megan took a breath, released it.

"Yours," she said. "And Annie Caulfield's."

Nimec stood there without saying anything.

"Pete, I'm sure it isn't news to you that Annie's flying out with the Senators," Megan said. "Good with words or not, you should talk to her before you leave. Or you'll miss your chance."

They were both silent, their eyes in solid contact across opposite sides of the desk.

"My chance," Nimec said finally.

"Yes."

"To talk."

"Yes."

"To Annie."

"Yes."

Nimec stared at her, his throat going dry all at once.

"About?" he said.

Megan waited to answer, looking at his nervous face, the barest suggestion of a smile on her lips.

"That's up to you, Deputy," she said.

"It's not that I don't want to help you," Granger said. "I'm wishing like hell I still could help. But with the herbie slamming us as bad as it did, and our field camps trying to get their heads up above the snow, MacTown's depending on me to check up on them."

"You can do it when we're out," Nimec said. "Seems to me that was almost exactly our original plan. I ride peter pilot while you make your rounds. And you detour us into the valley south of the notch."

Granger regarded him briefly, and then turned to watch a large rumbling dozer clear the chopper pad where his Bell remained half immersed in snow. Somnolent and dusky with winter's near onset, the cloudless sky under which they stood seemed entirely incapable of spewing the fury it had heaped upon the coast for the past three days.

"Flying isn't the problem," Granger said. "It's ground conditions that won't be the same now. Depending on what the camp teams need in the way of assistance, we could be stuck for hours every time I put her down."

"I can wait, give you a hand," Nimec said. "Our side trip won't take that much time."

Granger stood thinking his thoughts, his gaze following the bulldozer as it made a slow rolling circuit of the pad.

Nimec tried to understand his sudden hedging.

"Listen," Nimec said. "I realize you've got bosses with their own priorities. And that they must be edgier than usual because of the storm. But we can send them one of our own pilots if that's what it'll take for you to be available." He paused. "If Megan calls them, makes an official request, I guarantee they'll listen."

Granger watched the dozer's lowered scoop fill with snow and push it up high into one of several building mounds.

Nimec didn't press, giving him a chance to think things over.

About a minute later Granger faced him again.

"It's better she doesn't talk to the top dogs . . . you know how even the easiest solutions can get picked apart," he said. "We ought to stick to how we already worked things out."

Nimec looked at him.

"You saying we're on again?" he said.

"On," Granger said. "And keeping it between ourselves."

Nimec nodded. He didn't care how they did it, just as long as they were going.

"Whatever works for you," he said.

Bull Pass

Burkhart listened to Granger over their black phone line—and when Granger stopped talking, did not waste a moment telling him what needed to be done.

Granger wasn't surprised. In fact, he seemed quite ready.

"I set this up, take care of this thing, it'll be dangerous

for me afterward," he said. "You'll have to get me away from here. Off the continent . . . maybe to South America. And I'm going to need money. *Geld*. Plenty of it. We can decide on a figure later. What's important is that everything has to move very fast. *Sehr schnell*. That's how you say it in your language, right?"

Burkhart rubbed a fingertip over the mark on his cheek. The pilot was a low creature of venality and deceit. But then, where was his own claim to gallantry?

"Execute your task," he said. "I will see to the rest of the arrangements myself."

He terminated their call, put down the phone, and sat exceedingly still in his heated metal booth, the sounds of the subterranean mine loud around him.

The machines were grinding.

Sehr schnell.

EIGHTEEN

COLD CORNERS BASE, ANTARCTICA
MARCH 16, 2002

HIS PISTOL WAS A BERETTA 92 NINE-MILLIMETER, TOP
of the line, with a stainless-steel barrel, black-matte finish,
low recoil, and open-slide action. The same side arm used
by the U.S. armed services, it couldn't be beat for accuracy and reliability.

A handsome weapon.

Granger had never fired it except on practice ranges,
never killed anything bigger than a rabbit in his life. He
guessed that he was decent enough with a handgun, a
better shot than your average person, although popping
holes in a cardboard target that came gliding toward you
down the lane was a far cry from taking out a human
being. Or most likely was. The peculiar thing was that
Granger had found himself without any moral or emotional constraints about the ruse he'd worked out, a setup
that would have completely unstrung him once upon a
time.

Sure, he'd hoped it wouldn't be necessary. Granger
liked the money he was making hand over fist from the
Consortium. He liked being where he was, and the free-

dom of living on the ice—liked his freedom, *period*—and got a little bothered knowing he would have to lose his income stream, jeopardize his personal safety, and go on the run. But he'd banked plenty over the last few years, heaped up a nice financial cushion in numbered Swiss and Cayman Island accounts.

His concern was whether the snare would work. Conscience, guilt . . . he just didn't harbor those feelings. In fact, he'd discovered that part of him, a strong part, actually enjoyed running all the way home with the devil.

Peculiar thing.

Seated in the cockpit of his Bell chopper, Granger carefully adjusted his parka, tugging and smoothing it until he was confident the side-arm holster underneath made no visible bulge. An hour had passed since he'd agreed to give Pete Nimec his ride in the sky, a bit less since he'd phoned Burkhart on his secure mobile phone, and Granger was about ready to charge up the bird. He had laddered through all the routine steps of a preflight systems check, looking over the gauges, video displays, and digital readouts on his control panel, inputting coordinates into his onboard GPS unit, testing his navigation and communications equipment. Outside, the cleanup crews were still making a racket with their bucket loaders, but most of the storm's dumping of snow around the pad had been hauled off. Now Granger was only waiting for Nimec to return from Cold Corners One, where he'd gone to wrap up some unspecified last-minute affairs.

Granger had tried to figure out what it was about the UpLink crew that had irritated him from the day they broke ground in Antarctica and that now gave an undeniable appeal to the proposition of his sticking it sharply into their gut. Whenever he thought it over, his mind would turn back to something one of the old VXE-6 Ice Pirates he'd known had told him right around the time their unit was being dissolved. What the guy claimed was that he and a couple of his flyboy buddies had decided their ceremonial good-bye to the continent would be to stroll off a ski way on their final Herc run, squat down, and empty their bowels right there on a patch of ice, leaving behind freeze-dried commemorative monuments that would last longer than any footprints they could make. In fact, they would probably last forever.

Granger wasn't sure if the crewmen had ever gone ahead with their distinctive hail-and-farewells, or if it was the sort of notion that would have occurred to them after too many beers in a Cheech watering hole and been forgotten once they sobered up the morning after. And he supposed that wasn't important. It was the idea itself that had stayed with him. Granger remembered finding it funny in a crude sort of way. But there was also something more than a little bitter about it, something almost contemptuous, that had caused Granger to believe those flyboys had been eager for a parting shot. He hadn't known at whom or what. Maybe the cold hell they were vacating. Maybe their superiors and Air Guard replacements for making them feel expendable. Maybe all three. He'd really never cared enough to wonder or ask.

What Granger did know was that thinking about UpLink always left a comparably bitter taste in his mouth. He resented the fawning treatment they received from the Base Commander and NSF Directors at McMurdo, resented their instant prestige on the continent, especially resented how everybody jumped when their redheaded bitch-in-charge clicked her fingers, as if her entire perfect flock, hatched and delivered straight from the mother nest in San Jose, deserved whatever favors and assistance they wanted. He'd seen women like Megan Breen in action before, and they were very good at that—getting what they wanted by being nice but not *too* nice. Try taking it to a personal level, though, and they'd be all business, as Granger had told Chuck Trewillen that day at Marble Point. Breen wouldn't even catch a hint that a guy was interested in her unless he rated as a notable. It hadn't taken Granger long to see that he could never come into her radar . . . but he would have staked anything she was keeping her champion Pete Nimec from getting frostbitten at night during his visit to Cold Corners.

Granger reached toward his controls, hit a switch to fire the Bell's APU, and then settled back to let it warm. The auxiliary power unit would start his hydraulics, and it was important to be certain their line fluids were clear and circulating before he cranked the main turbines.

It occurred to Granger now that UpLink's closed-door, closed-mouth policy after the sabotage of their water-treatment facility had been what turned him onto his own drastic course. Nimec's reasons for wanting to go ahead with the Dry Valley overflight plainly weren't the same as they had been a little more than seventy-two hours ago. Couldn't be. At that stage there had been no apparent space between the hero's real and stated aims—he had wanted to begin looking for Alan Scarborough and the two beakers, who'd been thought to be victims of some kind of accident. But after the dome attack, the whole thrust of his search would have shifted. Breen and Nimec had learned they had enemies on the continent with a serious desire to shut down their operation, and would be figuring the lost S&R team had either fallen or been drawn into their hands. They would also figure those enemies were hidden somewhere in the rocks of Bull Pass. Yet Nimec had given Granger no tip-off that anything was different from before.

In asking himself why, Granger had decided it didn't mean *he* was under immediate suspicion, but was just further evidence of how UpLink would huddle up in secrecy when they were under fire. And when they were preparing to move. Even if he managed to steer Nimec away from the notch this time around, Granger knew the princely hero would return to investigate, probably with a Cold Corners pilot at the sticks, maybe going in with a whole damn squad of his own men.

No, he thought, Nimec wouldn't stop coming at it. Not unless he was stopped in his tracks. And that would itself barely postpone the inevitable.

UpLink, goddamn them . . .

UpLink International wouldn't stop coming.

Granger could read the writing on the wall, and intended to remove himself from the scene before his connection to Albedo was exposed. But he wanted to gain a lead, deal UpLink a blow that would send a major shock through its system, and convince Burkhart to provide him with money and an avenue of escape. But with or without those arrangements, he'd still do what he had to, and couldn't say that he had any scruples about it.

Aware of the Beretta's encouraging pressure against his side, Granger listened as the whir of the spinning APU filled his cabin. He was only a little anxious, and not in a particular hurry.

Nimec could take his time at Cold Corners One, squeeze in a final ounce of the redhead's exclusive hospitality.

His warm and cozy stay there was about to get cut short.

Annie Caulfield shut down her laptop, detached its modem cord from the telephone jack near her room's tiny desk, and sleeved the computer into her Timberland carry bag. Then she went across the room, put the Timberland on her bed, considered gathering her toiletries from the night stand, and instead sat thinking at the edge of her mattress.

Her face bore a troubled expression. She would not deny that part of it related to things left unfinished with Pete Nimec . . . a large part. But Annie's focus wasn't on her personal loose ends. She didn't think she had the right to turn it in that direction.

Minutes earlier, Annie had checked her e-mail and found a dashed-off reply to a note she'd sent to Jon Ketchum. Then she had scanned, in order, Goddard's public Internet and confidential Intranet sites for the latest SOHO updates.

Everything she'd read and seen on-line indicated the

solar flares that had been cooking on the far side of the sun—and heating up news lines around the world—were at last set to make their highly trumpeted appearance. It would almost surely be a brief one. But Annie had been persuaded it also would be dramatic . . . especially in Antarctica.

Given their high threshold of tolerance for challenging circumstances, she doubted the majority of polar bases would have much to worry about. In fact, she was sure their personnel would await the event with delirious anticipation, seeing it as an opportunity to gather scads of exceptional astrophysical data and enjoy one humdinger of a light show when the aurora australis got an energetic cosmic jolt. For most of them it would be like having ringside seats at an extravagant once-in-a-lifetime circus that came rolling into their backyard. Few to none would complain if the price of admission included a spell of erratic communications and ambiguous blips and ghosts on their radars that would be construed by imaginative Atlantis mappers as signs of the Lost Continent rising. While she realized power fluctuations and outages were a more serious potential consideration, Annie also knew virtually all of the ice stations had hardened electrical systems, and multiple backup generators that would kick in if their primaries were effected by the sun's demonstrative tizzy.

The situation at Cold Corners gave Annie pause, though. Its water supply plant was down, its security compromised . . . existing predicaments that would be magnified by what were only nuisance problems elsewhere. The last thing the crew here needed was to have their difficulties compounded, to become more isolated than was usually the case because of radio and satcom disturbances. And the last thing Annie wanted was to be leaving when they were in a pinch. Many of the researchers were longtime friends. There was Megan. And yes, there was Pete.

Annie sighed. Like it or not, she was shipping out, soon

and without any choice. But she still had time to make herself useful, talk to Meg about the latest info she'd gotten off the computer, give her recommendations on how to address some of the technical hiccups that might be expected during the solar outbursts. Her soap, dental floss, and makeup could wait till afterward to be tucked away in their luggage pouches.

She rose, strode to her door, started to pull it open.

And then blinked in surprise.

Pete Nimec stood in the partial opening, his hand raised in the air, frozen as if he'd been about to knock.

"Pete," she said, startled.

"Annie," he said, his eyes as surprised as hers.

They stood there in silence, her hand on the doorknob.

Nimec lowered his arm and indicated the parka he'd left on after hitching a ride back from the chopper pad aboard one of the big-wheel shuttles.

"The reason I'm wearing this is I was about to leave base—" He cut himself short. "Well, I'm pretty much on my way out . . . there's a helicopter waiting to take me into the valleys right now. . . ."

"I'd heard." Annie nodded toward her open carry bag. "It so happens I'm busy packing *myself*. . . ."

"Ah," he said. "If I'm getting in your way—"

"No, no. It was just a comment."

"Ah," he said.

"About the timing," she said.

"Right."

There was another beat of silence.

Nimec inhaled.

"Annie . . . can I come in a minute?" he said. "I'd like to talk. That is, I'd like to apologize for not . . . you know . . . talking to you sooner . . ."

"It isn't your fault." She opened the door a bit wider. "We've both had our hands full here at Cold Corners, and our paths just haven't crossed—"

Nimec was shaking his head.

"I don't mean talking to you *here*. I mean, well, before this particular occasion."

She looked at him, but said nothing.

"Months before this occasion," he said.

She remained quiet.

"I want to explain why I never called you," he said. "After you invited me for the Thanksgiving holiday—"

"You don't have to—"

"I do. Really. If you'll let me."

Annie stood watching Nimec another long moment. Then she nodded slowly, opened the door the rest of the way, and shut it behind him.

They faced each other in the room.

"Okay," Annie said, a step or two inside the door. "You were saying . . ."

Nimec swallowed hard, his throat even scratchier now than it had felt in Megan's office.

"Annie," he said, and halted. Which he guessed made it three, or maybe four times he'd already done that like a bumbling fool. "When we first met . . . in Florida, remember . . . ?"

"Yes, Pete," she said. "I told you I've been busy. But I think my recollection's fairly intact."

"Good," he said. "Of course, that is. Anyway, when we met . . ."

"In Florida . . ."

"Right . . . well, I knew right off we could never be friends."

She arched a puzzled eyebrow.

"Oh?"

Nimec shook his head, frustrated with himself. Had he just said what he *thought* he'd said?

He held up his hand.

"No, wait, that isn't what I mean," he said. "What I mean is that I didn't want to be *just* friends. That meeting you was special . . . I felt we really *clicked*, you know—"

"I know, Pete. I felt the same way," Annie said. "I thought we both realized it."

"Exactly," he said. *"Exactly . . ."*

"What surprised me was that you could choose to let something that special go."

Nimec's heart was racing in his chest.

"I didn't," he said.

"Pete—"

"I never let it go."

"Pete—"

"Not for a day. Not for a single minute—"

She gave him a look.

"Pete, is it only me, or are you aware it's been *months* since I've heard from you?"

"I am," he said. "I didn't intend—"

The sudden anger on her features stopped him.

"I don't care what you intended," she said. "You aren't even making sense. Did it occur to you . . . did you ever once in all those days and minutes of supposedly not letting go think it might be wise to *share* that information with me?"

Nimec looked at her.

"Annie," he said. "I was afraid."

She touched a hand to her forehead in disbelief, rolled her eyes.

"Come on," she said. "We aren't two college kids—"

"I know. I know that. But after my wife left me . . . I guess the idea of getting close to someone else . . . opening myself up to a woman—"

Annie flashed him another silencing glance.

"Pete, it isn't like I've been living in a paper bag for thirty-five years," she said. "I lost a husband. Lost my best friend aboard Orion. I understand those things. But that doesn't excuse—"

"I'm not asking to be excused," Nimec said hoarsely. He swallowed again, realized his throat was no longer dry. In fact, it had almost clogged with moisture. "I'm asking you for a second chance."

Annie was quiet. Nimec waited, trying in vain to read her expression.

"A second chance," she said.

He nodded.

Silence from Annie again. This time it seemed infinitely, torturously long.

Nimec's heart kept tripping away in his chest.

Then she met his eyes with her own, *locked* her eyes on his own.

"Okay," she said. "You've got it. I'm giving it to you. But I'm telling you very honestly there won't be a third."

Nimec pulled some air into his lungs. If he hadn't known better, he might have thought it had been an hour since he'd last caught a breath.

"I won't need a third," he said. "Won't let ancient history carry over into my life anymore . . . make *you* accountable for a bad divorce . . ."

"Pete, enough." Annie moved closer to him, reached out a hand, lightly touched his wrist. "We both have important things to do."

"*This* is important," he said. "Explaining why I wasted so much time—"

"It is, yes," she said, still touching him with her hand. All at once smiling gently. "And we'll pick up on it when we're back home. Over a quiet dinner. Maybe in front of a warm fireplace."

He stood there. Very conscious of her hand on his wrist.

"That'd be perfect," he said. "Soon as I get back, I promise—"

"*Shhhh,*" Annie said. And then leaned forward and kissed his lips, her own lips slightly parted, their mouths lingering together a moment before she pulled back, the taste of her remaining with him a good deal longer.

Nimec looked at her. She looked at him.

Both of them were silent now.

"Annie?" Nimec said after a while.

She nodded.
"I kind of know you and Megan have gotten tight. . . ."
She nodded again.
He took another deep breath.
"That part about me being afraid . . . ?"
"Will be our secret," she said.

Over Victoria Land, Antarctica

The Bell made a jarring launch from the USARP expedition camp where it had dropped its load of survival bags, having been forced to touch down at an angle in the steep-walled trench where the dome tents were clustered.

Nimec felt its sudden acceleration in his stomach as Granger throttled up. He held onto the sides of his tagalong seat though he was buckled and strapped in tight.

He glanced out his window. The scientific team that had called out for extra supplies—they had introduced themselves as micropaleontologists, mentioning something to Nimec about collecting flake-sized remnants of fossilized mollusks—stood waving at the bird in appreciation, arms high against a white background.

It struck him that Scarborough and his team must have looked much the same when Granger had become the last known person in the world to set eyes on them.

Then tents and expeditioners alike dwindled to vibrant orange specks under the chopper's skids, and blanked out of sight as Granger flared off above two spiring crystal-cathedral seracs.

"I'll have to see if we get any more urgent hails, but so far we're in good shape," he said. "One more scheduled inspection, a fill-up at the Marble Point fuel dump, and I think we'll be all right to head into the valleys."

Nimec turned his head from the window to look at him.

"I'll be here," he said.

Over Victoria Land, Antarctica

"The reason they use bamboo for wands is that it can bend a hell of a lot before it breaks, and is almost climate-proof . . . I think it has something to do with the fibre density," Granger said above the flap of his chopper's rotors. "You can spot them up ahead, straight out to starboard."

Nimec gazed down at the rows of marker wands with their orange and green flags. Granger had explained that they were planted to guide traversers and field parties across crevasse fields, steering them safely around the dangerous fissures. The purpose of his aerial survey, he'd said, was to make sure the bamboo staves hadn't toppled, gotten their flags shorn away, or been drifted over in the storm's gale-force winds.

"What's your verdict?" Nimec said. "They look in decent shape to me."

"Mostly, yeah," Granger said. "But I know this area, and pretty well know the exact location of the wands. I think a few of them at the margins of the zone might have gotten covered." He worked his cyclic and collective. "It wouldn't hurt to be safe. There's an outcrop a couple hundred yards outside the field that's flattened on top and makes for a good natural LZ. We can land on it, take a walk, check that the banners are exposed to sight. One bad step and somebody could fall right into one of those cracks."

"Not the sort of surprise a person would appreciate," Nimec said.

Granger's eyes flicked to his face.

"It sure isn't," Granger said. "You okay with us going down?"

"I don't see how we've got any other choice," Nimec said.

Getting from the platform where Granger lowered his skids to the first of the marker wands took them about twenty minutes. It was a tough walk for Nimec, his mountain-booted feet alternately sinking into deep snow and scuffling for traction on the slippery sheet ice.

Ahead of him, Granger was making easier progress in the snowshoes strapped over his own boots, moving with the balanced stride of someone practiced at their use.

"I know this must be tricky for you," he'd said when Nimec stumbled minutes before. "But if you aren't fitted for paddles that are the right weight and size, wearing them can make things worse."

Nimec had not commented. That was a discovery he'd made for himself after trying on a second set of aluminum snowshoes Granger kept in the chopper—spares that almost sent him sprawling, and soon wound up hanging over his shoulder by their strap.

The two men stopped now, the helicopter left well out of sight to their rear. Nimec looked at the gaudy red marker poking up out of the snow to his left. Then he wiped the fog of exhaled moisture off his goggles and browsed over the lines of bamboo staves stringing a long way past it into the distance. Their distribution in the groups that he could see appeared fairly even. Wind-rippled colored banners accented all of them, red ones indicating the boundaries of danger areas, green flags indicating the safer paths around them.

He looked over at Granger. The chopper pilot had his back to him and was staring across the crevasse field.

"You ought to have a peek through your binocs," Nimec said. "So far I'm not finding any problems."

Granger nodded, still looking out over the range, his probe chocked upright in the snow. Nimec saw him move his arm, reaching for what he assumed was the binocular case around his neck.

Then he turned toward Nimec, a Beretta pistol in his gloved hand, proving that assumption very wrong.

Nimec's eyes grew large.

"You want a problem," Granger said, "you've got it."

•   •   •

"What is this?" Nimec said. His gaze was fixed on Granger's drawn Beretta. "What the hell are you doing?"

Granger stood there pointing it at Nimec, his expression masked by his goggles and balaclava. "It's like I said. You came here looking for a problem. But sometimes you find ones you don't expect."

Nimec looked at Granger, remembered something that had occurred to him just a short while ago. When the chopper was lifting out of sight of the paleontologic expedition.

The last known person in the world to set eyes on Scarborough and his team.

The thought turned over in his mind with new, cutting significance.

"That day in Bull Pass," he said. "You didn't just happen to see our people. You were *scouting* them."

Granger held the gun steady.

"Forget about a confession from me," he said. "Won't happen. I've got nothing to *gain* from it." He shrugged. "You'll just have to leave this world holding on to all your questions."

Nimec lifted his eyes to Granger's covered face.

"No," he said. "Not about you."

Granger stiffened almost imperceptibly, the hand in which he clenched his gun tightening around its stippled rubber grip. Then he motioned its snout toward the crevasse zone beyond the marker.

"All right, hero," he said, pulling his probe out of the snow. "I'm taking you for another walk."

This time their walk was a short one. Moving behind Nimec, his gun held out between them, Granger suddenly ordered him to halt near a cluster of hazard wands some fifteen or twenty yards past the first red marker.

He sidled around him toward the red-flagged bamboo poles, never lowering the Beretta.

"Here," Granger said. "Let me show you something."

He inched closer to the poles, extended his probe beyond them, and grooved its tip through the snow. Testing, exploring, prodding.

Moments later Nimec heard a sound like a deep swoop of breath—a *giant*'s breath. Then the icy crust underneath the probe gave way in a great matted hunk, breaking apart as it spilled into a wide-open hole it had covered from sight.

Nimec stared into the crevasse exposed by the disintegrated snow bridge. Its jagged lips were about six feet apart and around the same length. He couldn't know how far down it went into the ice sheet, but the darkness filling it hinted at an evil drop.

Granger stood eying him from behind the snout of the Beretta.

"What you see is a pretty small crater," he said. "Deep and wide enough, though." He made a snorting sound that might have been intended as a laugh. "I always call holes like this *hag's mouths*. You curious why?"

Nimec looked at him and said nothing.

"It's because they're ugly," Granger said.

Nimec continued to say nothing.

"And because they're just the right size to be maneaters," Granger said.

Nimec just looked at him.

Granger jammed his probe into the snow, then snorted out another humorless burlesque of a laugh.

"What's wrong? Don't like my riddle?" he said. "Or maybe you're thinking about how you're going to miss another man-eater. Your friend Megan over at Cold Corners. She's got a *helluva* lot sweeter lips than the one that's about to gobble you up, huh?"

Nimec was silent.

"Well, okay. Whatever. No need to kiss and tell." Granger nodded to his left. "All you have to do is walk over to that hag's mouth over there. Right up to its edge. I'll take care of the rest."

Nimec looked at him. Looked at the gun between them. What was it Granger had said to him after he'd almost taken that spill in the snowshoes? *I know this has to be tricky.* It was yet another comment that had suddenly taken on new and unforeseen meaning.

Granger brought his gun up higher now.

"Do it, hero. Walk. Show me how brave you are," he said, and raised the pistol another few degrees, bringing it level with Nimec's chest. "Do it or I'll shoot you dead where you stand."

Tricky, Nimec thought.

He turned slightly, took a half step toward the crevasse. *Tricky.*

"You don't think I—" he began, giving voice to whatever words came into his mouth, intentionally breaking off, trying to sound like he'd really been about to say something as he feigned a slip on the ice and then thrust himself toward Granger in a sliding, lunging belly-dive.

His arms reached for Granger's legs now, grappling them below the knees, knocking him off balance before he could recover from his stunned surprise.

Granger teetered on his heels a second and fell over backward, driven by Nimec's weight and momentum. He grunted as the air went out of him, Nimec holding his legs in a tight clinch, his shoulders slamming hard onto the ice and snow.

Somehow his right hand maintained its grip on the Beretta. All in a heartbeat Nimec saw the pistol sweep down toward him, broke his clasp on Granger, and boosted himself halfway on top of him, reaching for the strap from which his rejected metal snowshoes hung around his shoulder.

Nimec swung the paddles at Granger's gun just as he squeezed the trigger, deflecting its barrel so the round fired harmlessly into space. He swung them twice again, hard, making contact both times, striking Granger on the wrist and knuckles.

Nimec heard Granger's exclamation of sudden pain, glimpsed the Beretta flying free of his fingers as they involuntarily released it, a black projectile hurtling off against the whiteness.

He also saw that both he and Granger had fallen precariously near the crevasse, their heads mere inches from its broken lip. Granger was heaving, grabbing, thrashing underneath him, his wild struggle to dislodge him moving their bodies closer to its edge—close enough for Nimec to hear miniature cascades of snow and ice spill down and away into its gaping emptiness.

He did not waste an instant. Pushing off with his toes, he clambered further up Granger's body, got fully on top of him now, and brought an elbow down on Granger's throat, *hacked* it into his throat, catching him squarely in the windpipe.

Granger made an *umphing* sound and went limp, sinking back into the snow, his chest seeming to collapse, his arms falling strengthlessly to his sides.

Nimec gulped a breath. Then he rose onto his knees, straddling Granger, bunching his fists around the collar of the man's parka to pull his head and shoulders out of the snow.

"You son of a bitch," he said. "Let's see what you've got to gain by talking now."

NINETEEN

COLD CORNERS BASE, ANTARCTICA
MARCH 17, 2002

MEGAN WATCHED PETE NIMEC AND RON WAYLON EN-
ter her office.

"Red dog," Nimec said, shouldering through the door
first.

She remained quiet behind the desk, where she'd sat
for over an hour, waiting for them to complete their latest
interrogation of Russ Granger and report on whether
they'd gotten anything out of him.

Waylon pulled up a chair opposite her. Nimec strode
over to the big Dry Valley satellite map.

She looked at him.

"I gather," she said, "you're going to explain what you
mean."

"Red dog," Nimec repeated. "It's the name of a card
game I learned—"

In your pool-shark days with your reprobate father, she
thought.

"—in pool halls when I was a kid," Nimec said. "My
old man used to play with some *Philly Inquirer* beat reporters. Everybody's dealt five face-down cards. Then the

dealer starts around the table, deals each player a card
face-up. If the player owns a higher card in the same suit,
he shows it and wins double his bet for that round. If he
doesn't, he tosses his hand and his stake gets added to the
pot. If they want to make the game more interesting, the
dealer *burns* a card from the top of the deck . . . shows it
to everybody, then tosses it to give the bank an edge."

Megan nodded.

"So Granger displayed a burn card when he let us know
Scar and Shevaun Bradley are alive," she said.

"Right."

"What's he shown you now?"

"The notch." Nimec stabbed a finger at the blue pin
identifying the area of Scout IV's disappearance. "They're
being held prisoner in the notch. At some kind of underground base."

Her eyes widened.

"Pete, that's incredible. . . ."

"Don't unbuckle your seat belt yet," he said. "He gave
us the exact location. There's some kind of tunnel or mine
shaft. He wouldn't tell us what's being dug up. Or stored.
I figure he knows, or has a damned good idea—"

"But that's another burn card he can show when it's
advantageous to him."

"Yeah. Granger's got a full deck. And he intends to use
it to win himself the sweetest deal possible with INR at
State, CIA, Interpol . . . whoever winds up with custody
of the slug once they can sort that out."

"Meanwhile he's playing UpLink . . ."

"Dealing us what he figures we want most . . ."

"The whereabouts of our *people,* in other words . . ."

"In exchange for our agreeing to testify that he was
cooperative when the time comes to face the music,"
Waylon said.

Megan looked from one man to the other.

"This explains a lot," she said. "Explains almost everything, in fact. Our rover coincidentally rolls too close to
the notch . . . we'd programmed it to explore the area . . .

and then whoever is out there in Bull Pass takes preemptive action. Disables or destroys it before we can receive telemetry that exposes their presence."

Nimec was nodding.

"Next our S&R team arrives," Megan said. "They pick up Scout's trail, follow it to where it ends—"

"Come too close to the notch *themselves* with Granger sounding the alert . . ."

"And stumble into the same concealed pitfall as the rover," Megan said.

Nimec and Waylon gave her near-synchronous nods. Then they were all silent for some moments.

"Why would they want to kill David Payton if they were going to let the others live?" Megan said.

"Granger swears he doesn't have any idea," Nimec said.

"And you believe him?"

Nimec shrugged.

"Hard to be sure, but my gut sense is he's on the level," he said.

Waylon looked at Megan.

"You know how Doc Payton was," he said. "I want to say the crew here got along with him. But the truth is there isn't anybody at CC that didn't have the urge to strangle him at least once." Waylon shook his head. "Don't get me wrong. It's terrible what happened to him. I wish it hadn't happened. But I'm thinking it's possible he could have done something to provoke it."

There was more silence.

"Okay," Megan said. "We have to make some decisions—"

"Like how we get Scarborough and Bradley out, you mean?" Nimec said.

Megan exchanged glances with him.

"You know what I mean," she said. "It isn't that simple. I won't allow any more of our own to find themselves in a situation where they're easy targets. There's a question of how we can accomplish it. Whether we should request help—"

"From who? And when's it going to reach us? I thought we went through this together once before. The boss got us the authority to act."

"No argument about that," Megan said. "But we have a small force here . . . and a slice of it's been allocated to recovering function at the desalinization plant."

"You know the pump kicked in for a little while this morning," Nimec said. It had been a good piece of news he'd gotten upon his return from Marble Point, where he and his rescue pilot had spent an overnight due to passing fog whiteout. "Don't ask me how the crew did it. For all I can tell they used string, scotch tape, and chewing gum. But they got it to show signs of life. And they figure to have some of its capacity back soon."

Megan looked at Waylon.

"How much?" she said. "And how soon?"

"I'm estimating we can get to almost a quarter of our regular freshwater output in a couple of days. That's with four or five of us on it round the clock." Waylon spread his hands. "I can't guarantee the pump'll *stay* up, but if we lose it again manpower won't matter. We've done about all we can with the parts we've cannibalized."

Megan shook her head.

"I don't know," she said. "There are other considerations to weigh. Before she left yesterday, Annie Caulfield advised me about a range of problems we can expect because of the solar flares— "

"Just another reason we should move fast."

"Pete, we've already felt some effects," she said. "Though they haven't even emerged from the far side of the sun, it appears we've already had some irregularities in our satellite and radio connections. Dead spots." Megan gestured toward her timed-out desktop computer. "I've experienced them myself. Annie provided an access code for a turnkey NASA Web site. A half hour ago I tried to log on and access the latest models for when the activity's going to peak. And couldn't. The data link broke on me. It's *still* fouled up. We might be looking at periods when our radio connections go partially or entirely down over the next couple of days . . . can you imagine what kind of tactical problems that would lead to in the field?"

Nimec nodded.

"Yeah," he said. "But it'd be an equal disadvantage. The other side would run into the same complications."

She shook her head. "Still . . ."

"I'm no world-beater," Nimec said. "I wouldn't take anybody out there to the Valleys without a solid plan."

"I'm not implying that. I trust you. But it's my job to measure the risks. Make the final decision. Nobody else can do it. I can't unload the responsibility. I *own* it. . . ."

She trailed off, her features tight with concentration.

Nimec watched her a moment. Then he stepped away from the map and softly rested a hand on her shoulder.

"Meg, listen," he said. "One thing I learned from the boss . . . from Gord . . . is that part of owning it is knowing when to trust somebody *enough* to let go."

Silence in the room.

Megan sat with her face turned up toward Nimec's as that silence spooled out between them like an invisible thread. Then she took a deep breath, seemed to hold it a moment, and released a long, deep sigh.

Nimec could feel her muscles loosen under his palm.

"You said you've come up with a plan?" she said.

"No," he said. "Not me."

She looked at him.

"Who?" she said.

Waylon thumbed his chest, moved his shaved head up and down in a single nod.

"You," she said.

He nodded again, his long-sword earrings gleaming softly under the fluorescent lights.

Megan half smiled.

"Tell it to me, Ron," she said.

"Sure," he said, "I was just waiting for you to ask."
And then he told her.

Bull Pass

Burkhart did not decide upon a conclusive plan of action
until several hours after Granger failed to report—convincing him the pilot's true failure was more critical than
that.

The plan's crucial elements, however, had germinated
in his mind much earlier. In fact, its rough contours had
emerged after his return to Bull Pass. He had known that
even Granger's success—his elimination of UpLink's
head of security—would only forestall the inevitable.

Looking backward, Burkhart could see the road to his
fall so clearly. With all veils of conceit and ambition lifted
from his eyes, now he could see. The destruction of
UpLink's robotic probe, his taking of its recovery team,
his exposed sabotage attempt and the bloodletting that followed, and at last, his hastily necessitated reliance on
Granger to do what Burkhart had recognized was far beyond the pilot's competence . . . from the day he'd set foot
on that road, and perhaps onto the many forking junctures
he had walked along the way, it now seemed there had
been something almost deterministic about where he was
headed

Gabriel Morgan was dead. The Albedo Consortium's
vast and elaborate underpinnings were on the verge of
complete breakdown, a thunderous crash that would send
legal and political ground quakes through scores of
nations.

What options remained before him then? What roads
on which to push toward success . . . or if not that, then
some little measure of self-redemption? There was no way
to erase—or substantially reduce—the evidence of the
uranium digging and transshipping operation in whatever
scant time was left to him. Not even if the mines were
razed would that evidence be concealed for long. He

could, perhaps, physically remove *himself* from it, arrange to be carried off in a small plane from one of the South American gateways . . . but that would mean abandoning all or most of his men.

They were men who had fought bravely beside him. Men who had been loyal and true to him in the darkest face of his own failure.

He would not do it.

Would not desert them.

Deep beneath the frozen earth, Burkhart had decided to make his stand in the pass above, and hold the high ground where he was certain the enemy would show his own resolute face.

Cold Corners Base

"These ATVs were shipped from Kaliningrad a few months back, when they ordered and got themselves updated models," Waylon was saying. "They're two-passenger, fully automatic, and have noise-dampened engines. Our field researchers love zipping around in them."

Megan stood beside Nimec and Waylon in the heated garage arch outside CC1, looking at the ten parked, neatly aligned vehicles, and remembering.

"They were used by Max Blackburn in Operation Politika," she said. "I was . . . we were together in Russia at the time." She paused and glanced at Nimec. "When you and I signed off on the upgrade request right before leaving San Jose, it came to me that the older vehicles might be perfect for the ice. Waste not, want not, you know?"

Nimec was quiet a moment. He had tried very hard to ignore the sadness in her voice as she'd spoken of Max.

"Their VVRS pintle guns," he said. "They were transported with the ATVs?"

Megan nodded.

"And stored away, yes. It's ironic, I suppose, that we

stripped down the weapons. It was the one feature we never thought we'd need here."

Nimec nodded thoughtfully.

"Waylon, you grab some men, take care of getting the guns remounted," he said. Then he turned to Megan. "In the meantime we better see about getting those extra choppers from MacTown."

Bull Pass

The cage door grated open, then shut with a dull clang.

Shevaun Bradley was startled. A while ago the echoing of the machines had stopped and left her in almost total silence. The sounds of the door seemed very loud against it.

Sitting on the cot that doubled as her chair and bed, her back against the wall of the enclosure, she lifted her eyes as the marked man came inside.

He was alone, unaccompanied by guards.

It was the first she had seen him since the time of the screaming in the black. The first instance in which he'd appeared without his guards.

He stepped over to the cot and stood watching her in silence.

She could see him easily now. The cage was no longer in darkness. Her conditions had improved after she'd talked to him, answered his questions. His men had returned to screw a bare lightbulb into an overhead socket and wheel in the cot. And the food had gotten better.

They hadn't brought Scarborough back, though. She hadn't heard anything from him.

Not since the time of those screams . . .

"You deceived me," the marked man said at once.

She stared at him in tense silence, trying to pretend she didn't know what he meant. Except she did, of course.

"It was an artful deception," he said. "The dome's outer cameras were precisely where you revealed they would be. But you neglected to mention the internal cameras."

She felt her heart pound in her chest, but said nothing.

"It was what you call a lie of omission, *nicht wahr*?" he said. "Is that not true?"

Bradley said nothing.

The marked man came closer to her. His hand slowly lowering toward the pistol holstered at his waist, hovering inches above its grip.

"You were loyal to your own. You showed courage. But your guile killed four of my comrades," he said. "Does the knowledge please you?"

She looked at him, but continued to say nothing.

"Does it *please* you?" he repeated with a vehemence that made her flinch.

"No," she said, her voice trembling as she gave her answer. "I'm not happy that men died."

The marked man scrutinized her features a moment, and then suddenly crouched in front of her.

His right hand still near his gun.

His face level with her face.

"I could kill you out of vengeance," he said. "Without pity or moral constriction. Do you believe me?"

"I believe you."

A pause.

He reached out his left hand, clamped her wrist in it, and forced her palm against the crescent birthmark on his cheek.

"Describe what you feel," he said.

Her heart was knocking. "I don't know—"

"Describe it to me," he said.

Bradley commanded herself not to cry, and the tears began streaming from her eyes.

"I don't know what to say," she told him. "I don't know what you want me to say. *I only feel your face.*"

He pressed her hand against his cheek for several more seconds, his eyes radiant with that terrible intensity.

Then he relaxed his grip on her, let her pull back.

"All right," he said. "Listen well, scientist. I'm going to tell you something you'll surely wish to remember. . . ."

Cold Corners Base

Nimec entered the water-treatment dome, strode to its central platform, asked the group working on the pump where he could find the man he was seeking, and was pointed in his direction.

"You Mark Rice?" Nimec said, approaching him from behind.

The man glanced up over his shoulder and nodded. He was crouched at a warped metal pipe-coupling near the platform, a small plasma cutter in his hand, a welding helmet and mask covering his head.

"I'd like to talk," Nimec said. "When you've got a minute."

"Got one right now."

Rice switched off the torch, rose, carefully set it down on the wheeled tool cart beside him, turned off the oxygen supply to his face mask, and raised its glass hatch.

"What can I do for you?" he said.

Nimec looked at him. A few spikes of hair showed over Rice's brow, sweaty despite the penetrating cold inside the dome. They were blond with dyed cobalt-blue streaks.

"I've seen your folder," Nimec said. "You were with the Sword detail in Ankara, my old friend Ghazi's section."

Rice nodded silently.

"Ghazi sent your team to flush those terrorists out of the mountains a couple, three years ago. On horseback."

Rice nodded again.

"Before UpLink, you were Army Ranger," Nimec said. "The 3/75th, right?"

"That's right."

"Saw your share of action in the service . . . Task Force Somalia, an anti-narc unit in Colombia . . ."

"Right."

"And earned some impressive commendations," Nimec said. "The Distinguished Service Cross, a couple of sharpshooter's medals . . ."

Rice flicked a Nomex-gloved hand into the air between them.

"With all due respect," he said. "It's been a long while since I wore a black beret. Or rode a horse—"

"Or fired a rifle," Nimec said.

Rice looked steadily at him.

"True," Rice said. "Before the attack on this plant the other night."

Nimec met his gaze. "You were going to resign from Sword until Rollie Thibodeau talked you out of it, and even then only agreed to stay if you could ship out to Cold Corners," he said. "Feel comfortable telling me the reason?"

Rice regarded him another moment, then shrugged.

"I didn't want to shoot anything anymore except with a camera," he said. "What I do here is mostly work for the beakers. Photographic ecosystem profiles. It suits me fine."

"And still puts that trained eye of yours to good use."

Rice made no comment.

"I need a sniper," Nimec said. "Someone who's dependable. Who won't make mistakes. A bunch of lives are going to be on the line. Mine's incidentally one of them."

Rice looked at him.

"The talk's been that you're going out to bring back the missing search team," Rice said.

Nimec gave him a nod. Their eyes were still in contact.

"I'm not a quitter," Rice said.

"Nobody thinks that."

Rice nodded.

"Go ahead and count me in," he said.

Bull Pass

Burkhart led his men from the ascending passage's mouth onto a black rock uplift, whipped by freezing wind, his boots stepping across striations that memorialized the labored seaward slide of ancient ice.

A hundred feet below him Bull Pass was congested with shadows. Faded orange, the sun floated on an almost even plane with his line of sight, giving the illusion that he could have squeezed it in his hand if only his reach were longer. It had been like that for days as wintry gloom made its onset.

His attention now, however, was captured by the writhing purple-red blot of light in the sky beside the sun. He had never before seen anything like it. Nor most certainly had any of the others.

Here was the first outward sign of the sun's advancing fever.

"Mein Gott," Langern said behind him, staring with awe at the bruisy radiance. *"Was ist das?"*

Burkhart turned to him.

"Der Gott des Krieges," he said. *"Kann sein, eh?"*

Langern's eyes remained wide behind his goggles.

"Ja, mein Herr," he said. *"Kann sein."*

Burkhart was silent. Then he tapped Langern's arm to stir him from his rapt absorption, motioning down at the pass.

"Hier müssen alle durchhalten," he said. *"Verstehen?"*

"Ja," Langern said, nodding to show he indeed understood.

This bitter windswept terrace was where they would position themselves for the enemy's arrival.

Cold Corners Base

Pete Nimec watched his hookup teams finish rigging their all-terrain vehicles to the pair of choppers requested from MacTown, each Sikorsky S-76 moments from bearing away its maximum sling-load of three vehicles. As the cargo hooks were slipped into their apex fittings, the wand men waved their static wands and the teams jumped off the ATVs to move out from under the downwash of lifting rotors.

Then the birds climbed from their hover, pulling slack from the sling legs, flying off against the strange, wavery orchid of color that had appeared in the sky near the slipping sun.

Nimec turned to Megan. His backpack heavy on his shoulders, loaded with his own gear, he was ready to join his strike force aboard one of the two UpLink helicopters on the pad.

"How you holding up?" he said.

"Fine." She lowered her eyes from the auroral radiance and studied his face. "I only wish I were going with you, if you want to know the truth."

Nimec smiled a little.

"You've been awful scrappy since I taught you to box," he said.

She gave his chest a light swat with her mittened hand.

"Fisticuffs are my thing," she said. "Before long I'll have to watch out for cauliflower face."

"I think," he said, "You mean 'cauliflower ear.' "

"Close enough."

They stood there facing each other.

"Got to head off," Nimec said, and nodded toward the waiting choppers.

"Yes," Megan said.

"You mind the store. There should be enough men here to—"

"I'm really okay," she said. "I'll be okay. And so will this base."

They stood a few seconds longer in the blowing cold. Then Megan stepped forward and hugged him.

"Thanks, Pete," she said, her voice catching, her arms tight around him. "Thanks very much."

Nimec cleared his throat.

"What for?" he said.

"Just for being you," Megan said.

Over Bull Pass

"We're seeing . . . *nk* . . . think the . . . *tch* . . . can . . . *sn* . . . us . . . down where . . . *sss* . . . *ssssss* . . . *sk* . . . "

"Chinstrap One, you're breaking up. Say again?"

"*Srks . . . siss . . .*"

"I'm losing you, Chinstrap One," the UpLink chopper pilot said as Nimec listened from the passenger seat. "Repeat your status. Over."

"*Crkrrsssss—*"

The pilot frowned, tried to reach the other MacTown bird. He was a wire-thin black man named Justin Smith who wore a sparse, tightly kinked chin beard and spoke with an occasionally strong peppering of a Caribbean accent. Nimec thought it sounded like Trinidad.

"Chinstrap Two, we've lost contact with Brother Penguin," he said, pronouncing the word Brother as Brudda. "We need to confirm you've made your tick mark. Acknowledge."

"*Ngg . . . you . . . rppttt—*"

"Say again—"

"*Still cnnttrd. Extnr . . . sssszzzdrr . . . rceee . . .*"

Nimec turned to Smith. "Snap, crackle, pop," Nimec snorted in disgust. "There any way to get a lock?"

Smith shook his head.

"Our radios are already hopping," he said. "The disturbance cuts across all bands."

"Try our own bird again," Nimec said. The trail ship carrying Waylon's team had peeled away toward its rendezvous moments earlier.

Smith radioed it, got more garbled noise, cursed under his breath.

Nimec wondered if Smith missed palm trees and white sand. "We'll have to forget about any of them reporting for now," Nimec said. "Keep our fingers crossed they're in position."

"They'll be doing the same for us."

"Yeah."

Nimec looked out his windscreen at the coiling lights in the sky. What had started out as an isolated purplish stain near the sun had become a moving, living rope of color across the horizon, twined with a glowy spectrum of greens, reds, and blues.

"Damned freakish," he said. "The weatherman says it'll be a sunny day, you can count on having to leave your house with an umbrella and galoshes. But solar flares, radio interference . . . *this* they can all get on the mark."

Smith flew in silence, making unconscious, minute adjustments to his sticks as a highway driver would to his steering wheel.

"Sir," he said after a while. "We're reaching the notch." His flight helmet dipped downward. "See it down there?"

Down dere.

Nimec's eyes traced the pass seaming its way between jagged mountain slopes, saw the dark shark's-tooth crosscut coming up fast.

He nodded. "The intercom working?"

Smith reached for a switch, and static burst loudly into the cabin.

"Sorry, sir," he said, and flicked off the com.

Nimec started unstrapping himself from his seat.

"Keep her steady," he said. "I'm going back to talk to Rice while my vocal cords can still transmit."

Bull Pass

Outside the tunnel entrance on the notch's spiny eastern shoulder, Langern thumbed off his radio handset, and then stood pensive and silent under the ribboning polar lights. He had scarcely spotted the helo through his binoculars before attempting to contact Burkhart, but all he had gotten from the handset was a senseless bark of static.

It was the same signal breakup he had received when he'd hailed Koenig on the western side of the notch, and Reymann's squad at the far end of the pass.

Meanwhile, the Bell helo was close enough now for its

UpLink markings to be seen with the unaided eye.

Zum Teufel mit ihnen, he thought. *Zum Teufel mit dem ganzen verfluchten Land.*

To the Devil with them. With this whole accursed land.

He turned toward the other men waiting on the crest with him, ordered them to stand to arms.

From this point forward they would be on their own.

The Sikorsky helicopter designated Chinstrap One after the ubiquitous chinstrap penguins of the peninsula had lowered its own "strap" of ATVs at the intersection of Bull Pass and McKelvey Valley—or the point where the shank of the valley system anchor would be seen to meet its ring end on a map. The pass walls were at their widest distance apart here, and katabatics weren't too bothersome a factor for the bird's pilot.

This was only one of the reasons the site was chosen for the linkup with Ron Waylon and his group. The other was because of its coordination with the separate rendezvous Sam Cruz's team was making elsewhere.

Dropped by the UpLink tail ship on its second hop, Waylon's team was waiting to receive the sling-load as Chinstrap One came in over the ridge and bellied low above their heads.

They took less than five minutes to get it unhooked and derigged.

Waylon stared up at the S-76, waved to the men in the cockpit as it lifted away into a sky swirling with brilliant color.

"Don't know if I'd want to be heading back up into *that* weirdness," said the man beside Waylon.

Waylon looked at him.

"Don't know if he'd want to be going where we are either," Waylon said.

Then he turned toward the ATVs and gestured for the others to mount up.

Within moments they were speeding south into the pass.

McKelvey Valley

"Chinstrap Two . . . *wvv* . . . *lzzzzt* . . . *tktyr* . . . brother . . . *gnnn*," came Justin Smith's voice over the radio. "*Wnud* . . . *confizzzz* . . . *tkmk* . . ."

Pulling pitch at the sticks of his Sikorsky, the Mac-Town pilot frowned as his UpLink counterpart's transmission was munched by static, incidentally noting the Carribean island accent. He thought it sounded like Jamaica.

"I'm not getting you," he answered into his headset. "Repeat."

"*Sayggggn*—"

"Still can't read you," said the MacTown pilot, his consternation deepening. He paused, tried to guess what the radio call was about, and went for the obvious—UpLink's lead bird would want a basic status report.

"External load successfully dropped and received," he said, hoping his message would be intelligible at the receiving end.

Bull Pass

On Burkhart's orders, the Light Strike Vehicle had waited just around the eastward bend of Bull Pass, hidden in shadow behind a toppled granite colonnade opposite Mount Cerberus's massif face, guarding its territory like the solitary feline hunter with which Shevaun Bradley had once associated it. A camouflaged leopard perhaps. Or a panther.

Now Ron Waylon's incursion team came shooting past, paired up in their three all-terrain vehicles, rusty sand reeling off from the spin of their tires as they hooked into the narrow stretch that led toward the notch and Wright Valley.

The LSV's crew continued to wait a short while longer, tending to their patience, allowing the little UpLink vehicles to gain some distance, get deeper into the trench.

Liquid jewels of color rained down from the narrow band of sky overhead, sliding over Cerberus's plated black flank in vivid, oily droplets.

Unglaublich, the man named Reymann told himself in his driver's seat, thinking he would never see anything like it again if he lived until the last day of the world.

Then he fisted the vehicle's clutch and pounced from behind the weather-chewed slope to spring his ambush.

Bull Pass

After overseeing the movement of the 150-ton haul trucks to their places in front of the mine entrance, Burkhart gathered the drivers and excavation crew together inside the shaft and detailed what he expected of them.

"No, it's impossible. We won't. You can't ask that of us!" one of the nervous forcmen said. A Canadian who had gained his experience in the uranium mines in Saskatchewan, he unnecessarily restated his objection in German. *"Das kommt nicht in Frage!"*

"What else would you wish to do?" Burkhart said, speaking perfect English.

"Get out of here!" The foreman's insistent shouting echoed in the gloom around them. *"We have to get the hell out!"*

Burkhart suddenly felt very tired.

"Out to where?" he asked quietly.

Over Bull Pass

It wasn't an M24 SWS. It wasn't the Barrett Light Fifty he'd used to take down armored troop carriers at long range in Mogadishu. It wasn't the slightly lighter Haskins of the sort favored by Green Beret spec-op shooters. It was a VVRS rifle, the original full-sized version, a little over a yard long, a little under ten pounds loaded, about the same size and weight as a standard M16A2 combat gun. Built for pouring out heavy fire with some resultant sacrifice in accuracy.

It was what Mark Rice had available to him, and he would have to make it work for him.

He knelt in position behind the slid-open starboard door panel of the Bell, wind screaming into the passenger/cargo compartment around him, his goggles off so he could keep his eye against the aperture of his scope mount.

The men below him on the ridge-back had opened up on the bird with their Sturmgewehr assault weapons as Smith wove evasively in the air above the notch, trying to avoid their fire and lower his skids. Rice rocked and swayed on one knee. He estimated there were five, possibly six opponents. They had traded their white winter cammo garb for something closer to desert dun. Some of them were sheltered behind boulders and rock projections. Others were in full view. All were firing at the unarmored bottom of the UpLink chopper's fuselage—the *ding* of metal on metal audible over the roar of wind and props as some of the rounds made contact.

Rice knew he had to take them out fast.

He inhaled, exhaled, squinting down the barrel. Then he triggered a shot at the center of a parka the color of coppery sand.

A shower of red and the parka tumbled away down the steep hillside.

Rice shifted his gun barrel. With that first trigger pull he had grooved into instinctive action. Later he would think of torn flesh and spilled blood. Later his gorge would rise at the waste and death. But right now these were no longer men down there, no longer even living creatures. These were targets. Simply targets.

He sighted between the crosshairs again, but momentarily lost his alignment as the chopper swung sideways to avoid an upward stream of bullets. Then he regained the mark, and fired.

There was more spraying blood and his target folded backward. Rice shifted to yet another, this one moving, breaking for cover, looking up at the chopper, *shooting up* at the chopper, making a target of Rice himself as it dashed toward a protective shield of rock. Rice released a breath, released a round, and got the target in mid-run.

Then he felt a hand on his shoulder, heard a raised voice behind his ear. Nimec.

"Hang on, Rice!" he said. "We're bringing her down!"

Langern volleyed continuous fire at the helicopter as it landed precariously on the windswept crest of the notch's southern slope and men came leaping from its passenger hold beneath the still-rotating blades.

Crouched behind a large boulder, Langern had seen three of his fellows die before its skids touched down, one of them bouncing down the slope like a rag doll.

The man in the cabin door had a falcon's eye, but now it would be his turn to be raked with death's talons.

Langern stopped shooting long enough to push a fresh magazine stack into his weapon, sprang up on the balls of his feet, and pushed himself from behind the boulder, his finger locked over his trigger, aiming directly for the sniper as he jumped from inside the helo.

Nimec did not pause to think. Could not afford to think. He saw one of the men on the hilltop bound from the protection of a boulder and make an outright charge for Rice, his weapon spitting bullets. He saw Rice standing with his eyes momentarily turned elsewhere, hunting out another source of fire. And he reacted.

Nimec's baby VVRS swept up from his side and rattled in his hand. The man went down onto the hard stone ridge, falling on his bullet-riddled chest, then rolling over onto his back, his lips moving faintly, his eyes staring skyward behind his snow goggles in the instant or two before life flickered out of them.

In the agitated heavens above Langern, the whorling auroral lights seemed to briefly assume the shape of a terrible multihued iris.

"Der Gott des Krieges," he muttered, gazing upward as he hitched his final breath.

Then the cold, chaotic eye drew closer and blinked shut around him.

Still exchanging light gunfire with the men hunkered behind the rocks, Nimec's team had gotten pitons and lines out of their rucksacks and were driving the metal anchors into the cliff head. Nimec didn't know how many of the ridge's defenders were left. Probably no more than two or three to judge from their fitful salvos.

Amid the clang of hammers and continued smatters of fire, he swept his eyes in a semicircle, seeking the tunnel entrance Granger had offered up information about.

Then, abruptly, he spotted it.

He called to Waylon over his headset, heard static crackle in return, didn't pause to consider the odds of his brief message having been communicated.

Grabbing Rice's shoulder, waving another two men over to them, he whirled toward the tunnel, turned on the high-powered tactical flashlight mounted under the barrel of his baby VVRS, and led the way inside.

Nimec's voice cut through the white noise in Waylon's earpiece like an isolated sun ray penetrating dense overcast.

"I'm headed into the tunnel, rappel team's on its way down," Nimec said. "Keep pushing forward, they're going to need cover."

"Got you, sir." Waylon heard a hack of static in his ear, and wondered whether his own response had slipped through the parted wave of electromagnetic interference. "Can see the notch in front of me."

And he could. It was an ugly, angular gash that looked like it had been hastily carved from the wall of the pass with a gigantic serrated butcher knife.

Waylon could also *hear* something of equivalent nastiness—the growl of a muscular engine at his rear, rising above the buzz of the two other Sword ATVs speeding along with him.

Something was coming on. And closing.

He tossed a glance over his shoulder at the man in his aft gunner's seat.

"What kind of problem have we got?" he shouted over the blasting wind.

The gunner turned to look, spotted the Light Attack Vehicle in pursuit.

"Bad one," he said.

Waylon eased off his accelerator and radioed out an urgent message to Sam Cruz.

Cruz didn't pick up Waylon's signal, but fortunately that wasn't imperative.

He knew the plan.

In the lead slot of the three-ATV incursion team that had met Chinstrap Two in McKelvey—dropped there so they would enter Bull Pass behind Waylon's men and guard their backsides—Cruz had spotted the Light Strike Vehicle up ahead moments after it launched from the pass's crumbled west wall.

As he sped forward at maximum horsepower, pushing within range of the opposition's militarized dune buggy, Cruz waved his accompanying vehicles into attack formation and hollered for his gunner to open fire.

The Light Strike Vehicle's driver had been outwitted and he knew it.

The motor-pack of ATVs that had appeared from McKelvey were gaining behind him like angry hornets. Reymann swerved to elude their firing guns, his own rear gunner turned toward them in his elevated weapons station, swinging his .50-caliber in wide arcs, disgorging a torrent of ammunition from its link feed-belt.

The hornet vehicles continued to close distance nonetheless, two of them splitting to his left and right while the third stayed at his rear and dodged the lashing machine gun volleys. There was no room for his larger vehicle to maneuver in the tight-walled pass. No time to use his grenade launcher as the hornets nimbly hopped alongside his flanks, trapping him between them. Nowhere for him to go but straight ahead toward the leading trio of ATVs that had now molted speed before him, their tail guns pouring ammunition in his direction.

Boxed-in, caught in a vicious four-way cross fire, Reymann was cursing under his breath with a mixture of astonishment and disbelief when a sleet of bullets knocked him back in his seat, turning his head and most of his body into a crimson mire.

One of Pete Nimec's biggest unanswered questions was resolved minutes after he entered the tunnel, Rice and the others following him down a metal stairwell into the darkness.

They had descended three long flights in a hurry when the beam of his tac light chanced on a kind of niche in the stone wall to his right—and then held there as he paused briefly on a landing.

The recess was filled with sealed steel drums.

Large fifty-five-gallon drums, stacked two and three high and going several rows deep into the surrounding rock.

Their warning labels were printed in various different languages, but it was easy enough to see they all said the same thing.

Nimec glanced over them.

De rebut Radioactif.
Radioaktiver Müll.
Reciduous radioactivos.
Scorrie radioative.

"Goddamn," Rice said. He stood slightly behind Nimec on the riveted metal landing, his own flash trained on one of the English drum labels. "Radioactive waste. They're storing *rad waste.*"

Nimec grunted. He doubted that was all they were do-

ing there. Before entering the tunnel, he'd looked down
from atop the ridge-back and noticed heavy equipment at
the bottom of the notch. Earth-hauling trucks. They were
stashing this stuff, true. Hoarding it deep in the ground.
But he had a feeling their operation would prove to be a
two-way street. That they were pulling something *out* of
the ground too.

He moved his eyes further down the stairs, angling his
tac light in that direction to illuminate the way.

"Come on," he said. "We'll worry about this later."

Burkhart waited in the dimness near the foot of the stairway, flattened against a rough stone wall on its right, his
Sturmgewehr angled toward its upper levels. One of his
men stood beside him, his back also to the cold stone.
Three more men were hugging the opposite wall. All wore
night-vision goggles.

They could hear the enemy sprinting downward.

Burkhart had counted three sets of footfalls. And while
he could not be certain of it, he would have wagered the
first of those sets belonged to the UpLink security chief . . .
Peter Nimec.

Burkhart had never met him, of course. But he believed
he understood him. The man had come from a world away
with only a single purpose, a single *mission,* and that was
to locate and rescue the vanished members of his organization. Nimec would care little at this stage for anything
besides, something Granger would have quickly realized
if he were captured—as the UpLink strike verified had
happened.

To what else could its timing and accuracy be attrib-
uted? Burkhart thought. He saw a flicker of light from
above now, pulled further back against the wall. There
was a great deal of information Granger had obviously
divulged. Enough to bring Nimec and his men here to
Bull Pass. To the notch. But his greatest bargaining chip
would have been the knowledge he possessed about the
whereabouts of the UpLink field team. And if he had told

Nimec about the tunnel—a fact made evident by the helicopter's landing on the ridge-back—then he would have surely told him its descending stairs were the fastest route to the cage in which the woman scientist was being held.

This man Peter Nimec . . .

A man who led on the ground, risked his life along with those who followed him . . .

Burkhart knew he would not delegate the actual rescue to others.

It would be Nimec leading the way down the stairs, just as Burkhart himself had chosen to meet him.

Nimec suddenly halted on the stairs and raised his hand, stalling up the three men behind him. He wasn't sure why. Or at least he couldn't have stated why. It might have been simple caution. Or that he'd noticed a trace of movement below, heard something below, a subtle forewarning that someone might be down there—except he wasn't even positive about that. But he told himself that they had better proceed very slowly until he knew.

"Hang back," he said, and glanced over his shoulder at Rice. "I want to check things ou—"

The first outpouring of fire from below silenced him mid-sentence.

Nimec ducked sideways as the gunfire split the darkness, throwing himself against the stairway's handrail, motioning for the others to do the same. He twisted his tac light to its flood setting, saw the figure of a man launch off the wall to the right of the bottom stair, and triggered a burst of return fire from his VVRS. The man slipped out of sight, into the shadows, but then Nimec saw another man swing his gun up at him. He released a tight hail of bullets, saw the man drop to the floor, or ground, or whatever the hell was waiting for him down there at the base of the stairs.

There was a second volley from the bottom, this time coming out of the darkness at his left. Rice had his gun

up, his own tactical light set on "spot," beaming a concentrated circle of brightness onto the center of the
shooter's chest.

He squeezed out a rapid burst and the man crumpled.

"Okay, move it!" Nimec shouted, bounding down the
stairs, leading his men down the stairs, thinking there was
no sense in them making stationary targets of themselves
here on these goddamned stairs at this point.

More movement as he reached the bottom landing—a
third gunner. Nimec raked the gloom with fire, heard an
agonized cry, saw a body fall straight from the knees, a
fine mist of blood glittering in the throw of his flash. At
the same moment one of the Sword ops racing down the
stairway behind him—Rice?—he wasn't sure in the confusion—loosed a sustained barrage and took out another
of the waiting shooters.

Silence then. Absolute silence.

Nimec took a quick glance back at his men, all of them
down on the lower landing with him now.

"Everybody okay?"

Three nods.

Nimec stood warily, moved his gun from side to side,
sweeping the area in front of the stairs with his tac light.
Four men lay dead below them, NVGs over their eyes.
He wondered if there had been any more waiting, thought
of the one who'd opened fire and slipped clear of his
initial return burst. Was he among those sprawled on the
ground?

He had no sooner asked himself that question than the
answer was violently delivered.

Burkhart sprang from where he'd concealed himself to the
right of the bottom landing, raised the barrel of his
weapon, released a crisp stream of fire. Bullets studded
the risers beneath Nimec, throwing up a bright shower of
sparks.

Nimec gestured his men back, his finger continuously
squeezing the trigger of his VVRS as he leaped down the

stairs and attempted to track the source of the volley with
its flash attachment.

Darting clear of his shots, Burkhart brought up his gun
for another staccato burst, heard a single sharp *tak!* as one
of his own bullets ricocheted off the handrail . . . and then
felt a slap on the upper left side of his chest, followed
immediately by a hot needle of heat in the same region.

His finger still looped around his rifle's trigger, Burkhart looked down at himself. Blood seeping through the
front of his parka where the rebounded bullet had struck
his heart, the strength seeping from his hand as shots continued to spurt from the Sturmgewehr's barrel in loose,
wildly straying patterns, he looked down at himself.

He could have almost smiled at the sublime jest as he
fell.

Nimec crouched beside the dying man, heard him struggling to say something to him, couldn't make out what it
was.

He leaned closer, removed the man's night-sight goggles, pulled the balaclava from his face, and for a moment
focused on an odd crescent-moon scar on the man's right
cheek.

"Die Ironie des Lebens," Burkhart said in German.

Nimec shook his head, unable to understand.

Burkhart realized his mistake. He pushed his head off
the stone ground, coughed up blood.

"The irony of life," he managed to say in English.

Or thought he did in his fading confusion.

In fact, the words never left his mouth.

EPILOGUE

"THE SISTER TOOK THE CHILD," SAID NAN AS GORRIE sat down at the table.

"What sister?"

"The Mackay infant. The sister will take him. Seems to be a fine family. The husband is an engineer."

"Good for him then," said Gorrie. A fresh loaf of bread sat wrapped in a napkin on a plate at the center of the table. "You baked this bread?" he asked, taking off the cloth and finding it warm.

"I did."

Gorrie broke out a thick piece and began buttering it. "Got home early from school?"

"No earlier than normal," said his wife.

"I was worried about the child," admitted Gorrie. "I was worried what he would think growing up."

"They wouldn't have told him."

"Not a thing to keep a secret," he told his wife. "Sort of thing can't be held inside. At least now he'll know the truth. Hard thing, but better than what he might have thought."

Nan busied herself at the stove. She'd made a roast and mashed potatoes—elaborate fixings for a weekday. She carved a few slices and presented a plate as properly as if they had been in a fine restaurant.

"What's all this, Nan?"

"We call it dinner," she said.

"Aye." He swirled a bit of gravy into the potatoes. She'd used an extra helping of butter in them, exactly as he liked them despite the doctor's warnings about cholesterol. "The runny tap in the loo?"

"Excuse me?"

"You're buttering me up for something, sweets. Out with it."

Instead of the laugh he expected, Nan sat down at her place with her elbows on the table, propping her chin in her hands. "Frank, now be honest—were you worried about the child?"

"As I told you."

"Did it make you—have you thought—do you feel as if . . ."

They would not have to have been married for so long for him to know exactly what she was thinking, but having been married for so long—twenty-six years that fall—they found it difficult to speak of certain subjects. The fact that in their case the number of these subjects was limited did not ease the difficulty.

"Very old rocks," Gorrie said softly.

"It is."

"To be honest, I hadn't given it a thought, not in that way. Just doing my job, as it had to be done."

She picked up a forkful of potatoes and ate slowly. When her mouth was empty, she said, "You would have made a lovely father. You still might."

Gorrie laughed. Then he looked into her face. She was no centerfold nudie girl, but Scotland was not the place for one. She was made of harder stuff—more beautiful in her way than any centerfold, he thought.

"Do you want a child, Nan?" he asked.

"Sometimes I think of it. But—" Her eyes glided from his and scanned the kitchen before returning. "I think I'm content, if that's the word."

"You would tell me if you changed your mind."

"I would."

"Forty's not too old these days."

"I wish I *were* forty. Is that what you're doing, slicing years from your age?"

"Just yours," said Gorrie, starting in on the meat.